The Dukedom in the Sun

The Dukedom in the Sun

Nancy Armstrong

Pearl Press

First published in Great Britain by Pearl Press

ISBN 978-0-9567697-0-1

Printed and bound by Good News Books, Ongar, Essex, England.

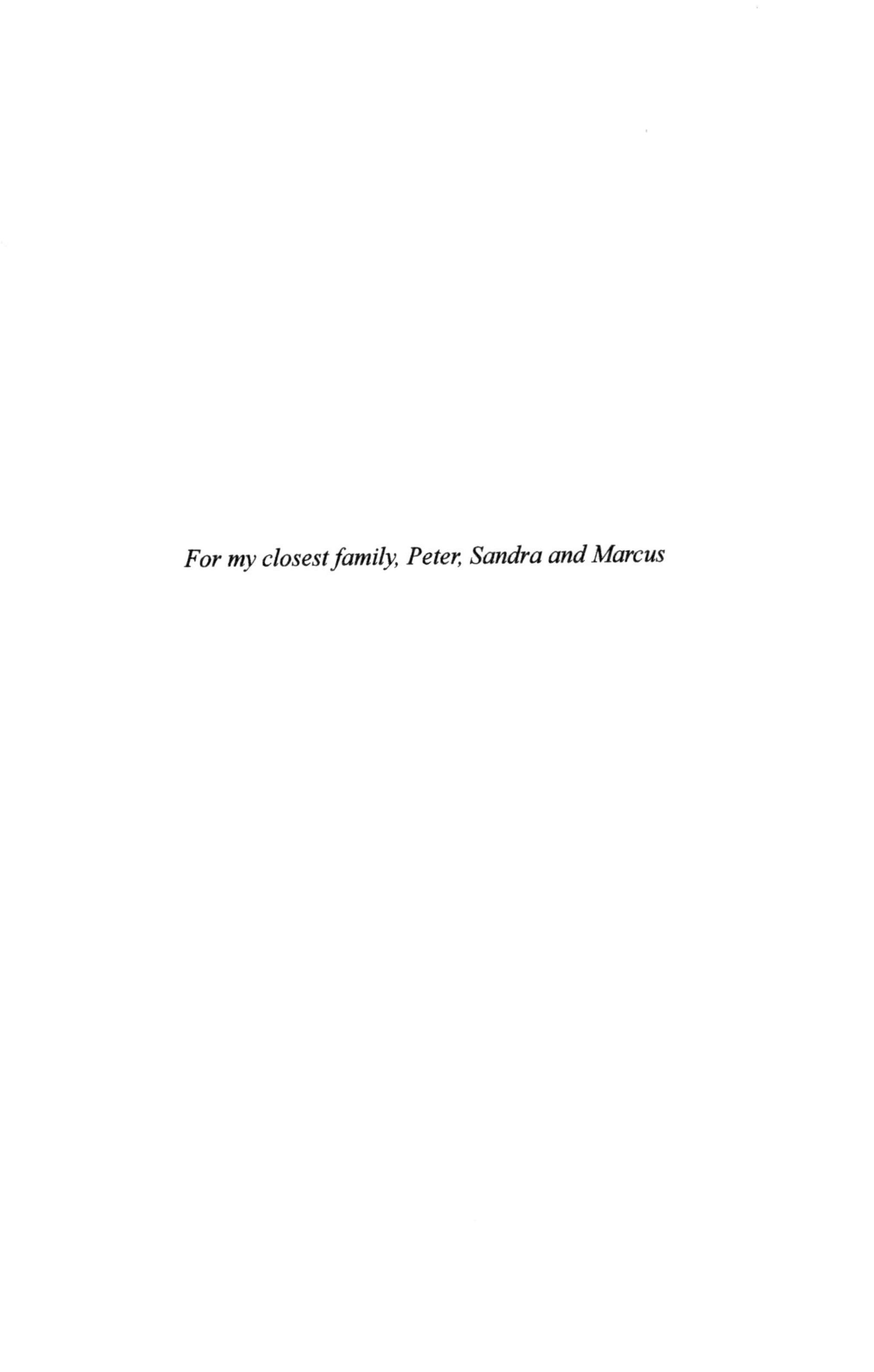

For my closest family, Peter, Sandra and Marcus

Acknowledgements

Especial thanks must go to my sister, Sheila, and her husband, Bill Oglethorpe, who saved my life after a heart attack, together with appreciation of all that was done for me by Judy Donell.

My cousin-by-marriage, the artist, Jane Duppa-Miller, urged that I 'should never give up' and therefore was behind this publication, and kind John Heaton took up the challenge and made all the difference in the publishing field.

My grateful thanks to you all.

CONTENTS

PART ONE

TANCRED DE HAUTEVILLE

The ship was filling with freezing water. The gale tore at them and they felt its bite deep within; they knew that if they didn't make landfall within a few hours they would all be dead. They were a company of soldiers, not sailors, helpless against the roar of the wind and the stinging salt of the fearful waves. Most were being vilely sick. Some slopped helplessly in the bowels of the reeking ship. Others dug their fingernails into the wooden planks to help keep a purchase, to prevent being washed overboard.

Their leader, Tancred de Hauteville, stood alongside the Master, searching the dark sea ahead - but it was dull, dark grey and angry. Not a fleck of seaweed or splash of colour in the night to give hint of a sanding shelf. The ship heeled in a sudden squall, her timbers screaming as she twisted. Two men fell against each other, their arms flailing. Mouths slack with wet despondency, they clung to each other for safety and comfort. Tancred, peering through the darkness, saw them grope and grasp and, himself, held on with sinews bulging until she righted. The ship's timbers squealed afresh.

The wind roared, then clamoured again, the turbulence was awe-inspiring. The Master exerted every ounce of his strength as the rudder bit. The whole ship shuddered in an unexpected pause, more frightening than its frenzied race through the waves. Several men caught their breath, instinctively making the sign of the cross.

The relatively still moment was shattered as another enormous wave smashed against the ship. Then the sea spun away to all points of the compass and they plunged down a precipice through the waves, with icy spume flying high above the mast on all sides.

Miraculously they rose again. Seawater cascaded away through the scuppers as wave after hissing wave foamed across the deck. A sucking sound heralded the approaching rollers. The cold was numbing. Every man wondered how much longer he could last against the onslaught.

The ship was forced to nose back into the sea, to try to make way. It was plainly too cumbersome, weighed down, water-logged. The men clung to anything they could hold. Some had lashed themselves to the rigging with their leather belts, turning their backs to the storm, hunched in soaking clothes. Others had pushed under the decking, hoping for shelter, but were cruelly punished by wind and water. The errant waves swilled around, like cats' paws catching mice. They were in constant danger of being prised out of their flimsy refuges and flung headlong into the storm.

The prow began to swing wildly and with increasing velocity as the screaming wind bore down. Those who dared to look knew they had nothing with which to combat the life-defying storm: most were helpless as babes, sick to the gut with both motion and fear. Worst of all was their lack of control. They could not stop their feet sliding on the deck, nor the deck shifting without reason beneath their strong brown toes, now blue with cold. Only the Master knew what to do. They were reluctant to trust him, but had no choice.

These Normans were hard, ruthless men in ordinary times. They were brilliant fighters, furiously loyal, tenacious as limpets - but with violent, explosive tempers when even minimally roused. To find themselves in such peril at this point in their long journey seemed such a futile waste. The mountainous seas were something they knew nothing of and against which they had no strength. Even their famed endurance was flagging as the wind notched up to another note of agony.

The altered pitch of the shrieking wind halted Tancred's mind from yearning about home. Earlier, when the storm began, he had resolved that when he was back under his own roof - by God! He would stay put, raise sons, and never cross the seas again. He loved his own land. He could not abide the feeling of a slipping, perilous base beneath his feet, nor the fear of a watery grave. A stinging wave slashed across his face, momentarily blinding him with salt. The ship lurched sideways like a staggering beast.

The terror continued.

Unexpectedly the Master howled at him,

'I smell land!'

The words were torn from his mouth as he struggled with the tiller, but he went on shouting to Tancred,

'Now the wind will change! It will drive us around the coast of the Gargano. We'll soon be safe. Tell them to bail out the water. Hurry! There's no time to lose!'

'Attention!' Tancred roared. 'Bail the ship!'

Some soaking men turned to listen: but not all could hear. He bellowed even louder,

'Hurry! Fight to save your lives - bail the ship! Use any method - but for God's sake empty the water out!'

'We must be foundering!' moaned a man. 'It's the end - oh, Lord Jesus help us ...'

Tancred, an enormous man, leaped forward two strides and hit the man with the back of his huge fist. His heavy ring split the corner of the man's mouth, from which bright blood gushed.

'Help yourself, you lazy fool. Get bailing - fast! We'll soon be safe if you get the water out - there's land ahead.'

The man's face stilled, incredulous, as blood dripped. Tancred went on, furiously.

'Do you want to live? Then work fast!'

'God will save us. Saint Michael has heard our prayers ...' croaked a limp young man, feeble with sickness, struggling to stand upright, 'He knows why we're here ...' shakily he cupped his frozen hands and began to scoop seawater out over the side of the ship.

'Saint Michael was a soldier, like yourselves,' shouted Tancred to all the others, 'so *behave* like soldiers and obey orders! Work! *Bail*!'

Every man threw himself into draining the water from the ship, developing a rhythm. The new air they took into their lungs steadied them. They settled down into a routine, shoulder to shoulder.

Gradually the wallowing ship emptied, slowly but steadily rising upwards like a sodden cork. The weathered sails were unfurled, piece by piece; control had passed to the Master once more. The old vessel beat towards the distant coast that only the Master knew lay ahead.

It had been a terrifying, wild ten days, building up to the nightmare of the tempest, which had lasted over two nights with a turbulent day in between. The whole group had expected balmy warmth and a gentle breeze - never a pounding storm. After all, they reasoned, hadn't they just ensured themselves a place in Heaven through their journey to the Holy Land? These Normans believed in an all-powerful God. Their race had sprung from a fertile ground of faith in magic, pagan Scandinavian in essence, but magic which was now inextricably interlinked with the teachings of the Church. Few knew exactly where magic had ended and God's will began; even fewer cared.

But, at the point of their death, Saint Michael had heard and acted, so they fervently believed in their simple hearts. They were convinced that he had reported back their plight to God, who had put out His hand

and stayed the climax.

As the skies began to change with the advent of dawn, the men could see the dangers more clearly. The immense waves had quietened down, yet the swell remained menacing. The wind had altered its high-pitched scream to a grumbling roar, occasionally faltering, until it lessened to an angry growl. The water which had swilled about in the ship had been removed and the men had secured what was left of the small but saturated cargo.

Tancred still stood like a rock by the Master, as a sign of his support. He loftily ignored the shivering men, one, at least, too mortified to look upwards, as they swiftly and safely drove towards the shores of the Gargano peninsula, the mountainous spur above the heel of Italy.

The weather was completely different after the Normans had landed. They took almost a week to rest and thoroughly enjoyed the now brilliant sunshine and heat rising from the ground. They were to recount the tale of the storm until they died. It was vividly remembered - without need for embroidery. There were about forty of them, and they had gathered no attendant women during their journeys, for they marched too fast and had too little money for anyone save themselves.

Amongst some of the first to leave Normandy on the pilgrimage to the holy places was Tancred de Hauteville, a hugely popular man, coming with several friends. They had agreed upon the special places that they were to visit. All had been rewarding: it was the highlight of their lives. Now, piety assuaged, Tancred and his friends were on the look-out for any opportunity to earn money as they travelled home again.

But first they were to make their visit to St. Michael's Cave near the top of Monte Gargano in Apulia, the very last holy place upon their lengthy list - and the most significant.

Before they travelled up the mountain to their longed-for destination, they sought out the Bishop of Sipontum, to be blessed.

They also gave thanks for their release from the grasp of death whilst at sea and asked for God's help in the days to come. The comatose old Bishop spoke kindly to them all; questioning them at length about the places they had seen and granted them a comfortable night under the stars in the episcopal cloisters.

Rested and well fed, the refreshed group started on their journey up the mountain, Monte Gargano, to the village wherein lay the church, as well as the grotto, a cave deep inside, dedicated to Saint Michael and All Angels. They were wildly excited to get there.

'There it is!' called out Gilbert, pointing. He was a small, lithe man, with a nutcracker face and long eyesight.

'Where? Where?' the men crowded about him.

'See that dark patch three-quarters up the side of the mountain, just below that rocky outcrop?'

The others nodded agreement, then eagerly began the long climb. The upwards paths - there were several, branching and joining up again randomly - were steep and narrow. Fortunately this day the men were only encumbered with water-skins and lamps, intent on a swift journey. No-one spoke, only the trickle of loose pebbles became their chattering accompaniment.

Alerted by the bishop, the leader of the Lombard rebels in Apulia awaited them in the village they sought: his name was Melus. The Normans knew nothing of his existence, but in the south of Italy his name was a household threat because he brought death and destruction in his wake.

Melus sat hidden in the shade of a great rock which was suspended above the steep slopes, overlooking the faraway group as they climbed towards him. He waited as, unmoving, a spider waits. He watched their actions as the distant blur turned into individuals, seeing how tightly they kept together on the open mountainside and how they closed ranks every now and again to rest - then, on some unheard word of command, set out again with an even tread, breathing as a team.

At last, hoped Melus, *at last* these might be the men he was seeking. His need for trained fighters was acute.

'I'll wait and watch,' thought Melus to himself, selecting a handful of nuts from his pouch, 'the climb will take them half a day. I can't afford to make a mistake - not this time.'

The Norman soldiers finally arrived at the small pilgrimage village. Before they marched in amongst the buildings they paused, as they always did, so that they could arrive in formation. They knew it impressed, imbuing their act with a sense of occasion, and it made them risky to challenge. One or two villagers glanced at them with scant curiosity. A string of children ran alongside until they all reached the clearing in front of the church. It was very quiet and very hot.

They washed themselves at the pool provided. Although the water was brackish it cooled them down as they dowsed their heads and washed their feet; eventually they left their swollen wrists hanging limply beneath the scummy surface. Cleansed and cooler, they looked around with fervent interest. The poverty and bareness surprised them. All the other holy centres further away in the Levant had been so showy and ostentatious. They wondered why there was such a contrast.

Tancred beckoned a watching boy to guard their water-skins. Then all formed up, hearts aflame to proceed. Months of marching were behind them and further weeks lay ahead before they would reach Normandy and home again, but the cave inside Monte Gargano had a magic repute which had held them in thrall from the beginning. At last the fateful moment was upon them. Each man had rehearsed what he was to pray. Several were frightened out of their wits at going inside, into the dark. Others were quivering with self-hypnotised emotions - of these they dared not speak out loud.

They all stood and faced the church, whose facade concealed the entrance to a steep downward path which travelled deep into the bowels of the mountain, leading to the cave which was decked out as a chapel dedicated to Saint Michael and All Angels. This was their dark destination; it had lured them like a magnet. Saint Michael, the warrior leader of the heavenly hosts against the forces of evil, and the main adversary of Satan, was their patron saint.

Tancred suddenly barked an order. The men, filled with genuine reverence, formed up in neat pairs and, with their small clay lamps in hand, marched smartly forward to seek out the first recorded place where Saint Michael had reputedly set foot on earth.

As the sound of the Normans' footsteps diminished Melus stretched, brushed the nut-dust from his garments, got to his feet and followed. Unhurriedly, stalking Tancred and his compatriots into the cave, he eventually found them kneeling on the wet rock floor, steady drips of icy water flicking onto their warm shoulders from the low, uneven roof above.

Some of the Normans had their faces in their prayerful hands, lost in private worlds. Others were gazing at the startling Byzantine statue of Saint Michael on the altar in a dim alcove. The legendary saint, stern and uncompromising, was seen with full shining armour and towering feathered wings, made of solid silver - which appeared almost to be moving in the flickering candlelight - one hand raised on high in blessing and an unsheathed sword by his side.

What a contrast Saint Michael seemed, they thought, to the men they had recently met. All they could remember during the past long months were the slovenly Arabs, the stunted Italian fishermen, the quarrelling Greeks and the salacious Byzantines ... they felt respect for none of them. To the Normans, Saint Michael stood there as an avenging warrior saint, looking not unlike themselves. For they, too, stood tall and straight; their swords were normally unsheathed in their capable hands and, as they gazed and prayed, these Normans, to a man, felt that they were appealing to a fellow Norman.

Melus waited in the shadows for a while, observing the men and watching their reactions: what mattered most to them, he wondered? What held their attention the longest? The dark obscurity of the cave? The effect of the lamplight, guttering and flickering, casting eccentric shadows on the rocky walls? Or even the antique tombs - some Roman - enfolded in cavities hollowed out by nature in the lee of the roof? Or the clergy, standing, waiting, until they could attract attention? No - unquestionably, he saw, it was the statue of Saint Michael that held them in thrall, their eyes glazing as they stared at the glistening silver, as if the saint was speaking personally to each man in turn. All doubts resolved, Melus knew at last how to approach them.

As the men gradually began to stir he strode decisively forward to stand foursquare in front of the ancient altar, allowing Saint Michael's statue to remain in full view. Alert, staring at him, the men all waited without moving a muscle. He, in return, gazed at each man.

Then, in a strong, commanding voice he spoke,

'Soldiers! Welcome! My name is Melus of Bari and I, too, am a soldier. When you have finished your devotions I ask you to meet me outside the church, for I have a proposition to make to you in the name of Saint Michael.'

By and by, the bemused men slowly climbed the many steps out of the cave and grouped themselves around Melus on a grassy terrace, a short distance from the church. He had paid some villagers to provide coarse bread and fruit for the visitors, so they were eating, and drinking spring water, lazing contentedly in the fresh air. Melus remained standing, elegantly leaning against a rock, his robes draped casually against the stone, grey on darker grey.

Tancred observed Melus from the corner of his eye. Why, he wondered, had Melus approached them on the mountain and not in Sipontum itself? For secrecy? And what did he want of them? Then Tancred looked speculatively around him, his gaze sweeping across the mountain to the horizon, taking in everything. He looked at the dark beech forest above, the *Foresta Umbra*, dense and wild; to the flourishing plain below and the industrious fishing boats out to sea. It seemed an intriguing land, busy and cultivated - perhaps the answer lay there?

And yet - and yet - the position from which Melus must have awaited them would have given him ample time to watch them, each and every one, but - more important - the group as a whole. Gradually the pieces of the puzzle began to change places and slot into a pattern. Tancred's agile mind tumbled like a juggler. He found a suitable place to stand and leaned against another rock, waiting for Melus to speak.

Melus continued to turn his patrician head from side to side, silent, his pale and high-bridged nose etched against the grey stone, sharp-eyed, watching. In repose his face was a face of iron, with bitter lines from nose to mouth, yet with the long upper lip of a wit. He had noticed Tancred's unrest and deduced it stemmed from his concern with tactics. *There's the leader!* He thought, *there's* the man who could be relied upon to plot and scheme, he knew how to plan ahead.

There was a hush. They all looked towards Melus.

'You must have travelled far?' Melus enquired in a gentle, caring tone.

There was silence. Of course they had - wasn't it obvious?

'Have you enough food? Can I provide you with more?' he went on, mildly.

Some men murmured amiably. Tancred said nothing.

Melus continued smoothly,

'An explanation is due to you all, so I'd better tell you who I am.'

'The soldier, Melus of Bari?' said the nutcracker-face, with an engaging grin.

'The soldier, Melus of Bari,' said Melus gravely, 'and leader of the

Lombard nation in the south.'

Oh! Thought Tancred - now this is *really* interesting! Swiftly he countered.

'Then where are your men?'

The group came alive at his sharp words. Some shot to their feet, reaching for their knives; others peered around the rocks and paths, but no sign of a soldier or men-at-arms could be seen.

Melus looked reproachfully at Tancred,

'I approach you in peace ...'

Tancred looked back at Melus and said, equally drily,

'Because you have none - no man left? *Is that it?* And you need us?'

Melus chuckled in apparent amusement, throwing up his hands in mock horror as he replied,

'You assume too much - too quickly! I *do* have an army, but they are scattered at this moment, at my request. I *did* have a notion of inviting someone to join me - but not quite yet! I'm far too experienced to rush into a situation without fully exploring every avenue first and getting to know my associates extremely well before I made an offer ... and *if* I made an offer ...'

'Well said,' growled Rainulf, Gilbert's elder brother, 'then would you like to tell us your intentions right from the beginning?'

Then he sat upon the rock behind him. Melus realised that some unspoken truce had been reached. He let out his breath, slightly eased the muscles of his neck and shoulders, fractionally lifted his chin and began to speak.

'Four or five hundred years ago,' he began, 'the Lombards were as disreputable a group of semi-barbarians as you Vikings were, when you came from the Norse lands to France - to make it your own Northland - Normandy.'

'That's insulting!' shouted a bearlike man, scrambling to his feet.

'Use your brains, man - *listen*!' said another, pulling him back, 'We've always been proud of our ancestors! There's nothing to be ashamed of by doing well ...'

Melus continued, scarcely drawing breath,

'And we Lombards did exactly what you Normans have been doing in France. We arrived in Italy from northern Germany, and established ourselves and prospered. We're a down-to-earth race, hard-headed and realistic. We called our part of Italy 'Lombardy' and our capital city was Pavia.'

'Aha,' breathed Tancred, 'you Lombards are known as 'the administrators', aren't you? The 'administrators and financiers'?'

'Why yes!' said Melus in delight, 'that's exactly what we are - administrators, law-makers and financiers: we're the backbone of any flourishing people! In other countries, when men fight amongst themselves their leaders call in a Lombard to make peace. This we do through compromise.'

'But something happened? What are you doing in Bari?'

'Not too fast,' laughed Melus, 'there's more to my story before I tell you what I'm doing here.'

'Continue, then, if you will,' said Gilbert, '*what* happened?'

'It was originally the fault of the Holy Roman Emperor, Charlemagne,' said Melus grimly, as if it had only just occurred. 'The Emperor Charlemagne swept down through Europe into Italy and captured Pavia - and our kingdom was at an end! But,' he added hastily, 'we spread out into other parts of this peninsula and created the duchies - rich dukedoms - named after our army units led by the duces.'

'So *that's* why they're called duchies!' said one Norman to his friend, 'I always wondered ...'

'Benevento, for instance, is one of our finest principalities today, together with Capua and Salerno, and our princes of these great cities are some of the most wealthy and powerful rulers in Italy.'

Melus paused: Tancred filled in immediately,

'And yet you approach us - *unknown men*? What else happened?'

'Ever since Charlemagne, a couple of centuries ago,' said Melus firmly, 'we Lombards have had a dream - a dream that the Lombards would one day rule the whole of Italy.'

'But your dream has turned into a nightmare?' asked Tancred maliciously.

'In a way,' sighed Melus, 'but pragmatic people like ourselves never give up!'

Tancred pressed him unflinchingly,

'I repeat - what *else* happened?'

Melus drew a long breath,

'It would take too long - now - to tell you everything that happened. Briefly - let me explain ... think of Italy as a cauldron, bubbling away, with a host of different nations fighting to establish themselves and take power. Roughly ... most of the coastline is occupied by the Byzantines and therefore ruled by the Emperor of the East in Constantinople. The Lombards only own pockets of land down the centre of the peninsula.'

'Don't leave out the Pope and the Church lands!' called out a bright-eyed man with dark hair, touching his thumb to his chin.

'Nor the smaller German rulers and theirs'!' called out another, rubbing the side of his nose with his finger.

'Nor the Saracens knocking at your shores,' said Tancred, 'when we were in the Holy Lands we endlessly heard of their plans to take over the south - to add to their conquest of Sicily.'

'You've all answered your own questions.' said Melus waspishly. 'We've been beset on all sides over the centuries. But we'll never give up! Germanic people never do!'

'Yet you approach us? What is your latest news - why are you so dedicated? Why do you call yourself the leader of the Lombards *in Bari*? You've not mentioned Bari since we were in St. Michael's cave!' Tancred, implacable, was like a dog worrying at a bone. '*Go on* - be more explicit!'

Melus answered without further ado, straight and to the point.

'The provinces of Apulia and Calabria are in turmoil. *It's our country*, yet the Byzantines from across the seas rule us with a rod of iron and tax us beyond reason. There's even a Byzantine Catapan who's Governor in Bari, assisted by Greeks. *Yet we're the ones who do all the work.* We Lombards arrange and construct the city's government - as we do elsewhere - and Lombard laws prevail. We work during all the hours God sends and then our profits are sent on to Constantinople. It's outrageous and it's unjust. Our citizens are seething with rage!'

'I see,' said Tancred, thoughtfully, 'it looks as if you've a crisis on your hands.'

'Exactly so.'

'Well something crucial must have happened,' said Rainulf sympathetically, 'what was it?'

Melus breathed hard.

'A most important Byzantine official was murdered in Bari. It gave us Lombards in Bari - and there are a lot of us - a chance to revolt. My brother-in-law, Dattus, and I got together an army and gained possession of the city.'

All looked up, impressed. There was a buzz of approval.

'And then?'

'The next year we took Ascoli.' The buzz altered to a hum.

They waited, eyebrows raised.

'Then we took Trani!' The hum deepened with respect. There was a pause. Melus appeared to hesitate.

'But then?' Tancred was merciless.

'Then a new Catapan arrived at Bari and bribed some Greeks to open the city gates. They re-took Bari ...'

'Yet you escaped?'

'I did. But ...'

'But - what?'

'But my wife and children were captured and sent as hostages to imprisonment at Constantinople.' Melus' face was set.

'So,' said Tancred slowly, 'you Lombards want to recapture Bari, throw out the Byzantines and get back your family?'

'We do,' said Melus, 'and I have my army ready to join me when I give the word. But we need inspiration - and I've been waiting about four years to meet you Normans, with your reputation as fierce fighters: you're just what we need - you could turn the tide for us!'

'Maybe,' said Tancred, 'but we don't come cheap!'

'Have you a better offer?' countered Melus slyly.

'Not yet,' said Tancred roughly, 'but then - you've not *made* any offer, either!'

'Nor I have,' said Melus. *'But I might.* Let's take time to reflect, shall we? Then let's meet at my castle at Benevento in two weeks' time? And take the discussion further? It's on your way home.'

The men looked at Tancred. He didn't speak, nor did his expression alter.

'I'll give you a feast ...' smiled Melus, grudgingly.

Tancred looked at the men,

'What d'you say?'

'Aye!' they roared in unison, and got up to march back to Sipontum.

When Tancred and his companions eventually marched into

Benevento they stood amazed at Trajan's triumphal arch and gaped at the magnificent castles owned by the wealthy Lombard aristocracy. Here and there they caught a glimpse of courts ablaze with Byzantine splendour and colour and they marvelled; clearly money was not going to be a problem.

Melus' own castle was not large - more a fortified keep with a moderately-sized Hall. Yet the impression the Normans received was of great brilliance of colour, for all the walls were gaily painted and gilt in patterns they had never seen before. Even the roof was coloured under a film of soot, for, as with all important Halls at that time, there was a central hearth and the smoke curled upwards and out of a hole in the roof.

The feast Melus provided was calculated to satisfy every appetite. All the servers were pretty girls - for a rare treat, rather than the normal men or boy servants - who had been instructed to please. They whisked about with the platters, twirling around as they placed the food upon the boards so that their bodies were entwined by their flimsy clothes, ankles gleaming: the Hall was very hot and the great door was left open to bring in some fresh air. The serving girls were mostly young, with distracting dark curls and moist eyes, who turned their heads languidly whenever a man seemed to favour them - and slipped alluringly away, just out of reach of plucking fingers.

Tancred found himself seated beside Melus, with Dattus on his other side. For a moment or two he felt imprisoned, but they set about to beguile him, speaking of everything bar the subject that concerned them. Flattered by their ministrations and casual, laughing conversation, Tancred soon felt at ease.

The food was overwhelming. First they were served with trenchers - large squares of day-old bread, taken from huge loaves, which soaked up the spicy sauces and gravies. They waited, drinking wine from cups made from horn, salivating, eager for the meat or fish. Soon some girls danced in with platters of small pastries filled with cod liver or beef marrow, which were wolfed down in a trice. Other girls brought dishes of boiled meat, sliced and swimming in a thin cinnamon sauce. Dishes of beef marrow fritters arrived, crisp around the sealed edges, and then small, three-legged cauldrons were set upon the boards in which fat, sinuous eels floated in a thick and spicy puree.

Following this was a bewildering choice of fresh-water fish in a cold green sauce flavoured with spices and sage; then bowls of saltwater fish fried in breadcrumbs. Finally heavy platters of whole roast kid were carried in by two girls at a time, the small animal glazed with honey and served with sprigs of rosemary.

Melus had kept his word. It was a veritable feast. They licked their lips and fell to in a rush. No-one had any idea when they would next have a meal.

In the dusky lamplight the colours of the food blended into a symphony of sea-and-sage greens and tawny browns, with all the intermediate shades of orange and grey and pastry rust. The golden sheen of light on auburn crackling deepened into the bronzes of aromatic sauces, until light and colour and smell fused into a gargantuan temptation.

Reaching forward, Melus filled Tancred's horn of wine for the fifth time; Tancred's mouth was crammed with food.

Melus looked across at the happy Normans, all at ease and eating heartily. He rapped upon the wooden board with the handle of his Arab-made knife,

'Eat! Eat! There's plenty more - this country is famed for its good food!'

'And naughty girls - maybe?' laughed a man.

'Girls know how to look after themselves in Benevento - but these girls are in my care today, so be discreet whilst you are under my roof ... their families trust me to look after them.'

The men looked at each other at the warning, and several hands fell away from caressing.

'You're a powerful man, it seems.' Tancred muttered indistinctly, gnawing on a bone.

'He is,' agreed Dattus, Melus' brother, 'you've no idea of the strength of his authority and command. He didn't become the leader of all the Lombards in Italy by default.'

The men nearby stopped their speech and listened; shortly all the men were quiet as they ate, their eyes on Melus. Expansively he appealed to the whole group,

'All life is a question of power - it always is! Who holds the reins - that's what matters, and whom a ruler can recruit as friend or ally. And power is rarely in the hands of one person for long ... is it?'

Tancred ruminated, as he swilled his wine and made inroads into the roast meats, that Melus and his brother had an engrossing flair for speech. He realised that they must be genuinely high-born and well-travelled, for they both spoke to the Normans in their own tongue.

'Tell us your aims ...' Tancred asked, 'tell us all what you hope to do in the future.'

'As I said when we last met, we Lombards have been dominated and crushed for too long, and it's unlawful and unjust. Our people are made to work so hard, for little reward, and then the Byzantine rulers tax us unmercifully - after which all our gold is sailed back to Constantinople; we see this daily and it maddens us. Apulia should be ours - *we were here first!* How dare they take our women and children away as hostages?'

It was clear that he had struck a chord within the Normans' minds; no race on earth was more independent than they.

'So that's what you want? Our help in regaining your land and cities?'

'We're not buying mercenaries ...'

'*Aren't you?* Aren't you offering to buy our skills as soldiers?' Rainulf shouted.

Melus spoke loudly,

'Stop thinking of only one day at a time! Instead - think of embarking on our campaign as power-sharing with us! *Power-sharing,*' he repeated, 'not calling one man 'master'! This way you keep your independence.'

A buzz of discussion arose from the Hall; the idea was new and intriguing. *Power-sharing?*

At Melus' signal the women cleared the dishes and set more food in front of them. Not one had expected a second course. As the women criss-crossed the Hall, first bringing in different fresh-water fish, roasted and garlanded with herbs, each man spoke earnestly to friends and neighbours about the opportunities opening up before them.

The maids carried in earthenware pots of broth thick with bacon, capon pasties and pasties of bream, and - with a flourish- a resplendent blanc-manger. Tancred found this to be a mound of shredded chicken mixed with wild rice which had been boiled in almond milk until soft ... then seasoned with sugar and garnished with fried almonds and preserved anise seeds. He picked and poked at it, nibbled the nuts, spat out the seeds, then ate all that was in the dish.

At a silent signal from Dattus the girls began to fade from the room. Melus rapped on the table again, loudly enough to gain attention,

'Life here, in the south, is very rich - as you may have noticed.'

Deliberately he looked about him, first at the overflowing tables, then at the comely girls as they left, and finally around his well-defended walls ... as if it was the first time he had ever seen these things. The men followed his gaze; they, too, had never seen the like. In over-populated Normandy they lived like peasants, often half-starved, with no chance of acquiring land.

'This small castle of mine is only used when I come to Benevento - you should see my castle at Bari, it's like a palace in comparison!'

They could well believe him.

'And such riches could be yours. Have you any idea of the fortunes available if we re-capture the ports of Brindisi and Bari? Their port taxes are huge. They are doorways to the East.'

Several men shook their heads. Melus had them in the palm of his hand, thought Tancred, they would follow any bait he offered.

'Fundamentally - let's capture Brindisi and Bari from the Byzantines and then organise the massive income from general trade. But - and this vital - *there's no time to be lost.*'

He drew breath and quickly got into his stride again.

'The roads are good: here at Benevento we are at the crossroads of the Via Appia and the Via Trajan, the two principal roads of the south; they were built by the Romans and they serve us just as well today.'

The older men nodded in understanding.

'The forests are stocked with fine timber - in fact, most of the uplands are covered with forests, and filled with game.'

He laughed as a man choked on a bone from the roasted meat, calling out.

'Take a drink - wash it away! We have abundant wine in this country - and as you can see we don't go hungry! There is unlimited olive oil, nuts in the forests, game - deer - wild boar - fruit - more variety, I believe, than you would find in Normandy.'

Tancred became even more thoughtful as Melus spoke, for there had been many days at home when there was scarcely enough food for the table. What a future Melus offered! Instead of being seriously impoverished they might be rich. They might even own land!

The women came again to clear away the bones and unused

trenchers, replacing the washed boards with yet a third course. This time there were lampreys with a hot sauce. Mouth-watering venison, sizzling and crackling. Triangular game fritters and minced-pork patties. Sturgeon and swordfish, cut thick as chunks of meat. And then the famous dish of frumenty ... which none of the Normans had tasted before. It was served with the venison, and was a thick pudding of whole-wheat grains and almond milk, enriched with egg-yolks and coloured with saffron.

'I'm going to be ill with all this rich food,' muttered Tancred, 'and I'll have trouble with the men on our journey home - hoping for another feast!'

'Speaking of illness,' said Dattus, 'our famous doctors in Benevento were trained in Sicily - the best - most civilised - doctors in Europe.'

'Never mind the doctors,' called one sturdy Norman, 'what about the women?' The crowd laughed as he winked at a pretty maid, they knew him well.

'The women? Well, it's difficult to say, there are so many of them and they're all different! A good proportion are very beautiful, especially the Greeks, although the Lombard ladies mostly have flaxen hair, if you prefer that type?'

'We love 'em all ...' breathed the man, happily.

'I hope you enjoy your share,' said Melus politely, 'but let's return to the matter on hand - the divisions of wealth and power should you join me?'

Swiftly Tancred pounced.

'Is this an offer?'

Melus paused for a fraction of a second, then nodded unsmiling. He raised his elegant hand for silence. The men fell quiet, leaned their elbows amongst the detritus and drank deeply.

'Let me be honest with you,' said Melus, 'we Lombards need you; we can't manage any longer on our own. I have a small army, but it's losing heart. Just think back to your pilgrimage to St. Michael's grotto, remember how it looked and has been affected by our Byzantine overlords? You men have been brave to go there at this time, but people in the south of Italy, even brigands, would have been frightened to try and stop such a forceful band of foot soldiers as you.'

The Normans looked at each other with pride, pleased that their worth was properly recognised.

Melus continued without a pause,

'Pope Benedict has recently given me his permission to choose a band of men, even foreigners, if I thought they would have the ability to help the Lombard cause. If you helped us,' he said, very slowly and loudly, 'you would be taking up arms for the sake of our mother Church.'

Several of the men crossed themselves at the Holy Father's name. Tancred admired Melus' strategy immensely; aware, too, that by seating him between the brothers, they had associated their leader with the Lombard cause throughout the evening.

'Even so,' Melus said, aggressively, withdrawing the carrot immediately, 'I don't really know what you are capable of: *it's as much of a risk for me as you!* It's even possible you'd be no use to us at all, but - at the very least - if you did agree to come and fight for our cause you'd be well rewarded. At the point of victory,' he recounted slowly, 'for every ten houses forfeited by the enemy - you Normans would have one. For every twenty golden vessels and lamps you would take an agreed share. You would have a daily wage, and salt, and your leaders would be given land in agreement with the Pope, and those of you who prefer a settled life would get the opportunity to work with Lombards in the administration of the cities.'

'Land!' murmured Tancred, *'land of my own!'*

Norman looked at Norman, wreathed in smiles: inwardly they gloated.

'But,' said Melus in a silky voice, 'perhaps I go too fast? Do I insult you? Perhaps you men already have enough land back at home - enough cattle? - enough gold?'

'Good God, we've no money at all!'

Tancred shouted with laughter, his massive shoulders shaking. His bellow broke the mounting tension, smashed the tissue of dreams the men were weaving in their minds, and brought them back to reality.

'We Normans have two main faults,' he said, 'we breed too fast and we quarrel too fiercely! But, as you've seen for yourself, we're strong and we're quick and we've unlimited energy. We all have reputations for being capable men-at-arms and some are good with swords and others good with horses. We may easily be tempted by your offer, for it gives us a chance for a wealthy future brought by our own fighting skills. But,' he said, leaning forward and thrusting his finger in Melus' face, *'never forget that our independence is paramount!* We'll fight when and where we want - and if we become disaffected, we'll walk away and fight for someone else!'

Melus stared at Tancred, incredulous, disbelieving. Then hurriedly, before it was too late, grasped his arm and shouted,

'Agreed!'

The men began to roar like the storm at sea, the sudden waves of noise echoing around the walls. They raised clenched fists above their heads and drummed their feet upon the floor.

'Then it's settled,' said Tancred, his voice rising above the bedlam, 'we'll come - but not until next year. That'll give us ample time. Confer with your fellow Lombards, speak to them about fair payment, and collect together your army again. In our turn we'll see our families, arm ourselves and bring extra men. As the Pope has sanctioned this cause,' he bellowed even louder, 'and as we first met in a holy place -

we'll fight for your cause in return for your promised rich rewards, and' he reached a crescendo, *'we'll do it in the name of Saint Michael!'*

So the preparations for the glorious adventure in Italy began.

In the castles and keeps and tiny hamlets of Normandy there was an air of excitement which surpassed anything that had gone before. The visions of gold to hoard, fine food to rest upon their tables, illustrious battles to win and deepening brotherhood ahead lifted all their hearts. The tales of their adventures spread far and wide across their homeland and became the highlight of minstrels' ballads; it resulted in their numbers being vastly increased, as friends and relations joined them.

All were thrilled to the marrow about the future - the fame, the money and the land: the opportunities were thrilling and the news spread right across northern Europe.

Swiftly the Norman hordes swept out again to their Lombard masters in Benevento and, with the element of surprise so wisely proposed by Melus, they gleefully took from the Byzantines hamlet after hamlet, town after town, steadily bearing southwards towards Bari, until many miles had been laid waste by this unstoppable - confident - army.

For well over a year they rampaged, victorious, raising Lombard hopes - although they cared more about their own. Tales of their brilliant successes winged their way back to Normandy.

Then they paused outside Bari, north, near the sea, preparing for the biggest prize. Brindisi would be the next stop.

But news travelled equally swiftly to the East. So the steely Byzantines left nothing to chance about their treasured ports. The Emperor in Constantinople sailed over a gargantuan army of fresh soldiers, far greater than was necessary, to combat these famed and ferocious raiders from Normandy.

At Cannae, north of Bari, the opposing forces finally met.

The battle that ensued was fought with high hopes to begin with, then fierce determination and finally in despair.

By the end, the Byzantine troops had massacred almost all of the Lombards and most of the Normans. It was a mighty bloodbath, and inevitable, for the Byzantines had outnumbered the daring incomers by many times. Melus and Dattus alone of the Lombards escaped, with a handful of Normans, but none of the Normans could bear to return to their homeland, it was too shameful. They remained in southern Italy, and they stayed there purely for themselves. They had had a taste of victory, of gold in their pockets and the lure of land to own ... being outlaws suited their characters admirably.

Gradually, over the years, their numbers increased. Normandy was still over-populated. The independent life of a brigand appeared glamorous from afar, so a steady trickle of opportunists travelled out to investigate.

They fought for themselves. They fought for friends. They fought for others when they fell out with their friends. They were disorganised and independent, clinging to the coat-tails of real power, which stemmed from a weak Pope and an absent Holy Roman Emperor. The area seethed with opportunities within the chaos.

But one key person was missing. One who could have created order and anticipated the problems of defeat, one who could have united them: Tancred de Hauteville, architect of it all, missed every adventure to come. He had his own battle in Hauteville-le-Guichard, his home in Normandy, and he lost.

The day before they were due to start Tancred rode out with a few friends into the forest, they had in their minds that they might never see their common land again. In Tancred's brain there was emotional turmoil; thoughts about the future fought with thoughts of the people he was leaving behind.

After a while he rode away from his friends, seeking complete peace, needing time for deliberation. It was a beautiful day, full of promise. He dismounted and sat against a fallen log covered with ivy, beneath a huge oak. With a few acorns tossing in his hand he leaned back against the wood, trying to assess the priorities. The sounds of the forest were all about him and the sun's rays slanted through the branches. He lifted his face towards the sun gratefully, closing his eyes, allowing the warmth to soak in until he almost dozed. In the distance he was aware of the clamour of his friends hunting - yet he was so deep in thought he really heard nothing, for all the scents and sounds were familiar.

He never knew - then - that someone had wounded a wild boar, which had escaped. He never knew that the boar had been deflected from its final race to safety by seeing a falling acorn through its scarlet, blood-soaked eye, handled by a man ... his enemy.

Too late Tancred sensed the wounded boar as it raced towards him, his great yellow tusks razor sharp and curving upwards in a half circle. He heard the animal's pounding hooves as he lifted his head, but he was blinded by the sun in his eyes.

As he leaped to his feet the boar smashed into him against the trunk of the oak. He screamed as he fell. Tancred lay on the forest floor, torn to a pulp, as the boar crashed into him again and again until he lost consciousness.

Later Tancred was laid, straightened out in agony, on his huge raised bed in the family castle. Broken, bleeding from a multitude of open wounds from the cruel tusks, he knew that both of his hips were broken and his right leg was crushed. Clearly he could no longer fight ... it would be a miracle if he ever stood on his two feet again.

Gilbert and Rainulf came to see him before they departed on their return journey to Italy and all the promised glory; they stood on either side of him. Such light as there seemed to be concentrated on the figure on the bed.

Tancred's pale eyes were unseeing in his paler face. He seemed as aloof as if he had been a denizen of another world, where there was neither sun nor wind. The cold room beyond him was a wild pattern of heavy shadows.

'I had such dreams ...' he muttered, blood trickling from his mouth. 'One day,' he moved slightly, his face clouded with pain, 'one day my sons will take my place. They can join you when they're old enough. I'll train my sons and send them to you - that I swear.'

'Aye,' they mumbled, hardly believing he would live, 'we'll take all your sons. But we'll miss you sorely.'

'I'll send them,' he repeated, 'my sons will live my life for me - eventually. Tell Melus. The battles with the Lombards may be over by then - but the prospects out there'll remain ... the princes ... the Pope ... the Emperor ... whatever happens - don't squander the opportunities!'

'Aye.'

'Then God go with you.'

PART TWO

ROBERT DE HAUTEVILLE

Robert de Hauteville was Tancred's sixth son; the eldest of a second marriage, which brought massive complications in its wake.

Tancred's first son was named William, then came Drogo, Humphrey, Geoffrey and Serlo. Several still-born children were born too, and some daughters - but they didn't count. Their mother was Muriella, slightly higher-born than Tancred, who had spurred him on to his voyage overseas, encouraging his ambitions. She dreamed he would return with plans for a magnificent future for them all. Instead she was left with a fragile invalid, continually in pain, who needed years of nursing - and even less money than before. They had a modest little castle in the vale of Cotentin in Normandy, south of Cherbourg. Muriella's own dowry had paid for some extensions at their castle and a luxury - a stone-built kitchen. But, whilst still a young woman, Muriella died 'from coughing' - so it was stated by contemporary scribes when documenting the Hauteville family; her early death was probably from pneumonia, brought on by exhaustion.

Five sons were not enough for Tancred; he wanted to be a power in the land, so he married again. He was an honourable man, in dread of any fault against the Church, so he refused to take a concubine; he swore that all his sons would make a place for themselves, in Normandy or even in Italy, so they must all legally bear the Hauteville name.

His second wife was the lady Fressenda, but her dowry was less than his first wife. She was so tall, so stately, with a fall of flaxen hair and big bones; she was a perfect match for Tancred. She dutifully behaved as a good step-mother to the first five sons, then happily continued to provide ten more children for her husband. These were Robert, Mauger, another William, Aubrey, Tancred, Humbert and Roger. Like her predecessor she gave birth to some daughters too; just as soon as possible all the girls were married off and left home.

In time all the twelve sons grew to stand over six feet - Robert became the tallest - and they became known as the 'family of giants'. They were immensely competitive, quarrelling continuously, furiously loyal to their mothers. Robert hated being the eldest of a *second* family, he felt diminished and undervalued and his elder brothers never let him forget his position.

One very cold day in midwinter, when Robert was just a child, he wandered out from their castle and made for the stables; there was always something going on there and he was bored with inaction. He heard the horses moving about in their stalls as he approached and cautiously looked through the opening to see who else was there. Immediately his attention was focussed on his elder half-brother, Drogo, who stood with his back to Robert, lazily twirling his long, thin dagger as he inspected Tancred's horse. The beautiful animal was half-asleep, held in its stall by a rope harness; it was a lovely sight with its dark-bay coat and a magnificent cream-coloured tail falling almost to the ground. What was impressive, too, was its size - everything in the stables appeared over-sized - because it had to carry such a huge man. Wounded Tancred and his beautiful horse were famous across the area and often spoken about in the local taverns with heartfelt admiration: Tancred was so proud of his glorious horse, it was his greatest treasure.

Drogo was Tancred's second son by his first wife - one of the chosen few in Robert's eyes. He was tall, handsome and charming when he wished to be, but he was also a tyrant, cunning, malicious and sly. Although able and athletic, with a scintillating brain, no-one trusted him for a moment. He stood out as especially devious in the Hauteville family of twelve thrusting brothers and enjoyed the fear he instilled in others. He especially revelled in the feeling of power; it was meat and drink to him.

This day it was painfully cold; snow had fallen for days, the hunt had been called off, and everyone was huddled indoors. Only Drogo stood in the stables. Time, thought Drogo, time to make some mischief - and arrange it so that someone else would take the blame - that would be amusing. He considered his options. He looked again at his father's horse, who suddenly grew tense, showing the whites of his eyes and laying flat his ears. A pair of stable-boys came noisily into view and stood behind Robert; Drogo turned to look at all three.

Robert's silent arrival inspired Drogo - *Robert would be the victim* - Drogo hated Robert, the newcomer, the first of Tancred's second marriage. Robert, although almost wordless in his presence, always looked at Drogo with an air of hostility and aggression. The moment they came near each other the air bristled with antagonism and just having Robert within reach made Drogo furiously savage.

Slowly Drogo lifted his dagger up into the air where, as he twisted and turned it, the razor-sharp blade flashed like a diamond in the light reflected from the snow outside. Drogo held the knife at arms' length and edged nearer the horse.

Two more swift steps and Drogo had his shoulder against the horse's body, pushing it hard against the wall, its head held by the rope. Then, like a streak of lightning, Drogo swooped forward and sliced off a great chunk of the horse's showy tail with his knife, and again, and again, until there was nothing left apart from the silky tresses in the icy mud at their feet. Each time Drogo sliced with his knife he roared aloud:

'NO, Robert!' or

'Don't DO that!' or

'Father will be FURIOUS! You'll be thrashed - I'll see to that!' or,

'Stop this immediately, *you upstart,* this only shows your mother's ill-breeding!'

The horse reared and screamed, thrumming his hooves against the wall as Drogo roared and sliced away. It was pandemonium. Robert gasped as he stood watching in the doorway, and as Drogo was thrusting his knife back into its sheath he turned and fled. He pelted as fast as he could into the castle. His father, Tancred, caught him as he raced indoors.

'Hold hard! What's this, young Robert? What have you done now? I heard Drogo shouting at you!'

'Nothing, sir.'

Robert was shaking, speechless with fear.

'Nothing?' shouted Drogo from the path outside, 'NOTHING?' He brandished a handful of the horse's tail in Tancred's face. 'Nothing? Only cut all the hair from your horse's tail!'

There was no escaping the fact that the hair in Drogo's fist was that of Tancred's horse - the colour was so unusual.

'By God, you'll pay for that' said Tancred, white with fury and removing his heavy belt. 'Come here - NOW!'

After the beating Drogo laughed quietly and beckoned his other brothers into a huddle. As he passed Robert, lying on the floor, he hissed at him.

'Don't dare to challenge us, Robert, we come first and always will.'

He knew, oh! How well he knew, those hurtful words shouted or hissed at him by all his elder half-brothers - he would never forget them.

As the snow was heaped against the castle's walls, so all the growing family decided to stay within its protection; each youngster had to find some way to occupy himself in the Hall, but they were all bored - bored and irritable. There was not enough food and the whole place was overcrowded and troublesome.

When Robert crept back to join them near the central hearth after his beating, his half-brothers hissed together for a while, watching him, taunting him, and whispering. When he didn't react, or cry, they changed tactics and suddenly rushed at the youngest baby of the extensive family, Roger, aiming to take away his plaything - a small pet badger. It was a deliberate dare to Robert, the stalwart eldest of Tancred's second family, to protect the boy.

The brothers twisted both baby Roger's arms, making him shriek and drop his pet. Terrified, the little badger ran around the Hall in circles, with the older boys trying to catch it. Robert instinctively raced to its rescue. It was bedlam.

The older boys pushed Robert aside, but he was boiling with fury and kicked and clawed at them, fighting, ungovernable with rage. His mother, Fressenda, miraculously lifted weeping Roger out from the scrum and took him away from harm, shouting at them all uselessly.

Robert defended the badger by the open fire. His nose ran with blood and his clothes were torn as his half-brothers hacked and kicked him back. Fressenda, powerless, called out to the lazy servants to help. Robert soon realised that it was inevitable that he would lose the battle so, with flaunting deliberation, he stamped on the badger's head and killed it, kicking its body into the fire. Holding his head high, he laughed.

Roger howled afresh. The older boys shouted in fury.

As the servants reluctantly answered Fressenda's call his enraged half-brothers, led by Drogo, caught Robert by the neck, forced his arms behind his back and dragged him outside the castle back to the stables. In the icy cold they wrestled with him, Humphrey, Drogo, Geoffrey and Serlo - but it was no match. Grim-faced he struggled, without uttering a word; his elders were clearly intent on teaching him a lesson he would never forget. The servants didn't bother to follow them - it was too cold and those older boys were too big and brutal.

In the stables they finally smashed Robert down to the ground but as he fought to pull himself away one of them - he never knew which – shouted,

'Oh, no, you don't!' then tore his loosened clothing from him.

He lay for a moment, stunned, face down in the horse's hair, his eyes wide with fear. Completely out of control, Drogo yelled,

'Look the other way, Robert, *we'll teach you to become a man!'*

His brothers surrounded him, holding his arms and his legs, baying like hounds surrounding a fox. Then they raped him. First Drogo, then Humphrey. Geoffrey and Serlo turned away. Finally, as he left, Drogo deliberately threw some horsehair onto Robert's unconscious face.

At the end of the day the stable boys helped him back into the castle. He never spoke about the incident to anyone, and his injured pride, and throughout all Robert's life he would try to forget that day, but without success.

'We'll teach you to become a man!'

There was a knife at the beginning as there would be a knife at the end.

JUDITH OF EVREUX

'Judith! Judith!'

A distraught nurse, calling softly, hurried through room after room in the huge castle at Evreux.

'Judith?'

The castle was half empty because the Great Count was away on Papal business. As the nurse hastened she grew more agitated, knowing that her punishment would mean instant dismissal if she couldn't find the child – or worse, if the child was damaged or dead. There were very few other servants in the area where the nurse searched, for all who could be spared were in the Great Bedchamber, awaiting the outcome of the drama unfolding before them.

The nurse called the child endlessly, and urgently, quietly, quietly, so no tell-tale would report her.

'Judith, sweet Judith, come to me! Our little game is over and we have to return to your mother – she's asking for you!'

The last thing she wanted was for the news to get out that the Count's only daughter was missing. Judith had never strayed before, she was always biddable, she knew nothing about naughtiness or being headstrong, she was only five years old and the only child in the castle, so knew nothing of bad behaviour. Her character was still totally unformed, apart from a tendency towards painful shyness; when in public she hid behind her mother's skirts or closed her eyes, distressed by vivid blushes which she couldn't control.

The nurse's tone was coaxing and loving, she called out in such a way that no-one, she hoped, would realise the serious nature of her quest.

'Judith! Let's play another game? You can choose . . .'

But there was no answer and silence hung in the air.

As the woman called the child, she hurriedly upturned leather cushions or rich fabric lying on the floor in every area, from clothing to horse-blankets – anything that could conceal a child. She peeped into boxes and chests and behind screens or bed-curtains or down twisting spiral stairs. There wouldn't have been a chance that the child was out of doors this cold evening for the Count's guards were trained to detect a living creature as small as a mouse if it had attempted to scurry through the castle's majestic gates.

The Count of Evreux, descendant of the Viking chieftain Rollo, and cousin of the Dukes of Normandy, was one of the richest, most powerful men in Europe, and one of the most formidable. He was crafty and devious, quick as lightning and ruthless. But he was also a reasonably fair man, for he believed in the power of the laws of the land, some of which he had personally drawn up. The laws had to be upheld: they had nothing to do with justice but everything to do with stability and as a leader of the community he was always seen to promote them. He was universally feared so he was instantly obeyed, and the nurse was terrified of him.

Little Judith was as delicate as a wind-flower, with long, silver-gold hair inherited from her Nordic ancestors. Unknown to her she was an heiress of such importance that almost no-one was of high enough birth to be permitted to speak to her: she had no friends, nor any playmates, and knew nothing of any interaction between people of her own age. Nor had she developed any form of curiosity – it was as if she was caught like a tiny insect in amber.

Her mother, who went from one pregnancy to the next, losing each child in between, kept Judith constantly by her side. She had had three miscarriages before Judith's birth, and countless miscarriages since. How Judith had clung to life, had remained in her mother's womb until full term, and then emerged so perfectly, was a miracle not to be repeated.

'She's a marvel, so tiny and looking so vulnerable, but she must have an inner strength to have survived,' said the Countess, 'now – is it possible that I could have another living child?' There was never an answer.

'Judith!' called the nurse again. 'Come child, come to me!' The castle rooms, too, remained silent.

Judith and her mother were inseparable. They murmured endearments to each other, stroked each other's skin and kissed each other's cheeks, all in all to each other. When it was time for the Countess to receive her husband at her bed to start another child, Judith would be taken to a room nearby for a few days and a maid would sit at her side as she slept. When her mother was with child again, or her father was away from the castle, Judith would stay by her mother all day long, in the shadow of her great headdress or behind the billow of her stiffened skirts, playing with tiny toys of immense value – of which she was unaware. There wasn't very much for them to speak about as Judith was too young to understand her mother's agonies as pregnancy after pregnancy ended in tears and stifled moans and emptiness.

Her mother, a great heiress herself, was merely a brood-mare for the Count. Yet, in some strange way that no-one could understand, the Count was exceedingly fond of his wife and was tender to her at all times. His greatest fault was being unable to put his feelings into words. Love, any true emotion, was not something one ever spoke of in high ranks of society.

He became, instead, only too ready to be invited again for intimacy with his wife, and lingered for days at her bedside until there was some hope of another child. He said very little to her; he was neither clumsy, nor hasty, nor cruel in any way – but he couldn't take his hands off her. She loved it.

The Count had been married before and had a grown son, Odo, who largely led his own life yet remained close to his father. His first wife had been a mistake, in the Count's eyes, for she produced only the one son when she was sixteen and was barren afterwards for years, withering away, hardly ever eating food, until one day she was found dead in bed, almost forgotten, only twenty-four years old.

After respectfully waiting a period of mourning the Count decided to marry a second wife. This time he chose with great care for the sake of his diplomatic plans, and selected a young heiress from the French court, many years younger than himself, and then found himself wildly – passionately – in love with her. He never fully explained to his second wife what he felt, nor could really understand his own emotions. *What he left out* intrigued his second wife enormously and there developed such a harmonious compatibility and affection between them that neither believed their own happiness. What had happened between them was an arrival, a jolting moment of recognition, as if they had walked through a door into the room of their lives.

Yet no other living child was born to them – bar Judith. And Judith and her father were never alone together. She was not expected to initiate a conversation and, to him, she was too young to notice. They had never exchanged a word: neither would have known what to say.

'Judith?'

Her nurse was frantic in her search, but there was no answer. So the nurse finally turned about in a circle and began to pace back to the Great Bedchamber, searching hopelessly where she had searched before. She concentrated on peering behind the heavy wall tapestries, woven with pure gold amongst the other brilliant colours, but most of them were too heavy for a child to have moved aside and got behind.

The Countess had, that day, aborted twins in their sixth month and, seemingly, couldn't save her own life either. It was clear to all that tended her that she was fading fast.

'Judith, Judith . . .' she herself whispered, her glorious hair unbound and wild across the pillow, 'come to me, my lovely babe. Let me see one last glimpse of you.'

Another rush of hot blood gushed out of her, leaving her suspended between life and death.

But Judith stayed where she was, only aware of the terrible atmosphere around her; she had closed her mind to reality. She was only two yards away, unseen, paralysed with fear of the unknown, crouched underneath her mother's bed. Heavy fabric was draped from ceiling to floor behind her mother's sumptuous bed, becoming a very private place for Judith. She knelt awkwardly on the floor in its folds, unheard and almost unhearing, all but forgotten except by the distraught nurse searching the castle. She had slipped into her hiding place some while ago when her nurse's back was momentarily turned.

All around the bed were her mother's serving women, tip-toeing, bringing silver bowls of warm water, fine linen cloths, pots of precious ointments and bunches of herbs. Judith could smell burning lavender across the room; a maid she couldn't see shrieked beneath her breath as she burned a finger, and an older voice said with authority,

'No, no! We'll cup her soon, but first try harder to stem that blood, she's lost far, far too much.'

Unaware of the great drama above her, Judith was trying to extricate one of her small legs, which was painfully pushed up against a piece of carved wood. First she had to pull her gown across her knees but it was made from such thick material that it wouldn't loosen. An inch here, an inch there, after what seemed a long time she gradually managed to straighten out her small leg with a sigh; then she rolled over on the floor to see what was happening in the room around her.

From under one side curtain she could see the rapidly moving skirts of the serving women and their big feet, flat feet, rosy bunions and dry heels, continuously passing to and fro. She could hear, too, the anxious, muted chatter between the serving women – and a man's deep voice, praying. She began to concentrate on the smell of those feet, the dust, the herbs on the wooden floor and, worst of all, the pervading – increasing – smell of blood. She wasn't sorry to be shut out as the daylight faded, because most of her semi-silent life was lived in a cocoon, a world away from normality.

Time went by and the room around Judith and her mother grew quieter and more still. She wanted her mother, she longed to be held in her gentle arms, but the smell of blood worried her so much that she couldn't make that last leap from under her mother's bed into her embrace. She had no idea at all what was wrong.

In the end there was a curious, breathless silence above her, more telling than a shout, and the crowd around the bed dropped to their knees in one long, mournful sigh, shutting out the remainder of the light for Judith. Claustrophobic in the dark, she couldn't bear the feeling of being trapped, so, as short prayers were being said, she wriggled down towards the light at the foot of the bed as each servant gradually departed from the room in tears. Two older women were left to straighten the Countess' body and the bedclothes and brush, for the last time, the Countess' beautiful hair.

As, together, they moved to lift the body onto fresh pillows Judith crept from her hiding place and stood upright, looking with horror at her mother's dead face, white as snow. She cried out,

'Maman – what's happened to her?'

The women turned to look at the child's tragic face and the tears beginning to form. One bowed her head, saying gently,

'Oh my poor child . . . she's gone, little one, she's gone for ever. This is a cruel way for you to see your dead mother.' She stood back, not daring to touch the crying child.

'Maman,' she whispered, 'don't go!' then whispered 'Where has she gone?'

As Judith began to sob into her own hands the other women began to clear away the mounds of cloths, sodden and stiff with blood. Two tiny shapes were reverently placed upon a silver dish and covered quietly with a fresh cloth and gently removed.

There was a sudden sound of hurrying feet as Judith's nurse appeared. She whispered urgently,

'Judith! I couldn't find you! Where have you been?'

'I've been in here,' said Judith faintly, 'I've not been anywhere else.'

The nurse could hardly believe her ears, but the child was so small that she could have become lost in a shadow. She brushed a little dust from the child's dress.

'Has word been sent to the Count?' She whispered to the priest.

'Yes. He's just now returned from business with the Pope, he'll be here shortly.'

'Then we must watch ourselves – the light will have gone out of his life.'

'Maman!' whispered Judith, now awash with tears, 'Maman … Maman … Don't leave me behind . . . don't leave me!'

But no-one dared to touch her in comfort as she stood, tiny but royally erect, alone – so alone - in the Great Bedchamber.

THE HAUTEVILLE FAMILY IN NORMANDY

Jacques swayed in the candlelight as he climbed the steps. Overburdened, he balanced a platter of meat upon his head, a skin of wine dragged down his other hand.

'God!' he thought, 'I'm so tired.'

Jacques was Robert de Hauteville's body-servant, but had been drawn in to help the general staff because the events that day were so important. He felt belittled by the work; he would have been happier standing guard behind Robert and watching. Robert, now in his twenties, depended on Jacques' eyes and reports.

Peppery Jacques was the same age, thin as a whiplash, with fiery red hair which curled in the rain. He was always eager to be first, impatient and volatile, ever ready to serve his master in any capacity. Sometimes his pale face, dusted with freckles, with its straight nose and curving nostrils, conveyed shocked disapproval without him moving an eyelash. Robert always knew Jacques' true opinions; Jacques had his own standards and they were very different from Robert's.

The Hall in Tancred's small castle was stuffy, even though the doors were flung wide open, for it had been built as a fortress and what openings it had were thin slits high up near the roof in the thick walls. In the kitchen and cloisters the air was dense with fumes; a careless cook had allowed fat to spill into the flames, burning meat and scorching Jacques' hand - it smarted fiercely, and he could feel a watery blister rising.

Tonight Jacques was disgusted by the reek of overturned mead and wine, he was acutely aware of it, mixed with the stink of rancid beer standing in open barrels. It all melded with the foetid odour from the carcass of a small sheep, green with mould, awaiting scouring before roasting. The whole area near the kitchens smelled sour. The rushes on the floors had been messy and muddy for many days; no-one had swilled the clutter through into the courtyard outside - knowing it would immediately be tramped back in again. These small signals indicated that the mistress of the house was slowly failing in her duties, but no-one dared supplant her, nor find fault - ageing Fressenda, Tancred's second wife, was too much liked. Jacques hated this state of affairs, reflecting that it dishonoured the family in front of guests.

It was eventide and, although it was early spring, there was a black frost. The many men here this day had met to discuss plans for the future, for Tancred was old and increasingly infirm after his terrible accident, and the small castle was bursting at the seams; it was time that some inmates should leave and ease the family's burden.

Thirteen years earlier, a year after Tancred's accident, his first son, William, had left for southern Italy, yearning after battles and glory and, hopefully, land. Two years afterwards William, in his turn, had sent for his four brothers - Humphrey, Drogo, Geoffrey and Serlo to join him. They had agreed to become a part of an army, where William was established in the service of the Lombard Prince of Capua, centred at Aversa. Tancred had been overjoyed that William had sent for all his available brothers. Robert was overjoyed to see the back of all his five half-brothers. They were like a running sore in his life. But he remained in Normandy, champing at the bit.

After years of fighting, first on one side and then on another, the enterprising Normans now had a fief of their own at Aversa, legally conferred on them by the Holy Roman Emperor. Now they had become almost respectable, and now they could see a clear objective - the acquisition of land for themselves in Italy. Tancred rejoiced for them, it was exactly what he had foreseen and wanted for himself: Normandy was very badly over-crowded and now, luckily, opportunities seemed to be opening up in southern Italy.

Today, Tancred wanted to have open discussions on this unique occasion, to show he had respect for the laws of the land, for he was, himself, still only an honorary commander of a modest group of ten knights in the militia of the Duke of Normandy and feared a conflict of interests. Norman laws were strictly adhered to, but how often had it happened that homage clashed with homage? Tancred had always been loyal to the core to Duke Robert of Normandy, but he had recently died and his bastard son, William, had not yet been totally acclaimed as his successor. Tancred knew there was a short, legal, breathing space in which other of his sons might legally escape to possible glory in Italy and win for themselves land, money and power. There was clearly no opening for them in Normandy – the overcrowding was crippling.

Wisely, with courteous good sense, Tancred had invited William of Normandy to witness - and take part in - their discussions today: what he had to say could lend authority to the enterprise; he still had further sons who were too young to leave; and putting their future in jeopardy was out of the question.

'The Bastard', William of Normandy, was now turning eighteen, acclaimed by the majority in Normandy as Duke, but he was always in great difficulty and danger, still universally known as 'the Bastard', and ever-threatened. He needed to secure his hold on his father's land; that was his first objective, before he looked elsewhere – perhaps England? Today he was at ease; this meeting could only touch him obliquely as he knew he had no lawful say in the outcome. The reason he had been invited was not lost on him, either.

It was William's habit to be in icy control, so fierce and tall and isolated; but on this occasion he was amongst real friends of his own age and choice. He lounged, long-legged, together with the Duppa de Uphaugh family, with whom he had travelled there, and who, it was known, might wish to take their chances in Italy, too.

Tancred was practical, wise and experienced, and lived in ever-deepening pain. He hoped his sons had absorbed his lavish advice, as there was little else he could do for all of them now. He thanked God that none were physically as disabled as he was: two huge yellow tusks hung starkly, low, just above their heads, over the doorway from which hunters left the castle. It was a conspicuous warning.

The modest meal was over at last, the atmosphere was humming with excitement: it was time for decisions. Tancred called out to the natural leader in the Hall,

'Robert! Have the servants clear the food - leave the wine - whilst I escort my lady to her room.'

Fressenda was slowly dying. No-one knew the cause, but all about her were disturbed by the appearance of her face, which had suddenly become lop-sided and set. White with fatigue and pain, her hands like dead fish, cold and wet, all she wanted was a little peace. Her last wish was to retire to the female order at the Monastery at St. Evroul-sur-Ouche, first to rest, then to die, going through the gates of Heaven as a carefree girl again. When Tancred rose, their youngest son, Roger, got up quickly to help his parents, and as his mother had expected, encouraged her to lean on his own strong arm, rather than his father's.

Whilst all three retired from the Hall Roger flicked a tentative backward glance at his eldest brother Robert. Robert scowled.

Young Roger, the youngest of all, was mortally afraid of Robert - everyone was - partly because of his size but mostly because of his personality. He knew Robert to be hard and forceful now, bred of frustration, but, as Robert was the eldest son of seven more boys in the second family, he had a natural leader's bearing and aspect; many people said that Robert was the man Tancred would have been.

Tancred and Robert looked alike, they bore their bodies in similar ways and were unaware that when they asked a question, father and son angled their heads to the same side, images of each other as they listened; they looked up, too, from under the same bleached and bushy eyebrows.

Roger hardly dared to approach his elder brother, but he watched him constantly, all the same, and learned much. He envied the bearded, blond giant, envied the way Robert would unleash a shout of laughter, wrestle with two men at a time, fight with his sword in either hand - ambidextrous, always the victor. Perhaps, one day, he would grow to be like him. To fourteen-year-old Roger, Robert was a god.

However, Robert epitomised conflict without uttering a word. He did not have Tancred's open geniality and ingrained trust. Tancred was always prepared to give the benefit of doubt; no-one expected the same liberality from Robert. It was no secret that Robert hated his elder brothers passionately, even in their absence.

Robert was now by far the tallest of the twelve 'Hauteville giants', who towered over the other short and stocky Normans. He always stood extra erect, head up, as if following the flight of migrant birds. His hair was thick, roughly cut, his clear skin was bronzed and all his features were in keeping with his height and weight - slightly over-sized. The shape of his mouth was clearly outlined, marked as though it was carved by a chisel: it could look classically beautiful.

Yet Robert was no boy - had scarcely ever been a boy - and had the air that innocence had left him far behind, long ago; it showed in his eyes and in the occasional curl of his lip, like a snarl. The look about him clearly said 'Don't trouble to tell me. I know it. I've done it.' World-weary, dangerously frustrated, his loud laugh now was often forced; his mouth made the noises of a laugh, yet most of the time his eyes remained stony. Never ignored or forgotten, Robert was a victim of his own physique. He knew he was a very big man, and was consumed with ambition. It was open to everyone.

Today, thought Robert, today was the day of crucial decisions and he needed to know exactly where he stood or he would openly rebel.

Always at the forefront, he blazed with a need to succeed. He had sulked for years at being kept at home, being boxed into the family, by law, because he required permission to leave - his father's and the Duke's. He was as tense as the highly-strung bow lying beneath his bench - he was frustrated beyond belief by his lack of advance so far: now the day, and release, may have come.

He beckoned to Jacques and ordered him to oversee the removing of the bones and the sopping coarse-grained trenchers - few beggars at their door would get much in leftovers today. The boards were salved and roughly wiped; the scene gradually altered from looking like a charnel-house. It appeared that several of the younger men there today were drunk, taking advantage of the occasion, for they were to have no say in the proceedings. Robert knew Jacques would take them, if necessary, regardless of their rank, by the scruff of their necks and dowse their heads in the freezing water butts outside. Hulked on the bench beside his father's chair he stared, oblivious, at his enormous young dog, Wolf; clearly he was in a dangerous frame of mind. Both showed the whites of their eyes.

Everyone was apprehensive about great Robert, and today, especially, they gave him a wide berth. When he gave orders they were swiftly obeyed: the servants flew about the Hall, thankful that they, too, might afterwards rest and eat their allotted portions. The sturdy benches were left around the walls, the food-stained boards hastily dismantled; only the roughly carved chair for Tancred was left in the centre of the long wall of the Hall. Finally the central fire was refuelled with logs, noisily, and sparks flew.

The servants withdrew, the other men sat on the benches, their wine in their fists, and their eyes on the giant, brooding Robert. The heavy doors were at long last slammed shut and a quick puff of black smoke swirled around the Hall, unable to escape until it made its meandering way up through the roof. Jacques silently took up his rightful place behind Robert and there he stood, watching.

Tancred limped, crabwise, into the Hall; he could not march at the head of his men, but he had forced himself to ride a horse with apparent ease so that he remained in the Duke's service. Roger, his thinner, silent shadow, followed his father and, rawboned and lanky, leaned against the wall behind him. Tancred settled laboriously into his chair, supporting himself with painful satisfaction; the crowd, bright-eyed, shuffled on their benches and gradually fell silent.

'My friends - greetings to you all. Welcome to you, William of Normandy, we're honoured by your presence. Welcome to the brothers and kinsmen of Theodor and Benedict Duppa de Uphaugh, and welcome to all of you others, friends and family, and all my fine sons and their knights!'

He bowed stiffly to each man as he mentioned his name; self-consciously they bowed deeper in return. The ceremonial was quaint, abnormal in this poor setting.

Their future lives hung in a balance.

Tancred spoke loudly, his voice filling the crowded Hall,

'Today is a day of decisions.'

His audience, waiting for the real meat of his words, growled their approval in their throats, some drumming their heels upon the floor. He went on,

'We Hautevilles have been fortunate. For we've been involved with my eldest sons' lives hundreds of miles away. We've remained in constant communication. This has given us a broad interest in the affairs of the world and an understanding of politics. We've become knowledgeable about the Church and our Pope and the Holy Roman Emperor - and of Italian domains.'

Tancred put his fist on the broad shoulder of his newly arrived fourth son, Geoffrey, who sat at his right hand. Geoffrey, like all the Hauteville men, was very tall, bronzed, and heavily lined, one of the least known members of the family, the fourth son of the first marriage.

He had done all that had been expected of him, but he had grown increasingly quiet; he hardly spoke - just smiled. All five brothers from Tancred's first marriage had been consulted as to which should return and take over the family's affairs when Tancred would die: Geoffrey had been selected. He seemed more suited to family life than warfare, and was pleased to come home; already he had picked out a woman to take as a wife.

Tancred turned back to the waiting crowd; his words were measured and slow, it was foreseen that he would make a grand occasion of the event.

'As you all know, many years ago my friends and I went on our pilgrimage to the East and later my friends, Gilbert and Rainulf, went back to fight in the lands south of Rome. But,' he grimaced as he momentarily looked down at his twisted leg, 'you all know what happened - my accident prevented me from returning to Italy at all. Later on Gilbert was killed and Rainulf took over the leadership.'

Every man sympathised with Tancred. It might have been better for such a vigorous man to have died. Year after year, twisted with pain, he had steeled himself to continue, waiting to send his sons to Italy in his place. Tancred hurried on, he loathed self-pity and hardly ever spoke of his tragedy - but his temper grew shorter day by day.

'Then, as you are aware, my eldest sons William, Drogo, Humphrey, Geoffrey and Serlo all travelled out too, to take up arms with Rainulf. They've done exceedingly well, above my greatest expectations - William even has a title! Their losses of men have been few and their numbers have increased tenfold over the years. Naturally they've learned much, watching the manoeuvres between the Pope, the Holy Roman Emperor, the Princes, the Greeks, the Saracens and the Byzantines from such close quarters. Now, so Geoffrey tells me, William has sent word that he wants new recruits!'

The Great Hall erupted with the sounds as if animals had been unleashed. The men shouted and laughed and cried out. Several men leapt to their feet, others drummed hard with their feet and their fists. Unsettled, Tancred shouted,

'Silence! Sit down! I haven't finished yet, I've more to say! Robert - make them quieten down.'

Robert got to his feet in one swift flashing movement, like a snake uncoiling. He stood, his hands upon his hips, his tree-like legs astride, and roared,

'*ENOUGH!*'

Everyone instantly subsided, falling back onto their benches with a resounding crash. Tancred rested his hand on Robert's shoulder gratefully: he sat between him and Geoffrey.

'I can't support you all, and you're perfectly aware of this. But your half-brothers need more men-at-arms now that my eldest son William, '*Iron-Arm' William*, is Count of Apulia.'

Tancred glowed in satisfaction; being on the periphery of a legend pleased him deeply. William justly deserved his nick-name. During the siege of Syracuse William, single-handed, had charged and killed the well-guarded Emir of Sicily. For this wild - unexpected - action he had attracted much glory and his new epithet.

'Geoffrey, here, who has also fought well in Sicily, has returned for good as my eventual heir, bringing the invitation from William. Be under no illusions. Expect life to be extremely hard! Be aware that the ways of the diverse people in the south will be difficult to understand. My five sons are still alive purely because they've stayed together as a pack - it's almost a miracle. So - never forget that treachery lies everywhere, *even between brother and brother'*.

His sons in the Hall eyed each other; one or two pursed their lips, nodding. Tancred continued, attempting to lighten the atmosphere,

'But my sons have been constant to Norman ideals. Of course

they've had to change allegiance several times - but they've always fought for Norman supremacy. And they've had some luck - Norman luck! Or is it Hauteville luck?'

The men gave tongue like hounds, relishing the thought. William of Normandy's mouth tightened imperceptibly as he stared at the floor, 'Hauteville luck' indeed, he thought, more like 'continuous Hauteville treachery.' Tancred swept on, not knowing he had offended his guest.

'My good Geoffrey will have my small estates when I die, as eldest son in this country; you all know he is to inherit. The remainder of you'll get nothing except a new sword and your horse. Never forget, either, to treat your horses well - wherever you go; they're especially scarce in the south.'

Few of those present realised that horses were so rare, they sometimes treated their own as cattle.

'Now, let me assure you all,' Tancred was in full flood, his aureole of silver hair flashing sparks in his enthusiasm, 'that you have a choice as to what you do and in which direction you travel. I hear that Rainulf's nephew, Richard, travels out to join his uncle at Aversa this year with forty or fifty men. If you wish to join him you must do so quickly.'

There was a sudden gust of laughter across the room. One of the Duppa de Uphaugh men called out good-naturedly,

'He'll never get there!'

Tancred laughed too; Richard, a man of unusual beauty, was known to ride so small a horse that his feet almost touched the ground.

'Be that as it may ... but he's popular and influential and you'd be safe with him. Remember - you'll probably never return home, and you have to make new friends and allies where you can, to safeguard your own future. But, before you make up your minds, I know that our guest William of Normandy is also looking for men of your calibre. His cause is nearer home - do you have anything to say, my lord Duke?'

William, broad-shouldered, russet hair low-fringed across his wide brow, rose slowly to his feet. All the older men saw the remarkable resemblance to his own father, the late Duke of Normandy, with his short, broad aquiline nose and his widely-spaced eyes. He spoke in a deep voice.

'Sir!' he bowed to Tancred, 'and worthy knights! I know all of you here today, I know you all well and I know that you're my comrades.'

The men looked solemnly at him. He went on,

'Yes, I do have urgent need of help. This, after all, *is your own country*.' He paused, as though - obliquely - accusing them of treachery by looking to Italy; some glanced away.

'I hope you'll all swear allegiance to me - one day - as Duke. One day, too, I'm sure my own eyes will turn abroad. I have plans to meet my cousin, Edward of England.'

There was the carrot, lightly held out, especially to the younger men.

'But these are early days for me, and there's a possible revolt upon my hands which I must deal with first.'

His eyes swept around the room, marking down whom he thought might be of use; he expected that they would refrain from choosing until he was legally elected their leader.

'Come with me, by all means. I'm afraid I can promise only small rewards until I'm more strongly established - it's the penalty of my youth! Should any of you care to join me - speak to me afterwards!'

William gracefully sat down again. Tancred murmured his appreciation. Now the conventions had all been observed and he'd been seen to do his duty towards William in public. He bowed a second time.

'And my thanks to you, my lord Duke.'

Tancred motioned to Jacques to fill William's wine to the brim. He turned back to the smoky room, to speak with greater confidence and ease to everyone there.

'So! In either case you'd go as trained fighters - either in this country with William of Normandy, or to join your half-brothers in the south. The choice is yours! What say you, Robert?'

Immediately Robert was on his feet, released, shouting. Everyone else was shouting, too.

'I go south to Italy! I've waited long enough!'

The whole Hall shuddered to silence.

Head and shoulders he stood above all the men present, desperate for a future. Every eye was upon him as he yelled at his father,

'I will go. I go to William 'Iron Arm'! *I demand it!'*

His demand was just and recognised. His voice beat like a drum, gathering momentum,

'I'll blaze the trail. I've waited far too long!'

Robert shouted again into the silence,

'I'll go with my own men. I'll take no younger relations this time. Not one. They must wait their turn. But I – I'm ready now - *I'll go tomorrow!*'

His voice roared so loudly that the whole Hall echoed.

Uproar broke out.

TANCRED AND ROBERT'S FAREWELL

None dare defy Robert's supremacy. They were shocked he had pushed everyone else aside so roughly, denying his younger brothers any chance of moving out with him. Tancred, too, was disappointed. Clearly the meeting was at an end.

William of Normandy made his farewells and several of the men joined him outside the castle, talking easily about the future - provisionally with him. It was clear that most of the Duppa de Uphaugh men would join William. Gradually the remaining men and boys in the Hall fell quiet, or spoke seriously in groups.

Under Jacques' direction the servants cleared the last platter and crumb and, silent as shadows, slipped wearily away. They left a fresh supply of wine at Tancred's elbow; it was a nightly ritual for, in his old age, and in pain, sleep was elusive. Family members withdrew to their quarters, prepared for sleep; a few disappointed young men chose to walk outside in the starry night, to clear the fumes. A long time passed. Quietly Jacques slipped into a small recess, deep in shadows, and sat down thankfully on the floor.

Tancred and Robert remained where they were, alone together for the last time, gazing mesmerically at the fire.

'Robert,' his father said, 'your life ahead's going to be fraught with torment and contradictions, never forget that a sharp mind is as vital as a sharp sword. *Think - always think* before you act, I implore you, you'll never regret it. And when in doubt, never give up! If you're convinced that you're right – then just think of another way around your problem. There is always a third way – and sometimes more.'

Tancred wanted to reach Robert, speak words through which he'd be forever remembered. Robert, in his turn, wanted practical help to prepare himself. He wanted so much for himself and now hope, like a juice mixed with fire, coursed through his veins: he prayed he wasn't too late.

'Now, tell me, father - one last time - how you and your friends went on that pilgrimage. I've forgotten the details, and they could be important. Tell me especially about Apulia and the Gargano, so that I'll go armed in my mind as well as with my sword.'

Tancred laughed.

He knew he was being flattered. But all their kind turned their situations to their own benefit and it was sensible of Robert to refresh his memory. He kicked a log, watching the sparks fly up and divide, then gestured to Robert to throw on several more from a nearby pile. Slowly Tancred reached out and refilled their wine, then looked down at Wolf, his head between his paws, well out of the reach of Robert's foot.

'You'd be wise to take Jacques, you know he's loyal - and you'd miss your dog - he could be useful.' Tancred said ambivalently, easing his hip which stabbed with never-ceasing pain. 'I wish I were you, starting out again tomorrow. But I can only live on through my sons - and, maybe, grandsons, too ...'

Tancred mused in the half-dark, revelling in his memories, knowing, too, that he would shortly fade from the scene and die. He dearly wanted to know if Robert succeeded, and how family friction might intervene.

Robert, sulky at the delay, moved impatiently. His father growled,

'Very well, very well, give me time.'

Tancred effectively retold what he could remember, re-living his adventures on his journey to the Holy Land and back.

He spoke of the people and the politics of those years, and estimated how they could have altered. He concentrated on the sights they had witnessed, especially the power of a sea-storm during their return journey. He explained how the enervating climate had affected local people, to their detriment, but not his sprightly companions; Norman men were famously resilient. For the longest period, he spoke of the opportunities available at that time, especially the chances, through battle, of conquering and owning land. Then he told Robert all about the feast at the Lombard's castle and the glory of the half-hidden courts at Benevento, which eventually led to the first glorious conquests by Normans and Lombards, two years later, followed by the awful defeat at Cannae. It was told like a troubadour's romance, tantamount to a marathon relay, as if he was handing on a torch.

For a while Tancred was young again. Finally he leaned back in his chair, staring into the dying embers of the fire, and all of a sudden fell asleep. Robert caught his wine before it spilled. Perhaps the old man could go no further, thought Robert, or, at his age, he needed the refreshment of a short rest.

He pushed some gnarled logs onto the fire; they were hoarily encrusted with lichen, grey-green, primeval, like monsters that had survived another age. The new chunks fell on half-burnt timber and quickly came alight, giving off added warmth and light. Soon their red-hot noses met together, pointing into the flames - they blazed, hissed, and spat out showers of burning sparks; whirlpools of white wood-ash fluffed out and danced in feathery, fan-shaped patterns over their surface.

As he, too, gazed into the fire in the stillness of the night, Robert remembered his childhood experiences with his half-brothers; now he was voluntarily joining these hated ones in a far-off country. Four - maybe more - against one! He had such a loathing of those men, a barrier he knew he would have to surmount if he was to be successful.

All at once the older man opened his bright blue eyes in their spider's web of creases, looked around him cautiously, and resumed,

'I wasn't asleep,' he said, yawning, 'I was just thinking.'

'That's just what I thought,' soothed Robert. 'But there's not a lot of time left for you to help me and there's so much I don't understand.'

He refilled his father's wine, saying as he gave it to him,

'What are the Lombards like? They sound very capable!'

'They're fierce, ambitious and ruthless. But they're very great administrators, too, and the first ones left a lasting imprint on the country.'

Tancred gulped his wine, twirling the vessel between the palms of his hands. Robert was surprised at his father's approval.

'In what way?'

'I don't know too much about them - but one thing I do know - it was they who created the duchies, named after their army units led by duces, and that system is used all over Italy today. That's what you must aim for, Robert, a duchy of your own.'

'A duchy!' Robert said scornfully, '*that won't be enough for me.*'

Tancred rumbled a wry guffaw.

'I rather doubt if the Emperor or His Holiness would give you one anyway!'

'Well, what's the position of the Church, then? She's powerful enough today, isn't she, to withstand everyone?'

'She'd like you to think so, but her power waxes and wanes in that troubled land. But, don't forget, the Bishop of Rome, as Patriarch of the West has only held the title of Pope for less than two hundred years - and these Popes have been having a colossal struggle to keep their position - with not much in the way of wealth behind them. They're contriving to consolidate their power, their position in the world is changing and they desperately need money - income - rents from land. They're spreading Saint Peter's nets for land across the earth; others can administer it, they really only want the rents! Believe me, the

Church's position is still perilous.'

Robert's eyes glittered.

'I can't wait to get there: I'm convinced that I have a destiny ...'

'Yes - *but not a holy cause!* That's not in your nature, is it? You're going for the rich pickings - *aren't you?* The gold and the power and land? And because there's nothing much for you here and I've filled your head with stories of my own dreams. Well - there's nothing wrong in that. But, tell me, if you want land and glory why not go east, my son? To the Baltic countries, or Prussia or Bohemia? At this moment you could go almost anywhere!'

'No, sire, I'd rather be warm - I'll go to the Mediterranean coastland and take up where you left off. I'll tread in your steps if I can.'

Tancred, warm himself with delight, tried one last delaying tactic,

'Are you sure you won't join William of Normandy?

'What! Fight for that youth? I'm too old Father, to take orders from a lad younger than myself. I know he needs all the help he can raise, and I know he has hopes of succession in England - if he ever gets that far! Let my younger brothers fight for him, I saw several of them talking earnestly to him this evening, but I fear he has a mountainous time ahead, to gain full control. Besides, William will only see me as a threat, for I'm stronger than he - and older ... he'd never trust me fully - and right he'd be! *I'm my own man.* The day will come when I'll acknowledge no man my master.'

Tancred mused, tired, yawning until his jaw cracked.

'Do you think that you could lead all the Normans in Italy in your turn? And settle there? Is that your intention?'

Tancred ached to be in Robert's shoes. Robert answered,

'Well, I'll have to bide my time to start with. I must get used to the climate. I must learn the language. I'll join my half-brothers first, yes, and much depends on what they want from me.' He continued, 'I'm a leader, father, I know that. *I can't take second place*. It's my pride: if I can't be first I don't want to live. And I swear to you I'll try to live up to your hopes. I'll get word to you somehow, over the years; but now I must get on my way. I'll send for some of the others in time, but I need trained men - not boys - so I'll have to rely on your experience! Send me the best, won't you? Let me know how they're developing?'

Tancred nodded in the half-light.

'Leave nothing to chance, Robert, rely on no-one but yourself. Test everything for yourself by sight, by hearing or by touch; test all weapons and women, all hunting falcons and dogs and men - test them all, especially the men. *Test them to breaking point.*'

Robert nodded in agreement. Tancred continued,

'Power has to be handled delicately, like a horse. Show your friends and allies their eventual reward - keep it forever dangling before their eyes - but be sure to remove it before they can seize it! Thus you'll keep them devoted and eager to serve, even if it creates an intolerable strain on them.'

Robert nodded; then went on.

'That's in the future, father. But, for the present, I must go with no burdens if I'm to look out for myself; that's why I'll take no novice soldier with me. Yes, we've a large family - I may take them all one day, even down to young Roger. It's up to you, sire – train them well!'

Tancred sat in thought for some time, then spoke so quietly that Jacques had to strain to hear,

'There's little chance of us meeting again, you and I. But I want to give you a keepsake, as the eldest son of my second family. Here - I give you my ring. I had two made which are alike. William, as my eldest son, has already been given one, and I wear the other - I've waited to give it to you, if you chose to go to Italy. You'll find the others will notice it - they may not be best pleased.'

With difficulty he pulled the ring from his hand.

'The design on it has been handed down from our Norse ancestors, for we share the symbol engraved upon it with our kinsmen, the Duppa de Uphaughs; as you've seen tonight, they're trusted friends of us all, including Duke William. Give this ring to your own son one day, it's a precious symbol of our strength - learn from it, it will help you ... and you have my blessing.'

Tancred handed over his thick silver ring, engraved with the device of a lion's paw surrounded by chains. Robert forced the warm metal onto his finger. He stared long at his father, wordlessly nodding his thanks. Then he slipped to his knees, and knelt before Tancred, who placed his hand upon his head, light as a feather, in benison.

Jacques shifted slightly, uncomfortable, his hand was still smarting, and the blister had burst.

Robert rose in one fluid movement and opened the great doors of the Hall. The night of black frost had turned to a crepuscular thaw.

It was dawn.

FRESSENDA IN THE CONVENT

Whilst Robert journeyed impulsively out to Italy Fressenda finally got her wish; she was given the chance to enter the convent of her choice in the complex owned by Odo, son of the great Duke of Evreux. By litter and by boat Fressenda and her maid, attended by Tancred and Roger, wended their way across the countryside; word had come at last that they had room for her. Suitable accommodation was scarce.

At long last, the lady Fressenda de Hauteville was carefully lowered onto her new bed by a throng of people, family and nuns alike, in a small but sunny room which faced onto the central courtyard and herb garden. Her old maid bustled around putting the few objects Fressenda had brought to comfort herself on shelves hung on the wall, and sturdy hooks, and buried others into a deep chest.

When left alone at last, the peace beggared description for Fressenda; only the quiet footfalls and murmurs of passing nuns in the House of Distinguished Guests, and occasional piercingly sweet birdsong, could now be heard; now and then there was also a faint clang of hammer on anvil in the distance.

From her blissfully soft and solitary bed she could see glimpses of fruit blossom in the orchards beyond, swaying in a slight breeze against the cobalt sky. She felt she had arrived in her own heaven at last and closed her weary eyes. Some little time later, awakening, she sensed another person holding her hand, and heard her cheerfully say,

'My lady, I'm Sister Sophia, and I'm hoping to make your life more comfortable!'

Fressenda tried to struggle up, but Sister Sophia gently pressed her frail shoulders back against the pillows.

'No! Don't move! You've had a very tiring journey and must now lie still…'

She laid her hand on Fressenda's clammy forehead and noted her semi-paralysed face.

'Our Guest-mistress is away at present, visiting the nunneries at Montivilliers and Cerisy, so I'm doing her work as well as my own.'

Fressenda appeared mystified, so Sophia explained,

'She's gone there specifically to see their leech-books and have them copied to bring them back here – I need them for my work.'

'And what is your work, Sister?'

'Oh dear! Has no-one explained who I am? I look after our sick guests and I oversee the infirmary – the lay servants do the menial work, of course, but I am also responsible for the pharmacy.'

Fressenda's eyes opened wider in surprise.

'That's a considerable amount of work, Sister – do you have sufficient help?' She could see that the nun was old.

Sister Sophia smiled happily, without a trace of vanity,

'Oh! Of course! *But how I enjoy it*; it's a wonderfully rewarding life! Thank the dear Lord that it's our Christian duty to care for the sick and comfort the lonely – not to mention feeding the hungry – for it's all meat and drink to me. We have a hospice here, and we also have an orphanage, and a small pharmacy. Luckily we have no need for a separate house for lepers … poor souls.'

She appeared to look inwardly, recalling past patients, then went on,

'And yes! *Of course* I have ample help, although I admit I could do with some more. I need someone special to aid me, who I could trust to deputise in the pharmacy. You see, our leech-books and herbals refer to the ingredients of ointments and salves by their Latin and Greek names, but all local people and most of the nuns call them by more familiar ones. You're right, it's a responsible job … I expect, if it's

God's will! I'll get a suitable assistant soon.'

Fressenda looked very pale as Sister Sophia bent over her comfortingly. As she prattled on she had been stroking her patient's arms from fingertips to shoulders, putting a bolster under her knees and raising up the foot of her bed.

'We'll let you rest for a few days, and feed you well. After that I'll examine you and see how I can help you.'

She stroked the back of Fressenda's hand and, with a final soft pat on it, quietly left the room.

'Tancred ... Roger ...' whispered Fressenda, and heard from the doorway,

'I'll ask them to come, they are waiting outside.'

And she dozed again.

The complex of St. Evroul-sur-Ouche was self-supporting in a detailed way; it had only been fully developed for a few years, and was owned by Odo de Grantmesnil, first and only son of the powerful Count of Evreux, cousin to the Dukes of Normandy. A great deal of money had come to him through his very rich and high-born mother at her untimely death. His father hadn't married a third time.

Odo, meanwhile, had poured almost all of his inheritance into building this monastic centre on some of his most fertile land; he was eager to make it affluent and well-known, and aimed to entice academics from other establishments to add to its lustre.

To increase his considerable income from wool, timber and grain, he had built both a monastery and a convent, so that they might share some of the facilities. There was a mill and a bakery which was common to both, as was the smithy and stables for oxen and horses. Both monastery and convent had their own separate walled gardens filled with herbs, for, amongst other charitable establishments, there were profitable male and female guesthouses and hospitals. Both had a pharmacy and an apothecary to see to the sick and make up the medicines. Each building was blessed at its completion, each pig and sheep and horse on its arrival and each living soul at every sunrise and sunset.

Vegetable plots and orchards were tilled and pruned by local labour, and beehives surrounded their boundaries. Sheep and goats were guarded, milked and shorn – not by the monks or nuns, but by the local shepherds, and cottage women spun and wove cloth. Near the river, which curled around the monastery lands, Odo had constructed a large pond, stocking several varieties of fish which grew plump in the still water. Beyond the river were hare warrens and in the forest was other game which either flew, or trotted along the ground or burrowed underneath. It was a well-knit organisation and became a model to others.

Odo's personal appearance pleased most people, for he tended to greet everyone with a smile. He was above average height and was beginning to grow corpulent. He was a gregarious and popular guest. Invitations came thick and fast, for people wanted to hear his never-repeated variety of stories or sly, pertinent jokes. When deep in thought it became obvious that he had a full and rather petulant lower lip, which often held the glisten of moisture, but at times like these, when he was thinking deeply, he was most valued for his integrity and silence – and he kept many a potent confidence. Women envied him his white hands, with their long, thin fingers; some people felt that he was a little too prone to giggle, but he summed up a situation fast and was never the butt of a derogatory remark – in his hearing.

Odo, as owner of the monastery, chose to be an unconsecrated Abbot and, in the first flush of youth, had plunged into the planning and management with boundless enthusiasm and success. But he had too agile a mind to stay in any backwater for long and, destined as he was to follow his father as Count one day, he began to enter boldly into politics, first on his father's coat-tails, encouraged by him – it was to his advantage – and then through his own cunning.

In order to devote time to this new enterprise of statesmanship, and travel extensively across the lands of the Holy Roman Emperor as well as those of the Pope, he first appointed a lady from a very distinguished Norman family, the Montgomerys, to be Abbess of the convent, forming a self-contained unit. Then he created a council of three: Dominic, Francis and Peter, to run the monastery and his all-male household during his absences. Dominic, as senior monk, supervised the monastery's 150 occupants and was empowered to make major decisions, both secular and religious. Francis was the chamberlain, who looked after his bed chamber and, as a consequence, became responsible for all finance because the bed chamber was heavily guarded and hence the safest place for treasure. Peter was the chancellor, Odo's principle household cleric and one of the few fully literate people, who acted in a secretarial capacity and dealt with all documents and written work.

Odo's rule was reasonable and surprisingly mild. The religious world of both monastery and convent was dominated by prayer, penance, work and learning, and there was genuine rejoicing on feast and saints' days. Wednesdays and Fridays were reserved for fasting. There was rest on Saturday, but from Saturday night right through the whole of Sunday the monks and nuns knelt or walked in prayer: although they were housed within a quarter of a mile of each other they seldom met.

Because Odo was learned and happy and rich he encouraged the arts and became an authority himself, having seen so many treasures on his travels. Manuscripts were written on music, art and literature in a forward-looking way; old tales and poetry were transcribed and religious Books of Hours were copied and illuminated. The monks and nuns were peaceful and content and grumbled in a natural way. Fressenda felt she lived in Heaven.

'Well, we've done a good deal, haven't we?' said Sister Sophia a few weeks later. Fressenda now sat on a stool, wrapped in a warm shawl and looking out of the window, the shutters thrown open. 'And I'm glad to say I've narrowed it down to 'half-dead disease'. That's why your face had been affected.'

Fressenda smiled, relieved.

'If this is 'half-dead disease' then I must have been quite ill when I arrived. The rest has done me good. What a comfort, though … 'half-dead disease' is to be expected at my age and, in these pleasant surroundings, my passing with heart worms is bound to be peaceful and easy. Thank you, Sister.'

'Not at all,' said Sophia, 'you're an easy patient because you're philosophical. Now – we've examined your waters, we've cupped you and bled you and purged you and I've just pronounced your disease. It's all done, and henceforth, within these walls, you may live your life exactly as you please.'

'No more cupping? No more bleeding and purging?'

'No more! In this convent it is our custom to show compassion – *I've no intention of hastening your end!* Now, tell me, how did you like that infusion of wild lettuce?'

Fressenda ruminated, licking her lips,

'I'm not sure what I liked best about it; the lettuce and wine were pleasant, but I think I liked the taste of honey best.'

'Good,' said Sophia briskly, 'it's good for the many malfunctions of the humours and it's good for the eyes, too. Naturally, our own bees made it. I'll bring you some more when you have your next meal.'

Then, with a brilliant smile illuminating her face, off rustled Sister Sophia, through the motes of sunshine, somehow transparent, rubbing her red, chapped hands in obvious pleasure with a frailty built to last.

ROBERT AT AVERSA

AVERSA! Rainulf's city, just north of Naples, a market for Norman mercenaries and centre point for the de Hauteville band of brothers. Robert turned in his saddle and looked back at his twenty men, some mounted, and his dog.

He had got there at last!

Aversa lay straight ahead in the sunshine. Smoke rose straight up in thc air in the windless, cloudless day, with the leaves on the trees lying limp, drooping listlessly against the branches. The first sight of the city surprised Robert, for it had no natural defences, apart from the fortifications which looked so very new - which they were. But once, when leading his horse, he bent down and crumbled some soil between his fingers and realised that the land was very rich. There were shade trees, too, and crops grew in an orderly fashion, so its cultivation was clearly organised by a practiced hand.

Inside the city was the famous castle and court of Rainulf, under whose banner his half-brothers fought; William, who had invited him there, Humphrey, Drogo and Serlo. Geoffrey remained in Normandy. Robert was confident of a bright future with them, swelling their successful band and expecting to sweep triumphantly with them through the south of Italy. As they were now so important he wondered which strip of land, which villages and hamlets they would grant him: maybe even a minor title?

As he passed between the buildings he was aware that never before had he seen so many people crammed together - the city teemed with life and everyone seemed so young. Robert was amazed to see that this town, built recently under Rainulf's direction, had so many buildings of stone. He had expected the houses and hovels to be made of wood, decorated inside and out. But here the majority were made of blocks of stone, most of which had been taken from local Roman ruins; feminine space was symbolically surrounded by masculine stone. The rare stone houses - unique, it seemed to him - inspired awe because of their very grandeur and they seemed immense.

Some of the buildings had carvings upon the lintels and corbels, doors and steps. The world of the carver's imagination showed monsters of pre-history, dreams of paradise, and infernal horrors of this world and the next. As a general rule, the carvings were painted and gilded, like the wooden carvings of Norseland and Normandy, which made it all more familiar.

At one house they paused to laugh when they saw a bas relief showing an arrogant noblewoman kicking her servant in the belly; in another place, by a merchant's doorway, were carvings of life size oxen in stone, a tribute to the animal world whose living brethren had hauled that very stone as well as providing the merchant's livelihood.

The churches were, as usual, built near running water, a direct means of communication with the womb of the world where it lay in the depths of the earth. Robert and his followers crossed themselves as they passed by these holy places, vowing to return and look within. At the moment there was just too much to take into their inquisitive minds.

They spoke to each other about how the city came to be Norman owned, and, in some ways, there was a sense of pride. Robert longed to pay homage to the legendary Rainulf, knowing that he was now very old and battle-weary - as old, in fact, as his father. Fairly recently the German Emperor had invested Rainulf with the lance and gonfalon of Aversa, making him a member of imperial nobility, a possessor of rights, and holding a title which could only be withdrawn from him by the Emperor himself. Afterwards Rainulf privately declared he had one clear objective - the Norman domination of the South.

As he jauntily rode through the town's western entrance, Robert was uneasily aware that his pockets were almost empty. But he was certain of recompense and that - in spite of a personal, very personal difference - his brothers would loyally welcome him and his young, keen soldiers. His blood pumped with excitement. The wealth and strength he could see about him was very different from the poverty he had left behind; he was amazed at it all.

He halted by the castle gate, dismounted and left his horse in Jacques' care. The soldiers at the gate were quick and sharp, looking up at Robert's enquiring face - which seemed slightly familiar,

'A new member of the Hauteville family, sir?' asked the astute one in command. He'd never seen a man so tall and broad.

'That's so.'

Robert looked about him with a air of genial propriety. The commander said,

'Your family are at Melfi over the mountains in Apulia, sir. They left word for you to travel on.'

'I see. And Rainulf?'

The commander looked him up and down, slowly.

'Our lord, the Count, is away, sick, in Sicily.'

Sensing rebuke for his familiarity, Robert wheeled about and strode back to his men. Jacques could see his flush of anger as Robert said to them all,

'We'll have to travel on to Melfi. We'll camp outside Aversa tonight. Meet me here at sunset.'

He was furious. He felt rebuffed that no arrangements had been made for him and his men at the castle. They would be on very short rations for the next few days; his companions scattered to find food.

Robert and Jacques walked through the town together, with Wolf loping ahead. Everything was crammed into the narrow space fenced in by the walls and closely guarded entrances and gates; churches, chapels, counting houses, the town hall, the dwellings of the town's leading citizens, the market places, the inns, the barracks and the castle. Life around them was ebullient, raucous and quarrelsome; restoration of order amongst the townspeople came through the ringing of the church bells, or the intervention of the town watch. The military had stricter rules of their own.

After they had paced through the majority of the town, they entered an inn with a half-dried bush hanging outside, it was crowded with people, but they gave way when Robert shouldered his way inside with his air of authority.

'Ale!' he said to the serving wench, 'Ale for two.'

She returned with a jug and two vessels, pertly saying,

'We only serve wine.'

'Food? Do you have food?'

'We've barley bread.'

'No more?'

'We could prepare mortrews.'

'Bring them, then, and bring sufficient.'

Robert and Jacques looked about them as they sat against the inner wall; it was cooler in the building, but dim, windowless, with only one lamp near the innkeeper. As they gulped their wine they talked, briefly, about the journey to come.

'I hadn't reckoned on the extra distance,' grumbled Robert.

'An added expense at this point,' sympathised Jacques.

Robert looked up from under his shaggy eyebrows; his flaxen hair shone like a lamp around his head and his golden beard curled luxuriantly down to his chest. Jacques changed the subject quickly.

'I wonder if they'll mix in ginger?'

'In a place like this? We'll be lucky if they give us white meat with the breadcrumbs - they'll probably only mix in eggs.'

'Aye.'

He was right - but they added plenty of pepper. Later, they found a fat cockroach drowned at the bottom of their next jug of wine. It was a deliberate insult to strangers. Later still, on looking once more at Robert, the inn-keeper decided not to overcharge him. Robert said,

'The next time I'm here you'll add in meat or fish.'

'Yessir!

'And ginger!'

'Mmmm.'

The innkeeper bowed and backed away. Jacques stepped on his bare foot as he passed by, and hoped he heard the crack of fractured bones.

'Men of prayer, men of war, and men of work - they're the worthwhile people,' observed Robert heavily, 'God made the clergy, knights and labourers, but the devil made townsmen and usurers.'

ROBERT AND DROGO

After a few days Drogo met him on arrival at the castle at Melfi in the Apennine Mountains.

Drogo! The most hated one; handsome, dark-complexioned and smiling.

The castle at Melfi was the Norman supreme headquarters in Apulia, their metropolis and citadel, jointly owned by all twelve Norman chiefs.

Without a second's pause Drogo accurately calculated the impact on his young knights of Robert's presence and size. The troops and the people, too, couldn't fail to be impressed; Robert topped him by at least a hand's span, and it did not make him happy. He paused momentarily, then clapped his young half-brother around the shoulders and formally kissed his cheek. His chamberlain immediately showed Robert to his quarters and found places for his men and horses.

Later that day, during a lavish meal, Drogo pointed out to him all the senior men who were installed there or passing through, but he didn't formally introduce him to the throng as his brother - or even mention his name to anyone there. This unsettled Robert a little. Although placed in the centre of the table, they sat apart from other men; a slight distance was set between them and their neighbours. Robert thought it was to allow them to speak privately after so many years. They attracted much attention, but no-one spoke to them.

Caustically, but with some attempt at humour, Drogo enquired about each member of the family back in Normandy. Their conversation was impersonal and easy, alighting mainly on generalities, and at the end Drogo tossed him a modest leather purse of money.

Robert felt a sudden incandescence of contentment and leaned back in his seat in the noisy castle's Hall, beginning to feel at peace with the world; he had a full belly and a fresh supply of money. It was a strange sensation, tranquility, and he savoured it. He wondered where the other brothers were, but didn't care to raise the subject until Drogo raised it himself. It wouldn't hurt, for once, to keep silent and follow someone else's lead.

The next mid-day Drogo sent for him. Then Drogo gestured that Jacques should stand outside the door. Reluctantly Robert gestured him to do so.

The atmosphere seemed friendly. They sat across a heavy table from each other, on which lay a fine silken carpet sent from Baghdad. Robert couldn't resist stroking the luxurious pile - it felt like a cat's fur - and was intrigued by the subtle colouring of the peculiar pattern, which writhed without ending like the tendrils of a vine.

As he did so, Drogo stared at Tancred's ring upon Robert's hand, his eyes hooded.

Wolf stretched himself out at Robert's feet and gave a deep sigh, whilst his master rested, his other arm along the open window's ledge, lolling in his seat, and looked outside. The shutters were thrown back to let in the fresh morning air, and a draught of jasmine scent, mixed with pine, wafted through the room. Jasmine and other creepers wound themselves up the castle's walls, and, as the town lay in the foothills of Monte Vulture, a burned out volcano which now was filled with fir trees, the scent of pine came from there.

'Where,' said Robert, in a friendly way - as equals – 'is William? I expected he'd be here.'

'I didn't want to spoil your first day,' Drogo replied, 'so I didn't tell you before. William, our famous 'Iron-Arm' hero, is at Venosa.'

'Venosa? Near here, in Apulia?'

'Yes.' He looked straight at Robert's face. 'Fresh in his grave.'

Shocked, Robert stared at Drogo, there was a lazy half-smile about his moist lips.

'Dead?'

'Naturally. Indeed. Dead. Poor William.' Drogo laughed softly, in satisfaction. Robert crossed himself, saying hastily,

'God rest his soul. Geoffrey didn't tell us William had died.'

'Geoffrey didn't know. He died two months ago.'

Robert pulled himself together sharply at Drogo's tone. He became suddenly aware that Drogo sat between himself and the doorway. He noticed that Drogo's chair looked rather like a throne. The atmosphere in the room had altered in some indefinable way.

Instinct made Wolf rise, alert under Robert's restraining hand. On looking around Robert also perceived that Drogo had stationed several men in the big room who, hitherto, had casually stood in groups, and spoke low, out of hearing - but who now stood at attention, and silent, watching them.

Drogo drawled,

'Did Geoffrey tell you that William had made a bargain with Rainulf? That he married Rainulf's niece? That, at the occasion of his marriage, he would be created Count of Apulia and Calabria - after he was elected chief of the Normans?'

'I knew he was married and was a Count - no more!'

'Then Geoffrey was remiss in not telling you the whole. His wife was the daughter of Duke Guy of Sorrento; that was five years ago.'

Robert gasped. Why had they not been told? Drogo drawled on,

'And did Geoffrey not tell you that William's election was the very first one when all Normans in the south peacefully, and jointly, elected their own leader?'

'No ... It seems like yesterday.' Robert was bewildered. 'So - do we Hautevilles own the city and fiefs of Sorrento, too?'

'Not 'we Hautevilles'. *Not you. Remember that.* My blood brothers and I share power. Sorrento is owned by one of our redoubtable Lombard partners, one of the last of the great Lombard princes of South Italy - Gaimar of Salerno.'

'Gaimar?'

'You really are very ignorant,' sneered Drogo, 'why didn't you question Geoffrey more closely when he returned?'

Inwardly Robert agreed with him, he had been guilty of living in a dream. Geoffrey had said hardly a word that would have been of use. He was bewildered at all the news of people he had never heard about before. Geoffrey's silence, now, looked premeditated. What else had he done? His loyalty must lie with his brother.

Drogo continued, as if teaching a retarded child,

'The Lombards have always been at the epicentre of our lives and exploits in Italy. When William was made Count, then Gaimar shared out between the twelve Norman chiefs all territories in the south which had already been conquered. As well as all those which might, in future, fall into our hands! The Lombards were - are - determined that the last Greek and Byzantine should finally be driven from the land. *And so are we.'*

It looked to Robert as though he might have arrived too late. He enquired hesitantly,

'Which fief did William receive?'

'Ascoli.'

'And Rainulf?'

'He's too old to be one of the twelve chiefs, and too senior. Even so, he was granted Sipontum and parts of Monte Gargano.'

'Understandable - as the sole remaining Norman who went there; father told me that the grotto cave of Saint Michael that they visited there was the high point of his trek to the Holy Lands.'

'True.'

'And you, Drogo?' asked Robert, with a grim set to his jaw.

'I received Venosa. I'm building a fine cathedral there in honour of the occasion. I'm transforming the old Lombard basilica into an abbey - of course it's going to be magnificent.'

'Of course.' repeated Robert thoughtfully.

'Incidentally, I married Gaimar's daughter a month ago.'

'I see.'

Yes thought Drogo, *you do*, and that's what worries me; you're too sharp. He went on,

'Humphrey has since become Count of Lavello.You haven't enquired about him as yet! But I'd watch him if I were you! He's - let's say he's a hard man. He's due back soon.'

'And brother Serlo?' Robert didn't want to be caught out again.

'Ah, Serlo,' said Drogo, 'Serlo's looking after our interests in Sicily at present.'

Robert asked suspiciously,

'How did William die?'

'No-one knows. That's God's truth.'

There was a long – doubtful - silence.

Robert found himself sitting upright in his seat, no longer lounging. His hand fell from touching the carpet. Two months ago, thought Robert, that gave Drogo time enough to seize overall power - but he ought to enquire. He did so politely,

'Have the Normans had another election for chief? Are you, in turn, Count of Apulia and Calabria?'

Arrogantly Drogo looked him full in the face, and made him wait for his answer. His dark eyes glittered and his thick lips closed over his tombstone teeth. When he was younger he had been one of the most captivating members of the family, slim and brooding. Middle age had thickened him and his profligate ways had coarsened his features. When he was tense he exuded a faint smell - fusty and sour, like a mouse. He knew his long pause had heightened Robert's anxiety, and it pleased him. Then,

'I am.'

Again silence fell. No-one moved. They eyed each other and Drogo felt as if he looked into the eyes of a snake before it struck. He had to look up when eye to eye with Robert. In turn, Robert suddenly remembered the day when it had been the other way about ... when Drogo had looked down on him and found him too attractive not to touch; *'We'll teach you to become a man!'* He grew cold.

'My congratulations,' he said, finding it difficult to force the words through his lips. 'Our father will be pleased. So - it appears that you and I are the only Hautevilles here at present?'

'We are.'

No land here, thought Robert, or titles - what a fool I've been, and how naïve I must seem!

The insubstantial picture that Geoffrey had painted for him, which Robert had held in his mind and embroidered throughout the lengthy journey, seemed to be false. He had never realised how important his elder half-brothers had become. He had wanted - expected - to be made much of, to stand beside a brother, Count and commander, and be recognised by all the other Normans as an Hauteville of some consequence. It had been a very long while since he had been under-dog.

And unpopular.

And certainly not needed here.

Robert receded into himself, giving himself time to muster up his deepest thoughts of self-preservation.

Drogo, rare for him, suddenly felt a frisson of self-doubt; his own close brothers, fiery men, were well understood by him. Now their solid block of support for him was drastically reduced: Geoffrey had left for good, William was dead and Serlo was fighting in Sicily. Something would have to be done about Robert, this greedy upstart of a half-brother.

'Let's go and look at the town, shall we? You'd like to see Melfi's delights, I'm sure. The inhabitants have learned to be most co-operative.'

Robert, mollified, was puzzled by Drogo's olive-branch. His brother seemed to blow hot and cold. It left him increasingly nervous. Together they swaggered out of the castle. No-one approached them, but everyone watched the extraordinary sight: who was this new man – taller than Drogo but not alike in looks?

Melfi was quite a different town from Aversa, for Aversa was situated on the rich plain and foothills near Naples and Melfi was built on top of a small but extinct volcano. The humidity of Aversa was almost forgotten in the mountain breezes of Melfi, cooled by nearby lakes and rivers. Both towns were built by the Normans, on ancient remains.

First Drogo showed Robert the town's fortified walls with pride. He pointed to places in the mountains where other towns lay hidden - naming them. He prodded an informative finger at the valleys below, where oxen ploughed, adjacent to small villages. Then he swept his arm dramatically northwards,

'The Gargano peninsula lies away over there, and Saint Michael's cave.'

Robert caught his breath, remembering Tancred's stories.

They turned into the centre of the town and, as day turned to night, soaked themselves in debauchery. Drogo paid.

Next midday Drogo sent word to Robert, inviting him to take part in his 'Games' in the castle's enclosure. Both were still half-drunk.

Robert was told to strip to his tunic and belt; there was a large crowd of men similarly attired. Drogo merely directed activities.

'What are we to do?' Robert asked a pleasant-faced man standing nearby. His name was Girard.

'When Drogo gives the signal you kill your opponent - or try to.' The man said in an even, unemotional tone.

'Kill him? *Why*?' Robert was stupefied, trying to shake the past evening's fumes from his brain.

'Why? To prove who's master - or, at least, to show Drogo where you stand upon the ladder.'

'By what rules do we fight?'

'There aren't any.' answered Girard, tersely.

'What a waste,' said Robert, 'to kill or maim when it isn't even wartime and there's nothing to be gained.'

'Yes,' said Girard, 'it's distasteful. It only occurs when a new man arrives; the quickest wins.'

They watched as various men competed, heaving and writhing on the ground, buffeting and slashing at each other. None died, but several men seemed badly injured.

Then Drogo called out, pointing,

'Your turn, I think.'

He didn't even give Robert's name, but turned away quickly as if disinterested.

Robert beat two men, one after the other, hearing their bones crack against his own until they cried out 'Pax!'

Then Drogo called in Girard to compete against him. Girard was smaller and slight. At the beginning Robert attempted to grasp Girard in his mighty arms like a bear; he quite liked the man and wished him no harm. But Girard was fleet of foot and twisted and ducked, then slithered away like an eel. For once Robert's height was a disadvantage and, as he lunged to catch Girard once more, the smaller man reached up and tangled his fingers in Robert's curly beard, yanking his head to one side with a swift and ferocious jerk.

As he slipped and fell heavily, Robert just caught sight of the rock which Girard had snatched up ... then felt incredible pain.

Robert awoke two days later in his own bed. His skull pulsated in a syncopated rhythm of its own. Jacques waited silently beside him. Wolf watched outside his door, showing the whites of his eyes. Eventually he muttered,

'Who was that man?'

'A distant kinsman of your own, sir, from Normandy,' Jacques said quietly. 'His name is Girard. He's won for himself a fief in this land, and he's known as Girard of Buonalbergo. He's universally popular.'

There was no reply.

The next day he was sent for again, to meet Drogo once more in his private room. Drogo smiled briefly at him with his mouth, the smile didn't reach his eyes. This time Robert wasn't invited to sit down.

'Robert! How's your head? How's your temper?'

'I'm well enough.' Robert growled.

'You lost.' said Drogo maliciously.

'I know,' Robert muttered through gritted teeth, 'it doesn't happen often.'

'A good thing no-one knew you're my half-brother - I can do without that shame.'

Robert flushed, reigning himself in.

'I see you've shaved your beard,' said Drogo, 'what a pity you didn't think of that before!'

Robert stared out of the window, his jaw set. In the past his beard had been much admired and he'd been proud of it. Drogo laughed, saying lightly,

'Well, what d'you intend to do now that you're out here in Apulia - and on my land?'

Robert's frown was part frustration, part apprehension.

'I came here because I was sent for! William ...'

'*William* sent for you?'

Robert was appalled.

'*Of course* William sent for me – he was the eldest! Wasn't it a joint decision?'

'William might have invited you - but I wasn't consulted. We choose our own men.'

The message came across loud and clear to Robert: he definitely wasn't wanted by Drogo. He decided to meet the opposition head on and clarify matter once and for all,

'Does this mean you've no need for me and my men?'

'I've never really thought about it,' Drogo drawled, 'but - as you appear to want a straight answer - well, I'm sure you can appreciate ... in the circumstances you'd be difficult to fit in.'

There was a lengthy pause. Neither man moved or spoke. Drogo gave up, having the advantage, and said,

'Now that William has died I've a great many men altogether. My problem is - to whom should I give any available rewards?'

Robert looked thoughtful, stayed silent. He hadn't thought about any problems Drogo might have had on William's death - only about the advantages.

'Look out from this window, Robert, to the men below.'

Obediently he did so. Dozens of people milled about below them.

'See that limping man with carrot-coloured hair? He was William's senior commander. And look at that man leading the grey mare - for twelve years he fought with William and was wounded twice. And look at that older fellow coming through the gate, for he came out with us when we first arrived. They've all petitioned me for land - as have many others - and it is their due.'

Pensively Robert observed them all. They had immediately stopped being soldiers and turned into personalities. Drogo continued,

'Available land is scarce - you must believe me. There's a very long line of battle-weary men who've earned a fief through their loyal service, and I'm hard-pressed to find anything for them, William's men - my men - who, do you think, has the pre-eminence? Even tough old Humphrey had to wait until last year to receive the county of Lavello, and he only got it because the previous incumbent died.'

Robert's spirits sank deep. Drogo watched his shoulders sag with some satisfaction.

'I will allow you to join my army,' said Drogo, 'on equal terms and footing with any other Norman knight. But I'll give you no land or title. You're young. You're inexperienced. And you're untried. If I discriminated in your favour there'd be a rebellion on my hands - from my own soldiers as well as William's.'

'But I ...'

'Can you speak the local language?'

'No - but I'll learn it.'

*'Some never can.*Do you know the names of the local barons - who's an enemy and who's a friend?'

'Not yet! I've only just arrived.'

'You never interrogated Geoffrey when you had the chance, did you? *Why ever not?* What use are you to me?'

'I'm strong ...'

'All you've successfully proved to me, Robert, however strong you believe you are, is that you can be beaten in unarmed combat by a man half your size.'

Robert leaped towards Drogo, his fist at the ready. With lightning speed Drogo's hand was on his knife.

'Stop!' he shouted. 'You crazy hothead! If you lay a finger on me you'll die!'

He pointed to the circle of men-at-arms now poised close behind Robert, each with a drawn sword in his hand.

'You insulted me!' Robert thundered back, without apology.

'I spoke the truth, as well you know, and many people witnessed your downfall.'

Robert said nothing.

'Well,' drawled Drogo patronisingly, 'I can't see why I should do anything for a loser.'

'But I'm your brother!' The words burst unwittingly from Robert's throat; he wished he hadn't spoken them.

'Half-brother.'

'Half-brother, then. Doesn't it count that we're related?'

'Yes,' said Drogo firmly, 'and it counts against you. Unity's one thing - nepotism's another. You can't expect good fortune to be handed to you as of right, *just because you wear our father's ring!*'

Robert glanced down at it. Tancred had been right. Drogo was piqued.

'So,' said Drogo, 'it's clear that you have a choice. Join me as an apprentice, a nobody, and work your way up - or go home!'

'Never,' said Robert, breathless with anger, *'never in my life* have I been a 'nobody', and I'm not starting now. I'll campaign on my own out here. I can see the day drawing near when we meet on opposite sides, can't you? You've a lot to learn about me, Drogo, and perhaps -

one day - *from me*, too.'

Drogo looked at the towering inferno of a half-brother he had been deliberately goading, who was almost speechless with rage and frustration. Robert was the most potent challenge he had met. He had spent some time the night before working out a plan to rid himself of Robert as quickly as possible, so, as part of his scheme, he appeared to make a lightning decision. He raised a restraining hand.

'Hold hard,' he said eventually, 'in my position as your overlord, for my father's sake, I'm prepared to be generous. This concession will only be granted to you the once; it could make or break you.'

He paused, as if in deep thought. Robert waited anxiously for the outcome.

'There's trouble in Calabria that needs immediate attention. I've reason to believe that an attack's to be made at any moment. To make an attack upon me, the enemy has to travel through a pass at a place named Scribla. D'you think you're strong enough to guard and hold the pass?'

'Who's the enemy?' Robert rasped.

'There's a choice! A report's come through that the Byzantines have been forced back from the coast by the Saracens and are coming towards my land - either the Byzantines or the Saracens will arrive - probably the former. Fight them off! Don't let them step one pace onto my territory. I've just been over there to see for myself - but had to return because of William's death and the election.'

'These are my duties?'

'Yes - stay and keep the pass open! Guard it - and turn any invader back. Make sure they know who's master in Calabria.'

Drogo saw the gleam in Robert's eye as he said throatily,

'I will.'

'Then leave tomorrow with your men.'

Robert nodded, thinking furiously.

'We'll need supplies.'

'They're available - look into the stores and choose wisely. It's hellishly hot, so take that into consideration.'

'And salt? If it's so hot we'll need extra!'

'I believe we're low on salt. You'll need to make a detour to the saltpans at Santa Margherita, on the coast north of Barletta. Collect what you need and hurry on.' Drogo drew breath. 'I would have sent some of William's experienced men, but you're fresher and they deserve a rest.'

He looked at Robert sternly, speaking with degrading emphasis,

'By a stroke of coincidence and *my unstinting charity* it seems, does it not, that you've been granted a temporary reprieve?'

It became clear that Robert could not bring himself to thank Drogo, so Drogo roared at him,

'And, in future, call me 'sire'!'

White-faced, at attention, Robert bowed. His future depended on it.

'Sire.' He said, with difficulty.

Drogo turned away contemptuously.

Within a day Robert had mustered his men and clattered out of the castle's courtyards. In silence he rode imperiously away, ignoring the many glances which followed the noisy display. He headed east to reach the coast. Drogo had sent a servant to his quarters with money for expenses. They had not met again.

ROBERT AND MATTEO

Sickened by the confrontation, Robert led his men away from Melfi to the coastline north of Bari, arriving at Santa Margherita's marshes. Although they first seemed to be travelling in exactly the opposite direction to their destination, without salt a man couldn't live, especially in great heat. Their journey took several days as they tracked across the plain.

Two thoughts chased in and out of his turbulent mind; to visit Monte Gargano and the chapel-cave of Saint Michael and to hurry on to action at Scribla. On this occasion he would have insufficient time to go around the coast of the Gargano peninsula and visit Saint Michael's cave, but it was near enough, now, and he would go later.

When they arrived at the coast the scene was a deep disappointment. The land, as far as they could see in all directions, was flat; and the aquamarine sea was as calm as a millpond. The saltpans appeared extensive, blindingly white in the brilliant sunshine, and a heavy smell of salt stung inside their noses and hung across all the sodden, malarial marshes near the beaches.

The evening after they had secured their supply of salt, Robert made his way alone towards the noise of the sea as it lap-lapped steadily in the otherwise still night. It was not long before he found himself walking on the sand, looking out to the gentle waves with their infinitesimal crestings of phosphorescence, disappearing like ropes of fireflies as each placid wavelet reached its diminutive climax.

He traced his steps by the safe-conduct of a full moon, which showed the long straight shore-line and a few sand dunes. Weary, he rested under the lea of a sandbank. He was cautious of the great round silver moon, which floated serenely through space, dimming the stars as it made them, and bathing the earth in splendour. He lifted a hand between the moon and his face, for fear of bad luck.

It was so light that he could see a single, small boat meandering towards the shore near him, the sail hardly lifted by the frail zephyrs of wind - the boat was merely being drawn to shore by the slow incoming tide. When it finally glided ashore, its owner jumped out ahead and pulled it up the sand as best he could.

'I see you,' called Robert form his vantage point, 'is this your home, or are you a stranger to Santa Margherita?'

'I am. I'm a stranger - but not from choice!' answered the sailor. 'And as you're abroad so late, will you help me secure my boat for the night?'

Unused to a request like this, but amused by the novelty, Robert stood up. To the sailor's eyes he seemed to grow like an immense tree, pushing his shadow before him on the opalescent ground.

'By Saint Nicholas,' he said, in awe, 'you're a giant! A veritable colossus!'

Between them the boat was swiftly pulled across the sand and its anchor chain tied to a stout eucalyptus branch. The top of the sailor's head scarcely reached Robert's shoulder, but he was clearly a strong man.

'Where are you bound?' He asked, seating himself again.

'My home port is Bari, but I have sailed off-course by the lack of wind, the wind just died down and I couldn't do anything about it.' The sailor seemed to repeat himself continuously.

'And your catch?'

'This time I've octopus and mussels and some poor shrimps.'

Robert knelt to look into the boat and saw a heap of grey slime oozing in the moonlight. The sailor hastily spat over his left shoulder and, when Robert looked questioningly at him, he smiled in a knowing way, rubbing the side of his nose with a finger.

'Return from whence you took - we sailors always do that.'

And spat again for good measure.

'Now I'm going to eat,' said he, 'will you join me? Will you eat with me?'

'I will gladly.'

Robert watched as the sailor gathered twigs from the beach's flotsam and from nearby bushes and quickly made a fire. Then he positioned a rickety iron tripod around it and fixed on this apex a thin chain with a hook, from which hung a small pot. Into the pot he poured some dark mixture from a pig's bladder, already prepared, then fetched a large flat loaf of bread from his boat.

'Will you lend me your knife?' He asked Robert: he had his own, well-worn, but he wanted to see Robert's as it might give a clue to his birthplace.

Robert handed over his knife, which the sailor examined with interest. After a while he said thoughtfully,

'This wasn't made here - no-one in these parts would make a knife like this. Where do you come from?'

As he hacked at the hard bread Robert answered, his face half in shadow - which hid his smile.

'I come from Normandy ...'

'Jesu! *Wouldn't you know it?* And I'm so far from home!' The man knelt, as if waiting for the blow.

'... and I mean you no harm. What's your name?'

'Matteo, Sir. Matteo, the sailor, from Bari.'

'Well, Matteo, your food seems to be ready.'

With a practised hand, Matteo pulled the pot of bubbling food away from the flames and placed it upon the sand between them. He handed over a chunk of bread and indicated the Robert should dip it into the pot. When the hot food and bread was in his mouth Robert let out a shout,

'God - it's hot! What are we eating?'

'Funghi - mushrooms - from the forests of Monte Gargano, cooked with fish and many, many chilies; don't you like it?'

'My mouth's on fire - but give me more!'

Contentedly Robert and Matteo sat together on the beach, sharing the furiously hot mixture and then cleaning out the last vestiges from the pot with the bread. All the while Matteo chattered about his wife and children and about the hard life of a sailor in a city beset with trouble. His solitary toil made him garrulous in company. He rambled on for hours and through his adept questioning Robert learned a great deal about Bari and its people.

Robert, rarely alone or without close companions, avoided speaking about himself and, after one or two abortive attempts, Matteo questioned him no more.

When the food was gone, Matteo began to hum as he packed away his pot, and then spontaneously raised his voice in song. He sang as he spoke and thought, as naturally as a gushing stream; the words were his own, adapted to age-old tunes. He sang about the tides and the waves, about dolphins and storms; he sang in thanks and supplication to Saint Nicholas, and he sang about his family and children. He sang from his simple heart and Robert was touched by his morality. It was a healing sound and he drank it in thirstily.

At last, as if he were about to settle for sleep, he sang in a low voice a chant like monks' plainsong - an offering of thanks to God - for life, and food, and 'good company'.

Before he walked away in the moonlight, Robert touched his new friend's shoulder,

'And my thanks to you also; maybe we'll meet again one day - and you will eat at my table.'

'I hope so, sir' said Matteo happily, as he watched his leviathan stroll away. 'I really hope so. But - before you go! Tell me your name?'

'I am Robert de Hauteville.'

Matteo unconsciously shivered in the hot night, ghouls walked over his grave.

ROBERT IN THE WILDERNESS

The journey to Scribla in Calabria involved retracing their steps across the Appennines, then bearing southwards through an unpopulated area. They travelled through a harsh agglomeration of hill and dale, chaos formed of rocks of every age, torn into gullies by earthquakes and other cataclysms of the past. For a time they found themselves lost in a maze of contorted ravines, winding about without any apparent system of watershed. Did the water flow north or south? Who could tell? They felt, for a while, that they were trapped in a box.

Guided by the sun, the route they followed crawled in and out of valleys, mounted upwards to heights of sun-scorched bracken and cistus, descended once more into dewy glades hemmed in by precipices and overhung by drooping fernery. It crossed streams of crystal clearness, rose afresh in endless gyrations under the pines only to vanish, yet again, into the twilight of deeper abysses, where it skirted the rivulets along precarious ledges, until some new obstruction blocked the way. So the track writhed about for long, long hours. At last, through information from a shepherd wearing a cloak like an Arabian burnous, they found their pass.

Robert ordered his men to find a reliable water supply first, near which they made a hidden camp. Then men were told to chase up some wandering goats which, hidden from any invaders, they roasted with salt and rosemary; rosemary and myrtle abounded in clumps all around them. At night they slept out in the open under the moon, and slapped at the mosquitoes as they sucked their flesh and dug their bites into young skin. Dutifully they kept watch, minute by minute, hour by hour.

Jacques grew thinner and lines began to show on his face, his red hair tightly curled in the heat and his eyes grew even more wary and sharp, he began to stand with his back to Robert's. Wolf took off on his own; silent, curious, as he slipped through the undergrowth and marked his own territory.

After a few days Robert fell sick with a fever; two others lay sweating like him, and shivered night and day. Jacques spent his time struggling to place cool cloths on Robert's head, pouring water into his dry mouth and waiting for the crisis. Wolf lay panting by his side, his tongue lolling out of his mouth and his yellow teeth gleaming.

Not before time Robert recovered, but he was to have recurring attacks for the remainder of his life. Jacques witnessed his anxiety that an attack might have come upon them whilst he lay ill, but neither a Byzantine nor a Saracen appeared upon the horizon. Jacques idly wondered what they might look like, and how they would be different from Normans. When all was well, Robert led them all in heartfelt prayer for their deliverance.

Day passed after dull day; not a soul was seen.

Two by two they guarded the pass. Occasionally they spoke to some villagers and bought their bread or wine, some poor goat's cheese or meat, but mostly they provided their own food. Only Jacques noticed the messages of spring - the golden flowers of the giant fennel which bloomed their brief delirious yellow passion against the grey-green foliage of the olives, and the patches of ruby-red poppy, and asphodels, pale and shadowy, past their prime.

To keep them all alert, Robert taught them some stratagems he recalled from life in Normandy, he also taught them about the tactics in battle and he learned with them some local Italian dialects. Before they slept he led them in Norman songs as each man in turn was sick for home, remembering friendships, good food and ale. Jacques became aware that Robert was creating deep bonds between them all, with hoops of iron discipline, that would be impossible to break apart.

As the weeks passed Robert became certain that he had been the victim of an elaborate and humiliating hoax. It was now plain that neither Byzantine nor Saracen would pass that way, or had even intended to do so. With no-one to question over Drogo's assertions he neither knew if they were lies or truth. He felt trapped and unable to move without breaking the terms of his agreed duty. Assessing his position proved difficult, especially as his supply of money was decreasing rapidly. He yearned for action - once or twice even daydreaming of what his life might have been if he had joined the Bastard, William. Yet he knew in his gut that he was right in his choice of the south.

Imperceptibly, the season began to change. The weather became hotter and hotter, the sun beat down and the land became dusty and dry: a hush began to fall on all things, birds rested during the day, great Pan seemed to brood over the earth and a deathlike stillness reigned. The only nearby shade was under the silvery olive-trees, up whose branches ran colonies of ants and beetles.

Still there was no movement. And they waited, sick with boredom and ill with recurrent bouts of fever; Robert, dangerous now, barely able to control his frustration, sent one of his men back to Drogo in Melfi for orders and money.

Three further weeks passed by before he trotted back into camp, accompanied by the Norman, Girard of Buonalbergo. The latter rode his horse easily, as if at one with the animal. Although slim and of average height, Girard had large white teeth of a kind to crack nuts with, and the full, wide, flexible mouth that denotes the generous talker. He greeted Robert in the same friendly manner in which they had spoken before they were forced to fight.

'Drogo tells me that you must stay where you are!' smiled Girard, unaware of Robert's bitterness. 'He says that he has news that the enemy might still attack, but he doesn't know when - he has had information that forces are gathering near the coast. He says he's confident that you can turn them back. He wished you well.'

'Is that all?'

'I'm afraid so.'

'He sends no money?'

'No.'

Robert, furious, turned on his heel and walked almost out of sight - to the spot where they had all, in turn, spied out the land over the past months. He sat down beneath a monolithic pine which crowned the apex of the pass - in old age it had grown monstrous. High-perched upon a lonely granite boulder, with roots writhing over the bare stone like the arms of an octopus, it sat firm and unmoved, deriding tempests and flinging fantastic limbs into the air - an emblem of tenacity in isolation.

So Robert sat himself apart, mirroring the loneliness of the tree, blindly facing over the empty pass, and the blue-green mountains all about him. He did not see their majestic beauty, he missed the tones of colour running down each valley, the light and shadows - he was sick with resentment. The scene in front of him blurred to lush Norman fields, oaks and hawthorn, and a friendly call from passing men.

Wolf lay at his feet, now and then looking uncertainly at his master. Jacques brought him food where he sat, and recognised the danger signs. In the group at camp Girard lounged, talking quietly with Robert's men about their homes, and what he, himself, had left behind in Normandy. Their siesta was uneasy as Robert continued in thought, torn between the safe but degrading harbour of dependency on Drogo and the dangers of total independence with no friends in power.

He had difficulty keeping fixed in his mind his original ambitions - but they could only be achieved out here, never in Normandy. He resolved to keep himself tightly in control this time, and to rely on no-one. Unaware, he twisted his ring about his finger, round and around, sightlessly.

Robert finally walked back to the group, calling Girard to him, speaking insolently,

'You showed courage coming here with Drogo's message! Weren't you afraid?'

'Not really ... I laid you out last time.'

'This time,' said Robert evenly, 'you're a puppet, my brother's mouth! It's a pity we aren't playing those famous games again, for you'd have got a knife between your ribs.'

Girard laughed lightly,

'Why so unpleasant? You have no need ... we are, after all, distantly related in some way.' Robert eyed him. Jacques saw that he was making an almighty effort not to hit Girard. Then Robert said, with gravel in his voice,

'Well, my official thanks for your trouble, bringing my brother's words. As you are intent on mentioning our kinship, perhaps you'd do me a kindness? Take back a message from me for Drogo - will you do that?'

Girard nodded his head in agreement.

'Tell Drogo - and tell him this in public - that I said to remind him that I'm an Hauteville, just like he is, and that *'Robert's been a man since childhood.''*

Girard repeated the crucial sentence. 'I'll tell him in front of everyone.'

'Good.'

So Girard then rode away, east, to deliver his incomprehensible message.

The moment he was out of sight Robert sat his men in a half-circle about him and said,

'I've considered our position with care; I don't believe there ever was a threat from anyone here! Certainly not from either Byzantines or Saracens - it seems too far from the coast. *I'm sure that we've been tricked.* I believe that there has been a change of heart and, in some strange way, my brother Drogo finds that I'm a threat.'

There was a low muttering from his men, and Jacques boldly said,

'Sire, you're right! I heard some of his servants say that when he first saw you, he said that you were *the one man he would rather not have met!'*

Wolf barked, and Robert looked down upon him with surprise as the sudden noise punctuated the quiet.

'I think,' he mused, 'if it was turnabout and I was Drogo, and saw myself arrive, I would be worried too - it's my accursed height, it intimidates people on first sight.'

In his heart Jacques agreed, and was grateful. Robert went on,

'As you all know, it was my eldest brother, Count William, who asked me to join him out here. But with him unexpectedly dead and buried I found myself in a quandary, for Drogo, in turn, offered me Scribla - nothing else! I'm certain, now, that it was a ploy to get me out of the way until, I suspect, he could confer with the others - Humphrey and Serlo. I think that's correct - don't you?'

He turned to Jacques, who agreed with a nod.

Robert spoke in a reasoning way to the people he now knew so well, there could be little hidden from each other. He resumed explaining his position,

'My brother got rid of me at once, by sending us here, so that I made no acquaintances or friends, nor upset his well-knit court. And he has robbed me. No! Not of money - but of time! Almost six precious months of my life ... it's clear to me that he wants to keep me out of his way. *I swear I'll get even for that - one day.'*

His voice began to rise confidently,

'Now - I want good food. I want to sleep under a roof, not under olive trees. I want to fill my own coffers with gold. I need to live my own life and call no-one my master - even my powerful half-brothers! I've decided to be independent, and make my own way in this country ... and Drogo can find others to guard his pass! I'm leaving; I'm leaving here, now! Will you come with me?'

Every man leapt to his feet and Wolf raced around them all, barking madly. Robert shouted on,

'Then let's be on our way – andiamo - let's go!'

His voice roared in crescendo, and the solitary pine watched them, indifferently, as they travelled away from the high but empty pass at Scribla in Calabria.

FRESSENDA AND SISTER SOPHIA

'I have a treat for you!!' Sister Sophia was glowing with pleasure. 'It's lovely news! In a day or two we're to have a visitor, the little Lady Judith of Evreux - did you know that?'

'No! Are we? Naturally I know of her lineage, but I only saw her once, at the funeral gathering of Duke Robert of Normandy. She's half-sister to your own Abbot, Odo de Grantmesnil, isn't she?'

'Indeed she is,' Sophia tucked a fold of the shawl around Fressenda's neck, 'and very generous she is, too, to this establishment - or, at the least, her father is, in her name – she's still very young. If it wouldn't tire you too much would you like her to sit with you? Although she's still unfledged, you'll find she's very adult in her ways. She has to be, poor child.'

'How exciting,' said Fressenda, with a happy laugh, 'after longing to be alone I find I now crave a visitor! Yes, do bring her in if she has the time. With my own daughters long gone, I seem to have been surrounded by men for so may years - to talk to a young girl would be delightful.'

'She'll make time - she knows you're here. And I think she could learn a lot from you. Especially fondness.'

'Ah,' said Fressenda quietly, leaning back in the soft sunshine, 'fondness has been in rather short supply in my life, but I'll do my best for this young woman if she comes.'

ROBERT'S CASTLE

Equally sunny was the scene in Calabria, where Robert had sped headlong across the countryside away from Scribla. Conditions were devastatingly harsh for him. Deliberately he travelled higher in the mountains, away from Drogo's land.

He selected a situation for his base which, he thought, would suit him well and not overstretch his means. Then he, with his men, spent the following few years building a small castle above the nearest town of San Marco Argentano. To get sufficient money to build, and to feed and clothe themselves, Robert was forced to turn into an accomplished robber.

One day he chose to rob a monastery. Monasteries should have money to hand, he thought.

'Eh? Jacques?'

'I disapprove, sir.'

'Are you hungry?'

'I am.'

'Then come along.'

'Naturally I'll be with you, sir.' said Jacques stiffly. 'But I still disapprove of robbing the Church.'

'You hypocrite.'

'Yessir.'

Robert and his soldiers formed up to look like a solemn funeral procession. They wound their way slowly up the mountain path to a hill-top monastery at Malvito, cursing the weight of the coffin under their breath. On arrival they sorrowfully pointed to the draped coffin and asked the Abbot,

'Father for pity's sake, may we have a requiem Mass in your sacred Chapel?'

'You may, my sons. You must have loved your friend very much to carry him so far.'

The groaning men wholeheartedly agreed. Quietly, unarmed, the group all shuffled inside, carrying the heavy coffin. They laid it reverently in front of the altar. Surrounded by the monks, the men knelt. The Abbot led the service.

With a shout the drapery of the coffin was flung back and Robert - the 'corpse' - leaped out, brandishing his broadsword. To the monks' astonishment he handed to the men the other swords upon which he'd been lying. They all began to threaten the horrified monks, slashing at them vigorously with their deadly weapons.

The Abbot cried out,

'Peace! Peace, *for God's sake! This is a consecrated place!'*

Robert glanced at Jacques and dropped the point of his sword to the ground.

'You shall have your peace. But on my terms!'

'On NO terms. This is MY monastery.'

Robert placed his sword across the Abbot's throat and drew a little blood.

'On the contrary - it's now MY monastery. Look about you!'

Without difficulty the Abbot could see all Robert's men with their swords to the monks' throats. He croaked,

'*What* terms?'

'In return for your lives ... *you do want to live, don't you?* ... and in exchange for all your available wealth - coins and furnishings, vestments and ecclesiastical treasures - I'll remain the rightful owner of the buildings here. *I'm master from now on!'*

The Abbot groaned,

'Not our vestments, sir! Please - not our precious, holy vestments!'

'As dispossessed men - why do you need vestments?'

'Well ...' the Abbot changed direction; at least Robert, the aggressor, was prepared to speak to him. 'What about our furnishings, sir - would you need those?'

'We've a castle to furnish,' said Robert, 'but I might come to an arrangement over your altar. We've no need of an altar.'

'*You* may have a castle, sir, but you've left us without a roof over our heads. Where would we put the altar?'

'You havc a point,' Robcrt said, keeping his blade hard against the Abbot's bloody throat, 'it seems to me you and your monks need to remain in this monastery. Don't you? And keep the altar in place?'

More blood trickled down onto the Abbot's vestments.

'We do. *We do. Please* take your sword away ...'

Robert lowered his sword.

'Then we'll have to talk about the rent you're going to pay me, won't we? It may be high.'

The Abbot blanched.

'Satisfied, Jacques?' Robert asked with a grin. Jacques lifted an eyebrow.

This was the beginning of many profitable tricks and forays, none of which did Robert any credit. He simply didn't care what anyone thought of him.

As food was scarce, he and his men scoured the countryside, looting far and wide. When they could find no more - they burned - first as threat, then as punishment if they were given nothing. They threatened murder. They held up travellers. When desperate, they destroyed farms and homes, monasteries and churches. They burned crops and stole pigs and horses. Sometimes, they would start by burning property or harvests, and then agree to put out the fire if sufficient money was handed over.

They used every deceit to gain advantage - goods, money and land. They became notorious. It all evolved into a legendary background as everyone survived on Robert's nimble wits. When they weren't living their legend they were building the castle. Robert had chosen the site for his castle strategically; there was only one path which approached it, corkscrewing its way upwards through curious groups of enormous rocks and sudden, cliff-like drops. Defence always came first. It was devised so that no sun would shine into the castle-dwellers' eyes if an attack came from this single approach. Behind, the mountain had been sliced away during an age-old earthquake, providing a sheer precipice. The ground all about his castle was covered with coarse, tufty grass. On one side there was a stream which, even in late summer, bubbled up from a spring among the rocks, with loose shale upon its banks. As it meandered to the village below it occasionally went underground. It was one of the many sources which fed a long, narrow lake nearby.

Across from the castle was a steep, wooded valley, filled with caves, some with piles of bleached bones left there, untouched by the superstitious local people. High above were clumps of trees, a mixture of pines, beech and holm oaks, giving shelter and firewood.

Robert stood with Jacques and Wolf as the last of the battlements were fixed in place. They watched in pride as a man above them waved an arm to show the work was done. Fifty men stood around him, culled from his half-brothers, one by one - opportunists, every one of them.

'It's time for action further afield,' said Robert, 'you men stay here and clean it all up. See to the horses. Fill the barn. Chop firewood. Get it ready in case of siege. Jacques and I will see what could be profitable. We'll return soon. But first - let's eat!'

ROBERT IN BRINDISI

Robert thought it might be profitable to travel back to Apulia, where his humiliation had taken place. With care they skirted his brothers' lands, and headed - not for Sipontum or the Monte Gargano, for they were pilgrimage places where you were expected to give, not take - but for the busy international crossroads of Brindisi. Here everyone travelling to Greece would stay, and here traders from the Levant would land, when visiting Rome or the north. Here, too, they might learn things to their advantage and, even if they had to steal it, they might eat a satisfying meal.

The city was large and bustling with activity; so they followed the crowds towards the harbour which was the centre of commerce then they took up places where they could observe their fellow men and see their diverse faces and clothing.

At the very end of the Via Appia Robert stood looking about him, under the soaring white marble column; silent, secret, unsmiling. Jacques and Wolf stayed some distance from him, watching the busy ships in the harbour and staring at heavily-laden passengers being unloaded from a large vessel just docked. It was a one-sailed open boat in which cargo and crew travelled exposed to the elements, and reminded Jacques of a Viking long ship.

Robert was lost in thought as his lengthy shadow plunged down the marble steps in front of him. The sun was setting behind him, leaving in shade the harbour lying below him, *curved liked the horns of an antler.* Suddenly a firm hand fell on his shoulder and Girard stood by his side.

Robert whipped his knife from his belt and held it to his throat.

'No! No - my friend - *for heaven's sake let's be at peace this time!'* He shouted, pushing him off.

Robert let him go, saying,

'Girard! You - again! *Can you never let me be?'*

'We meet by pure chance, Robert - my notorious kinsman!'

'Kinsman? *Since when?* If it's true I warn you not to trade on it.'

Robert glowered. Girard laughed, saying;

'Oh! *Come on!* How sullen you look! Let's go and have some wine together before you're tempted to take my head from my shoulders!'

The two men went to a nearby tavern by the sea, pushing their way steadily through the mill of travellers and beggars. The tavern was merely a booth, bare and temporary, surrounded by piles of fishing nets left on the sand. Both men were fair, with sunburnt skins; Girard was dressed more modishly, and Robert had a wilder look; all heads turned as he spoke, for his voice was deep and bell-like.

Robert allowed Girard to act as host, noting that he kept his money in a finely embroidered purse, hanging from his broad leather belt. With wine in front of them, and mussels shared from a pot, which they plucked out with wooden spoons and ate with bread, Girard pleasantly enquired,

'What's been happening to you these past few years? Apart from the mayhem you've created?'

'Are you mad? Do you think I'd tell you - my brother's puppet?'

'You've made a mistake, you know - I'm not any puppet of Drogo's, I just happened to be visiting Melfi when you arrived, recruiting soldiers for my own use. Then, when I came with his message - Drogo paid me to do so - I was on my way to Salerno on business anyway, and I agreed to make a slight detour. That's all. I found it most diverting, meeting another Hauteville warrior.'

Robert was hardly convinced. Girard went on,

'Anyway, just after I left you at Scribla - what a God-forsaken place that was, wasn't it? You decided that you'd had enough, didn't you? I came back, you know, to refresh my water skin, and found you hard at work packing your camp. So I waited in the shadows until you left, to see which way you'd go ... you travelled a different path from mine.'

'Did you tell Drogo?'

'I gave him your first message, the cryptic one, but as for telling him you'd left the pass - well, I thought he could work that out for himself, given time.'

Robert began to relax. Girard chattered on,

'Anyway, you made up a clever reply for your brothers, you wily creature! Humphrey and Serlo were both there when I told Drogo what you had to say, and Drogo seemed really put out when I told him you *'had been a man since childhood'*. They all looked perturbed. Drogo looked thunderstruck, and was on edge for days. What did you mean by it?'

'It was just a timely reminder about an event that happened many years ago. But I'm glad they remembered it.' He looked out across the sea, unfocussed, a thin smile on his lips. 'Yes, I think they'll all look at me with different eyes - now.'

'Well, whatever it meant, it certainly put the fox amongst the chickens and was full of guile. You really are as cunning as a fox! Crafty and devious! I'll give you a new name - henceforth I shall call you 'Guiscard'!

'Guiscard,' mused Robert, 'I think that's fair ...'

'It is. And, of course, you were quite right to leave; your brothers were using and testing you. Drogo received you, but the others knew you were coming; they stayed out of the way until Drogo could report what you were like. Once he'd met you, it became as clear as day that they'd made a mistake asking you to come, you became a challenge immediately.'

Robert felt gratified: his instinct had served him well.

'Is that so?' He said, with amusement in his eyes.

'Well,' said Girard, loftily, 'news isn't a one-way street, you know. Information from home filters out quite quickly, within a year or two at least, and just as much returns to Normandy; they'd been talking about your abilities quite openly for some time and it was clear you might be useful. But - not if there might be confrontation.'

Robert looked grim.

'I had hoped to be welcome, but I wasn't. In some odd way I was put at a disadvantage at Drogo's court ...' He couldn't bring himself to describe his devastating scene with Drogo.

Girard riposted, laughing,

'You certainly were. I suspect you lost your temper! And if you didn't, I'm sure you'd have let that implacable side of your nature ruin your chances if you had stayed any longer serving Drogo. You may be much bigger than me, Robert, *but at least I can laugh at life;* I'd advise you to do so too, if you want to survive.'

Robert found himself admiring Girard's courage in advising him, not many would have dared. This was a new life, he reminded himself, he had to try new attitudes.

'But,' said his companion, with mirth, 'after Drogo had taken one long, hard look at you he realised that you were too strong and dangerous if crossed, so he took up their prearranged plan and rapidly sent you into the wilderness. The message I conveyed to him endorsed their fears somehow, and I heard Drogo say to Humphrey 'Well, that's let the cat out of the bag', but I didn't know what he meant. Tell me, how have you fared?'

Robert told Girard all he wanted him to know.

He spoke of his men, his castle, his slowly increasing wealth and of some of his ambitions Girard listened intently, picking shreds of mussels from between his teeth with a fishbone toothpick. Robert went on,

'But I seem to have arrived at a crossroads and I can't progress any further.'

'What's your immediate problem? Lack of money?'

'Not altogether. Tancred, my father, impressed on me the three routes to success: ability, marriage and money. I've the ability, but I've certainly no marriage in view – anyway, I've no chance of meeting an heiress.'

Girard's eyes brightened.

'That sounds like an ultimatum to my own social skills! I know so many people out here, let me think about it, and work out who might fit the position. Let me think, now, who do I know that's *really* wealthy?'

It was the first time that anyone had held out a helping hand to him, and Robert was grateful. They agreed to meet the next day, and that night Robert and Jacques slept on the sandy shore some way from the town, wrapped in their threadbare cloaks.

When Girard met them at the same small booth his face was alight with merriment,

'I've had a *splendid* idea - it might solve your problem and it would also please me a great deal - the answer's under my own nose!'

Robert looked mystified, but waited.

'My aunt!'

'It isn't often you hear anyone say that,' Robert murmured, 'and, no doubt, your aunt may resolve my difficulties - but I'm not sure I could stomach an old woman for wife.'

Girard shook with laughter, but behind all the froth of his talk and manner there lurked, it seemed, an answer.

'I'd better explain from the beginning. You see, I come from a very large family, as you do; I'm the eldest of eight children. And so was my father before me - the eldest, I mean, the eldest of ten.'

'Normans breed like flies ...'

'Yes. Well ... my father's youngest sister, Alberada, is, in point of fact, younger than me. She's on a visit here from Normandy at the moment, so you can meet her. Why not go further - and marry her?'

'Marry your aunt Alberada? How much money has she got? And is it her own?'

'She has rather a lot, as it happens. She inherited land in Normandy from her grandmother, and her godfather, a bishop, left her an unexpectedly large portion of gold. Marry her! What do you say? It's an advantageous match and you'd get the money you need.'

Robert paused to think. This was heady opulence, the first appearance of unlooked-for good luck. Outside the booth, Jacques could see Robert's face light up as it once did in Normandy, and he was glad. Robert began to think aloud,

'That would mean more men and land - perhaps I'd better build another sturdy castle?'

'Don't be a fool,' said Girard sharply, 'keep your castle as a safe headquarters for the time being, it sounds well-built. The only thing that concerns me is that it's in Calabria, far too near your brother's land.'

'Don't tell me I've wasted two whole years building it for no good reason?'

'Building a castle is never a waste, and you're bound to find a good use for it one day when you've achieved your ambitions and are installed at Melfi or Aversa. I dare say you'll litter the south with your castles, given time!'

'That day can't come close enough!'

'Well, make a positive start: bring your troops straight over here to Apulia and fight your fellow Normans first, before you start on any Byzantines or Saracens - you know Norman ways and behaviour, and you're bound to be successful. How else do you think I managed to acquire Buonalbergo? *Start with the weakest of your own kind.'*

There was good sense in what Girard had to say. He went on,

'There's been so much turmoil in Apulia lately, especially since your half-brother William's death. Now both Gaimar and Rainulf have died as well, and your obnoxious half-brother Drogo has far too much to do. The Pope and the Emperor are meeting in Germany, trying to control this surge of greedy, lusty Normans, leaving everything in confusion all across southern Italy. Politically, it's a mess. No one person exercises real control - so the situation is wide open for you to step in!'

Robert stepped in immediately with a request,

'Then will *you* join me, knowing my ambitions?'

'Gladly,' said Girard, 'and I'll bring my own men; the rents from Buonalbergo will feed us all for a while.'

Robert immediately returned to the unsolved project,

'And what about your aunt?'

'Marry her! Take a chance!'

Robert paused, saying thoughtfully,

'Why don't you marry her yourself?'

'I'd like to, believe me, but it's impossible, I'm afraid, we're too closely related.'

Relieved, Robert went on,

'Ah - yes of course, aunt and nephew would be incest in the Church's eyes. What's she like?'

'She'd independent and adventurous in her ways, because of her money - which has brought her out on this visit.'

'Independence isn't a virtue in a wife.' Robert stated flatly.

'That's true - but you'd still have her money.'

'Anything else?'

'People respect her, and find her sweet.'

'Sweet? Good enough to bed, you mean?'

'And more …' said Girard, with a thoughtful look. Robert flashed a suspicious glance at him.

'After all,' said Girard, hastily, 'she's still under twenty, but she tends to be wayward, that's why she hasn't married before. If you want her money you'll have to take steps to impress her.'

'Well in truth, I've very little to offer her.' Robert was ruefully modest, but Girard contradicted him good-naturedly,

'Don't be a fool, have some confidence - leave it to me to present you in a favourable light! We don't want to lose the chance of our partnership, do we?'

'No - that's the most important aspect of the bargain.'

'Well,' said Girard, 'take it steadily with her, it won't be difficult. She has an aura of calm, and there's no malice in her.'

'A woman with money and no malice? Why hasn't she been taken already? Why didn't anyone marry her in Normandy?'

'She's been too discriminating - up to now, but plenty made an offer.'

'Then - *what the devil are we waiting for?*' said Robert, getting to his feet. 'Let's go and ask her!'

'Perhaps,' said Girard, carefully, 'a haircut, first?'

Robert flinched.

ROBERT AND ALBERADA

The lady Alberada was small, direct as a dart and competent. She had a Norman air of never dawdling, but making her way with purpose when on her feet. Neat and fastidious, she was economical with words and gestures. After due consideration, she set herself a course of action that she knew she could maintain, then followed it to the letter. She knew her own capabilities and, like so many small and happy people, was surrounded by an aura of self-composure and orderliness. It was reassuring.

She was staying at a small dwelling in the centre of Brindisi, which had a flat roof on which the occupants could take the air, however she was in the courtyard when Girard arrived, plagued by Venetian traders who had come out in the cool of the early evening, trying to interest her in their multitude of wares. She told a servant to send them away. As daylight began to fade, the pair walked up to the reception rooms, away from the noise and heat; eventually Girard led the conversation around to Robert, but failed to kindle her interest, asking her to meet and speak to him, several times she refused him.

'Please be gracious enough to meet him,' he said, lightly, 'he's recently arrived from Normandy and he's already built a small castle and made his presence felt. He'll go far, I'd wager my life on that.'

She shook her head. She had heard about this newest Hauteville, the tallest one.

'I'm truly not interested.'

He persisted,

'Look - he's down below; see if he pleases you or not, for my sake!

After all, you're independent, you can choose your own path; nobody can force you - and you've nothing to lose in being civil to my friend.'

'Oh, very well,' said Alberada, with supreme disinterest, 'if he's already here – and if that's the only way to get you to leave me alone – he can come up for a minute or so.'

At Girard's shout Robert strode in. He stood by the open door, looked across the room at Alberada and, suddenly breathless, said,

'Oh.'

'Good day,' said Alberada, quietly, 'and welcome.'

As they exchanged looks, a strange, fleeting expression crossed her face. Then,

'I understand you wish to marry me - unmet! Why?'

Startled by this businesslike frankness, Robert stared, taken aback. He saw a very small and slender girl, modestly dressed, standing solitary in the shadows of the room, her back to the open window. She had dark hair, which she wore in a coil about her head, and appeared to have enormous eyes - were they violet-coloured? He couldn't see clearly enough in the gloaming. Those eyes were fringed with thick lashes like sooty fingerprints; he was mesmerised by them, together with her sun-warmed skin and pointed chin. He felt that he had met her before, somewhere; there was a sense of recognition. It was uncanny.

He gathered himself and cleared his throat.

'You ask me why? Well, foremost I'd prefer to marry a woman, like you, from Normandy, from my own part of the world. We'd speak the same language; we might even know some of the same people. I'd know how to deal with you, and you'd know what to expect from me.'

'No other reason?'

'Your money?'

Alberada gave a throaty chuckle.

'Honest enough, I must say.'

'You asked me a question. I answered you.' Robert lifted an eyebrow. 'Wasn't that what you had in mind?'

'Some men might have taken a different approach.' Said Alberada, apparently still amused. 'However, as we're being so forthright, let's take turn about - *what's in this alliance for me?* Be honest again.'

Robert felt his reply might alter the course of his life, so he spoke slowly after deep thought.

'You'd receive a share in everything. I want money, land, and a high position out here. I have the ability, and I know that, once I've set my foot upon the ladder of success, there'd be no peak I couldn't conquer. I'm sure that's my destiny.'

His tone changed, became light, bantering.

'Have faith! Come with me and I'll conquer for you!'

'Prettily said. *What imagination!* Like coloured bubbles floating in the air ...'

Alberada paused in thought, twisting her long fingers in her belt. She crossed to the other side of the room and sat on a window seat in the last light of the day. She continued thoughtfully,

'But the higher you rise in the world out here, the less chance there would be a place for me. I sense that. In time, I wager, you'd want to leapfrog over me to an alliance with a woman of greater lineage and power. I don't know that I'd care to be your stepping stone.'

'I'm surprised that you think I'd be so base and craven.'

Robert's face changed with a slight twitch of his lips, as he lifted a quizzical eyebrow again and, unaware of the devastating charm he wrought on her, continued to speak,

'If you agreed to marry me, I'd respect your position until the day you died, and I'd look after you always.'

'Perhaps I know you better than you do yourself,' said Alberada dreamily, 'perhaps I have a destiny, too, but mine may be more precarious.'

She turned to look at Girard, who stood to one side, and he answered her questioning expression,

'Watch out, Alberada,' he said, 'I call Robert 'the Guiscard', 'the wily one'! See he doesn't trick you!'

'That comes well from you, Girard, when we're supposed to be joining forces and fighting together. *Don't you trust me yourself?'*

Robert was displeased with the jibe, yet Girard went on in an amiable way,

'No, I don't trust you fully because I know your ambitions may consume you. But I can take care of myself: it's Alberada we're speaking of this moment - *can she trust you?'*

Robert crossed the room to stand by Alberada's side,

'Yes,' he said, under his breath, 'they *are* violet.' His flesh tingled all over at the mere thistledown of the moment, puffed off into space. He thought of home.

Alberada looked up at him as he said quietly,

'Well, will you come with me? I can offer you very little at first, but there will be much to lay at your feet in time. Will you have me?'

She sat still and steady as a rock.

'Not now. I'll – I'll give you my answer within a week.'

Robert smiled one of his very rare, hesitant, smiles. Bending low, he took her slender hand gently in his and brushed the fingertips gravely with his lips, looking into those fathomless eyes.

'There's something about you ...' he began, but, confused, he walked away without finishing his sentence, shaking his head.

A week later Girard kept his appointment with Robert at the foot of the white marble column which marked the eastern end of the Via

Appia; Jacques looked anxiously into his good-humoured face as Robert leaped to his feet on his arrival.

'Let's go over and discover the verdict!' said Girard.

As they walked to the house where Alberada lived, sweat trickled down Robert's clean-shaven brown cheek. The sunshine was bright, and Robert sucked a lemon he had just plucked from a nearby bush.

Girard spoke like a waterfall, discussing this and that, but Robert had nothing to say in reply. He couldn't forget the sudden lurch he felt when he first had looked at Alberada; he didn't know what it was, but every time he thought of her he'd feel an echo of it. It alarmed him. He felt beyond control. He chewed his lip, deep in thought. Would it be better not to marry Alberada after all? Shouldn't he wait until he found a woman who had money - perhaps another of Girard's friends - but a woman he would never wish to touch? He had just spent a whole week thinking about Alberada, and he wanted to touch her very much indeed.

Equally disturbing was the fact he wanted to talk with her, laugh with her, and then to hold her in his arms; he shivered again at the foolish thought. He knew that when he much desired a thing, his temperament knocked flat all reason. He also knew that, to succeed, he needed to be ruthlessly determined; his inner soul ought never to be bound to any woman, it would weaken him. Alberada had unaccountably made him feel that he would like to know her, know her mind and heart, as well as her body: to be at peace with another human. His confusion was rare.

Later, when they finally arrived at the house, washed and in fresh clothes, he gloomily asked Girard to let him speak to Alberada in private. Girard smiled a knowing smile, but Robert didn't respond.

He found her on the rooftop, alone, sitting in the fresh, seaborne air. She wore a gown of some dark red stuff which made Robert think of glowing rubies. The smell of oriental spices wafted from a nearby building and, in the distance, there were sounds of Muslims at prayer. Alberada had tucked some fresh flowers in her hair and their scent drifted over them both. The night air was as warm as new milk.

He took her hand. They half-smiled, nervously. Again he felt dizzy, then in agitation, plunged into stumbling speech.

'I'm sorry, I must retract before it's too late: I find I can't marry you after all. I fear I've acted badly towards you.'

Her hand dropped. She stayed very still.

'Oh! May I know the reason?' She looked up at him.

'Girard was right. My goals are too far-reaching. I want the whole world for myself, and I've absolutely no scruples over getting what I want.'

He found himself distressed with the effort to be honest with her.

'I'm not a good man, Alberada, you deserve better. I've robbed and stolen and had more than my fair share of other crimes ...' nervously he gabbled on, running out of breath. Then started afresh shaking his head in frustration, 'I'm not the man for you, you're too gentle. And, I'm afraid, your assessment was quite correct. I ... I might put you aside if a better chance came my way, whatever I'd promised. So - now d'you see why we can't marry?'

Robert, touchy as an unshelled fish, ashamed, too, was astonished at the words which had poured out of him. Alberada answered him,

'So! Again you act the honourable man; not quite in keeping with the reputation I'd heard about. How curious! Yet, you wouldn't say all this unless you'd given it abundant consideration. I've a notion that you've some deeper feeling for me - some personal attraction - could this be so?'

'Yes - unfortunately. I didn't expect this.'

He spoke under his breath. Her arrow-like directness unnerved him, slid under his skin like a rapier.

'I've never had this sort of feeling before.' Then, louder, pushed on, 'Look - I need to marry someone that wouldn't distract me, make me lose my concentration on my career. If I put someone else first I'd never reach my goals because I'd grow careless and let my ambitions take second place.' He climbed out of the pit he had dug for himself. 'So - you see - I need someone I could shamelessly abuse ...'

Alberada interrupted, her eyebrows arched provocatively as she said flirtatiously,

'Someone absurdly rich, in a high position, that you could flagrantly exploit?'

Her eyes were alight with amusement. He met her mood accurately,

'Yes ... in a highly unprincipled way ...'

They laughed softly together, spirits soaring, lost in each other's eyes. Suddenly she blushed apricot across her pale cheeks, yet bravely continued to look into his face, saying,

'Well, shall I come to you in this - even more - honest way? And the day you meet your heiress I'd be prepared to step aside. Then you could further those worldly ambitions of yours. Shall I? And would you continue to look after me even when we part?'

'Are you saying you would *really* sacrifice yourself for me?'

'Yes. Yes, I would. I gave myself the time to think about it in earnest, although, I'll admit, I'd made up my mind the day we met.'

Robert breathed out in a husky voice,

'Then - you feel something for me, too?'

'I do. As we're being so deeply honest with each other, I'll confess that I haven't thought of anyone else since we met.'

Searching her face, Robert said shakily,

'Nor I.' then Robert took her small hand in his again and murmured, 'Alberada, you're gambling, do you realise that? You're taking a terrible chance – I know I'm a prodigious fighter, but I believe I'm bound to be a disastrous husband. You could do so much better.'

Alberada didn't hesitate, but spoke clearly,

'Just once in a lifetime I think one should make a leap into the dark. I'm willing to leap with you. I don't believe my heart will change over the years.'

'And,' said Robert, 'as the old wedding prayer goes - will you promise to be bonny and buxom at bed and at board?'

'I promise!'

Robert swept her into his arms, light as a feather. Then, tentatively, and with respect, he just touched her mouth with his.

'So, it's an honest way to start. When shall we marry?'

Alberada laid her head fleetingly against Robert's chest, then looked up at him again, deep into his eyes.

'When you please, Robert. But let's not wait too long. Say - a month?'

'Yes, definitely violet.' said Robert, lifting her chin.

Then, more confident, he bent and kissed her mouth differently, sensuously, until time stood still and, eventually, night fell.

ROBERT AND GIRARD

Girard and Robert again sat in the sandy tavern.

'We have a month,' said Robert, 'so - let's make our plans!'

'Which comes first,' said Girard, 'discussing which target you're aiming for? Or fetching our men? Or arming us all?'

'I've got it all worked out, and these are my reasons for what we'll do. Once I'm married I want to give Drogo the fright of his life. I want to give him a threefold message: first that I'm newly married, secondly that I have sufficient money to take him on and thirdly, thirdly ...' said Robert, 'that I'm coming for him personally. I've had enough time to think. Now I'll tell you what we'll do - and in what order.'

That set the pattern of their relationship and Robert's gradual ascent up the ladder of power in southern Italy. Alberada saw nothing of him until the day they wed. It was deliberate. He held himself on course with iron determination.

Their wedding day in Brindisi began very early and was short and sweet. Robert reined himself in all through the day, hardly speaking; hardly looking at his bride clad in diaphanous Sicilian silk, amethyst-coloured, shot with gold; hardly pausing before he placed her upon her horse, hurriedly rode with her back across the Apennines and installed her in his castle with her possessions, her maids, and her money, which she had with her at the marriage ceremony.

He allowed himself the luxury of just one short night with her. *And then he left her.*

He thought it best not to tell her what he meant to do – just in case it hadn't been a success. She would understand, he told himself, she knew his career couldn't be interrupted by sentimentality: he dared not tarry with her or take his eyes off his first major target...

'Oh no!' thought Alberada, wordlessly, as he accelerated out of sight. 'He doesn't waste time. But he'll be back.' Then set about making Robert's castle her own.

He sped along with a quantity of Alberada's money to join Girard, where they instantly began the final preparations to put his crucial plans into action. He intended to capture the legendary city of Cosenza, in the wilds of Calabria and many miles away from Venosa, where Drogo was desperately at work – for Drogo, now Count of Apulia, had been the proud and boastful overlord of Cosenza for some years.

There was an especially good reason for Robert to target Cosenza, because some Saracens, recognizing that Drogo was vastly over-stretched in Apulia, had arrived there first, swept in on a raiding party and captured Cosenza from Drogo's small holding army. Drogo was mad with anger, it was known all over the south within days that Drogo was foaming at the mouth with fury and frustration and was a laughing stock.

Now Robert aimed to nip Drogo's heels and win it for himself from the Saracens, who had never heard of him. Their guard must be down. Take Cosenza into his own hands, thought Robert, and Drogo would be bruised with a type of smarting sting he'd never forget.

'Our turn!' Robert grinned at Girard. 'Only hit a man when he's down ... *Drogo'll hate this!*'

So, with newly bought armour, horses and weapons, together with newly recruited Norman soldiers, Robert and Girard, who had brought with him two hundred fighting men, led their young and enthusiastic army against Cosenza, wearing their new shirts of mail, the freshly made chain links sparkling in the sunshine. They looked like gods.

They swept down onto the town and overcame it, citizens and Saracens alike, with such ferocity and lack of mercy that reports about the drama and cruelty of fire and sword, both used indiscriminately, gripped the imaginations of all the south for many years.

Until this time Robert's raids and skirmishes had been swift and punishing, followed by an equally fast withdrawal with the spoils. This had earned him a sour reputation of being merely a lawless robber, an amateur, and few of his gains on land proved permanent. To have conquered Cosenza was totally different.

Robert took no prisoners.

The spoils from the conquest of the city were immense, set against anything they had won before. Not only was there the money and city treasure, but there were the horses - some of which had originally been brought there by Drogo. To their delight two Lombard administrators were brought to their notice, trained by Drogo, who were prepared to swear allegiance to the victors and work under a group of senior soldiers left to guard the city. Most significant of all, there was the universal recognition of Robert as a warrior. Leaders from nearby settlements voluntarily came to surrender, rather than risk similar suffering.

Through their spies, Drogo, Humphrey and Serlo heard the disastrous news at once. The first-hand reports were frightening. Robert's half-brothers were informed over and over again with descriptions of the unceasing uproar of the battle, and the ensuing cruelty - which chilled their blood. The confusion engendered by the billowing smoke and raging fires never left the Cosenzans' memories either, and for years to come they displayed their burned flesh and lacerations.

Drogo sent a messenger to Robert without delay, thanking him,

'For re-taking Cosenza for him, Drogo, in the name of Hauteville.'

Robert laughed contemptuously and sent the messenger back with a message of his own,

'You had your chance. *Cosenza is mine!'*

ROBERT AND ALBERADA

Some weeks later, when all the city's problems were settled to his satisfaction, Robert returned, victorious, to Alberada. This time he stayed for a few months. This time he indulged himself, gave himself time to laze with her.

'I'm so glad you brought me here, especially now.' Alberada looked up at Robert, her eyes shining. 'I'll always think of this castle as a special place.'

She and Robert turned their heads together and gazed thoughtfully across the hillside, and over the valley, to his seemingly impenetrable castle above them. They were curled up beneath a beech tree, looking, too, obliquely down along the path of the little stream as it meandered to the long lake below. From where they sat they could just glimpse small patches of grass near the lake, bright with buttercups and orchids, shimmering in the sunshine. Happily she let her thoughts roam.

'It's so beautiful, isn't it? I love it here, it already feels like home.'

Robert gazed down at her memorable face, luminous with love, and gently touched her cheek. In these surroundings his face seemed to be always just about to smile, the lines of a smile being always about his lips; it happened nowhere else.

'You've already made it so, just by being here you've filled it with life'. He smoothed her skin with infinitely gentle fingers. 'I don't know how you do it, but you seem to transform ordinary, everyday objects, and arrange them in your own way so that the rooms look quite different - I think I'd always recognise a place where you had lived.'

He stroked her face from the delicately pointed chin to her, as yet untroubled forehead, smoothing his fingers up, slowly and gently, until they reached into her dark hair - then re-traced their steps and softly sent them up across her skin again; a shiver coursed down her legs. He felt her slight movement, and was satisfied.

'Have you noticed,' he said quietly, 'that in Normandy our castles are our homes, and we make them our own; whereas the people out here, especially the Saracens, wonder why anyone should expend thought and wealth on that which may be abandoned tomorrow? Perhaps that's because so many of them are nomads.'

'Mmmm.'

Alberada, with eyes closed, moved her head under his probing fingers, lithe as a cat, rolling her skull around in a languorous circle - she almost purred. As she did, Robert caught her face in his hand, held it still; her eyes opened languidly, lifted to his, fathomless pools of lavender.

'You're not to move unless I say so ...' he murmured, then slid his hand down to encircle her slender neck. Undeterred, grave and serious, she went on,

'Our home will be a refuge for you always, this I swear.' She outlined the shape of his lips with one slim finger. 'Somewhere for you to come back to, like a lodestar, some place where you know you'll always be safe, and where you can rest and be loved.'

'Ah! Love ... I need that. I need you. I really need you and I always will.'

Alberada touched his lips again. 'I mean it, Robert. Until I die you'll own my heart and, whatever happens, however wicked you are, my welcome and my love will never falter. Swear you'll always come home to me?'

Something in her face made Robert stop for one long heartbeat; then he said, huskily,

'I swear it.'

Her face changed again, relaxed.

Robert shifted his position on the grass, more free to touch his wife in new and different ways; ordinarily he couldn't bear to have her out of sight, when they were together he always wanted to touch her. 'Why,' he thought, 'I'm besotted with her!' He lifted a pin out of her hair, held it in his hand.

'It'll all come down if you do that.'

'I know.' He plucked out another pin and laid them both upon a broad leaf. Alberada shivered again, but wasn't cold.

'I'm glad you've become such friends with Girard.'

'Yes,' said Robert, playing with the pins, which had small jewels in their heads, 'I never thought I'd take on a partner so early in the game. But it's better, this way, than having one of my half-brothers.'

'But - somehow - he's not an equal, is he? You've worked out a legal alliance in a very friendly way, but there is no doubt who has precedence, Robert, everyone knows you're the leader.'

Alberada took up an errant strand of hair and united it with the rest, twisting it about until it stayed in place. Robert, turning the jewelled hairpins in his hands so that the sun made them glitter, said thoughtfully,

'I'm glad we're friends, he's a good man and I trust him, even if he's a bit on the lazy side. And he amuses me. But our affairs are pretty tightly fastened,' he said, with confidence, 'if anything terrible - final - should happen to either of us the other takes over, takes everything - *everything*! We both want to see that you're protected, too - you understand that? We love you so much, and we worry about your future.'

He handed back her hairpins carefully, which she laid upon the leaf with the others. He continued'

'Yes, I'm glad about our friendship, mostly because Girard's your nephew, it's because of you I'm glad, it makes us closer, somehow.'

Unexpectedly, his words sounded to her like poetry. Robert could do endless damage, exciting - tumultuous - damage, to her emotions with his hands and mouth and body, but he rarely expressed himself in speech. These words of his, spoken lazily in Robert's quietest voice, almost a deep-throated whisper, aroused another flurry of sensations.

'*Could* we be closer?' Alberada said faintly.

He smiled up at her, then turned away and lay full length at an angle to her seated body, putting his heavy head into her lap. She ran her fingers through his fair hair, close-cropped now, feeling the austere bones beneath.

'No, we couldn't. And, whatever happens, I'll remember this day for ever...'

'Because I've told you I'm having your child?' She blushed a rosy glow. He moved his head, burrowing lower.

'Because you've told me you're having my child' he asserted 'and for other things too. You'll have lots of children, but the first is always the most important!'

'That's because you're the first, Robert, in your family.'

'No,' said Robert, patiently. 'I may be the first of a second family. I'm not the first son my father ever had. Perhaps that's my trouble; I just can't bear being second.'

'I know, I know.' She soothed. 'You're the first and only man for me.'

She thought back over the months since their wedding, reminding herself of Robert's inner discord. In the beginning, furiously excited, he had mounted an onslaught on her body - taking, taking, until they were both drained; too often he found himself beyond his control, and it frightened him. But he had never loved before, never truly loved a woman for herself. He found himself facing turmoil in his dilemma, couldn't balance passion with peace; he couldn't get enough of her, night or day. There was so much to share, so much to pour out to her, in a way he'd never found in the past. Unexpectedly, too, he had wanted to know everything about her, especially her innermost thoughts; she had unlocked his hidden personality and now all his emotions poured out unchecked.

This discord within him was known only to her. He had found it almost impossible to reach a balance, to learn to understand himself, to reach a stable equilibrium between his mind and body. Unknown to him she had eased him along, never showing a flutter of her own problems, loving him beyond boundaries, understanding him completely: she acted purely on her instinct.

Now they lay quietly in the long grass, the whole day stretched before them, not moving. They were just daydreaming in their little backwater, like oysters in a lagoon. For a while they chatted, comfortably, discussing people they knew in Normandy. Robert told her all about his mother and her entry into a convent, then whiled away the time enlightening her how important Tancred had been to him, and about their final meeting when William of Normandy had been present in their small castle - and the many decisions that had been made: it all appeared a very long time ago. She, in turn, told him seemingly inconsequential facts about her brothers and sisters, wondering whether she would ever see them again. For a few brief moments a small group of tiny blue butterflies fluttered about their heads, then drifted out of sight.

'Life out here is a challenge beyond belief,' he said, speaking as if to himself, 'the stakes are so high. Issues have each to be judged on their own merits and any great man only fails because he's lost his touch for boldness. I must never forget that.'

For a moment he closed his eyes as he lay there, but it was not for long.

'The Pope, the Emperor - they're unpredictable, and unknown to us - Girard and me - at present. No ordinary man remains the same, either, events change him and he has to act in his own interests.' He gazed thoughtfully at Alberada. 'So will I, which sometimes makes me afraid; we're on the threshold of momentous events.'

'I understand.' she breathed, 'thank goodness you and I were born to speak the same language, so you can explain your actions to me.' Her hand rested lightly on his hair. 'It seems to me that your future is going to be like crossing a raging river, leaping from stepping-stone to stepping-stone, hoping not to fall into the deep. You're determined enough, but it's clearly very dangerous. Keep faith, sweetheart, that's what you asked of me! And I do. So, you must, too.'

Above them the foliage stirred now and then, as occasional breezes skittered down the valley, catching the leaves up, only to lay them down again where they had been a moment before. The noonday sun shone through the branches, making an ever-changing pattern on the grass, dappling their clothes with light and shade and making their skin shine gold. It was very quiet in their secluded grove, able to see, yet not be seen - they had discovered it some days ago when they had walked together down to the lake. Until then Robert had spent his life only thinking of things that mattered in his man's world, attack and defence, supplies and safety; now Alberada was opening his eyes to beauty and he felt he had been blind since birth - it was both wonderful and unsettling as he felt its emasculating pull.

'We've got to get on with our plans,' he said, 'but not quite yet. I need more time with you.' He lifted a lazy arm, finding the sun was glinting on the tiny jewels of another hairpin, and began to pull it out of her dark hair.

Alberada's face relaxed blissfully, and a secret smile played about her lips. For several moments she closed her eyes, the lashes thick upon her cheek, and Robert closed his, too, thinking the same thoughts. That meant she would have him with her for longer, she had been so afraid that every day - and every night - might be their last, that he would again be off to fight with Girard. Each day with Robert was a bonus, a gift of joy.

He moved to sit beside her, looming over her, his arms around her, holding her so close that she could feel the vital drum-beat of his heart. He tangled his fingers in her hair, pulling her head back gently as he, slowly, oh! so slowly, plucked the remainder of the pins from out of her hair and finally let it fall in a silken mass down to her waist.

'Oh, Alberada, my own Alberada...' He whispered, cheek against her cheek, 'Your gorgeous body isn't everything, you know, it's your spirit, too. We met as equals, as two parts of a whole: I'm sure we've known each other in some former life. We're an entity, whatever happens, no-one will ever part our hearts - or bodies.'

For both, his words were like coming home. It was like shutting out the world, knowing they were safe - that nothing, nobody, could come between them. They felt they were the only two people left in the world. He bent his head to nuzzle his mouth against her own and slowly, voluptuously, began to lick her lips, tasting faint salt, his free hand smoothing her throat, then bringing it down to loosen her gown away, very gently, from her shoulder and pull it down her arm.

'Oh, Robert ...' It was a whisper against his skin, but words failed her. 'I never knew I could feel like this.'

'Nor I. But don't let's hurry,' said he, 'let's take our time.'

And he pulled her gown further down and began to indulge in her beauty, very slowly, with mutual joy. To her, it was rapture and to him, unforgettable, sealing off a part of their life for ever.

He bent his head even lower, and parted his lips.

ROBERT PUTS PLANS IN PLACE

Two days later a raucously clamouring bell in the valley below heralded the approach of visitors. The moment it was heard, Jacques nimbly leapt up the steps to peer over the rooftop's wall. He called out loudly,

'Friends approach! It's our lord Girard and some men.'

Robert touched Alberada's cheek fondly.

'Friend he is indeed - yet I sense trouble.'

'I'll arrange some food and drink.' Alberada bustled off like a contented housewife. 'But isn't it nice to see him back, safe and sound?'

Girard swept in like a gale.

'I apologise for disturbing your idyll - but there's disturbing news.'

Girard sat himself across the hearth from Robert, his face alight with news.

'Tell me.'

'His Holiness has left Rome in state for Germany.'

'That's serious. His patience must be at an end.'

Girard nodded, reaching for a document hidden in his garments.

'My friend in papal circles sent me the text of Pope Leo's letter to the Emperor. It reads, '... *with an impiety which exceeds that of pagans, the Normans rise up against the Church of God, causing Christians to perish by new and hideous tortures, sparing neither women, children nor the aged, making no distinction between what is sacred and what is profane, despoiling churches, burning them and razing them to the ground.'* It's only too true, isn't it?'

'He must be appealing to the Emperor for military help at last - I'm willing to wager that the pair of them will sweep down one day and try to turn us all out of Italy. The situation for the western Church down here seems to be in greater jeopardy than I had imagined.'

'Yes,' Girard said thoughtfully, 'and it's all our own greedy fault.'

'Well ... not just yours and mine - there's Drogo and Humphrey and Richard of Aversa and ...'

'Yes! *Dozens* more Normans we don't even know about and haven't ever met. The problem is that Drogo simply can't control all the Norman forces in the south, especially as they're escalating - he's not strong enough. Brother Humphrey would have been better.'

'Not strong enough,' reiterated Robert grimly, 'but as unpleasant as they come.'

'Yes,' agreed Girard, 'they don't come nastier. He does the Church no good by allowing such freedom - he should discipline the newcomers.'

'That's the crux of the matter,' said Robert reflectively, 'we can't risk the welfare of our mother Church - and if we leave a loophole for the Byzantines and Saracens to return, it doesn't bear thinking about. Years and years of trying to throw them out for the sake of the Church will have been for nothing.'

'You're not the only one to think that way - your brothers Drogo and Humphrey have sent word that all Norman leaders must attend a meeting back in Melfi to discuss what's to be done.'

'How soon?'

'A month.'

'Where's Drogo now?'

'At Venosa, overseeing the building of the Abbey. It seems that he intends currying favour with His Holiness by pouring money into the church there. Instead - he ought to be out and about the land.'

'And Humphrey?'

'He's at Melfi, trying to discipline some of the Norman barons who've been the worst offenders.'

'Naturally we'll attend the meeting, don't you agree? Collective Norman business comes before my differences with Drogo - besides, I don't think he'll confront me there about Cosenza ... his ways are more devious.'

'You're right,' said Girard, reaching out for food, 'all the same, tactics have to be discussed in great detail in case the Emperor sends troops to reinforce His Holiness.'

'In the meanwhile - let's sharpen up our own troops, shall we?' There was a familiar gleam of excitement in Robert's eye. 'We've just got time, don't you think?'

'What's your plan?' said Girard apprehensively.

'The Byzantines in southern Calabria have sent out some insults to us; let's go and teach them a lesson – it'll give us some more practice, don't you think? Let's go south from here, deal with those fools and then swing north to Melfi. We haven't time to do much now, but we can frighten them in no uncertain way. They'll know we'll return.'

Girard rocked with laughter.

'You're incorrigible, Robert! Give me a day's rest first ... and I'll get a chance to speak to my aunt - if you can spare her?'

Robert put his hand on Girard's shoulder, saying amiably,

'Well ... just for a minute, that's all! If we're leaving so soon I want to make sure she doesn't forget me.'

The meeting ahead with Drogo, Humphrey, Serlo and his fellow Normans spelled intense conflict for Robert, but he was getting used to it.

As the months had raced by since his wedding, Robert had had scant time to call his own. He took one city, lost another - secured a third and found himself against a brick wall with the fourth. Back he went to the second and regained it, then put in an administration that survived and started afresh with the fourth. Confrontation followed confrontation, all were fraught with drama, the balance between success and failure was narrow. Girard was always by his side, shoulder to shoulder.

Bracing themselves, Robert and Girard travelled as planned, teaching their soldiers new tricks, and then turned northwards on a hasty last leg of their journey to the meeting of Normans at Melfi.

DROGO

When an unexpected episode involving Drogo occurred it was nothing of Robert's own doing - until the end. He did all he could, in the following years, to make up for Hauteville faults in the eyes of the Church - but it was a shameful affair. It all took place at Venosa.

Drogo had begun the building of the church, in the grounds of the Abbey of Santissima Trinità, several years previously; as he had boasted to Robert, it was in honour of his own levitation to become Count of Apulia. As time went by, and progress was so slow, Drogo had willfully decided to entrust the continuation of the buildings to the monks of the Benedictine Order. It had entertained Drogo to force them to build the church at a certain spot, for the position he had chosen for the most holy part was directly over a pagan temple to Hymenaeus, the ancient god of marriage.

Drogo had endlessly reminded these gentle celibates of all the pagan rites which must have occurred there, and had graphically told them salacious stories, much embroidered, which dismayed them deeply. He knew exactly how uncomfortable it had made these holy men to work there, but they had little choice - for he had paid out handsomely and they were not at liberty to refuse. The people in the town, however, and much of Apulia, were exasperated by the avarice and cruelty of all the warring Normans in the south - and were fast approaching an uprising against Drogo, lascivious and evil.

One of those monks in the Abbey was named Risus. He was lowly and happy in his work as a gifted stone carver; although he was very slow in his understanding, he was abidingly faithful to his beliefs. He was blessed by an engagingly captivating sister, Julia, who lived in the city two miles away. Julia was young, curvy and dimpled, and very fond of him and kept an eagle eye on his welfare.

As the walls of the Abbey church rose steadily over the years - space, stone and immensity being the attributes of holiness - Drogo occasionally made a detour to come and watch and comment. He always criticised the monks' slow progress, roaring at them that the church, and the Abbey itself, were *'to be a personal monument to him, so that his name would live forever'*. He crowed like a cock on a dung heap and the monks could hardly bear to fit together another stone; they would gladly build anything for the greater glory of God, but not for the glory of Drogo. Knowing full well how they felt, he forced them to carve his name, as donor, over the imposing entrance doors in over-large letters.

Then came the day when Drogo unexpectedly saw Julia, waving gaily to Risus as she delicately picked her way between the masons and their tools, bringing her brother a juicy bunch of grapes in a rush basket. The result was inevitable - Drogo, full of wine, lusted after Julia, whom he discovered was a virgin, and betrothed. But Julia, brave as a mountain lion, refused his first advances sharply. It amused Drogo even more to play out a cat and mouse game with her - his success, he knew, was a foregone conclusion: he soaped his greedy hands in anticipation. Just for a few weeks he had to leave Venosa, and go to deal with urgent business in distant Aversa. Julia, artless, thought that she was safe. But he returned and continued with his game, trying to persuade her by bribes, or sugary words; he could not make up his mind whether it would be more pleasurable to have her willingly or by force.

In the meanwhile Robert, inevitably, had discovered what was going on, as he had been having Drogo's footsteps followed with infinite care. Each brother had been allocated a reliable spy, ever since he had agonised about his future at the pass at Scribla. Each spy had been ordered to report every action and every rumour. Drogo's chase after Julia might be of infinitesimal importance, but primarily Robert, who was genuinely devout, didn't care for Drogo's tyrannical ways towards the monks. The extra pieces of gossip about Julia gave the story a new twist, which he - almost - discounted.

Whilst Robert and Girard travelled together to Melfi, it was agreed that Girard should journey on ahead with their troops, so that he could arrange for a suitable welcome for Robert when he arrived; they wanted to be seen as an important team ... and in no way afraid of confronting Drogo.

Robert made camp in the mountains between Venosa and Melfi, and sent Jacques to fetch his spy. There, in a little-known cave outside his camp, his spy recounted every detail, every nuance of Drogo's saga. Robert questioned him for a long while, until all the pieces of the puzzle were in place.

Robert learned more about Drogo's disgraceful treatment of the monks, and he heard about the carving of his own name above the church's porch instead of some Christian symbol. He was also told of the latest developments in the harassment of Julia; stressing her relationship to the simple-minded Risus - and how the townspeople were astonished that Julia had resisted Drogo so long and forcefully. A solution of sorts flashed across Robert's mind, the moment his spy told him that some form of climax seemed imminent. He tried to anticipate what Drogo might do at this point, with the meeting at Melfi so close, but had no idea if his timing would be sufficiently accurate.

Returning to camp, he told his soldiers that 'needing to plan advance strategies, he would remain in the mountains another day or two', which made them happy. Privately, he told Jacques that he was going alone to visit Venosa in secret, and he was to cover his absence. Jacques was bitterly angry to be left behind - and said so. But Robert was adamant, he left Jacques in charge of the camp, and then made him hold Wolf at bay and chain him up.

Riding down through the valleys between the woody mountains, watchful as a cat, Robert came stealthily into Venosa, alone and unseen, as the sun began to set. With unerring instinct he went to the half-built Abbey buildings and waited in the depth of the huge church, staring up at the first stars as they strained to penetrate the sky. He had never been there before.

All around him were the giant columns growing higher and higher, their function being to serve in God's house as lesser load-bearers in the service of a greater. The capitals of the columns were still to be carved and put in place, with tales of man's redemption. Robert had never looked closely at an unfinished church before, and it interested him greatly.

Previously he had made arrangements for this spy to bring the monk Risus to the church and told him to stay there. Robert found Risus on his knees in prayer. He touched the monk's shoulder. Risus looked up serenely.

'Your name is Risus?'

'It is, sir.'

'You're a stone-carver?'

'I am, sir.'

'Do you know who I am?'

'I've not seen you before, sir, but I was told to await Robert de Hauteville, the Guiscard. By the description I was given you must be him.'

He rose to his feet.

'That's correct. Do you know why I'm here?'

'No, sir.'

'I want you to work for me.'

'Oh no, sir! I can't do that ...'

'Why not?'

'I work only for the Church,' said Risus, agitated. His hands had risen as if to fend Robert off - they began to shake.

Robert said patiently,

'I want you to carve some stone capitals for this fine Abbey church. I will pay you to do so. Do you understand?'

Risus looked further confused.

'I don't need payment, sir, I'm a monk. I work for the glory of God. The Benedictine Order looks after my needs.'

'You can give my payment to the Benedictines then, it would help to buy more stone - what about that?'

'Very well, sir. As long as the Abbot sanctions it.'

Robert loomed over Risus, suddenly glaring at him; the bemused monk backed away in fright.

'Show me work you have carved in this church,' Robert said harshly, 'I want to see if it's of quality.'

The flustered monk's head turned from side to side in agitation, not knowing what to do. Robert took his arm in a steely grip.

'*Show me your work!* Especially the capitals of any columns but show me around this holy church in silence, for this is the house of God and we must respect it.'

Disconcerted and intimidated, Risus escorted Robert around the Abbey church, pointing in dumb show to carvings he had created. Fear rose like yeast inside him and he trembled.

Robert continued to manipulate Risus into the state of mind he required.

The unlikely pair wandered quietly all through the deserted building in the gloaming, stepping over tools and random blocks of stone, until Robert had the plan of the building clearly in his mind, and had chosen the area he thought would be crucial. Most important to him was the direction of the moonlight and where the shadows would be darkest.

Gradually, through sensitivity rather than reason, the naïve monk had become concerned by what seemed to him an atmosphere of conspiracy; even though he was bewildered, he held his tongue, too much in awe of Robert. The spy had been accurate, and Robert's assessment of Drogo's actions proved exact.

ROBERT AND DROGO

During that very same dusk Drogo had decided to teach Julia her final lesson. Moreover - to make it more theatrically enjoyable - he would rape her on the broad stone altar of the new church, and dedicate his act to Hymenaeus. Later on he might tell the monks about it, pretending it had happened centuries ago - just to see their faces. He told his court, with a conspiratorial grin,

'I insist on being alone this evening, to celebrate a personal and private Mass in my Abbey church, as it's the feast-day of San Lorenzo ... a saint most dear to me.'

Disbelieving, the members of his entourage hastily scattered through the town, relieved not be involved with whatever he did. They all stayed away until the following morning.

Carefully prepared, Drogo made arrangements to meet Julia in the moonlit - as yet roofless - church. This time, he threatened her that he would harm Risus, and send him very far away from her, if she disobeyed him or told another living soul. Drogo hadn't threatened her before. He was their liege lord; there was no higher authority to whom she could appeal: there was no way out but to comply and join him there.

At last the sun had gone and the whole church was in the early dark.

At the east end, standing in the now deep shadows behind one of the massive pillars, Robert, his eyes now accustomed to the semi-darkness, waited with baited breath as Drogo swaggered through the distant entrance. Drogo pulled Julia after him, and she protested at every step about his rough handling of her. They made their way slowly up the main aisle towards the altar. Julia dipped her head and made to kneel, several times, but Drogo jerked her up, anchored to her elbow...

Risus watched the scene too, not realising, at first, that his sister was to be Drogo's victim. He turned to Robert, begging,

'Let me return to the monastery, sir, it's too dark to look at capitals now - let alone see where to place them.'

For the first time for a long while Robert made a sound,

'Ssshh! Don't you see Count Drogo approaches? Keep quiet, if you value your life.'

'I can see very little, sir, it's too dark.' Risus' voice whined under his breath. 'Count Drogo, you said? Why is he here, at this time of night?'

'Silence! Don't utter one more sound,' growled Robert in his throat, *'or you'll never carve another pebble!'*

The approaching footsteps grew louder, Julia muttering under her breath and giving small cries of terror as Drogo dragged her forward.

When Drogo and Julia became fully visible to them both in a shaft of moonlight, Risus became frantic, mesmerised by horror. As he unconsciously clutched at Robert's clothes, he was swiftly twisted around and held roughly in a vice-like grip - Robert's hand over the monk's mouth.

Drogo and Julia were now at the most holy spot, by the altar. Julia, eyes wide with terror, remained where Drogo bade her stand, looking fearfully about her into the black shadows. Drogo drew out a beeswax candle from his pouch and lit it, placing it on one end of the long stone slab, whilst freakish shadows faintly crept up the walls and pillars nearby. In a grotesque caricature of a priest's humility, Drogo bowed to the altar, saying, with a giggle,

'Let the service begin!'

Robert, his face set, watched his half-brother and the girl he planned to ravish, then turned his attention to Risus. Discovering that the unfortunate monk had averted his eyes, he forced him around, made him watch the couple, pushing his head hard against the pillar, his left arm tight about his neck.

Then he began a monotonous whisper into Risus' ear, hypnotising the simple man until he was transfixed with fear. He told him that his sister was about to be raped in front of him, hissed to him tales about Drogo's many acts of wickedness, drummed his words into the man's skull by pressing it painfully against the pillar as he emphasised some point. Repeatedly he ground out how the rape would desecrate the holy place. He never stopped the monotonous harangue, continually rasping at him,

'Which is worse - the rape or the desecration of God's house?'

Risus became desperate under Robert's huge hands, one of which was holding his head to force him to watch, with the other clamped over his mouth so he wouldn't make a noise. He couldn't speak, nor could he turn away from the terrible drama so close by, yet he never thought to close his eyes.

As they watched and waited, Drogo went on harassing Julia in turn. His voice grew louder and higher pitched in the drama of his own making. She steadily resisted him, but with growing terror and a failing heart when she realised the enjoyment he was receiving through his protracted form of fore-play. Their voices rose in growing intensity.

Finally he hit her across her face.

'I've had my fill of words,' he said, 'now I'll have my fill of you.'

'No! I beg you ...'

'Yes,' he hissed, 'you knew this would happen before you came – you've been longing for it! Remove your clothes!'

She shook her head violently, remaining mute this time.

'Then I'll remove them from you,' he said thickly.

Julia tried to turn and run, but found that Drogo had trapped her against the carved stone altar.

One by one, and with ever-increasing flourishes, Drogo began to tear Julia's clothes from her. Off went her mantle, flying across the church until it hit a column and fell flatly to the ground. Then he snatched at the shoulder fastening of her gown, which ripped as she twisted away. He laughed as she tore at the garment, and pulled it down to her feet. She fell, but he dragged her back into his embrace and began to scratch and tear at the remainder of her clothing. He flung the scraps of torn fabric in every direction, until she was finally naked, white, sobbing with fear. Somehow, she had managed to keep a small blue veil clutched in her hand, useless as a butterfly's wing.

Risus, distraught, began gibbering with fright, imprisoned in Robert's arms, transfixed by the sight before them, his ears pounding with Robert's echoing - controlling - words. Never before had he seen a naked woman. Never before had he envisaged his sister unclothed.

With one exultant movement, Drogo lifted Julia effortlessly onto the altar. He fondled her, touched her pale skin, mottled blue by the cold night air, alternatively raked his nails across her back then sensuously caressed her full breasts and told her in detail, with mounting enthusiasm, exactly what he intended doing to her. She began to struggle furiously in his grasp, screaming yet not screaming, desperate for rescue but, at the same time, afraid the monks might see her nakedness. Drogo held her down. Quickly, hugely roused, he began to pull off his own clothes, letting them fall haphazardly to the ground, preparing to mount the stone slab.

'No! God help me! Please - please - don't! *I beg you ...*'

Julia finally cried out, clinging to her veil, brainlessly, as if it were a talisman to save her. Drogo laughed excitedly, his wet lower lip caught between his teeth and spittle gleaming on his chin.

'Look at him, man!' whispered Robert to Risus, 'He'll ravish Julia in this most holy place! Then he'll kill her. Then he'll kill you! Mark my words! God can't help her now - only you can - you!'

Risus, bewildered and terrified, was unable to grasp Robert's meaning.

'Drogo's alone, and he's unarmed.' Robert went grinding on, 'Here's my knife! Take it! Defend Julia! *Stop Drogo!* Kill him before he kills Julia - before he desecrates this holy place!'

Abruptly releasing the confused monk's head, he thrust the handle of his razor-sharp knife into Risus' unsuspecting grasp and pushed him forward, fast and hard, running behind him - guiding him. The monk fell forward into the patch of moonlight on the church floor, giving a muffled shriek.

Drogo saw him immediately, swinging around at the sudden noise, but in so doing he stumbled on his own fallen clothing, catching his foot in the armhole of his jerkin.

'It's him or you!' hissed Robert, following up behind Risus' black shadow as the monk uncertainly scrambled to his feet. Then he fiercely shoved Risus again, from behind, making him stumble further - right up to Drogo himself - in a tripping run.

As Drogo lifted his hand to defend himself against the fast-approaching monk, whose arms were flailing like a windmill, he saw moonlight flashing like lightning on the wicked steel. With a scream, Risus plunged the knife wildly into Drogo's body. He took no deliberate aim - he was beyond thought - but he thrust it up to the hilt into Drogo's groin. The moment he felt the flesh of his hand meet the hot flesh of Drogo's belly, he withdrew in terror. With a moaning gasp of horror, Risus tore the knife out, twisting it savagely as he did. Drogo's arterial blood spurted out like a fountain onto the altar.

Drogo instinctively clutched at the ragged lips of his wound with both hands, trying to hold all his guts together as the life-blood rhythmically washed down his naked legs, matted with curling hair, and seeped between his fleshy toes. There it settled, spreading in a widening arc across the floor. All around him hung the stench of mouse.

Drogo looked up at his assailant, and saw - not Risus, who had reeled away and fallen once more upon the floor, but, rising like a giant bat behind him, his half-brother Robert, staring at him piercingly. Their eyes met like flashing scimitars.

'I wouldn't dream of laying a finger on you myself,' said Robert, quietly and lazily, 'but the monk has made a man of you, too, hasn't he? *Sire?'*

Robert never forgot the sight of Drogo, was speechless as he drooped, his feet making sucking noises as he moved them, twitching, in his own clotting blood. There was nothing to be said, and Drogo's previously triumphant manhood now looked infinitely small, withdrawn into itself and wrinkled: it would do no more harm, now, to anyone - uselessly veiled in a thin film of spent semen.

Robert waited, hands loosely on hips - clean hands, untouched by crime in Norman law - while he watched the skin of Drogo's body become whiter and whiter as the pumping blood grew fainter.

Julia hastily re-clothed herself, after a fashion, hiccupping and sobbing all the while in shock. Every now and then she would make the sign of the cross, or touch Risus with concern, trying to make him get up from the paving stones. In time she was decently covered. Robert never looked at her - never looked from Drogo's face, now grey and distant in the faint candlelight as the fractured moon disappeared behind a cloud. Without hurrying, taking Julia by the hand, he led her from the church in silence.

When he returned to collect the monk he found him gibbering still, bubbles flowing down his chin, empty-eyed, clearly mad. Robert prised his knife from Risus' grip, wiped it clean on Drogo's cloak and turned his heel on his half-brother, draped against the stone altar, and gently led Risus away from the obscenity.

There had been a knife at the beginning, so there was a knife at the end.

An hour or so later Robert was back in the mountains with his rested company of men; no-one had seen him come or go, he had vanished and reappeared like a phantom.

The next day the whole company clattered into Melfi and were met by Girard. It was another two days before the news of Drogo's murder was brought to the city and there, with all the Normans of southern Italy attending the conference, Humphrey was duly elected Count of Apulia in Drogo's place.

Robert could not save Risus from a final and fearful death because Humphrey, after making rapid enquiries, made a rational addition between his dead brother, the pools of blood and a crazed monk: a decision about the murder could not be delayed for an instant if he was to gain, and retain, complete control of all who were gathered there. Whilst all the Normans were forced to witness the punishment, Humphrey, in order to 'relieve his grief' had Risus' arms and legs hacked off and thrown aside, and then had the torso buried alive within sight.

He was altogether unaware of Robert's part in Drogo's death. But Jacques knew.

JUDITH AND ROGER

The inhabitants of both the monastery and the convent at St. Evroul-sur-Ouche led lives so self-contained that only the Abbot's comings and goings linked them to the rest of the world. For Fressenda, as first the months and then the years swam by, her other outlet was through conversing with young Judith of Evreux, who told her of events in her own sphere of life. When first they met - the Mother Superior had taken pity on her state - the twelve-year-old was distant, for her life at her father's court was isolated; very rarely was she permitted to remain alone in any room with some form of acceptable companion, so to be alone with Fressenda in the convent was almost unheard of and, as a consequence, she was stiff and wary. Her visits were infrequent, being valued all the more for it, for everyone's lives were governed by the rules of Church and Court.

At the beginning, Fressenda showed interest and then affection, and very soon Judith was completely won over by her sympathetic charm. Although intensely shy and untried, Judith eventually confided that she revelled in the exuberance of the feasting and high festivals in her own home, even if she had to remain on one side as an onlooking puppet.

She regaled Fressenda with keen-eyed descriptions of household details, from the mistake made by some dairymaid to the colour of the newest lute-strings and ribbons brought by a passing singer.

The feast days of Christ the King and his saints, the tenants-in-chief of the Kingdom of God, were often made to coincide with the feast days of the Count of Evreux's Court. On these great festivals of the Church's year, marked by solemn celebrations in the House of God, the festivities in the Court gave the opportunity of taking council from the vassals; perhaps about a feud, or a campaign, or a marriage, within the Court itself or in the house of an enemy or vassal. The festivities would continue for several days and nights, and wound up with an orgy of drinking - from whose attendance Judith was excluded.

There seemed never a moment to spare as Judith grew older, learning to take her place, one day, as the lady of some exalted household. By the time she was fourteen, and of a marriageable age, her father had made her follow the steward's footsteps for hours as he dealt with all the household's affairs. Now that she was a little older, she occasionally dared to speak, to question the steward's words, and even made a suggestion of her own, now and then. But it was not often, and generally the suggestion had been a seed planted in her mind by the experienced Fressenda. She tried to persuade Judith to think for herself, and ever more gradually, she did.

By now, in mixed company at Court, Judith could control herself with ease when conditions were normal. She had schooled herself to float across a room as though there was no solid ground beneath her feet. She passed from place to place like a bejewelled butterfly new out of its chrysalis, and silently hovered, alighted for a fleeting moment, then migrated away again as if seeking nectar. When she spoke to courtiers and diplomats, churchmen and men-at-arms, she asked no leading questions, offered no opinions, but dutifully spoke words which were easy to forget. She had no female companions in whom she could relax, bar Fressenda.

Her young limbs were listless; it was considered stylish to appear languid. She waved her hands in gentle motions like the slow beating of a butterfly's wings, and her face remained closed and neutral from much practice. To the sharp observer she was permanently slightly out of focus. Nothing harsh or jagged marred her features; the sum of her was soft and fluttery, untried. Like the delicate butterfly she was well-nigh impossible to catch or pin down; she always took flight just in time, lifting herself effortlessly and drifting out of reach. It was maddening to try to engage her.

Well-schooled in etiquette, she was trained to be diplomatically ephemeral; she dared to make no move to step out of place. She expected nothing. She knew nothing of real pleasure, apart from the feel of her puppy's warm fur, and feared failing her father all the time. She had no substance. No-one knew her. She did not know herself. Deportment, bearing, behaviour and conformity in public were her only goals: freedom to be herself had never been an option.

Today Judith, as always, had brought gifts for the invalid to enjoy: a fat, creamy cheese, a basket of autumn fruit and a honeycomb. Fressenda was delighted, telling Judith that Sister Sophia would allow her to consume her favourite honey under the term of being 'medicinal'. They exchanged a conspiratorial bubble of laughter.

'I find everything to do with medicine all so bewildering - yet so engrossing.' said Judith, opening up to the older woman who was like a mother to her. 'But, of course, I hardly know anything about all those herbs and spices and salves and antidotes; unfortunately our household is so immense that we have a separate pharmacy and I'm sure the apothecary would be most annoyed if I spent time questioning him – justifiably he'd think that I was meddling.'

She settled more comfortably where she now sat, leaning back against the warm stone; she felt completely at ease with Fressenda - and wished her own mother had not died when she was so young - and missed the sisters she had never had. She wore an embroidered pale blue dress with a darker mantle, looking like the day and night sky, held together with cobwebby silver dreams. She had abandoned the large chair of state the nuns had carried into Fressenda's room, and tossed, instead, one of its leather cushions onto the broad windowsill and perched there.

Their discussion had ranged widely for a long time - mostly they had discussed household affairs. Judith questioned Fressenda about her own recipes for seething meat, then salting it down for the lean months of spring ahead. Talk about the seasons inevitably led to the castle's elaborate plans for Christmas, and then she asked the older woman to tell her of the different ways to make the heated and spiced red wine and honey - *clare* - which was lavishly given out on all feast days. Judith found she could unburden herself effortlessly to Fressenda, now. There was no-one in whom she could confide at home, it was too hazardous in that highly political Court, but in the relative no-man's-land of the convent, in Fressenda's loving interest, she could sometimes let slip her fears with the sovereign ease of semi-childhood.

'Yes, apothecaries can be difficult, can't they?' agreed Fressenda, 'They're in-betweens - neither family nor servants. But aren't they clever?'

'Indeed - yes! You know - once my father took me to see ours, and we found him making up some little pills. I watched him take this and that out of the jars and then mix up the ingredients - with such vehemence that I thought he was going to smash the mortar! Then he rubbed sweet almond oil over his hands and rolled the little pills between his fingers and put them out into the shade to dry; he made some for me in the shapes of the sun and the moon!'

'And did that make them more palatable?'

'I don't remember,' Judith smiled, 'but I did get better ...'

Fressenda, pale, but rested, glanced with increasing fondness at her visitor. In this sickroom there was no pretence at ceremony and Judith was now chatting freely, her hair a little tousled after her long ride from the castle at Evreux, and Fressenda saw a powdering of dust upon her fashionable shoes as she occasionally swung her foot.

Judith continued,

'Without meaning to presume, dear lady, do you ever hope for a miracle? Do you think you'll regain your health?'

'No. Not at my age. I'm quite ready for the cords to be cut.'

'But - if I could bring a reliquary for you to touch?'

'You're very sweet - but, no! God alone is the author of a miracle, the relic is only an occasion, and I'm sure in my heart that God is happy that I've done enough!'

Appreciating the suggestion with a smile, Fressenda continued,

'Have you ever thought of commissioning the monks to make a Herbal for Sister Sophia?'

Judith looked stricken.

'No! It's never crossed my mind. Do you think she would expect one? Is it my duty to purchase one for her? I would, if you think it proper ...'

'I've no idea,' confessed Fressenda, 'it's just that, at present - in my circumstances - we talk together quite a lot about diseases and Sister Sophia is so learned that she can understand herbals written in both Latin and Greek. Just recently the convent at Saint Amand near Rouen needed to build an extension and they left one of their most precious books on medicine in our convent's library as pledge for their loan. Sophia had a wonderful time studying that! It was amassed by that Christian, Janus Damascenus, who was a hospital director at Baghdad.'

'I can't even imagine where Baghdad is,' said Judith, unconcerned, 'somewhere in the East isn't it?'

'Indeed it is ...' said a male voice, which made both women jump, 'am I intruding?'

Fressenda gave a cry of joy and clasped her thin, lined hands,

'Oh! Roger! You've come!'

As he stepped smartly into the room Roger stopped, abruptly, shaken to the core. He had visited his mother in the convent before, many times, and knew how to find her room unaccompanied - and the loving welcome he would receive. But when he heard voices speaking he took it for granted that his mother's companion would have been a nursing nun. Never, for a moment, did he envisage seeing Judith of Evreux, daughter of the mighty Count, seated, alone, with his mother. Open-mouthed, he stood waiting, uncertain what to do. Then he bowed deeply to both ladies, smiling first at his mother, then looking quizzically at Judith from under his lashes, and kissed their hands. Bare-headed, he stood there, abashed and unnerved. To remain soundless, he had left his heavy outer clothes and shoes at the Visitor's Gate, padding through the building in a simple tunic and hose. Like all his brothers he was far taller than most men, but he was darker in colouring, and had enormous eyes in his bony face – filled with humour and understanding.

His mother murmured,

'May I present my son, Roger? I've spoken to you so often about him - and here he is, in person!'

'We've met,' said Judith, flustered, 'at least - we've often been in each other's company. But we've never been introduced ...'

She blushed, helpless and touching: the blood stained her cheeks, mounted to her forehead, spread in a warm wave over neck and ears. To spare her, Roger turned his head and looked out of the window, saying comfortingly,

'Six times. Since childhood, we've attended the same functions six times.'

'Well, well,' said Fressenda, smoothly, 'they do say that seven is a lucky number!'

There was a silence in the room.

Judith noticed Fressenda put a hand against her side, beneath her heart, and realised the sick woman was tiring rapidly, and looked in pain. It gave her a valid excuse to leave both mother and son together, yet she longed to remain.

'I have to see the Mother Superior, now,' she said, 'I think the High

Mass is over, and Vespers is near. If you'd give me permission I'll return to visit you again, madam, in a week or two?'

'You're very gracious, my dear child, and I'd be delighted if you would. My son will see you to the Mother Superior's chamber.'

From her bed Fressenda saw Judith and Roger drifting away from the Guest House, down the covered walk, which was reserved for exercise, and past a small corner of the herb garden; she hoped they were talking to each other, but she couldn't be sure. When Roger returned he didn't mention Judith, but Fressenda saw stars in his eyes.

'I see you like my lady Judith,' she opened the subject directly, 'I've grown very fond of her'.

'I'd like to make her 'my' Judith,' he replied, 'but my chances at present are almost nil.'

'Force the pace - make your own luck!' said his mother ambitiously. He sighed and shrugged his shoulders, then changed the subject,

'I've been speaking to the Mother Superior,' he said, 'you're in good hands - she seems to be very wise, as well as noble by birth.'

Fressenda took his strong lean hand as he sat beside her.

'Of course I am! Now, tell me everything! How's your father? What's happening at home? Have they finished the candle-making? With Christmas ahead you must all take care not to run low.' So the familiar small talk began until she drifted off to sleep with a quiet smile on her face and Roger, by and by, stole noiselessly away.

ROGER

Roger had been summoned to Italy. He was going by express command from his hero, Robert, recommended by his father, Tancred. It was spring and he was so excited he could hardly speak. On his way he aimed to make two detours, both an emotional luxury. The first was to the Castle of Evreux, the second was to visit his mother. He was apprehensive over both.

The castle was enormous, and dominated the area. Squads of highly trained soldiers guarded it on all sides, making Roger feel insignificant as he arrived with Pierre, his lone squire; he ruefully thought of the poor comparison with his own home.

Having only the one daughter annoyed the Count of Evreux, but she was treated like gold dust. Roger was determined to see Judith before he left, but felt his chances were slim.

Her father was a typical Norman leader, the type of dominant man who lived his life in the saddle - it was a life of immense and strenuous activity, passed in conflict, hunting and pilgrimage. Cool-headed, stern to the point of harshness, he had his wits about him and knew how to crack a joke with his subordinates. He was quick on the draw and ready with his tongue in company with other men, his talk and songs full of the joys of battle. When he was at home he became the clever diplomat, authoritarian and reserved, and when he was with women his behaviour altered even further, inaccessible, and aloof. Roger hardly expected to be allowed through the castle gates.

Several of Roger's brothers were in the service of William of Normandy, now officially elected Duke, and recorded to be serving him very well, which was a solace to their father. Yet Normandy was also agog with tales of Hauteville adventures in Italy; of the endless, mystifying battles; of their dealings with the Pope, which, almost always, were in some way involved with the universal fear of the German Emperor. Many families were directly associated with at least one man within the marauding bands of Normans in Calabria and Apulia, who kept re-balancing the swings of influence; but the Hauteville name was heard the most.

Robert's name was continually being mentioned; now known as 'Robert the Guiscard, 'the wily one', or 'the fox' - or, more often now, just 'Guiscard'. His covert political work was largely unknown, but most people guessed that much had occurred because his name was regularly being linked with the Pope or Emperor. Accounts of his assaults and atrocities during his multiple campaigns became greatly exaggerated, and were forgiven largely because his kinsmen admired his boldness and enterprise: stories which filtered back about Cosenza and many other conquests put heart into Tancred and Fressenda, and the younger brothers rejoiced.

It was known that Robert was becoming rich through his innumerable enterprises, that he kept only his growing band of Normans about him and that he plotted night and day, choosing a solitary course. Clearly he stood out as larger-than-life, and the wilder stories grew worse on being told again and again, and before they were able to be checked another story emerged and the self-perpetuating legend grew yet another dimension.

Roger had heard that his elder brother, like many of his countrymen, was made up of a mass of contradictions. He heard that Robert was capable of cold and ruthless violence, especially if anyone dared to come near his wife. He also knew that Robert was unpredictable and reckless, yet shrewd and calculating ... even painstaking. As an intensely physical character, his aims were limitless, his greed unbounded, and his preference for professional Norman soldiers was legend. Roger had no illusions about the future offered to him; he grasped the opportunity of joining his fabled elder brother with huge enthusiasm, elated to be attached to such an elite company.

Until recently all the family knew that Robert had hated and despised his elder half-brothers, convinced, with reason, that they were his enemies, having found them an entrenched and daunting band. But, as time had gone by, he was gaining the upper hand. He had therefore written to Tancred about his hard-won progress, and Tancred had suggested Roger as an aide for him; he was now fully trained and armed, and his loyalty was unshakeable. Robert immediately communicated with Roger, making no promises.

Robert, Tancred thought, was ready, too, to launch formidable attacks for power from a consolidated base. It was plain that he had ambitions to overcome Humphrey and Serlo and their allies. Young Roger would even up the psychological advantage for Robert when he arrived.

But Roger was set fast in a terrible dilemma; there was a confusion in his present life which had taken several years to intensify, and which had left him dizzy with frustration and indecision; it involved his adolescent emotions towards Judith. Roger found himself wholly distracted by his feelings for her. He had never dared voice those feelings, except to Fressenda. His case appeared hopeless, but he wanted to place his heart at her feet before he left.

The first occasion he had seen Judith was when they had been children, and he only saw her from afar, firmly placed upon a bench beside her father, the great Count, at a tournament. For a moment or two she had tried to hide from view, to clutch at her nurse, but her father forced the anxiety-ridden child to sit motionless, and bade her to remain there, unmoving in full sight of all the people. She had looked frightened, and there was something about her grave isolation that drew Roger's sympathy, but he never dreamed of speaking to her. Later, as they grew older, he watched out for her. Gossips at her Court slyly whispered to her that Roger could not tear his eyes from her; so, dazzled, she began to look out for him, too, very discreetly. Their glances spoke volumes; they never exchanged a word.

Over the years he and Judith had stood close to each other several times, observing all the conventions, and once, briefly, in Fressenda's sickroom, had spoken at last: she had worn a misty blue gown - he remembered every detail of it. On that occasion, just when they had the opportunity to talk naturally during their walk to the Mother Superior's rooms, words had failed them both, and all they managed was a thunderous silence. Judith again became aware that her skin was flushing a hot pink and she turned her face away from Roger, tongue-tied as he bowed low, and hung her head voicelessly until the Mother Superior's door was closed behind her.

Now he was to journey across Europe to an unknown and hostile land, with very little money but with bright prospects. There was no hope of taking Judith with him, although she was of marriageable age her relatives were too important and his station in life was far too lowly; he accepted those facts without question. But he longed to see her one last time before he left, and he had thought up a valid excuse to get into her presence: his mother had told him almost everything she knew about Judith, and he felt he knew her through and through.

As for her, she was so quiet, so grave and sweet, evidently nervous - did she ever think of him? Had his mother told Judith about him? He hoped she had. But he had to have one real conversation with her, however short, before he went away - perhaps for ever.

He was fully prepared and ready to leave for Italy. Fressenda found one last sum of money to clothe him in mail, and Tancred gave the last promised sword and fresh horse, which now champed at the bit. He had said his farewells, apart from the painful, final, parting from his mother. Now, somehow she just held onto life by a whisper, the thread almost severed, her body useless but her spirit not yet extinguished. She was quite ready to drift into the hereafter, but not until her youngest son had departed. He would soon see her for the last time. There were tears in his throat.

PART THREE

JUDITH AND ROGER AT THE CASTLE OF EVREUX

A servant spoke quietly to Judith,

'My lady, the young knight Roger de Hauteville wishes to have an audience with you.'

Judith looked with happiness mixed with astonishment across her face. There, in the crowd at the hugely populated castle of Evreux, stood Roger in shining armour. He had removed his helmet and wore a brown cloak over his suit of mail, which glinted silver: to her, he looked like a shimmering star, the substance of so many of her dreams. His eager face was taut with strain as he waited, not knowing if she would speak to him, or if she would even acknowledge him in such grandiose surroundings.

Judith had never thought he would come to her home - it was a brave thing to do: there must be a reason! Was Fressenda dead - was that the reason for his appearance here? Court gossip had informed her that he was off to Italy, and she had dreaded his going. Now here he was! Having braved the castle and her father's certain anger; he was standing across the room from her, a lone and military figure in the throng of colourful courtiers. Shocked, she accidentally dropped her tiny pet dog onto the floor, who squealed with shock and limped piteously away.

Judith glided towards him without another moment's pause. All the Court watched her. Her cream woollen gown trailed behind her across the flattened rushes, her silver-gold hair softly caught against her head with jewelled combs. When they came face to face her creamy cheeks suffused with pink because of her nervousness, the bane of her life: the situation was bizarre - abnormal - and she was thrown off-balance. Aware that she was blushing hotly, she turned her head in wretchedness and said stiffly,

'Well, sir knight, you are unexpected! But I wish you well.'

He looked at her with dismay. She sounded so stilted - perhaps because of the company they were in? Was she angry? His past daydreams of her had gone beyond reality - but he had never thought she would treat him to such coldness. For some moments he was sunk in the rich, egoistic despair of youth. He set his shoulders and said coolly,

'Thanks, my lady, I start my travels tomorrow. Perhaps, when I'm older I'll return.' He forced his luck as Fressenda had suggested. 'Would you agree to receive me when I do?'

They had got off onto the wrong foot. The weight of her inexperience numbed her. Demure, looking down, she gave her head a little unconscious shake; she had never spoken aloud to a strange man of his age before - a man she had secretly dreamed about for so long.

'Oh! Certainly. I don't think I'd ever forget you.' She said, almost to herself, then blushed deeply.

'Is that so? When I'm in Italy may I feel that you'd welcome me back?'

'*Of course!* But - must you go?' She bit her lip, amazed at herself for asking, and as she did so the ugly rash of colour across her face and neck slowly faded, leaving her pale and bright eyed at such a question.

'Yes, I must. My brother Robert the Guiscard has sent for me.

Besides, I've no future here, as you must know. But there is one thing that troubles me - it's the reason I'm here - and that's my mother. You've been so kind to her, visiting her at the convent - she's told me of your goodness. I can't bear the thought of leaving her at this time - she'll die before long, I know it. As she's in your brother's Order - can I ask you to look out for her? Would you go and visit her again, see she lacks nothing, and then send word to tell me how she is? Please?'

'Yes, of course, I'll be happy to visit her and attend to her needs.'

Judith glowed with pleasure. She had never been asked to do anything for anyone else before and became aware that the pleasant task would form an even stronger bond between them.

'My grateful thanks! That relieves my troubled mind. Now I can think of you both together - try to love her for me?'

'I will. I do already.'

She meant it. She looked up at last, right into his face. Her world stopped still for a moment, and her breath caught. Roger shakily murmured,

'Can we walk, my lady? Your attendants seem interested in us - it's a little daunting! Shall we go outside into the fresh air? It's a beautiful day.'

The sun shone down as they strolled on a grassy knoll within the castle walls, towards a wall against which many dark green fig trees grew. Although destructive to masonry, the trees displayed a deep intuition for the proximity of water, and as the Count of Evreux had a passion for their fruit, so the trees grew with abandon and the fruit was reserved for him alone.

As they gravitated towards the trees, both young people remembered the silent walk they took together at the convent, and Judith's shyness stifled her voice again. Several hounds lay panting in the heat, and the grass trodden by the soldiers gave off a rich aroma. Some of the court children were sedately throwing balls nearby, eyeing the young couple with ill-disguised curiosity, and a courtier strolled out to watch them unashamedly.

Roger and Judith just stood and looked at each other again, as if they couldn't get their fill. Their precipitate world was one of brief meetings and long partings, when decisions had to be immediate and binding, and any faint chance of happiness required to be grasped upon the wing. After so many years their chance had come at last. There seemed no need for speech, as if they'd reached an understanding.

'Judith ...' Roger began, looking into the face upturned like a flower. But at that moment a child's ball came bouncing towards them, accompanied by cries pleading to them to stop it rolling down the hill to the village below, through the open gateway.

Both moved to stop the ball at the identical moment. Accidentally Roger's arm brushed Judith's head as they bent down, scattered the intricate combs, and her hair cascaded down into a sweeping wave upon her shoulders and down her slender back. The ball rolled by; the children chased after it. They were left alone near the dark green shade.

'Why, Judith ...'

There was awe in his voice as he drew her aside in one swift movement amongst the leafy branches.

'Oh! Judith - how beautiful you are!'

Her hands went to his shoulders, holding him away for the moment, wondering why she felt so astonished. At once she sensed that it was the way that he looked at her; half-smiling and steady, with a gaze that was both a question and an answer. At last someone was taking her seriously, openly and as an equal. Small tremors lightly ran down her body, and the tips of her fingers trembled as she lifted her chin up high, to look him in the eyes. Roger, in turn, was aware of how difficult it must have been for Judith to raise her face and see, in one swift glance, what Roger was feeling; both of them with honesty, truth and immediacy. Young love blazed out like a heath catching fire, to be remembered always. And, without a second's thought, she was in his arms.

'By my faith - how I love you! How many years is it since I first set eyes on you? I fell in love with you then and I've thought of nothing else. Judith - look at me?'

She had never been in anyone's arms since her mother had died, it brought back vivid memories. Timidly, she raised her eyes, the lashes like a curtain of softest brown, and there was no mistaking what she felt. Her innocence and adoration was plain to see. His mouth came down on hers, gently at first, then harder and more demanding, until she began to draw away and then they stood, panting, out of breath.

'Tell me, then, tell me you care for me, too?' He demanded, breathlessly.

'Yes! Oh yes! I've been drawn to you for years. Now you're going away and I'll be left alone. It's too late! *It's too late to tell me!* How can I begin to bear it?' Inexperienced, untaught, she could think of no-one but herself.

'Can't you be patient with me? Is it asking too much - will you wait for me? I've so much to do, to fight, to earn money, to earn a high position before I return to you. But I will - I will! How patient can you be?'

He touched her cheek, she stilled his hand.

'I'd wait for you for ever, if need be. But don't leave it too long! Although he hasn't spoken to me yet my father is bound to have plans for me. I couldn't bear to be married to another man, to share his bed, to have his children, but I may be forced... I have my duty to him.'

'I'm damned if you will! You'll have no other man but me. Mine will be the only bed you share, mine your only children. Swear this, swear this now, and mix my blood with yours as a troth, as some customs have it when there's no time left!'

He put her gently aside, slid his sharp hunting knife from its sheath on his belt and carelessly cut a prominent vein throbbing in his wrist; the blood spurted out to sprinkle the ground like rain. Carefully, taking Judith's wrist he cut a tiny nick in her skin: when a drop of blood welled to the surface he rubbed their childish wrists together, mingling blood with blood.

'Swear it, Judith; swear you'll have no other man but me.'

'I swear it.'

'Make no mistake! *Are you perfectly sure?* You're in no doubt?'

'I am - why do you ask so many times?'

'I ask because you must fully realise that when two lovers plight their troth, as we're doing, this ceremony is as binding in the eyes of the Church as marriage itself!'

'Does this mean we are truly married? Or is it just an illusion - a dream?'

'Yes, Judith. We are. We're truly married, but we must keep it a secret until I return to claim you openly as my bride.'

'I'm afraid to stay here now. For pity's sake come back for me soon.'

She knew nothing of practicalities, always petted and praised, every whim indulged, she couldn't begin to understand that her hopes were impossible to achieve.

Neither of them was aware of the Count's servant watching them as closely as he could from the castle's keep, but his view was largely obscured. The courtier, too, had drifted closer, but found the leaves of the fig trees were too thick a curtain.

Roger bent his head and kissed her again. Softly he touched her lips, softly, slowly, gently. Then faster, harder, so intimately and deep that she felt as if she was falling into an abyss. She was carried away upon a wave, willingly, until she felt suffused, weightless, yet heavy with desire.

'Sir, it's time to go.'

Pierre, Roger's squire, had come up quietly behind them. He had turned to face the opposite direction when he spoke, quietly, as if to the sky.

'Oh no! *Don't go, Roger, don't go!* Don't leave me now...*don't leave me behind!'*

She was half fainting in his arms; each newly discovered emotion had followed another too fast. She buried her head against his chest and burst into a passion of tears, clinging to him. A fine trickle of blood ran down her arm and a thin gold chain around her throat entangled with the fastening of his cloak. He tried to unravel it, then restrained her clutching fingers.

'This chain of yours is binding us together - I can't get it loose!' A moment or so later he had freed it and held it in his hand, offering it to her. 'Let it be mine, please give this to me as a talisman and symbol, so it will bring me back to you. And then let me go.'

She lifted the fine chain with its elaborate gold cross over her head and arranged it about Roger's shoulders, smoothing it in place, tucking the cross out of sight.

'Take it. It was given to me by a blind woman - a witch, they said - many years ago. She told me then that my faith would be intertwined with my love, that I would have either one or the other. She said that, should I ever lose it or give it away I would have to make a choice, my faith or my love - but I was never to have both. So - I choose my love! Wear it until we meet again. God go with you - and come back for me soon.'

His strong arms held her close. They feasted their eyes once more upon each other. Then he took her hand in his, kissed the palm, and folded her fingers over it.

'My lady. May God protect you until we're together again.'

He strode across the grass to Pierre and the horses, leapt into the saddle and galloped down the pathway from the castle with his cloak streaming behind him... He never looked back.

She gazed after him, abandoned and desolate, tears coursing heedlessly down her white cheeks. She nervously fingered the void at her throat where her chain had once been, as she was to finger it, whenever agitated, for the remainder of her life. *Married, she thought, what would my father do if he ever got to know?*

JUDITH AT EVREUX

An anxious eighteen months passed for Judith, since Roger had ridden away, and now the Christmas season lay ahead. It was a time, so they said, of 'large tabling and belly-cheer', and provided overmuch work for everyone. Nowadays she co-operated more fully with the steward and his duties, seeing that the extra ale and mead and wine to be given out were to hand; they had estimated for half as much again to be shared by all at Pentecost, too, and Nativity and Assumption. The Hall was ready before time, highly decorated for the feasts, and fresh straw laid upon the floor. Freshly laundered cloths were prepared too, to be draped over the boards, and brand new bowls were bought for scented water for guests to wash their hands.

The steward grumbled at the cost, for it was his duty to account for the expenses of the household every night. Every day his other duties included taking delivery by tally from the larder, at the hands of the reeve, of flesh and fish of every kind. And it was also his business to know precisely how many loaves could be made from a quarter of wheat, and had to observe the pantler as he received this number from the baker. He considered Judith's decision for new finger-bowls to be an unnecessary extravagance. They were about to go to the dairy to count the holiday allocation of cheeses, when a servant came for Judith on her father's behalf.

Abruptly summoned, Judith found herself standing in front of her father. She was terrified of him, and it always became obvious. She thought he was cold towards her because her mother had died at the birth of still-born twins when she was a tiny child; she thought that, in some obscure way, it had been her fault. Guilt had always lain heavily upon her.

The Count of Evreux leaned back in his great chair, idly tapping the documents which lay in front of him with an overlong fingernail. A man of above average height, fair and thin, he had rather fixed and staring eyes, whilst all attention had to be focused on his wide and mobile mouth. His lips were thin and his teeth most prominent - his whole jaw seemed oversized, forcing his speech to appear guttural. To his eternal chagrin, he could not manage the letter 'r'. In the body of a word where it was negligible, he rolled it out as though it stood three deep. If he tackled it as an initial, his tongue seemed to cleave to his palate, and to yield only an 'l'. It infuriated him.

The Count was said to be slow - but deadly. His successes stemmed from his meticulous attention to detail, for he never left anything to chance. A great many people privately suspected that he had as many lawyers at his beck and call as his trained soldiers; his powers curled like tentacles through Norman laws. He had hardened like a rock after his beloved wife had died; his heart had withered away completely.

Absorbed by the many duties of his high position, he had never touched his daughter in affection - had never thrown her a ball or given her a plaything. As she grew older he had taken to speaking to her on occasion, but only because he was a firm believer in protocol and knew his lead was followed; he expected his court to be an exemplar, even rivalling Duke William's own. He had had her watched closely since Roger's visit; her worth to him was inestimable. He had never considered her as a person in her own right; nor did he now.

'How old are you now, Judith?'

Her head dropped with sudden fear, a curtain of hair sliding across her worried face, which seemed to shrink. Her father was looking at her as though he were selling a load of salt - and suddenly she began to review her situation with fresh eyes. He knew her age – of course he knew. What was he up to?

'Sixteen, father,' her voice faltered. She could feel her old enemy beginning to rise in itching pink patches on her arms and neck.

'I'm considering your future.' He sounded distant and appeared deep in thought. 'It's been a serious problem having only two children from my two wives, however high-born they were - and I've limited control over Odo; it leaves me with little to bargain.'

Judith felt she had no identity, as light as air, and as insubstantial. Without even looking at her, he shifted the documents in front of him, and said.

'Your betrothal is something I've been considering at length, and I have decided to speak to you about it. Negotiations are complicated; any false move would be costly.'

He looked at her with such a piercing gaze that she came out of her lethargy.

'I want to impress upon you that anything that might have happened to you in the past, any words said, any confidences exchanged, anything written that I don't know about - *anything* - is now beyond the law, because of your age. You begin another life, in our circles, at the age of sixteen. A belief in a strict adherence to our country's laws is paramount in our society, especially in the closed circle of the aristocracy to which we belong.'

With consummate ease he spoke to her, certain that his daughter knew nothing of the law. He did not need to specify what he meant. He looked across at her suddenly, and saw, with satisfaction, her stricken face.

'Don't be naïve, Judith - as my daughter you must know your worth, and the care I take of my assets.'

His long white fingers, heavy with glowing rings, beat a tattoo on the table.

Chilled to the bone, although a substantial open fire lay near, she remained motionless.

Her day dress of pale lichen green was sewn around the hem with small pearls and gold cording; several precious rings gleamed on her fingers and a net of gold and pearls half-hid her wheat-coloured hair. She wore her finery heedlessly, inherited wealth and security had never concerned her in the past, nor did she question its future. Yet the acquisitive gleam in her father's eye stopped her heart.

'The most advantageous alliance for our great name needs an explanation, Judith: never forget the words you hear today. When you are joined in marriage it is imperative that you always consider *my interests first* - this is why I am taking you into my confidence.'

Her father continued, as he contemplated her youthful skin and small-boned, agile body,

'There is no question of marriage into our own ducal family, of course. Duke William has enough on his hands and will most certainly have to marry into Flanders in time - besides, it's too close to home and my future power must come through political division. But Brittany? No... They lie at risk from the sea and are too far from active help. And Geoffrey Martel of Anjou is already satisfactorily married, which leaves us England, Blois-Champagne and Burgundy. I must be prudent in my choice, for the long boundary between France and Germany is, in many places, nebulous, with lordships intermingled there. Since many magnates hold fiefs and estates from both the French monarchy and the German Empire, I must take care to avoid those pockets of confusion.'

He leaned back against the carved chair, conscious of Judith's beauty and grace, knowing the time was ripe and, possibly, even a little late for effective breeding. He had deliberately waited to marry his only daughter, tentatively holding her out as bait again and again, but the teasing must wait no longer.

He began afresh to drum his fingers on the arm of his high chair as he concentrated, noticing Judith's hands that clasped and unclasped against the folds of her gown. Was she unduly agitated? He had been told by her nurse that she was easily upset, prone to tears at the slightest mishap, but he did not want to be near any emotional distress; he found it distasteful and associated it with only the lower bred.

'England is of no use to me and, anyway, I don't have sufficient ships to back up my investment. Only Champagne and Burgundy are left from which to choose.'

'Use.' 'Investment.' That is what he thinks of me.

Tap, tap-tap, tap-tap-tap.

With his chin cupped in his other hand the Count of Evreux sat staring into the distance, considering his only daughter's future allegiance as though he was playing a game of political chess: high-born women were the inevitable pawns across a European board.

Judith waited, cold with fear.

'Recently Henry Capet of Burgundy has helped our own good Duke William, so should you marry into that family he might see me as a rival, bidding for power.'

He smiled inwardly at the thought, knowing how often he had contemplated action but, on careful consideration, had drawn back.

'No. I think we should marry you into the House of Champagne! As it's east of Normandy it bridges a gap between Normandy, the King of France and the Holy Roman Emperor.... but it's safe! South of powerful Flanders, north of equally powerful Cluny, away from the conflagration of England, the Scots and Picts further north and Norway - and safe, too, from Viking invasion; yes ... I think Champagne will suit me.'

The Count neither bothered to invite Judith to sit, nor ask her an opinion - yet having had an explanation of the background to his choice was a rare compliment to her. He expected her to remember his views, to work always for her own family's good and not ask questions or create difficulties. He deliberately never mentioned that any son of hers, according to the law, would be entitled to inherit her mother's monies and properties.

'Off with you now!'

And, with a lifted finger, he dismissed her.

Tap, tap-tap, tap-tap-tap.

She still waited in front of him, unmoving, transparently white, transfixed like a rabbit in front of a stoat. Then an anger began to rise within her, but she controlled both her emotions and the expression on her face; if she was of any worth to him then she would make him rise to his feet to acknowledge her.

After a moment or two her father looked up only to see her still standing in front of him, stiff with pride and fear. With a sardonic smile, he half-rose to his feet. So - she wanted her presence felt, did she, now he had revealed his hand? He rather admired her. With a long, deep, look at his face she turned on her heel and slowly walked away. During this past half-hour she had become a woman.

JUDITH'S ESCAPE

In a private place within her rooms Judith threw herself onto a seat beside a window, which overlooked the spot where she and Roger had met; the daily sight had kept her memories bright and fresh. She knew her father's reputation as an extremely deep thinker and realized that if she was to save herself then she must think as deeply and carefully about her own preservation as he had about her sale. She was convinced, now, that her pact with Roger was no secret, and anyhow, was apparently illegal; the preservation of the law, however unjust, lay at the root of everyone's existence, from kings to serfs.

During the past months she had foolishly avoided facing up to the inevitable. Unaware of sharp reality she had daydreamed of waiting for Roger to return, rich and triumphant, to claim her. Meanwhile, meek, in the real world, she behaved as a dutiful daughter. She had no close companion in whom she could confide, and protocol forbade her talking about something so intimate to a serving-woman.

She dared not mention Roger whilst her father was assessing the strongest and wealthiest families, it would have been pointless. Now it was obvious she was to be disposed of quickly - her sumptuous wedding celebrations would be an elaborate front for diplomacy. There was no escape.

What could she do? Was there a choice? Reality appeared stark. No word had come from Roger in the past eighteen months. Yet the wise old Count, surrounded by spies, had known all along about Judith's encounter with Roger - and had laughed indulgently. But when the first of Roger's many letters had arrived for her, his mood changed and he savagely tossed it into the fire - followed, later, by all the others.

Roger, she thought, in her disappointment, might now be dead, she might never hear from him again - and yet he might send for her in time to come. What was her alternative to this hideous marriage? None ... bar going into a religious Order.

The Church! *A nun* - that was an acceptable avenue of escape, and used by many ladies of her rank. True, she was promised to Roger, but if she couldn't go to him it was obvious that there was little time to make a choice. There was not a moment to lose, if she were to escape from her father's net. Which was it to be? A child-bearing pawn in Champagne or a barren nun?

Judith fingered her cross-that-was-not-there, picturing it around Roger's neck, and realised the irony of the situation. Her 'religious' salvation, it was painfully apparent, lay in the hands of her only other near relation, her half-brother Odo, the powerful Abbot of the Monastery of St. Evroul-sur-Ouche. Although she had often visited Fressenda at the convent, she was hardly close to her brother - their paths rarely crossed, and when they did meet it was at some ceremonious event when little could be said. He was much older than her too.

If Roger should ever send for her word could have reached her through his mother in Odo's convent; she knew that Fressenda used to have regular news of all her sons in Italy - it had been her only comfort, to know he was alive and well. But shortly after Roger's departure Fressenda, her only friend, had died and her informal visits there had ceased.

If, on the other hand, she thought, she married into the House of Champagne she would be treated with immense respect, and her standard of living would be even greater than at Evreux, yet much would depend on how many children she could bear; especially how many sons. As time went by, she would be drawn into whirlpools of intrigue and disaffection, pulling her this way and that, until the unity of her father's world would be impaired if she spoke out of turn. She could envisage endless difficulties ahead. And she would never see or hear from Roger again. In her mind she thought that speed was essential, her father would never dream that she would make a move of any sort within twenty-four hours – *that* would be the key to her success.

Whichever way the dice was to be thrown, it would never be in her favour. Which, she deliberated, should she choose to be? A powerful lady while she lived in a foreign city, or the bride of Christ in the familiar convent in Normandy? She had never had to make any major choice before, anything greater than the colour of a new gown; now it seemed there really was no choice, no choice at all, she must act at once, before her father was shamed by sending envoys to Champagne: no one must become aware of that - she owed him a modicum of family loyalty at least. Her fear of the unknown became a deciding factor.

After much further thought, clear-headed now the die was cast and her plans had been made, down to the last detail, Judith wearily called her rosy young serving maid, Bertha, and took her into her confidence; it was a last, desperate, measure, and she had to risk trusting the girl.

Together they gathered up all her jewels, with as many gold coins as they could collect and carry, her Book of Hours and her finest clothes: her much-adored lap-dogs would have to be abandoned.

Later, Bertha slipped down the back turret stairs and out to the stables, where she selected three sturdy horses: a stupefying amount of money passed hands to keep a groom's mouth shut. Then, laughing, flirting, whilst the Court dined, she'd taken out wine to the guards at one of the smaller of the castle's gates, and watched the drugged liquid slip easily down their greedy, eager throats - until they were all senseless.

At dinner Judith had sat on her father's right hand. He had smiled at her a great deal, plying her with food, filling her goblet, and making it obvious to everyone present that she was much in favour. He had thrown down the gauntlet of his decision and was now preparing the ground meticulously. Several of the senior courtiers, used to her father, watched him with vigilance as they worked out the significance of his actions.

Judith, thought the more observant members of the court, looked curiously confident and worldly - not the trembling child they were used to; they instantly concluded that she had been informed about her future and would welcome a move away from her father to another Court - if that was his intention. Knowing him well, they especially watched his fingers tapping on the table in front of him, and the way his fingernails made indentations in the wood.

In her turn, Judith had taken great care in dressing in some of her newest and most fashionable clothes. By doing so, she reflected, it would look as though she had acquiesced to her father's plans and would represent him most handsomely in the future.

She wore an undergarment which was deep violet, above which she had a pleated scarlet tunic, with a hood - which she threw back to show the elaborate gold and enamelled combs in her hair. The tunic had sleeves striped with green silk and trimmed, at the wrists, with red-brown fur. A very heavy silver belt was clasped just above her slim hips. Her feet were shod in the newest - most frivolous - fashion of shoes, enriched with coloured ribbon laces; and more ribbons streamed from a multi-coloured head-dress, which flowed behind her and trailed to the ground.

As she sat at table, eating and drinking and playing up to her father, the remainder of the Court, out of the corners of their eyes, watched the tiny flashes of light sparking from the many rings on her fingers and thumbs, and noticed that her fingernails, like those of a sparrowhawk, were pared to resemble talons. She looked the acme of perfection, with her flawless performance: a pouting, lazy, icon of fashion who could hardly lift her golden goblet to sip the wine within – and she tottered in her dazzling shoes, hardly able to walk to her place at the high table without help.

The evening was brilliantly gay, with minstrels playing and wine flowing. Schooled for so long in unquestioning obedience, Judith forced herself to smile and nod and appear deeply interested in what her father had to say. In this way, she thought, he would take a few days before he made a move about her marriage, whilst she would try and beat him at his own game.

When it was over she retired to her rooms, yawning, walking slowly away with affected boredom. Her ladies dismissed, she bolted her door.

By morning there was no trace of Judith and Bertha at all, they had vanished without a trace. Gone, too, were her most beautiful clothes, including the ones she had worn the night before, and all her most precious possessions.

Aghast, the furious Count set out to find her.

THE BIRTH OF BOHEMUND

In Calabria, the rain clattered down, hour after hour, coating the walls of Robert's castle, bouncing into puddles, gathering into rivulets which swelled into streams and flooded the fields and paths. The beeches shuddered in the forests and the silvery firs twisted and strained in the wind, droplets falling off each pine needle, spattering on to the moss below. Autumn was coming in, as it generally did, weeping and wailing and wetting the land.

Inside the castle there was a cheerful fire in the centre of the Hall, the wind whistled and whooped in the chimney above in the roof, and the stone floor was damp. Men sat around the room, some whittled sticks whilst others mended harness. A few men gambled with dice, using carob beans for money, and others played board games with bone pegs. None played the pipe in case they disturbed Alberada, and some merely stared at the damp walls, daydreaming, waiting for the wind and rain to stop. Jacques paced nervously about, agitated, serving Robert. Wolf lay just inside the open door, nose on paws, ears pricked for sight of game.

Robert rose, paused uncertainly outside a door, then went into the private solar where Alberada rested. Her contractions were strong.

'How are you? How near is the birth of our son?' He worried about her face, which now looked drawn and thin. She smiled as brightly as ever, gesturing to him to sit beside her.

She grimaced with another contraction. Robert had a sudden insight into Alberada's deep-seated - but unspoken - fears; he now realised she was deathly afraid of the act of childbirth, of pain and of mortality. She badly needed reassurance. He continued to speak soothingly to her, holding her hands.

But Alberada turned away from Robert's hungry arms as her pains increased.

'You'd better leave me now Robert - please! Call my woman.'

Galvanised into action he shouted his orders so that even the wind and the rain seemed to quieten, and left Alberada to give birth to his child at last. It was a very protracted wait.

Robert moved about, restlessly, concerned - out of his mind as never before in his life: he would not leave her door. Jacques watched him, mirroring his anxiety. At last came the shouted words,

'A son! *You have your son!'*

Shouldering aside the unkempt midwife, Robert stumbled into the dim room which smelt of stale air and blood.

'Lights! Bring me a light! And throw open the shutters - let some fresh air in!' He held the rush light overhead and looked down at his exhausted wife who had been almost soundlessly in labour for over three days. Her hair was loose and wet, pushed from her face and straggling across the coverings of the bed. Her eyes were sunken, her cheeks ashen, her lips had a tinge of blue.

In her arms was a heavy baby, wrapped in cloths which left his big head bare; his dark curls rested against her neck, his eyes were closed.

'My son? Alberada – you look so ill…'

Alberada slowly opened her eyes and smiled radiantly at him, gesturing to the baby. 'I'll be alright now,' she sighed, 'here's your son.' He gazed at her, exalted, not taking his eyes from her tired face.

'It's Saint Mark's Day, isn't it? Or near enough?' she whispered. 'Let's have him christened Mark, shall we?'

'Whatever you will; we've not had a Mark in our family before.' Robert bent down and touched her hand.

'Now, let me take my son from you, I want to show him to my

men!'

She tried to lift the child, but the effort was too much for her. Robert bent and took the baby easily in his great hands. He held him close for an instant, then strode into the Hall with a look of enormous pride written all over his face.

'See my son ... my small giant! His name is to be Mark!'

His men shouted, clapped him on the back, and peered at the big newborn. One man called out,

'Maybe your son Mark will become another Bohemund one day!'

'After the legendary giant? I'm sure he will. And achieve fame!'

Robert held out the infant to Jacques, who took him expertly: the implicit trust of the gesture filled him with pleasure. He eyed Robert steadily. 'Let's pray he's the first of many!'

'Aye - and you must help me train him when the time comes.'

Jacques flushed, pleased once more, his freckles standing out against his pale skin, and returned the child to his father, making the sign of the cross upon his forehead. With great care Robert returned to Alberada's room, replacing their baby in her arms, anxiously enquiring,

'Is he all right? Is there anything amiss?'

'No, he's perfect."

'I'm so happy, Alberada. I've a loving wife, and a perfect child. It makes me afraid of how vulnerable I'm becoming.' Worry intermingled with his joy; how long was happiness to last?

'Don't ... don't spoil this precious moment; let it be. Just hold me close.'

Robert gathered up his wife and his firstborn in his strong arms. Mark opened his eyes for the first time and gave his father one long, straight look.

'My God - his eyes are violet, too!'

Not knowing why, and for the only time in his tough life, Robert wept, his tears fell onto his wife's pale face, but both she and the child had fallen asleep in his arms, safe and sound.

THE BATTLE OF CIVITATE

Late that evening Robert sat on a bench outside the castle, looking down the valley to the long lake as it disappeared into the trees. The rain had stopped, although droplets kept on plopping down from the leaves and pine needles. Overhead there was a rain-washed moon, now and then clouded by mist. A comforting warmth came up from the mossy ground which had blotted the water and was now springing back into shape. Cicadas began to thrum and call to each other and Robert eased himself against the stone wall and took stock.

It was unmistakable that he had done well. He knew he'd turned a corner in his life, following foundations which had been carefully laid. In the past years he had worked hard, making plans with Girard, meeting powerful people, gathering men and horses together, training them and, now and then, trusting some enough to delegate. There were endless battles. Naturally he was aware that there had been a certain amount of wrong-doing, of pillaging and burning, by his men, but there were fewer rapes and murders than before. Consolidation was imperative, he reasoned. The coffers were full enough thanks to Alberada's generosity - and the spoils from Cosenza and many lesser cities. There was food in the storehouse, and hay in the barns for the horses and there was grain for the coming year - and more; everything was now in its place and he could go ahead, in his relentless search for true power in the land. His initial conquest of Cosenza had turned the key, forcing open the door to his future. His latest battle, at Civitate, had prised open an almost impenetrable door to the Pope in person. All Europe had stopped and wondered at the astonishing outcome.

Now, deep in thought, Robert turned Tancred's heavy silver ring around his finger. He always reverted to fiddling with it at times of crisis and when he recalled Tancred's advice and wisdom. What, he pondered, was the significance of the ring's design? A lion's gamb, or paw, surrounded by chains? Were his responsibilities to chain him, as he had thought before? Was his love for Alberada meant to hamper him? No, he calculated afresh, the central part of the motif was the paw, and the interlinking chain surrounded and protected that. The lion, the king of all animals, shaped his own destiny with his paw - and so must he! He had to carve out his future with his own strong right hand. He had a young giant of a son, a devoted wife, enough gold to last a while, a fine castle and a good many trained fighters: it was a turning point in his life. One day, he promised himself, that ring would have to be given to his son, just as he had received it, at an appropriate moment.

He felt excitement rising; he knew his star was in the heavens and there was not time to linger or delay, for he asked advice from every fortune-teller and astrologer he could find. Now it was time for him to arrange to meet the Pope again, to offer his services, to place himself far higher up the ladder to success. This confident approach marked his search for real position and power: he knew his worth. Next month he would go to Rome, or Benevento, wherever the Pope might be. There, he knew, he would be welcomed. He had turned the most crucial corner and would respect the Church at last; it was an odd feeling.

And he had his first-born child – a son!

Robert stretched out his long legs as he leaned against his castle's walls, allowing his memory to stray back into the events of the recent weeks and the great battle of Civitate. That happened after his brother Count Humphrey had organised a hugely important conference at Melfi, after Drogo's untimely death. All the Normans in the country had attended the conference, whatever their allegiance. It was followed by a call to arms when the Pope demanded from the Normans 'the return of all the lands of Saint Peter,' which all the Normans rejected outright. It would leave them nothing.

Aided by the German Emperor, the Pope threatened war against all the Normans. The more senior people, such as the Hautevilles, under the discipline of Count Humphrey, were comparatively respectable; but clearly life for the native population had grown intolerable and they had finally banded together and appealed to the Pope to save them from the Norman invaders.

German-born Pope Leo IX, kind and saintly, responded to the peoples' pleas with sympathy and managed, after some considerable time, several years, to get together an army. This was so large and strong, especially with its contingent of seven hundred German infantry, that he was assured it would sweep the wretched Normans away for ever. It was the first time that Robert knew that there were over three hundred states in the Holy Roman Empire, and he now understood how the Emperor could be so generous with troops and money. At long last there was to be an ultimate contest between the Pope and the invading Normans. All Europe stood on the sidelines, watching, waiting, as the Pope's army slowly wended its way to the south and swept like a slow and inevitable tide towards the Normans near Foggia, in the plains of Apulia. They finally camped on farmland outside Civitate.

True to form, all the Normans banded together. Each small robber chief had presented himself to Count Humphrey or to Robert and handed over his men. All of them were eager for a battle, but most of them could scarcely believe that they were drawing their swords against 'God's Vicar on earth'. Crime and repentance alternated with astonishing rapidity, but – much more worrying – the Normans had brought insufficient food with them. They had expected to buy produce from the local people, but had been outwitted – they had been refused point blank.

With both armies in wait, Humphrey and Robert sent one last appeal to the Pope. They composed a dutiful letter, confessing their faults and promising him that the Normans would reform their ways if he would withdraw. *They did not wish to harm the Church in any way.* Besides, their army was much smaller than the Pope's.

Little did they realise that the Pope's army had, in turn, brought insufficient water with them, making it difficult in the great heat to postpone the conflict; it was mid-summer and incredibly hot. Nor did the Pope know the strength of the Normans' cavalry.

The Normans had always valued their horses, and their prodigious military successes were largely accounted for by their use of the stirrup, which had been introduced to northern Europe a century before. The stirrup permitted the Normans to wear extremely heavy armour, which rendered their bodies almost invulnerable, and whilst on horseback they were able to use both lance and battle-axe; it was an entirely different method of employing horses, and now they had to be much larger – known as 'destriers' – to take full weight, and charge as well.

The venerable old Pope, ensconced in the middle of his enormous multi-faceted army, sat and read the latest contrite document from the Normans, wavering between attack and forgiveness. All too visible in his long white robes, he was the very first Pope to wage war in person, and he was uncertain what to do. Accompanying him were almost all the non-Norman barons of southern Italy; the Duke of Gaeta, the Count of Aquino and the Count of Teano; Peter, Archbishop of Amalfi; detachments from Rome and the Sabine hills; detachments from the Campania and Apulia, from the Marsi and Ancona and Spoleto. They all waited for his decision.

Some typically tall, long-haired Germans jeered and gestured at the short Norman bowmen that they could see in front of them. Then they approached the elderly Pope and arrogantly addressed him,

'Command the Normans to leave Italy. Command them to lay down their arms here, and then return to the land from whence they came. If they refuse this – *then don't accept their peaceful proposals!'*

The Pope wavered again; at heart he was a peaceful man. He turned from the Germans to study the repentant Norman letter once more.

Unfortunately the German infantry chose just that moment to shout further insults at the Normans, calling out that,

'You're only little men who fight on horses!'

At that, both Humphrey and Robert rode out to the front of their soldiers, both well over six feet tall, in full armour, and astride their destriers.

The leaders of the Papal army blanched. The Pope had hesitated too long.

'DO YOU MEAN US?' roared Robert. His voice triggered off a surge of Norman fury.

It was later said of Robert that his battle-cry would turn back tens of thousands.

The Germans immediately hurried the Pope, protesting all the way, to safety behind the walls of nearby Civitate. When he was safe the combat took place. Success was governed by speed and timing and meticulous preparation by the Normans.

Orders were shouted out by the leaders and passed down the line. First the shorter men in the front knelt down and volley after volley of arrows were fired by the archers, as the Germans (and especially the Italians), unprepared after all, rushed too late to form up into squadrons. The Pope had never discussed a plan of action with anyone.

Then, at a second drum-beat signal, Humphrey and Robert together led the field of cavalry, followed by the rest of the horse-riding Norman knights. They all wore knee-length mail hauberks, carrying lances and elongated leather-covered shields. They all stood up in their stirrups and charged full-pelt at the enemy; it was a fearsome sight and the noise was tremendous.

The Normans swept through the Pope's Italian troops like iron birds.

The living turned and fled immediately, leaving the Germans to bear the whole brunt of the war. It became a massacre. After two days, although they fought brilliantly, not one German survived. The remainder of the Papal army gave in as the Norman cavalry ploughed inexorable through it. They showed no pity.

Once the outcome was known, Humphrey shouted out,

'Bring out the Pope'.

The cowardly city fathers of Civitate screamed back,

'We'll bring him – but his battle is nothing to do with us.'

They dragged the sad old man from behind the city's walls and across the fields, half-fainting, to throw him on the ground before the Hautevilles. Then the city fathers raced back to safety.

Humphrey and Robert advanced upon the Pope. To everyone's amazement they each took him by an arm and lifted him gently to his feet. Then they said,

'Forgive us, Holiness, forgive our sins.'

And both enormous men fell to their knees and bared their heads.

No-one could believe their eyes. After a slight pause, all the remaining soldiers followed suit, prostrating themselves on the battlefield in front of the Pope.

Trembling, exhausted, the Pope blessed them both, and then all the soldiers, telling them,

'If they would mend their ways.'

For Robert, there was a personal tragedy: Girard had been killed in the battle. But he had died as he had lived, with a gay laugh on his face and supported on both sides by friends. When they had buried him, Robert had the forethought to send Jacques back to inform Alberada, so she could mourn in peace before he returned, hopefully to be there at the time of their child's birth.

But, before Robert traveled back home he, and Humphrey and their men, escorted the Pope back to his own city of Benevento in the

Campagnia and then, at last, they all went home. It was a turning point in the status of all the Normans in the south. Their booty was immense, and Girard's men elected to remain with Robert, and all of Girard's money was in his safe-keeping.

Most of important of all was Robert's future allegiance to the Church and the Pope.

JUDITH IN THE FOREST

Deep in the forest, a few miles from Evreux, lived a woodcutter's widow, her husband had worked all his life for the Count of Evreux. Her moribund hut stood beneath an enormous oak beside a running spring in a small green valley; in winter months the spring swelled until it became a threat - changing to a small river which had to be forded. The wattle and daub cottage itself was untidily thatched with reeds from the river, and was just an open space inside, with no partition walls, the widow shared it with a few fowls and a goat penned to one side. The hearth was in the centre, with a jagged hole in the roof where the smoke eventually escaped. Her husband was long dead, and the widow didn't know how to make her circumstances any better as she had no sons. She did, however, have a niece, who visited her occasionally.

No roads came near, and the path the widow took was scarcely marked, for she was the only one who ventured there; once every three months she took a journey, to her it was immense, to walk the six miles to the Count's castle and be given her head-money - her widow's microscopic allowance. Then she bought her scant supplies, mainly rye or barley, and trudged back to live off her own small plot of land. Now and then the sounds of hunting in the forest could be heard, and occasionally some horsemen would splash up the bed of the river in winter, to avoid the thick undergrowth of the forest. No-one stopped to speak to the widow, for all they knew she might be deaf and dumb and, for certain, she would have nothing of interest to say to worldly people.

The lady Judith of Evreux, now clad in sombre brown, had travelled through the night with Bertha to the hut, which belonged to

Bertha's old aunt. It was within the Count's pale, and was even owned by him, although he had never seen it. Bertha, a country girl, suggested that they approached the hut for the final half a mile riding up the river banks, crossing and re-crossing the water several times, to look as though hunters had been that way. They rode past the silent, sleeping hut, then, a hundred yards above the spring, then they doubled back and came to it from behind.

Although it had been hasty, they had prepared for their escape with great care; Judith owed Bertha many a debt for her practicality. Amongst their heavily laden packs were containers with dye in them, and before they even approached the cottage door they dyed the horses' coats and then let them go, shackled loosely, in a grassy patch deep in the forest.

It took time to make the frightened widow understand the situation, but she learned considerably more quickly when Judith gave her a small pouch with a few copper coins inside. Originally, unthinking, she had told Bertha that she might give her future saviour a ring to recompense her. Bertha smiled indulgently and said,

'My lady, how do you think a poor peasant could wear a ring? And if she tried to sell it she would be put in jail for stealing it. And it might be recognised as yours in either case.'

Judith thought of her several large boxes of jewellery, overflowing with precious objects for adornment and display, and shook her head in disbelief.

'Then it must be money?' She took out some glinting gold.

'Yes, my lady. But only copper coins, for when she goes to buy her grain she never has more, and folk would be suspicious.'

'I don't think I own any coins of copper ...'

'I have, my lady, it's what you pay me each year.' And Bertha ran to fetch her tiny hoard, wrapped in a scrap of cloth.

Judith was so shocked by the amount that Bertha gave her that she sat and stared at it for moments. Then she swiftly searched around her rooms until she found every coin and all the jewels in her possession, to bring with them. Until now she had left the payment for anything she desired to the steward, and she had never bothered to ask the cost.

Dressed as poor country girls, heads bound with kerchiefs, Judith and Bertha tried to settle in the widow's hut. For Judith it was a terrible experience, and every day the contrast with her own past life became almost too much to bear. She couldn't believe that conditions such as these existed and, whereas now free, she felt totally imprisoned.

They both helped the woman with her daily chores, which were few, letting loose the chickens and milking the goat. Much of the time was spent gathering firewood, and when the frosts were over they tilled the ground to grow peas and beans, and later harvested them to make bean flour and add it to the barley when making coarse bread. Judith's beautiful nails no longer looked like a sparrow-hawk's talons. Now and then they trapped a hedgehog to bake in clay, or caught a rabbit for the pot, which gently bubbled night and day beside the hearth. Judith had never envisaged such poor food, such small portions and such little variety; it shocked her to the marrow. The treasures they had brought with them were now hidden down a disused well, and the rich harnesses and Judith's clothing first padded out the mattress they all shared, then were transferred to a small cave in the forest, near the widow's bees.

Bertha's nature was irrepressible. She was short and dark and bouncy; she walked with a lilt in her step, her curls bobbed and jiggled down her back; she gestured with her hands all the time and at scarcely any moment was she seen without a smiling face. Gossip and laughter were essentials to her, and she loved to touch things and people; an arm went around her aunt, smoothing her bent shoulders, the goat was embraced each morning, hens sat upon her lap at night before they slept beside the fire; she was a joy to them all, and lifted Judith's spirits.

Bertha's nature exasperated Judith as well, now all the rules of protocol had to be abandoned she was scared that Bertha would give away their secrets to any visitor - unbelieving that no visitor was ever likely to arrive. She had told Bertha that she should treat her as her sister, which she duly did, in a simple, unaffected way. But Judith had never had a sister herself, and, frantically worried as she was, she would try to control her with a pause or a look if she presumed too far. Their circumstances were so highly unusual that Judith had to judge and balance her reprimands with care, aware that loyalty was now a personal act of faith. Disclosure would have meant death to Bertha and her aunt within the hour; they became very close. Judith was taut with nervous strain.

Once some men came there, whereupon the toothless widow went to the low entrance, quavering, and they went away again, satisfied that she had seen nothing with her rheumy eyes, besides, they reasoned, the daughter of the great Count could never exist in such an inferior place.

The storm of anger which had poured out from the Count across his household and lands had been almost too terrible for words. What he most feared was that Judith had sought help from his first cousin, William of Normandy; but they had met several times since her disappearance, and William's manner gave no hint of subterfuge.

He had sent soldiers out to every boundary crossing, every ford of every river, interrogating everyone seen on the roads, searching every respectable dwelling which might have housed his rich, spoilt young daughter. It never occurred to him, even once, that she could have inherited his own abilities - that she had sufficient intellect to anticipate his way of thinking.

Then, when it seemed established that Judith had ridden clean out of his lands, the Count began again to send delegates and envoys to neighbouring states, cautiously enquiring if they had given her shelter, with veiled threats if they had been so foolish - yet leaving space if they had not, so that he, himself, would not appear foolish in turn. He used every particle of his political strength to find his daughter - his last pawn - and yet the weeks stretched on and no trace was found. In the end, cursing himself for speaking out his plans to her, he decided that she had managed to travel across the water to England, and was safe from him for ever.

In the meanwhile Judith stayed quietly at the hut, a mere six miles from her father's castle walls, intelligently patient. Neither she nor Bertha ventured out beyond the chickens' patch, nor showed a light at night and slept silently, sharing the same pallet. She had never shared anything before, let alone a bed, and she found Bertha's unconscious habit of clasping her in her plump arms maddening and deeply intrusive. Nor had she ever dreamed of sharing a room at night with a goat and some chickens - the alien lack of refinement dismayed her deeply but, being young and finding herself still safe from harm, she eventually learned to adapt.

Once a quarter the elderly widow travelled as usual to the nearest small town to collect her tiny supplies, and this she continued to do. Each time she joined the crones sitting on the steps of the small church for some hours, chatting about the days of their youth and gossiping about local events; it was her life's entertainment, and always had been. Now and then, when the commotion had died down somewhat, she heard what progress had been made in the search for the lady Judith, making no comments about the matter herself, and returned with enough information and extravagant stories to delight the two young women for a further period.

Some days later, Bertha would retell the stories to her companions, acting out each part in caricature, until they were almost ill with laughter, watching her. In time the simple stories became legends to them in Bertha's hands - 'the time the lad got caught on the roof', 'the day the bride found her husband to be the father, not the son,' - and so on; stories which were brought out for different occasions and enjoyed once more, all over again.

Then, after the widow's fourth visit, it seemed that no more surprise forays were being undertaken by the soldiers, but now the envoys were being sent in orderly processions instead. The Count, too, had been summoned to a Council at Rouen - and had departed in a furious display of strength and colour and a hullabaloo of silver horns.

On hearing this news, Judith decided that it would be safe to travel on to the convent at last and, one evening, she and Bertha quietly mounted their shaggy horses and crept away through the silent darkness.

The widow slept happily that night amongst her snuffling animals, smiling in her sleep, like a cat licking its whiskers after cream, with enough coins buried under her earthen floor to keep her fed and warm for the remainder of her days.

ROBERT AND POPE NICHOLAS II

Whilst Judith was in hiding, Robert de Hauteville was meeting the new Pope, Nicholas the Second, at Melfi. Nicholas had been in Italy thirteen years. Popes, thought Robert, were elected too late in life and lasted far too short a time; the state of affairs brought continual disruption and lack of stability.

Since the day of his son Mark's birth he had met two Popes, now he was to meet a third. He had met the first in Rome, before he had known Alberada, and was kept waiting for days, and was then refused an audience. On the second occasion he had fought the ailing Pope on the battlefield of Civitate and saved his life; it was a turning point in his life.

This time he came by invitation from the new Pope, Nicholas II, and he was being seen alone, and as an equal, with measured pomp and ceremony. Clearly this Pope respected his reputation: Robert was warily flattered. All the same, the meeting was to be in secret, held in the Norman's castle at Melfi.

Pope Nicholas was formerly Gerard, Bishop of Florence, and had, unusually, been elected outside Rome, at Sienna. His enthronement in the Lateran formally resolved internal Church conflict, because an aristocratic family in Rome - the Tusculans - had previously forced an illegal election, without imperial consultation, and amidst riots. Strong Nicholas arrived, the illegal Pope fled, and all Italy and the Empire watched to see how the new Pontiff would handle matters in the future. If he lived.

Nicholas was a big man with a plum-coloured face and a great beak of a nose, and his dry mauve lips were parted in a mirthless smile in which his teeth shone as yellow as old ivory. In his first quick look at him Robert had found something jarring in his penetrating eyes which were shining and stony.

His personal priest was another tall and powerfully built man with the large hooked nose of an oriental and whose nostrils distended as though they scented prey; he looked like a Greek, with a slightly Semitic strain in his ancestry. His eyes were deep-set, and a tufted eyebrow drooped over one which was turned out of place and glared with the glassy stare of the blind.

The Pope ushered Robert to a seat across a wide table, saying affably, 'Now we can be private!'

'Private?'

Robert gestured towards the priest. Pope Nicholas frowned.

'You'd prefer he withdrew?'

'In the circumstances - yes!'

Robert, aware of Nicholas' own reputation for strength, was determined to press every advantage he could. Besides, at this very moment, he had no idea why His Holiness had arranged this extra-secret meeting: he was very tense.

Nicholas made a slight dismissive gesture, his heavy amethyst ring winked once. The priest shuffled out sulkily: Robert had no doubt at all that he would be listening at the door.

Nicholas looked thoughtfully across at Robert de Hauteville; having supped in splendour they were now completely alone, and it was time for business.

'You've done well, Guiscard. And you've earned your nickname, you've accomplished a great deal in these past years, like your half-brother William 'Iron Arm' before you.'

Robert coloured slightly. The compliment had a cutting edge; he owed his half-brother nothing - but it was better than being compared to Drogo.

Nicholas continued, noticing Robert shifting slightly in his seat.

'But you've found it difficult out here? Perhaps because your brothers have respected you too well?'

So - the conversation was to be about his brothers, was it? The Pope had wasted no time in aggravating him.

'Respect? Hardly, Father!'

'Oh yes - don't have any delusions about that. They've been deathly afraid of you.'

'Physically, perhaps. Politically they've been too tough to compete with - so far. But I will, in time.'

'I believe you're wrong, Robert; my sources tell me they're convinced you'll seriously undermine all their holdings here, and very soon. Of course, just about everyone in power believes you're capable of sweeping the board, starting with your own family.' Robert grunted; the Pope took no heed. 'So - let me recap: Geoffrey is currently in Normandy as your father's heir, both Count William and Count Drogo are dead, Humphrey has been elected Count of Apulia, and Serlo is occupied in Sicily, with a scattering of petty titles. What even-handed escalation - eh? - in the short time you Hautevilles have been out here.'

He spoke fruitily, lazily. Without a word that could be called incitement Robert could sense that Nicholas was provoking him, goading him, trying to instill into him violence and resentment. The Pope continued;

'But I hear you have been totally independent of all of them - you haven't spent any time with them, and brotherly love has been sadly missing - isn't that so?'

Robert shifted uncomfortably in his seat. Love? Even 'hate' wasn't strong enough. He continued to say nothing. Nicholas spoke with confidence.

'You've nothing to fear from me, you can confide in me freely -

after all, *I am a priest.*'

Still Robert remained silent. He was conscious of watching a master negotiator at work and the technique intrigued him; it would be better to say nothing than make a mistake. Nicholas murmured silkily.

'You know, I've made a study of you recently and I believe that maybe, given the right circumstances, I could help you.'

'Oh?'

The wind was rising audibly; the susurration of the encircling woods about the castle at Melfi surged upwards like a great sea. The priest must be finding it difficult to hear their words. Robert's mind was racing, trying to anticipate the Pope's moves - they had not met before that night. Robert looked into his eyes, almost amused.

'What circumstances?'

'I'll be more direct. But, first, tell me - what is it that you want most out here? Land? Money? Revenge? Those are the usual reasons.'

At his own words the Pope laughed a quiet chuckling laugh in which there was little mirth. Robert murmured thoughtfully,

'Revenge would be sweet; of course, I've a score to settle. But what I aim to have is power - real power. And land. All Normans lust after land.'

The Pope contemplated Robert who, for a brief unguarded moment, looked like a visionary. He was leaning forward in his seat, unseeing: his face was still, he had left his body behind in the richly furnished chair. Then, with a start, he returned to the present, eyeing his questioner, holding his fair head with its beaked nose at a proud angle, like a falcon about to be unhooded and sent after the quarry from the wrist of a falconer.

'Power is what we all want, Guiscard, in varying degrees, but some of us need power, too, as a trust for greater, more worthy goals.'

Robert waited, lounging back again in his chair, mentally now locked into full attention. The Pope's voice grew louder.

'Personally, I need power for the Church, for the Christians in western Europe and especially for the position of the papacy - which is precarious. Our Church of Rome has spent many years freeing herself from the power of the Roman nobles; you may have heard that I've finally bested the mighty Tusculan family?'

Robert nodded; the Pope's actions had deeply impressed him. The Pope went on,

'Now we have to free ourselves from the enveloping power of the Holy Roman Emperor - only then can we be self-governing.'

Robert showed amazement,

'But Father, I thought the Holy Roman Empire was the supreme protector of the Church! The *spiritual* world is yours, the *secular* world is the Emperor's - isn't that so?'

The Pontiff drew in a deep breath, his voice having risen loud, and said more quietly,

'That has been the case since Charlemagne's time, and Popes are elected by both the Empire and the Church. But the power of each Pope can't be absolute if it has to be divided, and sub-divided, the way mine is today. You see - for the good of the Church - I believe that all Popes should be men of religious convictions as well as of military strength, not merely suitable pawns chosen equally by both the Church and the Emperor.'

Robert smothered a laugh.

'You - a pawn? The last person, I should have thought ...'

'All Popes, all future Popes I mean.' Nicholas continued eagerly. 'It must be obvious that any dissipation through a dual choice with the Emperor means that the Church will always be the loser, always waiting on imperial superiority! *This must stop!*'

Robert stared.

'How can you stop the elections? Surely the law ...'

'The law?' thundered Nicholas, 'Don't confuse the law with justice! I aim to use it as a tool!'

'Then it would have to be changed, wouldn't it? What is your plan?'

The Pontiff drew a deep breath.

'My plan is revolutionary and I tell you this in strictest confidence.' He glared at Robert, who bowed his head in acquiescence. *'My plan is that the Church alone should choose the Pope through equal votes by the cardinals.'*

He paused, spent.

Robert sat waiting, unmoving. A shiver of nerves cascaded like a waterfall down his back, pinching through the muscles, and sped away.

'You'd force a change by canonical law? Is this in your power?'

'It is. I aim to call a conference for that very purpose here at Melfi.'

'But, Holiness, the dangers are inestimable ...'

'Not if I time it right!'

Time! It was always that. As long as the choice was yours. The Pope's old eyes looked sly. There was a thin crease to his bluish lips as if to indicate the smile he would not permit himself in public, yet his hands hidden in his robes were tightly clenched.

'You see, Robert, our Emperor Henry is not yet of age: he's a minor in law!' His voice had lowered to a whisper, as if he, too, did not want his priest to hear. 'That's my trump card! Until he is legally of age, he has no casting vote in Church matters. I've almost two years to call the conference and ratify the findings, and change the law - it's just enough.'

How clever, how diabolically clever, thought Robert as he leaned back in his seat, mentally applauding Nicholas' astuteness. But there must be more ... otherwise the Pope would never have taken the risk of telling him this. What was his own part in the Church's future? He decided to take the initiative.

'That may be so, but he's still the leader of a mighty force, law or no law! In fact, his imperial military strength is much greater than yours, isn't it?'

The Pope paused: how right he had been to gamble on opportunist Robert, who had immediately seen his only weakness. Robert continued, grinding on, making his advantage felt.

'And should the Emperor's representatives at the conference stand against you, as they'd have little to fear, then you'd be beaten - and the choice of Pope would forever be taken from the Church's hands! It would be a disaster for you. So how do you propose to confront the Emperor's strength?'

'By further strength! *Yours*!'

Nicholas and Robert glared at each other. Both were big men, both were determined; a threatening silence reigned, broken only by the crumbling and settling of huge logs in the fireplace. Astounded, Robert exclaimed,

'You'd go to war against the Emperor?'

'There really wouldn't be any need - the Church's safety would be assured if it was known that you - you! - stood alongside me. Everyone fears you and your army here in the south, and the Emperor has been alerted to your threat. But you'd need to stand steadily beside the Church for *all time*, not just for one battle ...'

'So my help - *my help* - is essential to your cause?'

'The cause of our mother Church! Don't you realise - you wouldn't be sitting here at all if you hadn't shown your mettle in '53, when you massacred Pope Leo's army at Civitate, and then offered unlimited sanctuary and aid to the saintly old man? It showed both your strength of purpose and your essential reverence for the Church.'

'That old story! That's in the past ...'

'The Church has a long memory, my son.'

Robert reiterated,

'But *my* help? Mine alone? Not the help of Humphrey and Serlo?'

'Yes, your help alone. Then - would there be any doubt that you were greater than those others if I chose you rather than them? You would have overtaken them in the eyes of the world. Would that be revenge enough?'

Robert sat brooding, chin on fist, elbow on knee: the prospect appeared before him like a giant sunflower uncurling, opening up in the strong Italian sunshine. Quietly the Pope persevered,

'Naturally, my son, you'd have to swear an oath of allegiance to me first ...'

Ah! Yes, of course! There was always a price. Robert continued to sit in thought. Without knowing, he ground his back teeth together, so that there came from them the little dry squeak of a pointer travelling over a slate. All he could think of were the consequences. *Power*! At last it was within his grasp ... perhaps his only chance! He steadied his heady thoughts.

'And, your Holiness, *in return*, whatever the outcome of the conference - what would be the rewards?'

'You'd not do this for the Church alone ... for her universal good?'

'No.'

The Pope raised his heavy eyelids and stared at Robert's arrogant face, his large dark eyes full of cold malice. Without turning his head he said in even tones,

'And what would you expect?'

'My brothers' honours, when each man died.'

'To be Count of Apulia?'

'And more - that's not enough!'

'How much more?'

'Duke of Apulia and Calabria,' said Robert, thinking about Tancred, 'and, in time, Duke of Sicily! And I'd need it all in writing!'

'Mother of God!' Nicholas paused, and then said, 'Why do you mention Sicily?'

'Because Sicily is paramount to the Church; Serlo's fought there for years to keep a balance - stability. We need to get rid of the Arabs and restore Christianity to the island. Until then Rome isn't safe.'

Nicholas had noticed Robert's use of the word 'we'.

'Yes,' he said 'we do.'

'Well,' said Robert, with confidence, 'I'm your man! That's my goal.'

'You demand a lot of me ... the Church, that is.'

'We both know I would gain no titles regarding Sicily until I'd proved myself there - and Serlo seems to be flagging - so you're risking nothing. As for the others, I've earned them and I've nothing to lose in demanding. Now that you've brought it all out into the open you're the one with the greater need!'

'Perhaps not that much ...'

'You're wrong, Holiness - you do need me that much! And you need me for the quality I've just shown - my confidence and thrust - and my reputation for cruelty! There are limits, let me remind you, as to what you could do, as head of the Church ... but I, Robert Guiscard, recognise no boundaries at all, as well you know!'

'Are you threatening me?'

'As if I would ... ' His voice was quiet, but clear.

The Pope remained still. There was a tense pause, he seemed to be gathering together some loose ends in his mind. In a level voice he resumed,

'I'd brook no delay if I acceded to your terms. In addition - you'd have to swear your allegiance here, tonight. The document is already prepared.'

'You're very sure of me, then?'

The Pope nodded, solemnly.

'I am.'

Robert went on,

'Then it's agreed, so long as you sign my letter of appointment at the same moment. Don't forget to have your priest prepare the titles too.'

'You'd want to consult no-one?'

'No.'

'Not even your wife?'

'Alberada? What has she to do with it?' Robert intuitively tensed. Why did the Pope mention her?

'It's a pity not to have a wife you'd wish to consult.'

'No leader consults a woman.'

'If she was sufficiently important he would.'

Robert disliked the drift of the conversation. He stayed silent. The Pope continued, in silky tones.

'To become Count, then Duke, would give you immense power ... great riches ...land, and influence in affairs of state. And you'd have leap-frogged so many, many people! But before you make a final decision I need to speak to you of your rather disastrous marriage.'

'*Disastrous*?' Robert clenched his fists, dark hollows and harsh cords marring the jut of his sunburned throat, and a network of fine lines revealed themselves about his mouth. Nicholas' voice grew quieter as he spoke again; his voice fostered a thin strain of world-weary cynicism,

'For some while - I told you I'd made a study of you recently - I've been concerned that your marriage seems to contravene the consanguinity laws.'

'*What*?'

'You're too closely related to Alberada!'

'No!'

'Through your mother's lineage you're third cousins, didn't you know? Think of what happened to William of Normandy. He was rightly accused of incest, you know - his wife, too, was a distant relation and their punishment was excommunication, for a while, until he came to heel.'

'Excommunication? Sweet Jesu! You can't - I had no idea ...' Robert looked suddenly deflated. Nicholas pressed on with his advantage,

'In normal life, with little people, it would make small difference. But in public life I couldn't tolerate it - breaking the Church's laws - especially as we're both pledged to uphold them!' The Pope paused. Then continued, so slow was every word that it stood with a separate menace in his sentences. 'And if - if - we're to be so closely allied it would be completely out of the question.'

So - it had come to that, had it? Robert spoke in tones that were distantly cold, exquisitely formal,

'The price - now – for my help and titles is to be my sworn allegiance and *my marriage annulled?'*

'It is. You'd be my champion, acknowledged by all.'

Oh God! To gain military and financial power of such magnitude was to lose beloved Alberada: fate had him by the throat too soon ... far too soon. But then - there was the matter of revenge as well. She would understand - wouldn't she? Wouldn't she? She had, up to now.

His dishevelled head drooped to his chest with the abrupt movement of a marionette. He was sure he'd manage to find a way to keep her - there must be some way.

'I'll give you an hour to decide.'

Nicholas rose, swept quietly out of the chamber. As his face turned from Robert there were deep hollows in his cheeks, as if he had sucked them in and was biting them in an intense and murderous excitement. His pompous face, congested with angry blood, now grew red as the wattles of a turkey, and his washed-out blue eyes glittered.

The trickle of wax that dripped over the edge of the candle on the table in front of Robert dripped the colour of crystal, clouded, and then solidified as a bead of yellow-white. His options, too, had trickled and stopped.

As Robert desperately weighed the situation the wind outside had risen to a rushing, roaring storm. It beat against the castle - a clamorous sea; and all the woodland around rustled and sighed with the perpetual song of an undertow along a pebble shore, amid the booming of breakers. The wind gradually increased in fury: the air was full of the noise of its own passing, of the roaring with which it shattered itself against the hills. The trees creaked and groaned, boughs and hedges whispered and chattered, to everything a tongue was given with which to sing the might of the great wind or moan its frenzy.

Robert mourned, lost himself in reverie, in his land of erstwhile dreams, a blind search for human support. The fire collapsed with a crash; the tapestries billowed a little in a stray draught that had crept into the room and could not escape.

Oh! Alberada...

Aeons later, the high altar in the darkened chapel of the castle at Melfi sat in golden radiance amid the gloom, but Robert's voice was strong as it rang out, witnessed by cardinals and priests, and the lone figure of Jacques in the shadows. Then, with distaste, he kissed the trembling, swollen fingers that were heavy with great rings and not over-clean.

ROBERT AND HUMPHREY

'I can't go back to my wife - not yet! I can't face her: not until I've worked out some solution so that we can stay together.'

Miserably Robert looked at Jacques, who, as witness, had had it explained to him. Jacques stood across the room of the inn in which they were staying a few days after the crucial meeting with the Pope at Melfi. He had never seen Robert so distressed. Grave, he looked away from Robert's tortured face.

'You'll have to see her some time - to explain. Wouldn't it be better, sire, to do so quickly, before she hears from others?'

'It would be better if I found some legal loophole so that I could keep the power - and keep Alberada.'

Jacques noticed that the word 'power' preceded the name of his wife; it seemed significant. Robert and Alberada had been married five years now, five years of apparent great happiness, they were devoted to each other, but Jacques knew Robert's impatience for progress.

'Well,' Jacques reasoned, 'you can't ask anyone in the Church - that's obvious.'

'No ... yet who else knows about canonical law?'

'The Emperor? Or his advisors, at least?'

'I can't ask them, either, not at this stage.'

'What about your half-brother, Count Humphrey?'

'Humphrey - perhaps! Of course I couldn't tell him about the main thrust of my meeting with His Holiness.'

Jacques turned back to look at Robert, who now looked a little less anxious, the promise of action was calming him a little.

'Before we go on to Aversa, sire - why don't you speak to the Benedictine monks at Venosa? They're not far away.' Robert brightened, visibly.

'That's a very good idea! But I'll have to go in secret. Let's leave the men behind, so they'll assume I'm still in conference with His Holiness. It'll only take a day or so, if we ride fast.'

Apart from swearing his oath of allegiance to the Pope, Robert had extracted a promise from him that His Holiness would come to the ancient city of Venosa high up in the forested mountains of Apulia, and bless the family tomb that Robert had recently built within the new abbey church; Hauteville gold had paid for the whole building. Flattered, and unaware of how significant his action would be to Robert, the Pope was just about to do so. Robert, religious in his own way, was thankful and relieved.

As they rode swiftly and silently through the mountains of Apulia Robert's thoughts veered wildly between the conference with the Pope and his coming meeting with Alberada. Never had he felt so ashamed in his life. Several times his horse nearly fell; once a great branch almost swept him from his horse's back; Jacques could see the inner turmoil reflected in Robert's actions; he had never ridden so carelessly.

As they neared Venosa, memories of Drogo's death also passed through Robert's mind.

Just recently, when the church was finished, and consecrated by the local Bishop in front of many mountain people and the monks, Robert had lost no time in arranging to have Drogo's name obliterated from its place. The monks were gladdened, and he smiled briefly when he saw the empty space.

Then he established a family tomb, erected near the entrance to the church; somehow, to him, it seemed the right resting place, a dubious penance for multiple Hauteville transgressions.

First he had William's body brought from where it had formerly been buried in a small church in the town of Venosa itself, and laid it inside, then Drogo's. Eventually he planned to bury that of Humphrey, the notorious sadist, when he would die. He was not concerned with Serlo, who he hadn't seen for many years. He shed no tears for his half-brothers, nor pretended to, but, to the monks' confusion, as each body was interred, he loudly declaimed,

'Well, *that's another man, made - and dead.'*

When all was over, Robert handed over a large sum of money to the Benedictines and told the monks that he, as well, must one day be buried there, but - *laid on top of them*. And that was an order. Without a blink or murmur, they agreed.

During the service of the consecration of the church, in his innermost heart Robert determined that, once he had both the time and money, he would himself build a magnificent cathedral to the glory of God, unsullied by any sin - probably at Salerno, which he now had in his sights. Pope Nicholas' arrival to come and bless the Hauteville tomb assuaged some of his guilt: perhaps it would wipe some stain of blood from it. Most crimes he forgot at once - but never crimes against the Church. This time he had been personally involved. Even so, he felt the monks owed him a small favour.

In spite of his oath to the Pope, he spoke to the Abbot throughout two long days, explaining how desperately he needed to retain Alberada as his wife. The Abbot told him that, although they felt obliged to him, there was nothing they could do to help him: the law was exact, and they could find no loophole for him. Robert was caught in a trap of his own choosing. He would have to break the news to Alberada.

Lashed into a fury, he set out on another breakneck ride, to seek advice from ageing Humphrey at Aversa.

A week later, after the meeting at Melfi and the abortive discussion at Venosa, the colossal dog, Wolf, trotted through the door into the Hall at Aversa. He bayed once, a great, dignified, as if exiled royal creature and people moved aside. They looked surprised, knowing that Robert the Guiscard would follow if his dog came in. No announcement had been made of his imminent arrival.

There was the sound of marching feet outside as his disciplined soldiers fell to and the clang of metal as swords were unsheathed in salute, then came the clopping of horses' hooves and the sudden crystal call from a pipe. Humphrey strode to the door to welcome his unwanted guest. He had recently heard whispers, only whispers that the new Pope and Robert had set up as allies; it bode no good.

Humphrey was also ill at ease to know a story was being spread abroad about Robert's latest exploit - one that again did the Hauteville family no honour: it was over a month old and Robert had just about forgotten about it. It had been reported to Humphrey that Robert had gone out to meet an adversary, shouting out that he was prepared to discuss a peace, his men in solid ranks behind. When they met in open ground to debate a truce, Robert had reached out smiling, to clasp arms with his opponent. Towering above the surprised man, instead of the welcome suggested, Robert jerked him from his horse and dragged him through the mud to his camp. It was outrageous.

Then, with hideous precision and obvious enjoyment, he personally tore his teeth out, one by one - demands for a ransom growing higher and higher as each one was pulled from the screaming, bloody mouth. When Robert declared his intention of starting on his toe-nails the man succumbed and fainted. Without a blow exchanged, or an arrow wasted, Robert had made a handsome fortune from that one encounter.

He, himself, encouraged the retelling of the story, which seemed to him mere harmless child's play, and considered he had taught the man a well-needed lesson, adding to his legend: he wanted people to realise that nothing would stop him in his striving for power - not a great city's forces not a puny man with twenty foot soldiers, they were all grist to his mill. Humphrey felt he was too old to be taken in by his own half-brother's swindles, but - even so - he chose to be watchful.

Robert stamped into Humphrey's Hall, surrounded by his men, approached his elder brother and saluted him with gusto. All was pandemonium as hosts and guests made friendly overtures, it seemed to everyone that Robert had no intention of making trouble this time - yet was he to be feared more when in high good humour? In his turn, he looked about himself avariciously, at the high roof, the thick walls, the laden tables and the wall-hangings, comparing it to his own castle.

By happy coincidence, there was a feast arranged for that day. Robert was placed on one side of Humphrey, Jacques stolidly behind him and Wolf lying at his feet. A small group of musicians were herded to a corner of the Hall; Robert noticed that they played no Norman tunes, the music sounded, instead, as if it had started out from Constantinople. Oriental ways, thought Robert, seemed to have taken over the family - he liked it himself; not just the music, but the food and clothes were oriental at times, and so were many of the women, half-veiled in the shadows - in the Persian way.

On the other side of Humphrey at the spectacular banquet that evening sat a special guest, Sichelgaita, a Lombard lady, sister of Prince Gisulf, of the ruling family of Salerno. Robert thought again of his cathedral. Sichelgaita was a striking woman, broad, big-boned, almost six feet tall, with heavy flaxen hair in plaits and an athletic, fluid body. She had no smiles for Robert when he courteously saluted her, - 'Princess!' - But spoke the obligatory words and inclined her head. She sat, silent, with an air of withdrawn haughtiness. He was immediately reminded of a popular roundelay when he looked briefly at her, it went,

'Woman is the gate of the Devil, the path of wickedness, the sting of the serpent - in a word, a perilous object,'

Humphrey spoke in a probing way, as he carved a choice slice of meat and loaded it onto Robert's full platter.

'I was told about your victim who lost all his teeth, and now I hear you've added yet more to your coffers on your journey here by ambushing a group of wealthy merchants and extracting some heavy ransoms from them - is this true?'

'Yes, I took what I wanted - I always do - people know this now. I suppose I was in luck. But this part of the country is pitifully poor, isn't it?'

'You've only brought it on yourself, Robert, with your policies of burning as you conquer. That famine in Calabria, three poor harvests after each other, your own heavy hand on the people – no wonder that they're in a state of revolt against you .'

'I've little interest in consolidation at present, or the time for it, that must take care of itself. Perhaps when my young brother Roger arrives I can leave those matters in his charge; our father sent word that he's clear-headed, and could be useful. In the meanwhile let's just admit that I have a healthy appetite - especially for your good food!' He reached for more.

Humphrey and Robert spoke together for a while, exchanging views on affairs in the south. Each was aware how the family of brothers had used all the tricks they knew to keep Robert away from their seat of power, but now Count Humphrey, like an old lion, with Serlo, was the last of them, growing old and wary of this new, powerful contender.

Robert made no secret of his great admiration for the castle, which he voiced loudly; Humphrey saw that as a threat, which it was. He had also understood the half-concealed warning about the awaited Roger; one brother could be followed by another ... and another; there were several still left in Normandy, straining at the leash with greed, who might be plucked from Duke William of Normandy's grasp.

'I've come to you for advice, Humphrey. I had an audience with the Pope last month and he has warned me about the outcome of my marriage to Alberada. It is causing me great distress for she's a good wife to me. Do you have any knowledge on canonical law? Or has anyone in your entourage?'

Humphrey looked up in surprise. Robert's statement was very abrupt, which must mean he was deeply troubled.

'You're distant blood relations, is that it?'

'So he says. They've discussed the matter at a recent Council - the laws of consanguinity are being made more rigid. I was unaware that her mother was a remote cousin of mine in Normandy.'

'Might that mean excommunication for you both?'

'So I'm led to believe.'

'So - you're confronted with an ultimatum? Either excommunication or annulment?'

'Yes. The first ruins my plans, the second ruins my family, it's not easy to decide - the choice is grim.'

'You have a child, I believe?'

'Yes, my gigantic son Mark - no other - yet.'

'I see - that makes your decision even more bleak.'

Robert spoke under his breath,

'What do you know of canonical law? Is there any course of action open to me?'

'I can make enquiries: but Pope Nicholas is a cunning man and I very much doubt that he'd leave an open door for your escape.' His words sounded incontrovertible.

Robert's heart plummeted.

SICHELGAITA

Suddenly a dwarf, round and dimpled, rolled into view on the floor, tumbling and somersaulting, squeaking like a mouse. Wolf, startled, pulled himself up and stared at the strange sight. The dwarf darted towards him, patted a paw, and dashed away, giggling infectiously. Wolf's head was aslant, his ears pricked. The squeaking dwarf ran forward again, patted another paw and stroked his fur. Wolf rumbled a growl. The dwarf, warned, ran and danced and walked on his hands - then ran forward and patted the dog again. Wolf flopped down onto the floor, the dwarf flopped down beside him, crooning to him and running his tiny fingers through his fur.

'That's unusual!' Robert pointed to his dog.

'And unusual for my dwarf, too,' lied Sichelgaita, who had schooled him for days.

Together they watched the huge dog and the tiny dwarf, until, in triumph, the dwarf made the dog stand and jumped upon his back. For a few steps Wolf bore him there, then shrugged him off. They tumbled together on the floor, until finally the dog slumped in an untidy heap and the dwarf almost disappeared in his long and matted fur, lying back and laughing. It seemed they had made friends.

'I've never seen that before!'

Out of the noise an instrument played, and there was the Court musician making a musical ballad of it all.

'Your dog and my dwarf! They make a strange pair.'

Sichelgaita smouldered with gratification, content that her careful plans were going right. As she bent intently over her goblet of wine, an earring swung forward from amid the studied mass of her honey-coloured hair, as she intended, and flashed like a drop of falling water in the candle-lit radiance of the Hall.

Robert looked at her, long and searchingly - the size of her! The strength! And her many links with affairs of state. *How useful.* Her glinting earring went unnoticed.

'It's a pity you're a woman! I would have enjoyed a fight with you otherwise.'

She looked at him, first with amazement, then with curiosity. What an extraordinary remark to make! Yet there was no hint of rudeness, or flirtation, in his tone, so he must have meant what he said. She countered his remark in a confident voice, part-filled with laughter.

'And it's a pity you're married, I'd have enjoyed being your strong right hand!'

Because of her unrestrained laughter, Robert quickly became conventional. They uttered pleasantries for a while, until politics began to dominate their conversation; Sichelgaita proved time and time again that she was both knowledgeable and astute. Robert was impressed by her grasp of the political scene in the south, of her knowledge of military forces and where they were deployed; at times she knew far more than he did. Eventually, Robert said

'You Lombards hate us now, don't you? Your hopes for domination in the south are over, now, since the battle of Civitate? *On the wrong side?'*

'It's tragic,' said Sichelgaita, 'especially because you've betrayed our trust so often ever since Gaimar died.'

Robert laughed carelessly.

'Now we're your overlords in turn you're all sullen and discontented with us aren't you? But Norman ways won't change, you know, we're fighters through and through. Sichelgaita - I would have thought that you, of all people, could understand that?'

She nodded, suddenly serious. Robert continued, planning his course far in advance in his mind,

'Even though we have no legal ties, can't we agree upon some form of political partnership? I could certainly use your help in reconciling the Lombards and Normans. You know about my conquests and battles as well as anyone. Now I've agreed to champion the Pope - I'm in agreement with his plans.'

Sichelgaita pounced on the idea, murmuring smoothly,

'It's difficult to discuss this here. Let's meet tomorrow? I can ride to the bridge by noon. Come without your men; this is between ourselves.'

Robert nodded thoughtfully. What a strange woman, he thought, who had the height of a man, was strong and bold, and suggested meeting him, alone, to discuss politics! Most women preferred to keep away from him. How different she was from Alberada, who was soft and needed protecting and made him smile ... and ... he shut her from his thoughts. They were unbearable.

A tall man awaited Robert at the bridge next day, astride a heavy horse with unusual piebald markings. He wore leather leggings and a rough jacket, but all at once Robert noticed a gleam of yellow hair under a head covering and realised it was Sichelgaita. He greeted her with renewed interest.

'What! A man's clothing?'

'Naturally! If I came as a woman there would be talk which I don't want. Besides, how do you think I could ride astride in a gown? When I go on campaigns with my brother I always dress as a man. At other times I can assure you I'm all woman.'

She bit her lip, regretting those last words. But Robert hadn't listened to them.

'You've actually gone on campaigns with Prince Gisulf?'

'Several.'

'But not as a fighting soldier, surely?'

'Well, of course! What would be the point, otherwise? Besides, I enjoy it.'

Robert eyed her afresh. She continued, unflattered;

'But don't let's talk about him – you know how he hates you Normans – he thinks you're barbarians.'

'And so we are! And as the illegal Pope Stephen has just died, and my friend Pope Nicholas II has taken his place, I should think that your scheming brother feels he could do with a great many more friends and allies at present?' Robert glanced at Sichelgaita's face, aware she knew his purpose behind his taunting words. She replied with honesty,

'I suppose so. On the one hand we have you wretched Hautevilles overstretched across the south of Italy, both in Calabria and Apulia, with most of the people rebelling against you, so hungry that some are selling their children into slavery and others forced to make bread with weeds from the river. On the other hand there's my unfortunate brother who is struggling hard to keep you and your cursed brothers under control - after all, he is your suzerain chief. His territories of Capua, Sorrento, Amalfi and Gaeta are far less trouble to him than you Hautevilles!'

Robert countered, pleased that she disliked Humphrey,

'But your brother's own lands are fairly safe now. Salerno is a fine city; I've seen it several times. I'd like to own land there.'

'Don't you believe it,' said Sichelgaita, 'he's very hard put to keep control.'

Both had dismounted and began to lead their horses along the river bank, talking with deep concentration as they strolled. Wolf sniffed about for small game, snuffling into rabbit burrows and lapping water. Jacques, unknown to Robert, watched them both from a nearby hill-top.

Not since he had discussed his future with his father had Robert felt so at ease with a man - as he thought of her - for Sichelgaita had a dazzling grasp of statesmanship and knew better than most precisely what was happening in Italy. They talked of the new Pope, of the Emperor, of threats and raids from other warring nations, of trade and prosperity: never once did Robert think of Sichelgaita as a woman.

Sichelgaita sensed this, playing her trump cards of intrigue and political acumen, because she had long planned to have Robert for herself. She'd heard of his exploits for years, and once caught a glimpse of him. At that moment she knew that Robert should belong to her. She was tired of appearing abnormal because of her height and strength, she knew she had a fine brain and she despised most men: the others she didn't think about, or, if she did, she used them. Now, having schemed with care, she had finally met the famed Robert de Hauteville in person and she was overthrown by his magnetism.

He was inches taller than her, fluid in motion, and fast in action; that he was casually cruel and lacked any form of chivalry didn't matter to her at all - there was only one real obstacle: his marriage.

Sichelgaita rose from the soggy bank on which she had been sitting; they had been speaking for several hours and now she wanted to bring her business neatly to a close.

'To become anyone of great importance in this world you have to have the right connections. Money equates power, of course, and is all very well, *but good blood is paramount* - and makes breeding prospects better. Don't let's forget how essential it is to be well-bred; it opens up so many avenues through marriage alliances.'

She glanced up at him with a straight look, forcefully driving on,

'As I see it you must nurture your friendship with the Pope, he's essential to all your ambitions. But,' she emphasised, 'it's obvious that you'll never achieve anything important if you're excommunicated.'

Robert's face twisted momentarily. She developed her stratagem, her nostrils scenting triumph,

'I know, as well as you do, that William of Normandy has been excommunicated - and others - but they all come back into the fold in the end. What a pity that His Holiness disapproves of your marriage to Alberada - that might make a lot of trouble for you in the future: you had better resolve that matter. And quickly…'

Robert looked unseeingly across the water meadows, thinking for a long time. Then, very quietly, he said,

'Do I understand the true and deeper meaning of your words?'

He turned and looked squarely at Sichelgaita in her rough man's clothing. He saw her size, her strength, her fine brain. He also was aware of her lineage, her famous relations, her considerable wealth and her close ties with the Prince of Salerno and all his allies,

'You think my marriage should be dissolved? That my son Mark - Bohemund - should be considered a bastard? That we, you and I together, might unite the Norman and Lombard ruling families across the whole of this part of the world? *Is that what you're saying?'*

Sichelgaita tried no feminine wiles at all, she knew that any union between her and Robert would be wholly political; yet she knew her great worth to anyone hungry for status. She'd heard that he was unduly fond of Alberada, but she also sensed his saturation with ambition and his willingness to sacrifice anyone who stood in his way. Alberada, she was convinced, would never figure in their lives.

She brushed a fly from her face, nodded unsmiling, shrewdly vowing that he never would know how attracted she was to him - as long as she had him as a partner, then stipulated,

'If we married it would have to be a totally equal partnership. I would insist on being told all your plans. Unless with child I would expect to go on campaigns with you - and if you cheated me I would use all my far-reaching power to pay you in kind! This must be understood between us before we enter any pacts. I'll tolerate no double-dealing.'

Sichelgaita laughed gaily as she looked directly into Robert's cool eyes. She had his measure and was just as ruthless.

What a woman! What ferocity she had - what a reliable comrade she would make ... he couldn't bear to think of Alberada. Nor Mark. No-one, it seemed, would be able to help him remain with Alberada as husband; it was too late, the Pope had forced his hand. Yet - perhaps Alberada would agree to stay with him as concubine? After all, she had promised him his freedom.

Suddenly he brightened at the thought; said with conviction,

'Agreed!'

Mounting their horses they wheeled and rode at a spanking pace back to the castle, Wolf loping at their heels. Sichelgaita laughed to herself in triumph: two could be winners - two could be equally ambitious.

On arrival she changed her clothes and came back to find Robert in the Hall.

'We must drink a toast to our pact. It may take some time, and getting consent from my brother will be difficult - I know he'll make irksome conditions. But let's return here in six months to sign all the necessary documents and take our wedding vows? All the eyes of Europe will be on us that day - don't you agree? Together we'll conquer the south!'

They raised their wine to make their toasts; Robert was inwardly triumphant that he'd arranged this right under Humphrey's nose.

Now, with no further delay, Robert would have to face Alberada, and that was all he could think of. In spite of her magnificent clothes and remarkable jewels, her fabled lineage and promises for the future, Sichelgaita's smiling face became merely a dull, uninteresting blur.

ALBERADA

During their five years together, Alberada had concentrated entirely on her husband's comfort: she trained herself to be the most caring and considerate support to him.

Should he return to her bruised or exhausted from battle, she would have a special hot bath ready for him to lie in. Whilst he was away, she would either gather locally - or send for - hollyhock and mallow, the worts from danewort to bresswort, chamomile and heyhove, water speedwell, scabious, bugloss and wild flax - and several other flowers and leaves. She would watch his great body lying in the green-brown water, with all the pungent scent rising like a cloud above him, and then hand him a goblet of thin opium to drink. When his eyes began to droop, she would help him to their great bed and let him sleep for days until he awoke again, mended and whole.

On other occasions, she regularly massaged his body with scented olive oil, and when he was fully clothed afterwards she was pleased to see how clean his garments were, washed and bleached by the fullers until they looked like new. She looked after the castle servants, preventing quarrels and bad language, so Robert never became annoyed by raised voices. And she saw to it that when they went to bed all lamps and candles were safely extinguished and the copper *couvre-feu* covered the fire on the hearth, to be re-kindled by bellows the following morning.

She gave Robert all the food he liked the best, carrying out all the normal housewifely duties such as overseeing the salting and drying of meat and fish, and the making of sauces and preserves Robert favoured the most. When he was at home there was a wonderful pungent smell of charcoal braziers in the kitchens, and peat or wood fires in the Hall. Even when his favourite sweet food was placed before him, she arranged flowers on it, roses or violets, which were dipped in thick honey, or primroses or iris for decoration.

But, this day, looking out from the ramparts of Robert's first-built – favourite – castle, looking fondly down upon the sight of father and much smaller and adoring son, Alberada knew in her bones that something momentous had happened to Robert. Since their return from Aversa, she had a premonition that some form of disaster lurked in waiting for her. There was an ominous atmosphere; even Jacques couldn't look her in the eye.

She watched as Robert tilted Mark's chin upwards with a firm finger, seeking for something in his four-year-old face - for something that was not only the repetition and physical structure of another face, but a shadow across the years of a remembered expression. Yes! The sunny child was Hauteville through and through, but with Alberada's eyes and hair. Robert locked the sight in his emotions, mourning; his shoulders sagged. Alberada saw the gesture with a sense of shock. It looked so conclusive and despairing.

'So soon?' She asked herself. 'A brief six years - was that all?'

She suspected that her lovely idyll had ended. A wave of desolation engulfed her as she looked down at them both.

What had she done? Where had she gone wrong? She could think of no one action of hers that could have triggered off such a disaster, so it must be something beyond her control. For a few minutes she leaned against the warm stone, drawing a veil across her face, enclosing herself against misfortune, like a woman from the east.

Then, straightening her slender shoulders, she decided to face whatever critical situation awaited her. She sent word to Robert, courteously inviting him to come and speak in the cooler air; she had a chair brought for him, and, herself, sat upon a stool, below him. He looked wholly dejected.

She ran her small hand over Wolf's rough head; she, Robert and Jacques were the only people he would allow to touch him, her husband thought ... until that dwarf: Robert shivered in the sun. Alberada opened the conversation quite briskly,

'My husband, you know I love you more than any other person in the world. So - I think we'd better not waste time. You promised me honesty when we were in Brindisi, and now I ask it of you - what, exactly, has happened to upset you?'

'It's the Pope.'

He stretched his legs in front of him, wondering how to tell her everything, which words to choose. He could not meet her eyes, but looked at a curl of her hair.

'I know you've seen the Pope,' she said, calmly, yet feeling breathless with fear, 'I thought your meeting was a triumph?'

He swallowed.

'Well, as you know, I went to see him - I've told you all about that, and the promises he made about my titles and so on ... but there's something else ...'

He could not continue. She took his hand, smoothing it, and put the palm of her own small hand against his cheek.

'Go on, I'm listening.'

'It seems he's strengthened the laws of consanguinity. He's to have a Council at Melfi, to declare these new laws, but he's agreed to hold his hand until we've settled matters between us. You see,' he paused, looking away from Alberada's violet eyes to the ground with a sudden flush of shame, 'we're too closely related. Your father was one of my cousins through my mother's family. I didn't know - did you? There are so many of us! But the Pope had made enquiries and states that our marriage is uncanonical.'

'Uncanonical? What a curious word! But how does that affect us?'

'He calls our relationship 'incest', and I find that - not a curious word, but a very ugly word.'

She was offended and appalled.

'It is certainly an unpleasant word, especially if His Holiness decides to repeat it in public for his own ends, and I don't care for it either. But it simply doesn't matter, not in our private lives - does it?'

Robert was silent.

'Ah! So there's more to it than that, is there? What about that promised honesty between us? Have you so short a memory?'

His face was grimly set, his heart twisted.

'I swore that I'd always look after you, and I will. And our boy.'

'Is that the best you can do, Robert? Am I worth only half-truths?'

He told her more. After thirteen years - almost fourteen - of fighting all the way, that suddenly there was a chink of light. He told her of the lures of immense power; the threat of excommunication; the chances to get even with his brother; the riches; the titles, far higher than any Hauteville before - they were all spread in front of her like a shining sea, gloriously buoyant for him but in which she could only splash about until she drowned.

She bowed her head, this moment had always been in her thoughts since the day she had accepted him, yet promised his release. In the end she cradled his face in her hands and kissed it, saying lightly,

'So our marriage is to be annulled, is it? At least we've had almost six really happy years together!'

'In my heart I'll always be married to you.'

Her thoughts turned to realistic issues, saying,

'What will happen to us, Mark and me?'

He replied, quickly,

'I swore I'd look after you for ever. You'll stay here, of course, and I'll provide for you most handsomely - never fear.'

'Will you visit us?' She probed wistfully. 'Visit us often?'

'Try to keep me away!'

Jacques had unexpectedly arrived in their exclusive domain, delivering Mark to his parents by allowing him to ride upon his back; they were laughing together. Yet - he now stood within earshot, which was out of the ordinary for him, patiently whittling some small arrows for the boy. Clearly he could hear what they were saying. Alberada sensed something was very wrong - too many unfamiliar things were happening. Uneasily, she said,

'Robert, I don't know what it is - but I think there's more. Confess?' Artlessly, she smiled at him. Robert hedged again,

'I shall take Mark with me.'

'No!' She wailed. 'He's still a child – he's only four, and he's all I'll have left of you - he's ours, yours and mine.'

'I need my first-born with me.' He looked stony.

She wept, then; tears running down her face, eyelashes thickening into points; then put her face in her hands and sobbed, under her breath,

'Don't do this to me, Robert, I can't bear it. Not both of you at the same time.'

Robert sat still, as Alberada wept. He put his hand upon her shoulder to comfort her - he couldn't bear to watch her in tears. They sat for a long time, Robert like a monolith, Alberada shuddering with sobs.

'Oh! No - no - no, I can't bear it! If only Girard were here to help me - he wouldn't have let you do this to me.' She cried, rocking on her stool, as if abandoned. Robert looked away, his arms falling to his side.

'Sire?'

Robert looked up to see Jacques beckon him to one side. After a moment - thinking that Jacques was rescuing him from Alberada's passion - he went to stand by Jacques in gratitude, asking roughly,

'What is it?'

Jacques swallowed once.

'My lord - Mark needs his mother. It would be a pity,' he said, very quietly, 'if, at this juncture, the Pope got to hear of your brother's murder - and your part in it - wouldn't it? I doubt if the lady Sichelgaita would be gratified, either. She might change her mind about marrying you.'

Bravely he looked openly at Robert, taking the greatest risk of his life; the skin stretched tightly across the bridge of his freckled nose, as he laid a gentle, caressing hand on Mark's head. Robert, stunned, stared at Jacques. It was flawless blackmail. He chose not to speak; to voice his thoughts would give them credence. He lifted he hand to strike Jacques, but again Alberada called out,

'No! Robert - what has Jacques done?'

Dumbfounded, Robert lowered his mighty fist, motioned Jacques and Mark away and knew himself finally beaten. Gruffly, he muttered,

'You'd better keep Mark, then, until he's grown.'

She stared at him in astonishment. What had Jacques said to him? If she had been less tormented she would have questioned Robert further; instead, she threw her arms about his neck. Robert muttered,

'Oh! This is hopeless. I can't keep secrets from you; I'll have to tell you everything.'

She shrank back in horror; what more was to come?

'So - tell me, if you please.'

Looking away, over the castle's walls, he spoke as if to the hills and the woods, wishing they could cover him up and spare him from Alberada's tear-washed eyes.

'I'm to be married - that's the core of it.'

She blanched, incredulous, steadying herself by putting her hand against the wall.

'I can't believe it! To whom?'

Robert replied, unemotionally,

'Oh! She's the lady Sichelgaita, the sister to Prince Gisulf of Salerno - have you heard of her?'

'I think so ... isn't she a giantess?'

'Yes. I'm only marrying her because then we can take the rest of Calabria and Apulia. Then, somehow - somehow! I'll contrive to take Sicily.'

Stung with jealousy, she hissed,

'And you wanted my son - our son - to give to her?'

'No - no! I wanted Mark with me so that I'd have something of you always close to me.'

Robert looked ashen; the misunderstanding had shaken him deeply.

'It'll be so difficult for me for a while, for Sichelgaita's brother will hold a heavy hand over me - already he's insisted that I bring our more exasperating allies to heel, so I've been asked to discipline them. It's his condition for the marriage; then it can go ahead. Not until then can we really be allies. His alliance is crucial to my future.'

'And - what about my future?' thought Alberada, but said nothing.

Robert looked miserable, then, reaching for her hand said, with his face in Alberada's shoulder,

'Christ! How I'm hating this! The Pope will annul our marriage after I write and tell him you're agreeable.'

'First - tell me what does Sichelgaita look like?'

'Tall, strong, healthy - like a soldier.'

'And as a woman?'

'A woman? Gracious God, how can anyone think of her as a woman? Not I! There'll never be any other love in my life except you'

'Poor soul,' said Alberada, 'how she may suffer. Yet it's no consolation to me. Now, tell me what you intend for us? May we stay here, where you and I have been so happy - for so short a time? Is it still our home - yours, Mark's and mine?'

'Yes, yes. I've already told you that's arranged. I said I would always look after you, and I will - I've made my pledge; this will always be our home. And, Alberada, you will always be the core of my heart. May I visit you at times? And make love to you again and again?'

'Often, my love. Oh! Often!'

Suddenly, she wept afresh.

Then he lifted her slight form into his arms, and they sat entwined, silent, as the evening sky darkened and the birds quietened and were still.

ROGER AT AVERSA

Roger stood in a patch of shade at the side of the town's central square: Pierre his silent shadow. At last he had arrived at Aversa after a very long and hungry journey from his home, there had been many unforeseen delays, and he was keen to join his brother Robert.

He had travelled as far as Rome with some of the young Duppa de Uphaugh family, with whom he'd grown up, but they were messengers for William of Normandy and had left him, hoping to have an audience with the Pope. The journey out had been harsh - once they had been attacked, and there was much sickness - but he was with trustworthy companions, which made it all more pleasant. Even so, he was aware that he had left his youth behind during the experience and many of his illusions. There wasn't an ounce of spare fat on his lanky body.

He went to drink from the clear cord of water trickling from the fountain jaws of a lion's head, green now with mildew and mosses. Behind him, as he strolled forward, a cloud of dingy sparrows drifted to the ground, like leaves, from all quarters: they followed hopping in his footsteps, just as leaves travel briskly and jerkily before a puff of wind.

Aversa was Hauteville territory, but, before he took his final step and walked through those castle gates he felt he had wanted to sound out everyday opinions; Tancred had impressed upon him to be ever vigilant. The city was teeming with people, many of them clearly of Norman origin. Some of them looked with curiosity at him when he arrived, sensing that in spite of his appearance of poverty, with his height, he might be yet another relation of Humphrey's and Robert's. But they were careful not to enquire.

He turned to a group of bystanders,

'Robert de Hauteville? Does anyone here know him, - or are in his service?'

Some of the men about him drew aside, afraid, but a small wizened man with only one huge tooth cackled delightedly.

'The Guiscard? How could we forget him? He's our Count Humphrey's brother.'

Roger pressed on,

'What's his reputation? I've been travelling for many months, so I know very little about him.'

The little man shifted his feet in a dancing movement in front of him, eyes darting about him, gleefully playing to a gathering audience.

'The great warrior, Robert Guiscard? Isn't he the brightest star to come into our heavens for many a year?'

His friends about him murmured like angry bees.

'Isn't he destined to govern a kingdom - this friend of His Holiness?' The friends muttered and sighed in despair.

'The bets are on him in this city ... because our cruel Count Humphrey grows older and we doubt if he'll hold his own much longer. Robert's already had three major battles behind him and half the land is in his pocket already.'

The exasperated friends spat or held up one finger as an insult.

'But – is he liked?' Roger still had a faint thread of hope.

'What? *Liked?* Do you know of *any* overlord who's liked as a man? Can you care for a snake? Would you fondle a scorpion? He wouldn't be so successful if anybody liked him.' He cackled again.

'Is that all? I heard he was a great man - in Normandy he was popular.'

'Is he now? As citizens of Aversa we admire him, of course. Yes, we admire him, for he's done some extraordinary deeds. I suppose he's a great man - what do you others think?'

He appealed to the crowd, who backed away, muttering under their breath, then continued,

'Physically he's a giant so he's unafraid of anyone in the world. And he's mad with ambition and he'll do anything - anything! - for money!'

The little man sounded bitter, as he pulled out an empty purse and allowed the dust from it to fly in the breeze.

'But he's a bad man, a very bad man - he's a man without honour: he can't have any true friends, even though he's signed treaties with the Pope and others, for no-one would trust him a hand's breadth ... not if they've any sense.'

Roger turned away sadly, realising that most of the dishonourable stories must be true, the loathsome reputation that had spread as far as Normandy had been earned. Pale faces swam expectantly towards him from the crowd, realising that he, too, must have some connection with the Hautevilles. But, as you may see fishes do around bait in dim water, each one checked suddenly and swam away with a face expressing piscine distaste. Roger imagined that the barbs of a hook must protrude somewhere from his person. He made up his mind that he must be doubly careful, saying to Pierre,

'You hear what they say? You've never met my brother, so take heed of what you hear and see today. Whether my brother and I will remain friends is in the balance. I'll have to prove myself to him first, I expect, but I must take care not to become a threat. So - I take your loyalty to me for granted, Pierre, as you're a man of religion and you've sworn an oath to me with your hand on the Gospels, but, be warned - watch your back!'

'Tsk, tsk,' Said Pierre, his nose in the air. Roger glanced at him in warning, but couldn't resist an inward chuckle.

Pierre was a slender, uneasy man, with a narrow melancholy face. He had a disconcerting method of conversation - looking at a fire, or a tree, as he spoke, appearing to pontificate rather than address his companion.

'I don't like …' he started, and subsided before Roger's glance.

'No,' said Roger quickly, 'you don't like anything much! Today's a great day, so if you continue to complain I shall think that you're weary of serving me.'

Pierre looked away, and the edges of his mouth turned down.

Standing in the shade, and wiping the water from his mouth, Roger was reluctant to go immediately to the castle to meet Robert face to face: besides, it looked a though there was to be significant action out here in the square today. He was uncertain what to do if his eldest brother didn't approve of him, for then he would be on his own and friendless, and Robert would make a very bad enemy. Yet, he brightened; surely Robert wouldn't treat him badly after sending for him - would he? He remembered that you could never be sure with Robert; thinking that, now he was so powerful, he might be even trickier to deal with. Nor, he felt ruefully, could he go back home with his tail between his legs. If he had neither money nor position, then there would be no chance of claiming Judith for his own.

There was an immediate stirring in the crowd as some soldiers came riding into the square in formation, the sun glinting on pieces of armour: they weren't equipped for formal battle, but they displayed all the aggression they could muster just the same. Behind came foot-soldiers, and then some soldiers who carried huge banners of various colours on long poles.

Finally, at the head of another, much larger, group of fighting men, came Robert, huge in his oversized saddle - gold ornaments glinting on his gigantic stirrups. Roger's heart leapt at the resplendent sight of his hero-brother, magnificently dressed, displaying a heavy gold chain across his shoulders as he confidently lounged on his great charger. He drew up in the centre of the square, the men in formation around him.

It was an enormously impressive sight. They seemed to be waiting for someone.

The men and women who had gathered in the square patiently went on waiting and watching: surely all of Aversa was now in one place? Whatever was to happen, thought Roger, would be momentous! Today's events were one of the most exciting things to happen for months and months, and the citizens would go on recounting everything for years ahead. Except at very rare intervals, the troubled affairs of the country never entered their minds - still less could they control them. But, today, it was all being acted out in their very midst.

Roger and Pierre listened to some fat old women, who sat gossiping by humble merchandise for sale - scrawny chickens, little bundles of vegetables, or tiny portions of goats' cheese wrapped in bladders; they could understand a part of what the people said, but not all. In every city of the world the sight was familiar, as the women, young and old, relayed the tales of a passing peddler, repeating over and over again what he had said, and embellished it with their own versions until there was scarcely anything left of the original. Today, the ballad-makers were on tiptoe with anticipation - today there would be something new to sing about. One small girl detached herself from her sluttish mother and stood staring at Roger, bemused by his height, her dark eyes round and lovely on either side of a pinched nose, with a scarlet drip-line running from it to the open upper lip.

Roger noticed that most of the men were pressed against the walls of the castle, which was made from stone, or against the wooden walls of the tiny houses and huts which were built at the bottom of those walls, to keep out of the way of kicking hooves or a mailed fist. Roger moved to join them, Pierre a few steps away.

In the milling crowds, which grew larger by the minute, a man with sweetmeats pushed past, selling his wares; another sold nuts and several men were there with wine skins or fruit. By the fountain stood a lady of some standing, her fat baby guzzling and nuzzling against her fat wet-nurse, whilst she looked pointedly the other way. The sun beat down on them all out of a cornflower blue sky, and birds sat on the ledges of the buildings, cooing, and stepping delicately amongst their own droppings.

Roger gradually became aware of the sense of all the whispering around him, for everyone gestured as they spoke,

'They say there's to be a marriage here today!'

'No, no, you're wrong; the Guiscard is to have some awful prisoners killed - dangerous men: look at all his soldiers and their armour!'

'How could that be? Their swords aren't drawn and he's not in armour himself.'

'Besides, there's no executioner, no fire has been built, and they're all arranged in formation.'

'I tell you, it's a wedding!'

'But who could be the bride?'

'Come to that - who the bridegroom? Count Humphrey's a widower now, and there's plenty of juice in him still, I wager!'

'No, if the Guiscard is dressed so richly it could only be an envoy of His Holiness.'

Roger remained motionless in his isolation. He was intensely hungry and longed for food.

A man carrying a tray of bread laughed,

'Well, whoever it is - it's good for trade this fine day.'

Roger, very tall and very thin, continued to watch his brother and his impressive band of men. A goat trod on his foot, he wiped sweat from his eyes. Then he sensed a hand stealthily feeling amongst his clothes, trying to steal his money - and he smiled grimly to himself, for there was none left. The only thing of value he had was the cross around his neck, now hidden. He stepped back suddenly, ground his heel on a man's instep and crashed his thin elbow into the fellow's stomach. The man screamed, Roger turned, twisted the hopeful thief around lazily and, placing a hand under his wobbling chin, hit him precisely on the jaw. The man fell like a stone; Roger's timing had been immaculate.

'I don't care for thieves. Tell him when he wakes!'

Pierre chirruped to himself, fussily,

'Such impudence,' he muttered, 'to try and rob an Hauteville!'

The sudden movement and noise came to the attention of Robert, who looked across the square and saw a tall, thin, brown young man standing out amongst the crowd, with another man at his feet, unconscious, and someone, who was obviously his servant, alertly standing back to back in defence of his young brother. Immediately he rode across, Wolf jumping up besides him and placing his great paws on Roger's shoulders, and Jacques, grinning broadly, fell in a few steps behind.

'Roger! Good man! So you're here at last.'

'Yes, sir, it's me right enough - but what seems to be happening? I've only just arrived.'

'It's my wedding day!'

'How auspicious! I wish you happiness - but ... I thought you were already married?'

'I can't stop now, my bride is about to arrive for the ceremonies. Come to the castle, Jacques will care for you - I shall be too busy. But perhaps we can talk tomorrow? You must tell me all your news, too!'

With a grand wave Robert wheeled about just as a colourful group of people noisily came in procession into the square. The crowd heaved forward, like corn in the wind.

'Poor Robert,' sympathised Roger, 'his wife must have died. How quick he's been to take another. I wonder who she is.'

Peering through the crowds, aided by his height, Roger saw that all the brilliantly dressed people were escorting an important lady seated in a palanquin. As they drew nearer, Roger noticed that her skin was the flushed warm white of a moonstone, and her eyes glinted green.

She was very richly dressed in brocade, wrapped in a loose gown of green and silver, with a scarf as fine as sea-foam hiding her shoulders. Her thick gold hair was caught up in a jewelled net, and, so Roger saw, when she came close to Robert, she stretched in voluptuous luxury - but Robert had turned away momentarily and was counting her attendant men-at-arms. She smiled intimately up at him, then yawned, and her teeth showed against the red of her lips as white as those of a puppy - yet Robert hardly glanced at her. Her face clouded. But, just in time, he bowed before her, with utmost ceremony, and his soldiers stood straight as arrows - and looked as deadly.

She had a spectacular court with her, women clothed in brilliant silks, sent from Sicily, wearing garments of great variety. After them, and inserted in the procession before her small army, were attendant servants and a capering dwarf - who tried to ride the palanquin with her. She shoved him off, and immediately Roger became aware of her great size: seated, you could not see her height.

'Well,' he thought, 'she'll be a worthy mate for Robert!'

Soldier after soldier now wheeled about her; Roger had a quick and uncomfortable feeling that all the show in front of them masked hidden and competitive power, rather than partnership.

Suddenly a yellow banner was thrown into the sky, twirling crazily as it rose and fell, followed by another of blue and then one of red. Soon about twenty were shooting up skywards, their carriers forming a rough circle; tiny bells were fixed to the banners, sewn along the edges, which sent out a noise like a thousand birds cheeping at dusk.

A kettle drum took up a beat, and then another, and the banners were hurled upwards in concert, and caught when they fell with deft movements to prevent them slipping into the dust. To begin with each banner-carrier threw his own up high into the air, catching it himself, waiting for the leader to signal the next throw. Then the rhythm grew faster, and, at a shout, each man threw across to his neighbour, catching the new colour as it fluttered fast to the earth.

Robert's horse began skittering sideways across the square, clearly impatient, as he waited for the welcoming performance to be appreciated by Sichelgaita. As if a signal had been given, and just as quickly as it had begun, the banners were caught one last time and swiftly furled. The watching crowd howled their approval, and the throwers bowed gravely to the wedding party and to their friends in the crowd.

Robert athletically dismounted to greet his bride and her party; Roger saw at once that he had guessed right, the descending bride was very tall, coming up, with her hair so intricately arranged in its jewelled net, almost to Robert's steely mouth.

All at once several people took up a tune on their pipes, the young in the crowd began to dance and skip, the older ones looked on with knowing patience, beating time with their fingers on their knees. The dancers and musicians took their places on either side of the wedding group as the multifaceted crowd slowly moved from the square towards the large church, the soldiers forming a guarded path to the entrance. Roger followed in their wake with Pierre.

'So, we've arrived to witness a pretty important event it seems - although I wonder what's happened to Robert's first wife. I wonder how she died. Ah well, we'll find out in time, I dare say. I wish to God it was my own wedding day! Anyway, we'll eat well tonight I'm sure, and about time, too.'

'The food won't be good,' grumbled Pierre, 'it'll be filled with queer spices and funny tastes ...'

'If you think your squeaks of protest are going to make any difference, you are sadly mistaken - you ungrateful wretch!'

'No, sir, I tell you - now we've arrived I can't make up my mind if we're in the lands around the Western Pope or in Constantinople.'

'Oh! Stop it! You've never even been to Constantinople! Just be glad we'll be able to wash and eat our fill,' returned Roger, 'and look at all those pretty girls!'

'Humph,' muttered Pierre, 'most of them look like trollops - not good Christian women.'

'You should have stayed at Mont Saint Michel, with your own family,' barked Roger, impatiently, elbowing his way through the crowd to take a place in Robert's wake, 'and, even then, you'd not be satisfied, I wager. Come along, now - we've a part to play.'

Ostentatiously, Pierre crossed himself, and Roger hid another smile.

JUDITH

As Roger joined Robert in the magnificent wedding celebrations at Aversa, Judith was entering a new phase of her life too. Roger marched boldly forward into starshine as Judith trailed into the dusk.

Her journey was soon to be at an end, and safe haven was in sight, her brother Odo's familiar convent loomed up before her against the midnight sky, and the bell that Bertha pulled jangled harshly, as if angry at being disturbed. Judith waited, her hood pulled across her face. She was exhausted, more from nervous strain than anything else; the surveillance of her father's men taxed her, but she had chosen her route through the night with care and there had been no confrontation.

Some while later she made Bertha ring the bell again: the nuns must have been at prayer. When she had been staying at the widow's miserable hut she had asked why so many nails had been knocked into the wooden framework of her door, and had it explained to her by the lively Bertha that they were there to interrupt a witch's progress. The doorway itself looked on to the small stream, and Bertha told her that water, too was an interrupter - witches can't cross running water either. Although she faced a holy convent's door, Judith was intrigued to discover heavy iron nails rammed home into this door, too, and the whole monastery complex was surrounded by water: clearly no-one was taking any chances.

After another long wait, she and Bertha could hear footsteps grow closer. A little panel in the door slid back and, in the moonlight, Judith could just see a face, plump as a dove, with moist lips, which peered at her through the iron grille. If it had not been the door of a convent Judith would have thought it was a man's face - so strong was the beard which sprouted from the wrinkled chin.

Judith took a ring from her thumb and asked her to take it to the Mother Superior; it took some time to make her understand that she wanted someone in authority - as the old nun kept shaking her head and telling Judith to go away. At last she agreed.

Some time passed, Judith continued to hide her face, looking at the heavy stone walls, creeper covered; she was thinking of the last time she had ventured there in state, to attend Fressenda's sad funeral - partly on Roger's behalf. She missed her sympathetic presence bitterly.

The old nun finally opened the heavy door, beckoned, then led them along a deserted cloister surrounding the shadowy herb garden. Their horses were tied by the outer door, and the flagstones inside were cold to their feet. Judith felt alien and alone, in spite of the convent's familiarity.

The waiting Mother Superior was very old and stately: there was a calm and serenity about her such as Judith had never seen before. Whilst they made their greetings she told the nun to leave. Bertha was told to leave, too, and went to stand impatiently outside the door. Smiling, she said,

'You can take off your disguise, my lady Judith, you know that no-one will harm you on these premises. After all, you're a familiar visitor here, considering the times you came to visit the lady Fressenda in the Guest House before her death. Tell me what brings you this time? And why don't you want to be recognised? Is it because you escaped from Evreux?'

Judith obediently told her about her father, and about his careful plans for the impending marriage. It was pointless to lie. But she didn't mention the exact locality of the widow's hut, and the Mother Superior agreed it would be best she didn't know. Then she told her about Roger, and her terrible dilemma.

The Abbess seemed to understand and listened very patiently, once exclaiming,

'My poor child!'

As Judith described her love for Roger, she murmured,

'More than forty years ago, I loved a man.'

And when Judith spoke of her father, her eyes looked towards the window as she reminisced,

'I was nearly Normandy's bride, myself, but that was at a different generation.'

When Judith had completed her story she enquired,

'You came here because of your brother Odo, didn't you?'

'Yes, Mother, partly. Also because of the lady Fressenda; I knew you had been so kind to her - and others - and she was contented here'

'But - do you think your brother, our Abbot, would take your part against his father? You see, I don't think your father would agree that you're married *in the eyes of the law*, and he'd make you renounce your vows to Roger de Hauteville. He sent his men to search this convent almost from the start, and it was an unpleasant time - I shouldn't like it to happen again.'

'Does Odo have to know that I'm here?'

'Naturally! We may be separate entities, this convent and the monastery, but I'm afraid you're too important to keep silent about. However, you're very fortunate; he's away at the Council of Rouen. I believe your Father is there too, isn't he?'

Judith had heard of the possibility, through gossip picked up by Bertha's old aunt in the market-place, but didn't know for certain.

The Abbess continued,

'I don't know how long it will be until Abbot Odo de Grantmesnil returns. It appears that, in spite of the conference, the Pope's Legate was himself called away to Lombardy after it began. It may be months

- even years! Obviously I'll take you in until the storm breaks over my head!'

'I don't mean to make trouble for you.' Judith flushed and pent-up tears flooded her eyes.

A steely look came into the Abbess' own.

'Even after all these years I don't think anyone would touch me - a Montgomery. I'm still a power in this land.'

'I've come to take my vows.' Judith's tired face was awash with tears of exhaustion and nervous strain. 'If I don't, my father will either marry me off or kill me for defying him.'

Not knowing the complicated procedures within individual convents, for many had differing rules, Judith had been prepared to drop to her knees there and then.

'Good Heavens – *no*! You can't do that without endless preparation and thought. But I understand your concern. For the immediate present you may remain as my personal guest - but, for your safety and anonymity, you'll wear a habit, and sleep in a nun's cell, as if you were visiting from another convent. Keep to your cell; in a nun's habit no-one will suspect who you are.'

Judith sighed with relief. The elderly Abbess went on,

'You may keep your servant too; she can take the horses to the monastery stables, and then join the other servants here: tell her to keep silent!'

Judith wondered how anyone could keep Bertha from blabbing and gossiping, but determined to be stern and threaten her with fearful descriptions of her father's wrath if they were caught. The Mother Superior continued, quietly,

'During meals I want you to speak, if you must, in a low tone. In this convent we don't have the rule of silence, nor do we use a system of signs when you want food: I find the dumb pandemonium at some convents' dinner tables more mirth-provoking than speech, so I forbid it here. Until this day you've been a visitor to the rooms of the honoured guests, or the orphanage, or the hospital - but you've never met the ordinary nuns in the convent, so they don't know you; guard your tongue.'

With surprise, Judith realised that she was right.

'Then I'll be safe ...' she said.

'Not entirely,' said the kindly Abbess, 'you'll be safe enough once you have that disguise and a new name. It will be months before you take all your vows - if you ever do! In the meanwhile I can arrange some official protection right away.'

Judith fell to her knees, white as a ghost.

'My thanks - my thanks ...'

The Abbess gave a throaty chuckle.

'Well, my child, by the look of you - perhaps your new name should be 'Humiliata'!'

Once Bertha had been dispatched, with dire warning, Judith was taken, secretly and silently, to the storeroom. Here she was given an off-white habit of coarse wool, two undershifts, very harsh to the skin, a rope girdle, and a wooden rosary. She was shown how to tie the stiff coif with which her hair had to be covered except when she was alone. With a wry smile the Abbess then led her to a remote cell.

The cells opened off either side of a dark passage; each door had a heavy iron lock and a little panel which slid back from the outside. Judith's cell was very small, one side taken up by a plank bed which had no pallet, just a sole covering of coarse fabric. The high window was covered with a grating; there was a simple black crucifix over the bed and a three-legged stool. The Abbess left her then, as the first whispers of the dawn began to break far away over the hills and nearby birds heralded its awakening. In spite of the lack of comfort, Judith pitched onto the hard bed and was asleep within seconds.

Between Nones and Vespers the next day the Mother Superior and Judith met again in the Abbess' room. It was furnished with two massive carved chairs, some plain stools and a long table: woven hangings covered one wall; there were gilt leather cushions and matching window seats, and a generous sprinkling of lavender flowers lay underfoot.

Both women held silver goblets filled with deep red wine in their hands and they toasted their toes at a crackling log fire. Judith was at her ease, rested and fed; the familiar wealth in the room was an enormous relief after the previous year's dire poverty and discomfort. She felt in limbo.

'I have the impression,' said the Abbess gently, 'that you don't know very much about this monastery?'

'I feel ashamed - but you're right.'

'Well, why should you? After all, Odo is years older than you, and he built and endowed it quite a long time ago.'

Judith seemed perplexed.

'I didn't know he was a religious man, is he supposed to be?'

'No, he's not - and he doesn't have to be, my dear, so long as he's got the money! There's no disgrace in that, it's within our laws. He's an Abbot, after all, not a consecrated Bishop. There's a very big difference.'

'I see.' said Judith, dubiously.

'I doubt if you do! Let me try and explain.'

The Mother Superior helped herself to some salted nuts in a silver dish.

'Think of it this way: first of all, by endowing this monastery and its nunnery, Odo has obviously reserved for himself a fine place in heaven ...' she twinkled, as she looked across at the girl opposite; then went on,

'In the meanwhile, whilst in this world, Odo has provided for many, as well as developing a fresh centre for Christian culture. Added to that, he has a thriving financial business here, in the centre of his own land. He's built sturdy stone buildings - stone, mark you! Not flimsy wooden ones, these will last for many years. And, from the land around and the work of the monks and nuns, he receives a splendid income.'

She stopped, to sip more wine and went on with her explanation.

'There's a place for everyone, you know. Abbot Odo has his diplomatic work outside the monastery for the Pope, and he goes hunting and also makes his gastronomic tours - as well as overseeing the important functions of this monastery; whilst the monks do their own special work here, as well as exacting the rents or tributes for him from all his serfs and vassals in the adjacent villages.'

She nibbled another nut and continued,

'Landowners like Odo and your father accrue money from several sources - rents from land or from houses, perquisites from fairs and mills and woods, sale of farm produce and payments from boarders in both the monastery and the convent. Each nun and monk, in turn, has personally donated large sums to the Order: we see to that, Odo and I, we're very selective who we take in.'

She pursed her mouth, thinking back over some of her more difficult choices. Judith was surprised, and said,

'You, personally, choose the nuns? Can't they choose where to go themselves?'

'No, they can't!' snapped the Abbess. 'I'm very particular - I prefer to concentrate on aristocrats in this convent - and preferably literate ones at that - although they do tend to be indolent. Their servants do the menial tasks. That provides work and shelter for even more people.'

Interested, Judith enquired,

'And the Order? Under what rule are you disciplined?'

'At present we owe allegiance to no other body, we've made our own regulations - but, one day, when both Odo and I are dead, the convent may join with the Cluniacs.'

'What about the monks? Do they work harder than the nuns?'

'Yes, in some ways, the monks do work conscientiously, I admit. In the main they oversee the local peasant farmers, and give much-needed manual work; the payment for the peasants is made up partly of money and partly of food.'

Pointing to the wine they drank the Mother Superior said,

'I don't suppose you've ever seen the vineyards over the hill? No? Nor noticed the sheep and calves around us? Yet you've drunk some milk. And haven't you ever looked at our tilled fields and neat copses on your visits here?'

Judith became more and more uncomfortable; in her past isolation, she'd rarely thought or looked beyond herself. The older woman continued,

'Well, at least you must have heard the humming bees and seen the many flowers from which they take their pollen? The monks in charge of our honey work very hard!'

'But - madam - Mother - I thought the monks only came to monasteries because of their faith?'

'Some do. Yet there are scholars here who work in our archives and library, and artists, too, who paint our breviaries and Books of Hours. Some of these we sell to rich people or wealthy religious houses. To others we sell the wheat and timber, honey and fruit - or we grind flour for most of the area around here in our windmills and water-mills ... '

'But,' Judith persisted, 'isn't the monks' *faith* of paramount importance?'

'Yes, of course! But faith is experienced! The monks have an attitude of reverence, reticence and love, rather than theory or theology, and no-one has come here to suffer! We're monks and nuns, not martyrs!'

'How true - almost everyone looks contented here. I suppose that's why I like it.' Judith smiled. The Abbess continued her explanation,

'Think of these great buildings, Judith, and all the people in them, as if you were looking at a honeycomb. In each section there are worker bees following different occupations, yet the whole - the comb- is held together by a common faith.'

Judith held her head aslant, listening attentively.

'However, faith apart, the most important thing in a monastic house is the liturgy. Much of our waking hours have to be spent singing in the choir - speaking the praise of our Lord, mulling over devotional literature or engaged in private prayer.'

'There doesn't seem much time for sleep!' said Judith demurely.

'Sometimes there isn't.' said the Abbess, wearily. 'But I have the power to excuse a nun her duties for an endless number of reasons.' She leaned back against her chair and rested. Some little while later she resumed,

'I don't believe you realise as yet how often we're at prayer? Matins at two in the morning, then Prime at daybreak, around six o'clock. After breakfast we have Masses at nine and again at eleven. Lunch is at noontide, followed by Nones at two in the afternoon. Vespers is at four, supper at six, and the last service of the day, Compline, is at seven. We don't aim to waste much time, because we're at work all the hours in between, apart from our sleep between Compline and Matins. And then certain people speak of the 'monotony of the cloister'!'

Judith, herself, was lost in thought for quite a long time, comparing her precious leisured and self-indulgent life at the castle, followed by the boredom and utter monotony of the widow's shack, to the life of a nun.

'What's the purpose of your strict routine?'

'Why, my dear, it's simple; to learn humility, obedience and prayerfulness - in other words - holiness. That way we get to heaven.'

'It seems a hard way to live ...'

'Nonsense!' the Abbess spat out the word. 'We nuns didn't *escape* here - we haven't rejected life. *We chose it!'*

Judith put down her wine and picked up a plum, which she ate delicately, like a bird.

Judith thought back over her brief - egocentric - life and what she had done with her time. Mostly, she realised, she had busied herself in the pursuit of fashion, so she could always appear the most modishly dressed at court on feast days and holidays. New Year, Twelfth Night, the May Games - were all highlights in the castle's calendar. The Feast of Saint Nicholas was an especially festive time, when they could expect the 'thriftless, shiftless player-folk' to enliven their days. Then she would sit by the Count's side, and the court would murmur their admiration over her clothes. Normally, she remained silent, but everyone noticed her shining eyes. Christmas, and the saints' days around that period, were relatively religious, and they all answered the priests' call; holidays were more light-hearted.

Occasionally, she went out hunting and hawking, when her father invited her to accompany him, but when there was dancing or gaming at tables she generally stayed aloof: her father kept a very close watch over whom she spoke to, with whom she gossiped. Her pet dogs, all tiny creatures, gave her the most comfort and joy, and she had had some of them painted into the borders of her Book of Hours.

So her clothing and its accessories took much of her life. In order to while away the time, as she daydreamed of Roger, she also spent many hours embroidering silken purses and tassels, cushions and belts for herself. Now she was dressed in a scratchy habit and was bewildered by her change of circumstances; she felt like an actor in a play.

'You never thought to marry?' She enquired, politely, speaking as a social equal.

'I was an extremely rich heiress, Judith: You know, full well, my lineage as a Montgomery. I was accustomed to directing my own affairs in relative freedom and I knew I wouldn't take kindly to the constraints of being governed by a man. So, I kept my freedom, kept my own money, and agreed to become Mother Superior and Abbess here.'

'But - what about love?'

'Pish - sentimental rubbish! Love is pure, it's what we offer God, and quite another thing from marriage,' said the Abbess, crisply, 'they've got little to do with each other. Perhaps you're thinking of lust?'

Judith coloured.

The Mother Superior put down her goblet and looked piercingly at her.

'As your father has a fine library, can you read Latin and Greek?'

'I can, Mother.'

'And can you write them, as well as read?'

'Not as well, Mother, but passably. I find Greek more difficult.'

'Good,' said the Mother Superior briskly, 'you're just what Sister Sophia's been waiting for.'

A bell tolled. They both rose to their feet. The elderly nun touched Judith's arm,

'I'll explain what I mean after Compline tonight.'

They walked demurely off to the chapel, Judith trailing behind her protector, perplexed and uncertain. Yet soon the peace that wrapped itself around the convent like a cloak enveloped her and she was stilled.

JUDITH AND SISTER SOPHIA

Sister Sophia was busy making a list,

'Rose, mustard, fennel, rosemary, sage, mint, pennyroyal and lily.'

She ticked off the items as she counted the jars.

'Peony, balsam, yarrow and wolf's teazle. They're all here.'

Judith looked up from her bench.

'Then we'll have to buy the others?'

'Yes! We will - make another list! I'll have to send away for ginger and cinnamon, aniseed, cassis, cloves, liquorice, olive oil and scammery. We can make our own vinegar.'

Judith was sent scurrying off to fetch more pots and jars; Sister Sophia, sworn to secrecy, would trust no-one else now that Judith was here. In the past Sister Sophia had been colourless, having a pale face with shadows under the eyes and faint grey lines that curved with the curve of the wings of her nostrils; it was a mournful face, but with dreaming eyes - and a smile, rarely seen, which lit up like a light. Now she seemed to smile all the time and the lines ran upwards towards the line of her coif. She turned back to her Herbal, looking at the illustrations, then reading out loud some descriptions,

'Comfrey is produced on moors and on fields and also on meadows - but there's none nearer than Saint Lô - we must make a note of that. And 'groundsel is produced on roofs and about walls', luckily we have plenty here, but we've run out of the powdered variety, which we ground up during the season. Oh Judith! Having you here - to help me like this - means I can really make time to study - thanks be to God'

Fingering it Judith said,

'I've never examined a Herbal before, although I believe my father has several.'

'Well, I shouldn't wonder...being who you are. And you've not read a leech-book either, I dare say?'

She pushed a heavy manuscript towards Judith, saying fearfully,

'You'll take care of it, won't you? It's such a precious document.'

Judith hardly dared to open it. In the past she had used her family's library of about two hundred books without a thought. Alone, and friendless, she had spent many of her hours reading the books in the library – all entirely handwritten - and had virtually schooled herself; but she had never considered the books' rarity or cost. Here, in front of an anxious pharmacist, she balked at turning a page. Sister Sophia explained, prodding Judith's arm in her enthusiasm,

'You see, it's written in two parts. The first part deals with the outside of the body, from top to toes; the second part writes of internal maladies.' She pulled forward another, smaller, document. 'Then we have this Book of Wounds - but, sad to say, that's a trifle old-fashioned now. And - apart from the Herbal, for medicines, salves, ointments, plasters and normal treatment, I generally refer to our equally precious copy of Galen's book. Our Mother Superior brought that with her when she came. It's invaluable.'

Judith was overcome by the nun's scholarship, her expertise had no boundaries. She watched as Sophia moved across to a pestle and mortar in another part of the large room, and pounded at some green mixture inside that she had been working on all morning, adding dried bark, and saying under her breath,

'I mustn't forget my other list for the gardening nuns to plant ... now - that's celandine and wood lettuce, agrimony, yarrow, lemon verbena and dill - and I mustn't leave out the saxifrage and parsley - add them, Judith, dear child, add those, together with southernwood. If only ...'

'If only?' Judith repeated, poised above the growing list.

'If only I could get hold of some betony! They say 'sell your coat and buy betony' - but that's out of our reach, I'm afraid. It's wonderful when curing eye diseases.'

On the one hand Judith was trying to make the lists for Sophia, yet on the other she was attempting to strain what looked like curds into a row of little pots. The walls were lined with shelves, and on them, ranged in orderly precision, were pottery jars lettered in Latin, a row of pestles and mortars, little sacks of seeds, and bundles of twigs tied up with thread. Outside the window lay the precious herb garden.

Expecting the weeks to pass slowly, Judith had found she had never been so busy in her life. The Order, not strictly enclosed, was surprisingly liberal; everyone was given work to do, whether nursing the sick, taking food to the crippled poor, or helping in a dozen different ways in the convent. Less active nuns remained in the convent buildings, spinning, and embroidering vestments and altar cloths.

The Mother Superior had been infinitely careful over Judith's welfare, and keeping her out of sight. Bertha, too, was enjoying her life - untrammelled with habit or prayer times; she was permitted to serve Judith when possible, so that Judith often was spared the publicity of the refectory, and occasionally the two young women whispered their secret thoughts and hopes like conspirators in Judith's lonely cell. On several occasions Bertha whispered the stories from their days in the shack, acting them out again, and Judith found herself convulsed with laughter, holding her hands over her mouth as she rocked and spluttered. Now and then Bertha slipped in a new story culled from convent gossip, but Judith found herself more restrained with those: they were too close to her fear.

Judith's silver and jewellery, fine clothes and possessions were placed, unopened, in chests in the strong-room; the Abbess wanted no responsibility of knowing what lay therein. One impressive jewel had been extracted by Judith, and was given outright to the Abbess, who caressed it - then placed it in the chapel. Her horses joined others in the monastery paddocks, and Judith was permitted to use her richly decorated Book of Hours - but only in her cell; for a long time she never realised what a concession that had been. Now and then she would examine the painted miniatures of her little lap-dogs in the borders, remembering the feel of their tiny bodies warmly asleep upon her lap, or the way their miniscule faces would look intelligently up to her face, anticipating her thoughts almost before she had them, shivering. She missed them deeply, and dared not think of their fate at her father's hands.

One day the Abbess sent for her, saying, mildly,

'I promised I would talk to you about your role in this convent. Let us discuss it now, for I have a spare hour of time.'

Judith had been worried for days, so she acquiesced with relief. Her nervous rash began to itch along her arms and her neck mottled pink.

'Reverend Mother ...'

'You're not here,' she interrupted, 'because you want to become a nun - are you? You're here because it's politically inconvenient to be elsewhere ...'

'Well – yes - but - am I safe here?'

'Let me be honest with you, Judith. All our lives are governed by the laws of the land, which is just, for otherwise there'd be anarchy. No-one is really safe, anywhere, unless they're dead - which would mean that they'd be outside the law. Naturally I'd like to have you as one of our nuns - partly because I'm growing fond of you, but equally because the dowry you would bring could be immense. But it wouldn't work - *God vomits up the lukewarm!* You'd be miserable without a hint of a vocation. You ought to look for another way.'

'But - have pity! I've seen some others here who couldn't possibly be religious people?'

Judith's eyes pleaded, willing the Abbess to tuck her safely under her religious wing.

'Of course you're right,' agreed the Abbess, heartily, 'and I sometimes think my nunnery is a house of secrets! We have the deformed, and some with incurable illnesses - and several who are either half-wits or deaf; and it's difficult to differentiate between an imbecile and a madwoman - until they become violent. But they can't help themselves, they're hardly in this world, and their families have paid us to look after them; no-one is waiting to pounce on them outside! But that doesn't mean Judith that *you* could join our oddities - you're highly intelligent, you can't delude yourself you're carrying the cross.'

'I feel there's no other outlet for me if I'm to save my own life. I don't know where else to go until Roger comes to fetch me.' Tears stood in her eyes. 'You've other strange people here, as well - why don't you ask them to leave?'

'Yes, we have two concubines here, no longer desired, and several illegitimate children, either from lapsed clergy or from men of great importance - but, naturally, I can't tell you which! I've had to take a vow of silence about them.' The Abbess chuckled. 'Convents are becoming more lax, I'm afraid, but we make our own rules here. You must understand that I have to be an autocrat - the Order is new and fresh and I'm the first Mother Superior, so I have to set the rules. I'll take no political refugees! But I will take a variety of boarders - if they are prepared to pay.'

'I can pay! Anything you ask! You know that!'

'And so you can, whilst you're in hiding as a boarder.'

Judith relaxed, thankful that the Abbess was so strong.

'Now, Judith,' said the Abbess firmly, 'living in hiding isn't any solution to your problem - which you must honestly face! And I'm not taking your money as a nun if you aren't going to be one ... I'm not dishonest! I think we'd better wait and see exactly what your brother has in mind for you on his return; if your father doesn't know where you are then your brother should bear responsibility for you.'

Judith shuddered. The mother Superior carried on, making certain that Judith knew her choices.

'Bear in mind that there's an order in our ways for a girl to become a nun; first a girl becomes a postulant, and can leave of her own accord at any time - or be sent away as being unsuitable. Then the girl can become a noviate proper, for one calendar year and a day; then - and only then - can a noviate take her solemn vows. Do you understand?'

'Yes, Mother. But what if - when he returns - my brother wants me to return to our father?'

'Then you'll have to go! Unless you're a professed nun, of course, which means you're dead in the eyes of the law. He wouldn't want you then. If,' said the Mother Superior, slowly and clearly, as Judith shrank into her seat, 'you had told your father, the powerful Count of Evreux, that you preferred a life in the cloister - he wouldn't have entertained *that* idea for a moment, because he had a use for you.'

Judith stared at the old nun.

'But,' she went on, 'if he was eventually forced to send you to a convent for disobedience he would have sent you to the far greater monastery at Evreux, which he owns, and which he has handsomely endowed.'

Judith nodded. The Mother Superior continued,

'But you have chosen to hide in your brother's smaller monastery here at St. Evroul-sur-Ouche, which would bitterly anger your father should he know: have you *any idea how much trouble you are causing ... and for how many people?'*

Judith was aghast, for she had never considered anyone else in her plans.

'Yet, if you return to your father's jurisdiction, and marry where he commands, Judith, an enormous fortune awaits you. Otherwise you'll never share in your father's vast estate. Think carefully, my child, you don't have many options.'

'But - at what cost! However, if I become a noviate - what then? Wouldn't I be halfway between a nun and a free woman? Couldn't I wear the habit, yet refrain to take any oath or make any profession until my brother comes? Would I be safe, then?'

The Abbess fingered her chin.

'You would ... and let me reassure you that if your father came to hear that you were here, this convent would protect you until the weight of the law brought you to book. However,' she wagged her finger, 'if, *after a year and a day*, and you decided you could *not* take your vows, and your family went to law, insisting you leave this House - then I couldn't prevent the law taking its course. You can't remain here in limbo. You will have to make up your mind at some point.'

'Then - if I became a noviate today - would I be guaranteed a year and a day of safe haven here?' Judith implored.

'You would. But - if your father threatened you here - you must swear to me that either you'd leave immediately by your own will, or you'd have to be professed at the end of the year, there is no other choice - for a certificate would be required from a Bishop to testify that you had freely taken your vows, to show your family. Until then - you'll be at risk. *And I will not endure any violence in this holy House.*'

And so it was agreed, and Judith became a noviate.

Judith had been in fear of her life to such an extent that she was deliberately hiding her longing for Roger, even from herself. From now on she was in greater turmoil, set fast in the discipline of the convent, but watching the hours tick away until she would be forced to take her vows. Worry fed on itself and in the end so destroyed her morale that less than an ant became a burden - and she became equally concerned that she might be going mad. All her waking thoughts now turned to Roger, and whether she could be saved by him before the end of the coming year. To make the time fly faster, she redoubled her efforts for Sister Sophia, soaking up her instructions like a sponge.

Almost a year later, word filtered through that Odo de Grantmesnil was expected back within the month. That day Judith fainted clean away in the pharmacy, and the Mother Superior began to look with worried eyes at her legal documents.

Later that evening the Abbess came to her cell, stood by Judith's bed, and looked down at her with immense sympathy in her face.

'So - you've heard? Abbot Odo's returning.'

Judith nodded miserably, tears trickling into her unbound hair.

'The time he takes to arrive all depends upon the weather and the food, your brother eats well, and if there's bad food wherever he is now he'll hasten back here: he's already sent word to his cooks.'

The Mother Superior smiled affectionately at Judith, trying, by her words, to comfort her a little. Judith tried to smile in return, but her face was white with anxiety.

'You're worrying about the time you have left, aren't you?' questioned the Abbess gently. 'It's almost a year - I've been counting, too.'

'I've seventeen days to go. I can't be professed before that day, and I don't want to take my vows. But it doesn't look as though Roger will come for me in time - does it?'

'No, my child, no, it does not.' The elderly woman laid her hand gently on the young woman's head, sympathy pouring from her. 'At present no-one in your family knows you're here, but Odo will have to be told on his arrival; what do you mean to do now?' The Abbess patted the shining hair. 'I can protect you whilst I live, but I'm afraid I'm getting very old and frail, and I don't know how much resistance there is left in me.'

Judith looked closely at the tall noblewoman who stood beside her and saw her now transparent skin, the blue veins showing too prominently, the controlled but trembling limbs - and the slight milky coating over her eyes. She had never realised how old the Mother Superior was! Bound up with her own troubles she had never bothered to look carefully at the condition of other people. The Abbess was clearly signalling that she was unwell. Who would replace her? Would the unknown Cluniacs be so caring?

She swung her legs to the ground and sat up, took the Abbess' thin hand in both of hers and wept afresh.

'You've been a true mother to me ...'

The Abbess sharply withdrew her hand, saying wryly,

'Now then - enough of that! No sentimentality, if you please. I've merely done my duty.'

Judith drew back, a little affronted and uncertain what to say. The Abbess smoothly carried on, reluctant to show the depth of her feelings for the hapless girl.

'Odo isn't a bad man, you know - just very rich, very fat and rather liable to put off uncomfortable decisions - being a diplomat. If you thought positively, you'd thank goodness he's been away so long - it's given you time, after all, time to learn and be calm - and almost time to become a nun. You still feel you have no vocation, after all this while?'

'No, I have no true vocation. You were quite right, I couldn't become a nun through deep conviction, I only thought to be one in order to be safe from harm. I was so frightened. I know I wear the habit of a noviate, but once I made my oath to Roger I've remained convinced that I'm still his wife in the eyes of the Church.'

Judith rubbed her wrist where once, in times gone by, her blood had run freely together with Roger's. It seemed a lifetime ago.

'And I hope I am.' She said, defiantly.

She was bewildered by Roger's lack of communication. He had

still sent no word, and now almost three years had passed since their last meeting. Was he dead? With Fressenda now buried Judith had no way of telling, and gossip was slow to filter through to the convent. Everything would have to be decided in the next few days - when Odo came.

Judith prayed that he wouldn't be accompanied by their father.

ROBERT AND SICHELGAITA IN ROME

For the Guiscard and Roger, out in Italy, it had been a similar tense and dramatic span of time.

Robert's fortunes had fluctuated back and forth after the battle at Civitate; all he wished to do was consolidate his holdings, but the devastated people of Apulia were unforgiving of his continued onslaughts on them and resisted him at every step.

Once, in a series of giant strides, he captured Minervino, Otranto and Gallipoli, one after the other. Then Humphrey sent for him, as his heir: he was dying.

The moment Robert had buried Humphrey in the family tomb at Venosa, there was an immediate election and Robert - with the papal agreement in his pouch - was created Count of Apulia. At the same time, all Humphrey's personal estates were imperiously accepted by him and he took over Humphrey's men and castles. In just fifteen years, Robert de Hauteville had become the greatest landowner and the most powerful figure in all South Italy. He was forty-two.

Although Robert - Guiscard - Count - was supreme, there were several contenders for power stepping on his heels. But none of them could approach Robert in wealth, or power, or prestige. When Roger had arrived Robert, now ennobled to Count, rejoiced, and for a while they became very close. They left almost immediately, to subdue the majority of western Calabria. Then Count Robert was swiftly recalled to Apulia, and he had sufficient confidence to leave young Roger in charge. Robert had felt that, with each step forward he took, there was an equal step back. As he consolidated one area, so another flared up. Roger's allegiance was crucial to him.

Now and then he sent Roger away to fight for him, and when he returned in triumph, instead of thanking him and making much of him, he would turn on his younger brother in a savage way. Jealousy lay at the base of much of the abuse he heaped upon him, but he was fair enough to realise that he was treating Roger in exactly the same way that his elder brothers had treated him - as a threat. Roger was bewildered. But he kept on serving Robert, relentless in his loyalty, as he began, legitimately, to accumulate money and men for himself. Roger was twenty-six.

Up and down the peninsula the brothers raged, quelling insurrections all over the country, especially during the period when there had been a famine; at that time the peasants and the people rebelled, loudly claiming that 'it was the Hautevilles fault' that it hadn't rained and the grain had died on the stem, and that if they returned to being subjects of the Pope the rain would fall again!

Robert's marriage to Sichelgaita made a considerable difference to his status, bringing in, as it did, most handsomely, the Lombard connections and stability. In time, almost all of Apulia and Calabria were under Robert's thumb, except the port of Bari, where Robert's traditional enemies stubbornly refused to lie down.

Back and forth the battles swung, and gradually they began to reclaim all their land and garrisons on a more equal footing: Robert was cold with anger that he had had to acknowledge Sichelgaita's political help through her brother, and equally resentful of Roger's able assistance - mainly winning his battles for Robert through enthusiasm and experimentation.

Powerful Count though he indubitably was, there was never a moment's rest for Robert. His nerves were poised on a razor's edge.

'Jacques?'

'Sire?'

'An eagle is a powerful omen of good fortune, isn't it?'

'Indeed it is.'

'Then come and look at this, I want a witness.'

Through the open window near him, and out of a brilliant blue sky, Robert and Jacques watched an eagle waver, then scream and finally wheel away. In another room, Sichelgaita could hear her husband speaking to his servant and wished he had been speaking to her.

As a younger woman, Sichelgaita had clumped and strode, uncoordinated. Constantly, she continued to knock into things, and it painfully embarrassed her. With the haughty bloodline of an aristocrat - and a Lombard one at that - it engendered Germanic pride and confidence and a thrusting chin. But her hidden self longed in vain for affection and compassion. She was a voluptuary, destined for denial: it made her rigid with self-control. Awareness became her goal, so that she would avoid making a fool of herself in public.

Sichelgaita never leaned back in her seat. She sat forward, her fleshy arms with their thick and furry down placed firmly on the surface in front of her. Her head aslant, she would look enquiringly at the person in front of her. 'Yes?' She would bark. 'Yes? And then?' It intimidated peopled. Frightened, they felt obliged to reply.

When she had finished with them, like a praying mantis, she would turn in satisfaction and, then, accidentally knock the contents of her goblet into her lap. Being a princess born, she would imperiously storm from the gathering with the liquid streaming down her garments, daring anyone, with angry eyes, to comment or to laugh. They never did.

Thrusting out her lower lip she would stump out of the door, wishing some gallant man would tenderly escort her - to no avail. She never gave up hope, but time dimmed her expectations. From Robert, now, she expected nothing at all - but a tiny spark of hope still refused to be quenched. At least they would spend the coming day together.

In Rome this day it was still early, the air smelled of freshly watered streets, sawdust on stone and freshly-baked bread. The brown Tiber, swarming with craft, meandered seawards, and the traders hurried over the wooden bridges to the crowded wharves or busy markets and haggled over their dues. Some songbirds sung piercingly sweet in their reed cages. There was an eager air of expectancy along the rutted and dusty roads, for it was rumoured that today the Holy Father was to have important visitors. That would be good for trade, and give everyone something new to gossip about, and the jongleurs and ballad-makers would, most certainly, have something fresh with which to make some new songs.

The inn was crammed with too many people, thought Robert, as he sprawled on the great rumpled bed, conscious of Sichelgaita's maids next door, all the while giggling, calling, bumping and shrieking with excitement; at least he was alone at last amongst the stained coverings and his wife's hot and eager body was gone.

She was always ready for him when he needed intercourse, but after it was all over he would turn immediately from her and sleep heavily. He had never kissed her, nor spoken during the act; sometimes he had thrust himself upon her, carelessly, pushed forward over a chair or backed up against a door, deliberately diminishing her by the insult. She, in turn, had learned never to initiate, nor be tender, nor touch him afterwards - shrinking from his look of physical disgust. They performed swiftly, briefly, an ugly, urgent act like copulating beasts: it gave neither of them pleasure - only temporary release.

Robert looked across the room at all his waiting finery, and gloated to himself,

'I've come far! This is what I wanted.'

When his election and ennoblement had been signed and sealed, and before the day was out, Count Robert had written a lengthy letter to Tancred, who was ill in Normandy. It pleased him very much to have a reply, in his father's hand; but with the short and shakily written letter came an accompanying one from Geoffrey, to say that their father was dead - at least he had known of his success. That set the seal.

Whilst he was thinking, Robert was preparing the day ahead with thoroughness, washing, and then dressing. Jacques handed him his sumptuous leather casket filled with gold and jewels. Robert pointed to a heavy gold chain, which Jacques fastened round his neck; if only, he thought, Alberada was here beside him to share his triumph. When speaking about politics with Sichelgaita he could hold a normal conversation - even be stimulated by her energetic ideas, lightning swift, and proposed plans - but that was all. Physically the comparison between her and Alberada sickened him, he was ever conscious of it, and he could never tell her what was in his heart; it would, he felt, open up his defences. Gradually, but very obviously, their relationship had come to a crossroads.

Slowly, weighed down by all the unaccustomed clothes and jewels, he walked across the stifling room and looked out into the street, saying to Jacques over his shoulder,

'It's a pity Mark's not here.'

'Yes, sire. He's far too young.'

'Yes.' Robert began to put on some rings.

'My lord - you'd better know - I thrashed him recently.' said Jacques, 'You would have wished it.'

Robert stared.

'You thrashed my son?'

'Yes, sire, he was stupid, he risked his horse's life. They're too valuable - and this was the stallion.'

Robert recalled his father's own words. Their horses were of immense importance to them and their destriers had helped them win many battles; he and Roger had recently set up breeding stables.

'Ah. Well - you were right to do so. But he's handling his bow better, isn't he?'

'Yes, and he rides well now, too. And how he's grown! He's a good boy, healthy - tall - he'll be a fine man one day. But he misses you.'

'Yes, I know.'

Robert pictured Mark, young Bohemund, in his mind, and the times the two of them and Alberada had sat by the fireside on those few rare occasions when he escaped home to Calabria and talked and laughed, and talked some more. Then he would tell Mark all about the Hautevilles and their friends, bidding him never to forget, like the handing down of old Norse legends. When he was busy he left Jacques to carry on his training.

Robert put on the last jewels as Jacques handed them to him, proud to appear rich and successful. This time, he thought excitedly, this time his audience with the Pope was to be in public. He had notched up another peg in power. Today's meeting promised to be vastly important in such a public place, but he had no idea what the new Pope could want of him; he had to wait and see. He pushed through the adjoining door into a confusion of luxury strewn over the bleakness of the room.

Every level space was covered with rainbow clothes of all sorts, or toilet articles, candles and boxes. Another bed was spread with a profusion of cushions and discarded furs; food and drinks were piled on the window ledges. In one corner a silver basin was full of cold yellow water, on whose surface floated a thin grey scum of soap. In another place a hand-mirror was propped against a shelf; clearly Sichelgaita had sat before it as her ladies dressed her, had regarded herself in it, and - like Narcissus - had admired her own coiffure and the powdered perfection of her features.

'Ahhhh! Madam - you look so fine! - So rich! - So splendid!'

Never, thought Robert, 'So beautiful!' *That* he would say to Alberada.

He watched her looking critically at herself in the polished metal mirror, framed in carved ivory. They were quite right, of course: with careful planning, she did look fine and splendid. Dressed in Sicilian-woven ruby eskalaton, garlanded in gold necklaces, her thick yellow hair plaited and mounted into a crown-shape, woven through with pearls, she towered above all the other women in the room.

But no man had ever called her beautiful. The sight of her thickened body nauseated him, reminding him of what they'd done in bed the night before, after he had tried to hold a picture of Alberada in his mind at the time - but failed, and their act of coition had developed into a near-brawl. He was disgusted at himself; if only he could learn to lead two totally separate lives.

Robert strode further into the room, shouting at her women and threw his silk-lined cloak upon the bed; he wouldn't wear it until the last moment, it was too hot. Old Wolf whined at the door, scratched with his long claws - but was left outside. Sichelgaita's women tumbled from the room at the sight of him. There was a painful pause.

She hollowed her shoulders so that the curves of her throat and bosom were emphasised, smiling expectantly, but cautiously. She waited. Robert said nothing about her appearance. Deliberately he looked out into the street instead, watching the crowds milling about. Both knew he had intentionally insulted her, not even paid a compliment. It was her due.

She looked at her husband in his splendour, the epitome of power, and a tingling thrill ran through her body; dressed or naked he never failed to make her body weak with desire. Her blood ran to water each time she watched his long legs walk towards her, or saw his heavy hands grasp a goblet, and if his hair touched her face shivers ran about all over the surface of her skin. His indifference set her nerves jangling, the more so because she knew it was unassumed - she felt powerless, knowing she couldn't attract him, intuitively knowing that his heart, too, remained with Alberada. She had been wildly wrong in her guess that Robert would soon have forgotten his first wife.

Every muscle in her face tightened in resentment. She, too, said nothing: she might have been made of stone.

'We'll speak today of trivialities - no more!' he said harshly. 'There'll be a certain pattern to our conduct and conversation - I've worked it out with Roger.'

'No Papal blessing for our marriage?'

He wheeled round in astonishment,

'Why do you want that? We're lawfully married, aren't we? That's all that was necessary!'

Willfully she pouted.

'But you've not bought me a ring - let me wear your silver ring for today? His Holiness will notice.'

Robert looked at her in growing amazement and irritation.

'What are you saying? You own plenty of rings! This is my family ring!'

'Aren't I a member of your family?'

'No, by God, you're not!'

'I see ...' she glared at him, trembling; she was extraordinarily angry: she thrust up her chin aggressively.

Robert stared at her.

'You look like a murderess, *Princess* - but don't dream of threatening me! There is no denying that you've come from a greater family than mine - we all know it: you needn't rub my nose in it. But - one day, one day,' his knuckles were white against the bedpost, 'mine will be far greater.'

'And then I'll be of it, *my Lord Count*?' She said, sarcastically, with gritted teeth.

He turned aside, speaking without a shadow of interest in his voice.

'I think not.'

She glared at him in the mirror, her fingers picking fiercely at the jewels sewn upon her gown. There was a screaming silence in the room.

Robert, grim face set, was inwardly seething, determined not to let Sichelgaita have the satisfaction of knowing it. Vacant-eyed, as his wife watched, he thought back in frustration to when he had married Alberada, and given her the best he could afford, a gold ring with an amethyst glowing deep within, echoing her eyes.

'My only love,' she had said, and he had known it to be true.

Later, when Mark was born he had draped her slender neck with rubies set in filigreed gold, and hung in her tiny earlobes earrings to match, and gave her gold pins for her hair, one by one. She had looked up at him with such adoration that, even today, the memory made his heart lurch in pain. Twisting the ring on his finger he remembered how he had taken it off, once, and placed it on Alberada's own, where it had hung loose, bracelet-like - and they had laughed together. Should that ring be put on Sichelgaita's finger it would have to be jammed on, man-like - no! He couldn't bear the thought - not after Alberada. He vowed to leave the ring to Mark: Mark would understand.

In his silent reverie he meditated yet again that marriage to sweet Alberada had been a fatal mistake, had weakened him - he'd loved her to distraction, loved her still. He could never understand why Sichelgaita was so loyal to him, in public she never faltered. He wondered about her motives: he thought she only wanted complete control, as he did.

And Sichelgaita *wanted his ring!* Had asked for it! Or another! Alberada had never asked for anything. But he would give her another ring now, all the same. Or perhaps two matching bracelets, again in gold and amethysts, with his family symbol inside, to show where she belonged; or some pretty new hairpins, with tiny green emeralds set in their crests - they'd look lovely in her dark hair. Perhaps, after this important meeting, he could steal some time to be with her and Mark again? Time was always his enemy. But here, in Rome, he could buy her jewels, and Sichelgaita could rot, empty-handed.

He wrenched his thoughts away, blank-faced, carelessly walking out of their room ahead of her, leaving Sichelgaita to follow him alone. The Pope was more important.

'Come on, come on!' he shouted impatiently as he left, 'I'm waiting no longer. If you're not outside immediately I'll see the Pope alone.'

He knew he did not mean it – politically she was too valuable...

'You can wait in the street until I'm ready,' she roared back, *'you're nothing without me!'*

Sichelgaita meant every syllable.

Robert slammed a door behind him so hard that a large chip of wood cracked off the edge.

Immediately Sichelgaita's maid came to help her, but so furious a face was turned upon her that the girl blanched and vanished: after a few minutes Sichelgaita strode down alone.

ROBERT, SICHELGAITA, ROGER AND THE POPE

In the square outside the inn a great crowd had gathered to stare. Robert drew in a deep draught of fresh air, untainted by the sickly sweet spices and unguents of his wife's room, and steadied himself. He looked at the crowds, knew they admired and envied him, but his smile was missing, and the eyes that caught Sichelgaita's eyes as she joined him, and held them mesmerised, and were as cold as any snake's. She was still incredibly angry, her face flushed and the sinews of her neck stood out like ropes, but she bit her lips and remained silent.

A hush fell upon the onlookers: Robert and Sichelgaita towered over them all, and the crowd marvelled over their immense size as they made ready with their companions, soldiers and servants. Youthful Roger stood to one side, at the head of the court and his own contingent of men - Count Robert counted them, thoughtfully. Pierre, close behind, was stammering with excitement at the probability of seeing the Holy Father - it was the most wonderful thing to happen in his life: he forgot to complain about the inn.

'Look at her clothes,' said a scrawny young woman with a baby in her arms, pointing at Sichelgaita, 'and those jewels sewn upon them!'

'And his,' said a man holding a donkey, steadying its load of wood, longing to touch Robert's gold chain 'and the Count's sword! It's the biggest I've ever seen.'

A fat old dame, chins wobbling, well used to watching and listening, wiped a trickle of sweat on her cheek, saying,

'She's got a sword, too, did you know? At their last battle she stood side by side with him, shoulder to shoulder, wearing armour and fighting. Amazing, isn't it? A Princess, a mother and a fighter?'

'Well, she's big enough, she'd frighten anyone ...'

'Where was that? It wasn't around here, was it?'

The knowledgeable old crone snickered,

'They say 'twas in Sicily.'

The gossipers quietened as the Guiscard's party suddenly thrust on their way, a lone drummer beginning a beat which quickened their footsteps, leaving the lazy crowd in their wake like froth in a glass.

As they marched through the streets, crowded with wooden houses on all sides, Robert was perfectly aware that a storm was sweeping across the sea of restless anger that lay within Sichelgaita's soul - knew that if she had been out of the public eye she would have raged about their rooms like a wild thing in a cage. But they both managed to control their emotions, shutting out the previous scene like closing a door, and concentrating upon the meeting with the Pope instead. They fell into step.

The Papal Hall was large and airy, and chatter swelled and deepened into the humming of an admiring crowd as their party approached. Slender windows soared to the roof, too high to reach or see through. The walls were hung with colourful fabrics, some interwoven with precious metals, glinting in the light. Flags, attached to painted wooden handles, were gathered into careless bundles, and there were nosegays of herbs for everyone. The new Pope's men stood vigilantly around the walls, the officers in their distinctive clothes here and there punctuating the scene.

No one was taking any chances today.

With a boastful flourish of trumpets Robert entered with his party: Roger stood behind him; Jacques and Pierre remained near the entrance. Wolf, too old now, was left behind.

Standing by the huge doors Robert stopped and made his bows to the whole gathering of people in the Hall. Sichelgaita, skillfully concealing her anger, sketched a curtsey with easy leisureliness, then lightly placed her hand on his, keeping an appropriate distance between their bodies, as they slowly paced up the central open space. Tall, stately, and with great presence, they deliberately took a long time - fractionally longer than was their due. Fifty muscular men, carefully counted out, followed them, headed by Roger. Then came a sprinkling of Sichelgaita's ladies - as a clear reminder of her own importance; then servants laden with gifts. No foot soldiers were brought. Robert had been invited with utmost courtesy, he had not sought an audience - he'd make sure no-one was in any doubt about that. And he knew all the tricks, for he had employed them in the past, one by one.

At the bottom of the long flight of steps they stopped again, and this time knelt. They made a spectacular pair. The new Pope, his shiny red face, the colour of underdone beef, split in a smile in which his eyes did not join, beckoned them to greet him, and finally they were seated - but on massive folding stools, beneath his throne.

Robert, Count of Apulia, casually looked about the Hall, supremely assured. He knew that the scale of their magnificent reception was in honour of his abilities. But he also knew that, in part, it was due to Sichelgaita and her connections: she had been here before, in front of a previous Pontiff, with her brother Gisulf, the Prince of Salerno. But the day was his - the most powerful leader in the land. He owned vast tracts. He was rich and cruel. Yet the power which suffused him was mainly through his unfailing confidence. He smelt of it ... his height and breadth alone threatening beyond measure - anyone could see he knew his own worth.

Then Robert turned to concentrate on the Pope himself. Personally, he could hold a balance between Pope and Holy Roman Emperor; he knew that - if it ever came to confrontation. Each would have to be played like a fish: give a little here, take a little there; he determined to remain an unknown quantity in their lives. They both needed him.

And he needed them both. But - one at a time, thought Robert, I would rather divide them, than allow them to join forces against me.

What did His Holiness want of him today? His honeyed words at the beginning of the Audience gave no trace of his requirements. That meant the request would be made later, and in secret, its significance probably as deadly as an asp. The present compliments must be added up, so he could gauge the size of the favour required. Then he could work out the size of the reward he expected. What an amusing game diplomacy could be; and, occasionally, how predictable. But dangerous. He stretched his legs comfortably in front of him. This was going to take some time.

Two days passed. They had eaten succulent food, been entertained handsomely and exchanged suitable gifts. Both he and Sichelgaita had managed to smile at the right times, and speak the correct words, seeming comfortable and relaxed, yet attending to all minute details of etiquette. Together with Roger, they worked as an unbroken team.

Now Robert and Roger were closeted with the Pope and his political priest, in a lofty room, with locked doors. The moment had come.

The Pope looked Robert straight in the eye and said, very quietly, pausing between each word,

'I - want - Bari!'

So that was it at last!

Like lightning Roger created the planned diversion, leaving Robert space to think.

'Holiness ...'

The Pope turned at the urgency in Roger's voice. He had noted that both brothers had a family likeness, but that the elder was far heavier, broader, harder. Something about Roger appealed to him, however - a softness - and, perhaps, humour. It seemed a novel idea that there might be one solitary, presentable soul in the devious Hauteville family, but he rather doubted his judgment.

'Yes, my son?' He said, courteously, in spite of the interruption, determined to be pleasant at all costs, 'What is it?'

'Your pardon, Father, but - before we start - could you ...' Roger felt inside his rich garments, then slowly pulled out his gold chain and hanging cross. Carefully lifting them over his head he handed them to the Pope.

'You want me to bless this?'

'Please ...' Roger bent his head reverently.

'Curious.' His Holiness stared at the cross for a moment. 'Was this made locally?'

'No, Father, it was made in Normandy.'

'Made for you? It looks rathcr dclicate.'

'How perceptive you are, Father. You're quite right; it was made for a lady. A lady I hope to make my wife.'

Roger continued to play for time, as Robert had instructed him to do.

'Can you tell me her name?' The Pope enquired, with a smile meant to charm.

Damn him, thought Roger, that's none of his business: but I fell into his trap like a babe. I can't avoid an answer.

'She's ... the lady Judith of Evreux.'

'Of powerful family, no less.'

The Pope did not pretend the name was unknown to him - he knew the family were part of William of Normandy's coterie. He allowed his mind to stray, momentarily, thinking of the permutations of such an alliance and how the Church could benefit.

'I suppose you've heard of the trouble between her brother, Abbot Odo de Grantmesnil and Duke William of Normandy?'

'No, Holiness, what trouble is that?'

Roger, desperate for news of Judith, spoke without a tremor in his voice, as if he did not care.

'Well, it's all to do with an off-shoot of the agreement made between Pope Nicholas II and your brother, here, at Melfi ... which resulted in the power of the Church emasculating the power of the Emperor - as it was designed to do.'

The Pope smirked, and gestured towards Robert, deep in a well of thought.

'But the inevitable consequences have now gone further down the succession and have upset the balance of power between the Emperor and his vassal states in Germany and elsewhere. A lot of mistakes have been made, mainly by the Emperor's mother - as you know, he's still a minor. As power waxes and wanes between Church and Emperor, then the same thing happens between the vassal states - so the power is now changing hands further west. Also,' the Pope took a deep breath, 'King Henry I of France has died, and so has Geoffrey Martel - there is a civil war in the state of Maine and, needless to day, Duke William of Normandy is poised to conquer the state - his old enemy!'

A movement from his Cardinal behind him pulled him up, and made him conscious that his words were running away with him. He finished,

'But we really haven't time to go into that further now - we've more important business which is nearer to hand! I'd be happy to talk to you about its ramifications later, if you like - but the nub of it is, I hear, that William and Odo de Grantmesnil had a furious quarrel - and now William's after his blood. I wouldn't care to be in Abbot Odo's shoes! Odo won't fight for him, which isn't surprising.'

Roger was anxious to prolong the conversation, but the Pope blessed Judith's cross, which Roger carefully replaced, with true gratitude. Somehow, he hoped, it might bring her closer. He recalled Judith's words, 'Her faith or her love - she couldn't have them both.'

He wished he hadn't been forced to speak her name in front of Robert.

Robert was not listening at all. His mind was flashing with permutations: Roger was doing well in laying a trail away from him.

Lombards, Byzantines, Saracens - was Bari destined, at last, to fall into the western Pope's hands? Emperors, Popes, Strategos - the Adriatic port had changed hands innumerable times since history began. Now, it seemed, the Pope wanted the Byzantines out for ever; obviously he couldn't manage this alone, he needed Hauteville help.

For a moment or two Robert set his mind to the position as a whole. One glaring fact worried him: the Normans were not sea-farers; they had no knowledge of ships, or warfare under sail. Bari had a long-developed sea trade, but no Norman ships had entered into her port as far as he knew. That meant, if a land siege was fruitless, he and Roger would have the challenge of learning a new aspect to battle - the remainder would be worked through by normal siege tactics. This time the conquest of Bari must be final.

This time the password had to be 'patience'.

It was bound to be a long siege. An enclosure would have to be built around the city. Their soldiers would have to be left in place - perhaps for years. Ships. Sailors. Diplomacy. Time. It would be extremely expensive.

The Pope observed Robert out of the corner of his eye as he blessed the cross, watched the Guiscard swiftly marshalling his thoughts. 'The wily one', how right! Cunning as a fox.

Apart from money, ran Robert's thoughts, what would the Church have to pay? Gold, of course. Land, too, and port revenues. Titles - he would insist on that; perhaps a new title for Roger. He'd earned it.

The Pope's thoughts were about the Emperor: although young, how pleased he'd be! No-one would ever know about a private conversation their ambassadors had six months ago, ostensibly to discuss Church outposts in Spain, yet, in reality, to debate how to dislodge Robert and the Hautevilles. This time, thought His Holiness, Robert would be tied up for so long that both Pope and Emperor could go about their affairs without serious interference. The Emperor needed time to unravel his many difficulties in Germany: the Church needed to consolidate matters in Italy. Count Robert would be firmly tied up in Bari, whatever the cost. It ought to suit everyone.

There was a sudden glint in the Pope's eye.

Robert's thoughts cut off immediately, like a knife through silk. That glint was not admiration at his quick appraisal; it was some form of satisfaction. Why? What else was the Pope to gain? More important than a port? Of course! Time was the crucial word. *His time* - his occupied time! The Pope wanted him out of his way. Perhaps - the Emperor, too? They must have made some private pact. What an accolade! He was too powerful!

He knew exactly what he would do now. They would settle down to discuss the problems in minute detail, make a careful reckoning, and arrange the rewards. He would be generous, offer to share the costs. Then sign the contracts. When the battle was won for western Christianity there would be some small legal clause in that contract that would let him claim the administration of the whole city for the Hautevilles, which would bring in huge revenues. The Pope would grant him that: in the eyes of the world the Church only wanted to make sure of domination over the city - which would mean *all Italy would be, for the first time, under the Pope of Rome and the Emperor.* The Church would collect money from the people in other ways; they were well-known.

In the meanwhile, as soon as his party had left Rome, a final letter of thanks would be delivered to His Holiness, cheerfully assuring him that, as he, Robert, had so much confidence in the outcome - and as he had so many other affairs to attend to - the man to be in charge would not be himself ... but Roger! Roger could earn any further privileges - *let Roger work for them* - he'd be well rewarded and would be in a position to marry anyone he pleased! He was intrigued, too, at possible links with William of Normandy - although they seemed slight at this stage.

Not only that, though Robert, with a feeling of relief, he would know exactly where Roger was, too, all the time, so he would never get the chance to compete against him. And he, himself, would be free to do as he thought fit to enrich his own life - in every way. What was sauce for the goose, thought Robert, was sauce for the gander.

He would wish His Holiness long life, good health.

Thoughtfully turned his head, forced himself to look at the floor: he knew faces could be read...

His eyes glinted, too, unseen. Time, indeed! They could plot their way to hell for all he cared - Bari would be a very important siege indeed.

'Holy Father,' he began, smoothly, almost gaily, appearing to shoulder aside his concentration of the past minutes, 'what an interesting proposition! Let's forget girlish crosses and discuss the possibilities. Shall we call in our Secretaries to put our deliberations down?'

In just thirteen years Robert had become the greatest landowner and the most powerful man in all southern Italy: he was not going to allow this new Pope to forget the fact. It had never been easy, but as simply as day follows night he had forced the issue after his meeting with Pope Nicholas, and demanded every concession. Now Roger was by his side, steady as a rock and between them they would spread their net successfully across the land.

Only one city had escaped them both - Bari. It was too powerful for them to have captured single-handed - they would have been overstretched, with all their other pressing problems. But here was the Pope, asking them to be his allies in taking the highly independent port. Apart from every other consideration, that would more than halve the cost! He was almost placing Bari in their hands as a gift: presumably he thought the Hauteville brothers couldn't conquer the city, for, whenever taken in the past, the people had shrugged off their rulers within months and regained autonomy almost immediately: in their hearts the Bariots believed they were invincible, their spirits were too tough to be broken.

Also, thought Robert, by suggesting the campaign himself, with the Hautevilles in charge, unwittingly the Pope had given Robert the upper hand - especially now that Robert had guessed his real motives. He smiled and stretched, and Roger, by his side, understood that their tactics had won for them a huge advantage, and, as if he had had a signal, copied his actions.

By the movements of their bodies, their smiles and apparent easy confidence, the Pope instantly recognised that the balance of power had shifted into Hauteville hands in some subtle way: the die was cast and the contrived control over Robert seemed to have slipped from his grasp like the unexpected disappearance of an eel.

He was also unaware, at that moment, that he had unwittingly put the Normans into the position of posing as champions in a Holy War. But Robert knew it, and was determined that no-one else would ever forget it.

JUDITH AND ODO

Judith was awash in a sea of terror mixed with hopelessness; much of this came through ignorance, and was exaggerated by the hours of daydreaming she spent, alone, in her cell. She had hypnotised herself into a vacuum. She cowered as Odo reached out to pat her awkwardly on her slight shoulder.

'Gentle lady, sister ... there is no time for all the niceties, but - there must be some plain speaking between us. And we must do it now.' Judith looked at her brother, listened to his staccato voice, not hearing what he said - deathly afraid for herself, horror widening her eyes; she felt bleak and vacant, dispossessed. 'You've been a complete fool. But I understand why.'

Confused, she couldn't believe what she was hearing; she felt the blood draining from her body as her imagination soared, crazily. For days, since his return, she had dreaded the moment when she was to meet her half-brother face to face. At least she knew he was alone, their father remaining safely in his castle at Evreux. A nun had waited for her after chapel that morning, standing there like a statue as the congregation filed through the doors. She beckoned to Judith, and then whispered low,

'The Abbot requires your presence. Holy Mother says you must go to him at once. But - first - go and see her in her chamber.'

Woebegone, she had blindly returned to her cell, stumbled to her knees, unable to form any sort of prayer. Shaking, she rose, then lay prostrate across her bed for some time - she didn't know how long. Finally, she had found the courage to get up and prepare to see Odo: she had cleansed her face, pulled back her hair beneath her coif. She wondered vaguely if this was to be her last time alone - alive. Her greatest fear was not just for her own life: she was panic-stricken that he would have her taken to some building and then have her walled in, to suffocate until she died.

'Breathe deeply: one, two, three ... breathe deeply ... one, two, three ... breathe deeply.'

Sister Sophia had taught her some methods by which she might control her nerves - perhaps for just this moment in her life. Encouraged, she had practiced them daily and found the routine helped. She steadied as she dragged the air into her lungs, then finally lifted her chin and straightened her shoulders.

Accompanied by the Mother Superior, eyes down, hands linked, drab woollen robe trailing behind her, she walked demurely to the nearby monastery building. Every step was a conscious effort, as she placed one foot in front of the other - the older woman gently guiding her. Her skin crawled with her nervous rash at its worst, her forearms shook. *Her forearms!* Why did her forearms shake like this? She pressed them by her side, feeling her ribs below, pulling her elbows back until they almost touched behind her. The bones in her fingers felt thin and brittle. Her shoulder blades ached. It seemed bitterly cold.

At last they were there, within Odo's magnificent rooms, filled with light and colour and delectable smells of a meal recently eaten. He had greeted the Mother Superior with gentle affection and much respect, placing her in a chair by the fire, for it was late November, and seeing that she had both food and drink at hand.

Would he imprison her? Wondered Judith, as she stood alone in the centre of the room. Would he have a wall built about her living body until there was no light, no air, no life? That was her greatest dread: it was a penalty used for family traitors - especially when they had conveniently dropped out of sight for several years. Or would he bury her alive strapped down in a coffin? She knew that that was often done too.

Odo repeated,

'There must be plain speaking between us!' Then he turned to her, went to embrace her and smiled at her - kindly.

The room spun around her as she fainted limply onto the floor at her brother's feet.

'Dear God!' He muttered, 'what on earth is the matter with her?'

The Abbess was quick to kneel down beside her.

'She faints too often,' she said, 'it's becoming a very bad habit.'

Some moments passed as they revived her, lifted her up in their arms, burnt feathers beneath her nose and gave her something cool to drink. Finally they helped her onto a window seat.

Solely occupied by his own troubles, Odo could wait no longer and said breathlessly,

'You may be in some trouble, but - I do assure you - I am in greater difficulties.'

She seemed to be half dreaming, half conscious. What was he saying? Trouble - what trouble? His trouble? Why?

'Don't worry; it's nothing to do with you. But I'm in desperate straights myself. Duke William of Normandy is infuriated with me because I've refused to go to war by his side!'

Judith focused her eyes upon her brother at last, began to listen to his words - astonished to find him talking to her as an equal. She watched him as he walked about the room, nervously - the way she would walk about, herself, when agitated - picking up his wine from one table, smoothing the folds of his rich gown, pawing the fur of a chair cover. He turned to face her, and said,

'Our cousin William wants to take control of Maine!'

Struggling for composure and wiping away a tear, she asked,

'Why – why does he reach out to Maine?'

'You wouldn't understand, you're too innocent of the ways of the world - of affairs of state ... government ... '

Judith interrupted him, raising her voice,

'Please answer me.'

Odo was taken aback by the strength of Judith's assertive tone, he had no idea she could speak so decisively: he replied amiably,

'Because Henry and Geoffrey are dead.'

'Will you explain further? Remember, I've not recently been at court.' It was a massive understatement; she thought ruefully, comparing her cell to the luxury of her apartment in her castle home. Odo took another long draught of wine from a heavily jewelled goblet and greedily stuffed a couple of chicken patties into his mouth with plump fingers.

'Well, Judith - I'll give you the background, but it'll have to be in brief. For the past fourteen years Duke William's authority here in Normandy has always been disputed and there've been continual wars. Amongst others, he's fought his overlord, King Henry I of France, and he's fought Geoffrey Martell, Count of Anjou - his greatest rival in the west. Now - King Henry is dead, and, by pure chance, Geoffrey Martel died within three months of him - which means, to put it simply, both Anjou and Maine have been plunged into armed conflict. It follows that William expects to profit by all this and he's called upon his closest friends and relations to come to his aid. But I refused to go and fight in Maine - it would complicate my allegiance to the Pope, who is unhappy over William's aims - and that, my dear sister, is why we quarrelled!'

Looking at the man who now sat before her, as wide as he was tall, with wobbling jowls and perspiration trickling down the side of his cheek, Judith could well understand why Odo didn't want to fight. He was exceptionally wealthy and wholly lacked the combative nature of most Normans; he loved to eat and drink, laugh and gossip with his many friends. His eyes grew rounder as he stared at her,

'Perhaps I'm in even greater danger than you!'

'You are? I thought that I ...'

'Well, you've been a silly little fool, of course, the Mother Superior has explained it all to me - not a dutiful daughter at all, but that's not of any importance ...'

She flared with indignation. She had spent almost two years in a convent, a virtual prison, and was within two days of taking her vows to be 'the bride of Christ' - was that *'of no importance'*? But her brother blethered on hoarsely,

'William told me that he expected me to be at the border within ten days - with my men. But I won't go! *I won't fight for him!* Our quarrel was abominably public, too - but I'm not bound to him other than by blood, and my first allegiance lies with the Pope; he knows that. So I'm getting out of his way and leaving here at once; I've decided to travel to Rome - and seek papal protection. I have a document from His Holiness which protects me whenever I'm travelling on Church affairs.'

Rome! Quick as a flash Judith was out of her seat and ran up to him and clutched his plump arm.

'Take me with you!' she cried out, 'it's my way to escape, too! We could travel together. I must - *it is essential* that I escape to Rome with you!'

Her brother pushed her away from him, dismayed, thinking of the many complications it would entail to have women in his party. It was out of the question.

'I can't take a woman all that way,' he spluttered, 'even though I sympathise with you.'

Judith looked crestfallen.

'You can't leave her here, either.'

Brother and sister swung round to look at the older woman by the fire. She went on, her voice becoming stronger as she spoke,

'Once the great Count has word that you've met her, but left her here in your nunnery - and not escorted her back to him at Evreux, then you'd find yourself in even greater trouble when you returned.' The Mother Superior spoke with authority. 'I think it's plain that both of you are very much afraid of your father and what he is capable of doing?'

'But I ... I haven't got the time,' stammered Odo, 'not if I'm to be sure to be well out of Normandy before the ten days are up! Besides, I may be away for years - there's so much to put in order before I leave - if I'm to live comfortably.'

'Well ... ' said the Abbess, thoughtfully, 'you might be a trifle safer if word got about that you'd had an urgent message from the Pope, inviting you to Rome; what about that? It's feasible, after this past Council at Rouen, and the Holy Father would be glad of your report. William couldn't stop you leaving legitimately - nor would he ever go against the Pope a second time, now that the excommunication trouble has just been resolved. And - perhaps I could put that gossip about, through my influential friends – who wouldn't mention the source.'

Relieved, Odo grasped the Abbess' hands.

'You have my deepest gratitude, and I accept. But William will never forget that I defied him in so public a manner, in front of all the delegates at Rouen, all the same. He said I'd made him look foolish.'

'Time enough to think of that when you get back, then you can make amends.' Said the Abbess firmly, 'I think there is no question about it - you should take Judith with you.'

Judith became alight with excitement, walking around the room with small, nervous steps, unaware she was moving. Then, convinced that her brother would do as the Mother Superior had proposed, she said,

'Do I travel as a nun, or as your sister?'

'Ah,' said the Abbess, slowly, 'now - that needs thought.'

There was a long interval, as they waited for the tired old woman to speak.

Judith sat down again, having noticed a faint nerve twitching on the Mother Superior's lined forehead. Yet her nervousness continued to betray her, as she obliviously tapped and twitched her skirt the way her father tapped his long nail. Odo finished his wine and poured out another generous draught. The Abbess stirred.

'I think I have the answer.'

At her quiet words they turned to her expectantly.

'Judith is still only a noviate, which is no protection to her outside these walls, and many greedy watchers would inform Evreux of her whereabouts, knowing the ransom your father has offered, the moment she is seen.'

Judith's heart fell; she grasped the folds of her skirt with clenched hands like claws.

'And,' said the Abbess, 'no nun may ever leave the cloister bounds without the written permission of the Superior.'

Neither brother nor sister could see where these words were leading.

'I have decided that I could write out a double document to state that Judith is a Sister at the Convent of St. Evroul-sur-Ouche - it's just possible, you've only a day or so to wait - and that both the Abbot and the Mother Superior give you licence to travel to our sister convent at Rome in order to study pharmacy for a period of three years. We could add, 'It being of a straiter order of religion and observance, not for a frivolous or empty reason, but that she may lead a life altogether and entirely harder'.'

'It would be a trick, then - a forgery? You wouldn't make me take my vows in reality?'

'No. Judith, we wouldn't make you take your vows - *we couldn't make* you take any vows by force - we wouldn't want to. But, on the right day, the three of us would have to sit alone in the chapel for some time, as if you were taking your vows in actuality. As the Abbot's sister there could be exceptional dispensation that your vows could be taken in private - that has happened on several previous occasions in other exclusive convents. All the convent's congregation has been witness that you've been a noviate for the required length of time - whether or not they guessed that you were the Abbot's sister.'

'And then I'd be lawfully travelling to Rome?'

'In the eyes of the world, yes. Only the three of us would know the wearing of your habit was a disguise.'

'And what would be the purpose of a double, rather than a single document? Why *'double'*?' asked Odo, who was very good with documents, as painstaking as his father. The Abbess looked at him with a knowing eye.

'It would be for Judith's double protection: only the three of us would know of the two documents' existence, and I would keep one safely locked up in the convent. If anything happened to her before she reached Rome then I'd know where the responsibility lay, and this document would give evidence of intrigue.'

She paused, briefly, aware that this was an open threat to the Abbot, and he understood. He nodded, not unused to small transgressions against the law.

'Judith will carry the other document with her, on her person; should anything happen to your party on the journey, she, at least, would have the full protection of the Church, not only from assailants, but from her father - or his men. The document would prove that she was beyond his jurisdiction.'

Again, she looked at Odo. He knew, then, that it would be pointless to send word about Judith by a swift messenger to the great Count before they left - for his signature would already be on the document - the Abbess would have seen to that - and he would be a proven conspirator. He shuddered at the thought of what troubles that would bring. She went on,

'Then, once Judith is safely in Rome, in our sister convent, and if she married Roger - which we all devoutly hope she'll do - if she can find him - she must return the document to me, accompanied by a certificate signed by both of you to tell me Judith is safe. I, in turn, can match the document with the one in my keeping for proof, see that the pattern of their division into two is exact and accurate, and then destroy them both. This protects us all.'

She smiled benignly at the younger pair; neither would ever know how long it had taken her to think out the solution, she had been working it out for weeks. She continued,

'All three of us will instantly sign both documents, which will be written on one long piece of parchment. Then I, as unrelated author, *and only* I, will cut it across, between the two areas of text, in my own pattern - so that, if pieced together again, the two pieces will fit snugly and accurately, and can be proved to be no forgery. Now can you see why I insist upon a double document?'

Judith sagged with relief, breathless.

PREPARATIONS: JUDITH AND SISTER SOPHIA

Odo was agreeable to the Abbess' plans - and said so at once; all he wanted was to set off as quickly as possible - out of William's long reach. He worried about no-one but himself, and always had done: it was a rich man's way.

He told Judith the day and time when he hoped to leave, and what she might bring with her. He also agreed to find time to come to the convent two days hence, clad in his richest clothes, as if the private ceremony was genuinely translating her into a professed nun. The consecrated Bishop, who would normally have carried out the ceremony, could wait alone in the Abbess' rooms, out of sight , and never know - or be told - what was going on. He had never met Judith, and had been away at the Council of Rouen, on and off, for almost two years - and he would, anyway, be left behind in Normandy whilst Odo raced to Rome.

Judith, for her part, became elated, thanking the Abbess with tumbling - grateful - words. At a stroke the Abbess seemed to have solved most of her problems, and - if they left Normandy safely - had saved her from her father's wrath.

'How quickly can you prepare the documents?' She enquired, taking the Abbess' hand and leading her from the room. 'And how can I help?'

'I don't leave important things like that to chance, my dear,' said the Abbess dryly, 'they are already done and I'll make Odo sign them this night.'

She leaned very heavily on Judith's arm. She knew with certainty, that she would be dead within weeks, Sister Sophia had already assured her of the fact, so all the risks she took would never come to roost in this life; she was also supremely confident that, in the next world, they would deal with her graciously: after all, she reasoned, Judith was not a nun in her care, but the sister of the powerful Abbot - let him take responsibility! A faint smile twitched in her cheek.

'One last thing,' said the Abbess into Judith's ear as they slowly walked back to the nunnery, turning their heads from the chill wind and treading with care on the wet cobbles,

'I'll prepare another document before you go, which we'll both sign - and get Sister Sophia to witness our signatures, to prove beyond doubt that you never took your vows in the first place; then you'll still be your father's sole female heir, whether or not you find Roger. But you can't take that with you, it would be an invitation for murder. There will only be the one copy - it's a risk you'll have to take.'

Three days later Bertha held out a travelling cloak of brown cloth, lined with squirrel fur, for Judith's approval: it had lain in their boxes for over two years, and Judith greeted it with joy.

'And you, Bertha? Do you have a warm cloak?'

'No, my lady; I had a shawl.'

'Then go to the market and buy something warm and thick - but be careful with the colouring, grey or brown, we must avoid being noticed as we travel.' She handed her money.

Her concern for others was new and unnoticed by her. In the beginning, sleeping uncomfortably on the same pallet on the floor with her serving maid, she learned what life for other people might be like. Following that, during the weary months in the convent she had learned more about caring for others less able to help themselves, mostly from the selflessness of Sister Sophia.

Bertha beamed with joy. A new cloak! The convent had never occupied her very much; the nuns were quiet and always busy, the servants were permitted to be freer ... but all of them were women! Bertha had a healthy appetite for male company, and she missed some of the soldiers at the castle. The chance to travel to Rome was most exciting. She had no idea at all where it was or why they were going, nor cared.

'I wish I could change all my clothes and get back to normal.' Judith grumbled, unconvincingly.

'Yes, my lady, these robes don't suit you - but they'll protect you, wherever you are, especially in such a large party of men ...'

'I think people will remember that Odo de Grantmesnil was travelling with a nun. It will be an unusual sight, for he normally only has men as companions.'

Judith could see that the Abbess' plans had many facets, all designed to throw a protective net about her as she left Normandy and rode to Rome. When her father heard the news he would unhesitatingly take it for granted that she was beyond the law, constitutionally dead. And useless to him.

'Now - has the Abbess released our bags and boxes?'

'Yes, madam. It's a wonder how we got them here in the first place ... there's so much! And the horses are fresh. I took them to the Abbot's men, so they could groom them like their own.'

Bertha smiled mischievously at Judith, who stopped herself from chiding her with the words she was going to use; of course Bertha wanted the company of men - it was only natural. She had no troubles, political or otherwise, to hamper her. She knew nothing about any documents. She was as free as a bird, and just as natural.

Although unaware of its contents, Sister Sophia had duly witnessed the Abbess' and Judith's signatures on the most secret document of all; then Judith gravely watched it being buried in the centre of the many rolls of parchment and other confidential papers in a vast chest. Judith's interest quickened, as she said to the Abbess, who was manipulating a huge and intricate form of lock,

'Are all those documents to do with the nuns' vows?'

'No, not all, but some of them are.'

'What are the others?'

'Well, we have rent rolls here, and proofs of title to our land ... those types of documents. And wills, and findings from law-suits, and so on.'

'If anyone forced you to open this chest - it would take quite a long time to find my little disclaimer, wouldn't it?'

'It would. Especially as I've enclosed it within the documents concerning my own entry into this convent. I think it will be safe.'

'And the double document?'

'It will be given to you as you leave. Odo has signed both, and so have I.'

Judith accompanied Sister Sophia back to the pharmacy with the carefully-chosen words, which the Mother Superior had advised her to use,

'I'm travelling with my brother to our sister convent in Rome: there I aim to study medicine. I'll be professed by then, so I'll naturally be dressed as a nun.' she said, reluctant to lie to a woman she cared for - but she did it for the protection of them both, 'yet I ought to travel with a box of pills and potions and herbs, don't you think? Besides, I know how to use them now, don't I?'

Immensely saddened by the news of Judith's imminent departure, Sister Sophia gave her all the medication she could spare, packing it tightly into soft bundles. She gave careful directions on how to mix them, cautioned her about some plants, and reminded her of others: then she made Judith repeat her words over, several times, questioning her exhaustively, so that she'd make no mistakes. She wanted their sister convent in Rome to be impressed by one of her pupils.

'I can't afford to give you the leech-books,' said the nun, 'nor the Book of Wounds, I'm afraid. We need them here.'

'Nor the copy of Galen?' Judith laughed, conspicuously carefree, in a way the nun had not heard her laugh before.

'Nor the copy of Galen.' They smiled at each other.

'But - I'll give you this ...'

Taking a small leather bottle from a high cupboard, which she unlocked with difficulty, she placed it into Judith's hand.

'This is one of my most precious phials. Use it only in the direst emergency, only in the most grave of circumstances - it's an antidote against poison! It's a remedy of great virtue and rarity, in fact it's my greatest treasure in this pharmacy, and I really oughtn't to let it leave the premises.' She pressed it into Judith's hands, then went on, 'But I doubt if we'll have much call for it in this holy convent!'

Judith took the little lumpy leather bottle in her hands with gratitude, and stowed it in the box. It was obviously full of liquid, for she could hear it swishing inside, bound around the stopper with wax and thread, and wrapped in further cloth, securing it. The nun addressed her, rather briskly, to hide her feelings.

'I've grown fond of you, my child, since you and I have worked together - I admit it, although I shouldn't! And I want to protect you, if I can, in the desperate world outside these cloisters. So, if the time comes when it's necessary for you to use this, take it all, don't leave a drop in the bottle - and guard it carefully as you travel. God go with you!'

She made the sign of the cross, and then kissed Judith gently, on both cheeks - rosy with new life coursing through them. Then she mournfully watched Judith walk out of the room for the last time, grateful, eyes shining with excitement, arms filled with remedies. Her own old eyes misted with tears - how she would miss her - but new patients waited so she must hurry to them and resume their care.

JUDITH AND ODO

On the appointed day Judith and Bertha were ready far in advance of the Abbot. Odo had to bring so much with him, to ensure his comfort as he travelled, and also when he arrived at Rome. But he needed to leave the monastery in a manner that would bring credence to the story that he was visiting the Pope; furniture had to remain, and precious hangings, and all the chapel's consecrated vessels and reliquaries: the Bishop would take care of those until he returned. Dominic, his senior monk, would remain, as usual, to care for the monastery; and so would his Chamberlain, Francis. Peter, his Chancellor, he would take with him. He knew about all his legal affairs, and would be invaluable.

Leaving nothing to chance, however, he arranged for various personal documents to be wrapped together in folios. All the coins he could gather together jingled in sacks; his lavish personal plate rasped together, even when wrapped in linen, and his rich clothes and vestments filled many receptacles, the exteriors of which were coated with tar to keep out moisture.

Everything was then most prudently apportioned and packed onto horses and mules so that the accidental loss of one animal wouldn't seriously harm his future. He had travelled so often, and so far, that packing it all up efficiently was done in a well-known system. Finally, his especial tastes in food and wine were pushed into every cranny. Living well and comfortably when travelling was a challenge he felt he could accept, and his staff were accustomed to his ways. Just as soon as they were safely out of Normandy he would try and stay at inns - but first they must race away as fast as they could, to gain ground between himself and Duke William and cross borders.

He thanked God that his monastery lay in the Bishopric of Lisieux, rather than that of Evreux ... for he wanted to avoid contact with his father. Both William and the Count hounding him at the same time would be too fearful - and Judith would be forfeit. At last they were ready to go. It was even more bitterly cold; dread winter was poised before them.

Judith sat on her horse with mixed sensations. This was the second time she had run away. Leaving her family home had been a sudden frantic dash: but she had always been truly frightened of her father, so she missed no-one in the castle - only her adored little dogs.

This time she was adventuring much further into the unknown, conscious that she was doing so illicitly, in disobedience of her father, and with forged papers to ensure her safe passage as a nun - which she was not. To be discovered, or captured, would put many other lives in jeopardy besides herself.

And what would happen when she arrived at Rome? Where was it, exactly? She knew it was south and south again - but had never had the route made clear. Would her brother help her further? Could she rely on him? And would Roger be there - or would she hear of his whereabouts when she arrived? Or had he even died? And if he had, what then? Would the de Hauteville family help her themselves?

Oh well! she conjectured, with a light-hearted smile, there would be time enough to think of all the disasters if they happened - later!

Finally, at Odo's command, she dug her heels into her horse's flanks, seeing, from the corner of her eye, a blessing hand raised for a last brief moment at the convent's window.

When they started off they were a large, unwieldy party; too many men-at-arms, too many horses, too many wagons. Judith and Bertha were the only women, openly in their roles of mistress and maid again; they were protectively placed in the centre of the long procession.

When the sun had vanished the clouds had grown more leaden, and a shrill sour wind whispered in the high hedges. It was not the ideal time for travelling when they set out. The moon rose high, white and cold in a leaden sky, and the ground sparkled as if with powdered glass. Judith felt terrified again, now she was so exposed in the open country, away from the protection of the convent; and the freezing weather evoked a cold danger that beat against her inner world.

The dark stuff of her cloak was misted with pin-point globules. It was silver-grey in the night light - insubstantial: a wet, shining film covered her other garments. Behind her, as they travelled, the land seemed blotted out in the freezing mist - it was as if a magic thorn-thicket had drifted in the wake of a Norse fairy tale, closing in behind her, so that she could never go back to the world of reality - but only forward into a land of new dreams.

Judith imagined an army speeding after them, terrible and shrill. But almost at once the air became full of snowflakes - thick white whirling feathers that reduced the world of spacious sky and covered all the party's churning tracks. Silently they rode on through the night, when occasionally, fitfully, it snowed again.

The next day, in the early sunshine, snowflakes lay like crystallised sugar on the green banks of the road, and ice crunched in the ruts beneath the horses' hooves. A frozen pond, away from the sun, lay grey among the alders; the snow blanketed densely white on the fields, blue-grey in the shadows of hedge and tree, and all was hushed.

Now and again they stopped, eating as they sat in their saddles, not daring to dismount; there was an impatient stamping of heavy hooves, and the juicy sound of horses sucking at a stream.

They followed a path running through the land along a river as it curved between a line of bare willows and alder thickets. The water still ran swiftly but not very deep, and glassy icicles hung from low boughs that dipped their tips into its dark flood-like trailing fingers.

In their wake slipped a grey shadow, a hooded small man,

unremarkable, keeping forever out of sight. He was one of Duke William's spies. From the moment of the quarrel he had been sent to watch Odo's moves. Once away from Norman territory, he had further orders to carry out.

One evening they halted for the night by a barn, looking across a strip of common dropping abruptly to a valley, beyond which the moors mounted to a high ridge, black against a fading sky: here their lookouts might keep watch. The white, heath-covered hills glowed like hot coals where the dipping sun caught their rounded sides, and the hollows were filled with luminous shadows. The thick white cruddled surface of the fallen snow was like the skin of a corpse, more sinister than the black clouds that rolled across it.

Judith ached from head to foot, as, for several nights, they had all slept beneath bushes, fully dressed: she had pillowed her head on her saddle. Through the night small country sounds eddied about them, and once an owl swerved through the darkness and plunged into a hedge abruptly with the noise of a diver meeting water: but, unhearing, they all slept on - save Duke William's conscientious watcher, who cat-napped.

So, day after day, they continued south and south again, avoiding William's land; sometimes eastwards, to disguise their paths; sometimes south-west; but always, with increasing hope, to political and religious friends in the sunnier warmth. In time they left the snow behind and now the frost was melting all around them in the sun with a faint crackling sound like that of a million tiny flames.

The weather changed again, the paths now shone with recent rain: a sudden gust of wind would shake the wet branches, and the drops fringing the leaves scattered onto soaking heads; the horses' legs were masked with mud. Sometimes it was completely still, then the trees never stirred; the silver trunks of the birches had a naked look through their mesh of purple twigs. Mostly they travelled in silence, speaking only when their party had settled for the meal at night.

A broken shaft to a wagon halted their journey for a day or two. Everyone was glad of the rest. Horses cropped the grass. Bertha hurriedly washed some clothes out of sight. The men slept or spoke. To one side a small tented camp was hastily set up for Odo and Judith and the cooks created a tasty meal.

Blowing pouts of air at his drink of hot mulled wine, Odo remarked,

'We're out of William's influence here, I believe, although he's such a clever devil I won't feel safe until I've the walls of Rome around me.'

Judith asked, with genuine interest,

'What pleases you - about being an Abbot? Living in monasteries?'

'Everything, I suppose! It suits my nature. I relish all my five senses.' He gulped down the wine and called for more.

'But you're not a religious man, are you?'

'God forbid!' He rocked on his stool, chuckles rising to his mouth like bubbles.

'The Abbess told me how you gained your income, but I can't think that any of that would be of true interest to you, you'll probably leave the fine points to your Secretary. Then - what does amuse you about being an Abbot?'

Odo was intrigued by Judith's insistence.

'I'm a very rich man, but I need protection against the might and power of our father; owning a monastery affords me that and, as you know, gave me the lawful excuse to run away to Rome.'

'And there the Pope will guard you?'

'For a while. But, in my present position, I can roll as a guest from one monastery to another whenever I please. In Normandy, especially, we seem to be cresting the wave in a new way of life - monasteries abound, haven't you noticed? Countless new ones are being built. The whole land seems to be shaking off the robes of age and putting on the white mantle of the churches: I'm in no doubt that William will make use of that fact one day, and make pretend that some new conquest of his is a religious crusade.'

'But,' said Judith, not letting the subject get away from her, 'where is the fun in the monasteries? Do you just go to avail yourself of the fine food and wine?'

'Well - I rarely attend the prayers! But, Judith, life is most diverting in the best monasteries; I suppose, at heart, I just adore gossip! I hear every piece of tittle-tattle, political and religious - and a great many secrets are told me after good wine. I keep up with all the saints - they're a cult now, you know - all the newest stories and legends, I know who's got the best relics - who's bought what - and, sometimes - whom! I've got intimate links across the Channel in England, too, and I've often travelled there. But I find Rome more entertaining.'

'When you were last in Rome - or even in Rouen? Did you hear any news about the Hautevilles?' She asked in trepidation.

Odo, enjoying himself, proceeded to spend considerable time telling Judith all he knew about the family's exploits: he mentioned Roger several times. She felt re-born.

That night she slept like a babe.

Their steady journey progressed. They followed streams, then broader rivers. The present one was grey and shining, and dotted with flotsam. Judith stared down on the grey waters in which thin sunshine drowned itself. There was a sudden rain shiver along the valley like a shaken muslin veil, and the drenched trees dripped tearfully on to the path. Gradually the sun came blinking out, spring-like, behind some slender silver shafts of birch trees; highlighting the delicate net of quivering leaf that spread between the green of fern and grass and the deepening blue of morning sky.

Still they hurried on, relentlessly, following the generous contours of the land, the line marked by an unseen bubbling stream along which a small bird flew swiftly and dipped quickly.

Towards the end of that day, months after their departure, they came to a shallow valley enclosed by low wooded hills. Narrow green meadows ran its length under a bluff fringed with oak and beech and evergreen, and bounded on the other side by another swift stream. The rains had swollen its rush, and the hungry waters had gnawed at the banks, so that, between each pair of guardian trees stooping over it, a shallow arc of earth and grass had slid down towards the devouring current. Downstream the party halted, made camp, then gratefully rested out of the wet.

THE SHADOW

Their grey shadow, William's man, came slowly down a gentle slope to the valley, wrapped in a cloud of silent obscurity, following the course of a rivulet across whose hurrying surface thin dark lines were drawn from the tips of floating weed. He cautiously edged his way towards the swift stream, and climbed down the muddy bank, between a holly and an old willow that leaned over the water, straining at the anchorage of its roots, where much cut brushwood had been thrown. Just above the water level there was a hollow in the pile, where some larger saplings had fallen and bore the burden of a tangled roof of twig and bramble and brush, as high as the bank top. It was secret and secluded, and offered some protection from the cold and wet. He crept into the spiky bed, fitting it as snugly as a tortoise fits his shell, and lay within, hidden - as always - from sight.

Meanwhile Judith stared across the meadow, not discerning the stippling of a plane tree's leaves against the pale sky, and never noticing a single scavenging magpie as he rose with a flutter of white tail. The hedgerow was full of wild flowers, pale in the dying day: in the darker patches of the wide pasturage faint-hued marsh flowers became yet fainter: the stillness was disturbed by no human sound nearby, only the tired bedtime flutter of birds: they reinforced the atmosphere of suspended time.

She felt calm at last, and spoke with growing ease to her brother. She noticed, too, that her habit of blushing seemed tamed at last; she was learning to control her emotions. Their grey shadow rested as well, then slept.

Judith and Odo had become more familiar with each other by now and found, much to their surprise, that they enjoyed each other's company a great deal. Once Odo said,

'Was your experience at the convent very dreadful?'

'No. My own company was my worst enemy. In my isolation I learned that I was too high-born and indulged - even cossetted - to fit in easily into a noviate's life, devoted to God, and I had really no vocation to be a nun. I learned when I was there that no-one will be a genuinely devout nun unless she's touched with fire. I learned, too, to think for myself.'

'You learned a lot ...'

'Most of all, I learned to be honest, I believe. The Mother Superior and Sister Sophia taught me self-worth by making me enquire conscientiously into my deepest problems.'

Odo put his podgy hand on Judith's sleeve, saying fondly,

'I'll do anything to help you find Roger when we get to Rome, Judith; I have a host of influential friends.'

'I'm glad to know that. I trust you.'

'In the meanwhile, I have a secret to tell you.' He leaned forward and whispered, for a long while, in his sister's receptive ear. Now and then she protested, but he spoke some more, until, at last, she nodded her head in agreement. Then he gave her a small piece of parchment, heavy with waxen seals.

'Don't let Peter see this, unless it's needed. He had nothing to do with its preparation.'

The journey south had been difficult, and was prolonged for months. Sometimes it was for rest, at others because the terrain was strenuous and demanding, or sufficient boats were hard to hire for travel down rivers, or because Odo had met friends and wished to stay with them.

They had to travel via areas where William of Normandy had no alliances, where he was neither liked, nor even tolerated. The long summer days swam by like leaves upon a stream until, at last, they entered Avignon in brilliant sunshine, relieved that they were both safe.

No-one had noticed their grey shadow as they journeyed, until he began to mix with the crowd of people; gradually his face became familiar to everyone. Sometimes, at night, he lay in the bracken near enough to smell their cooking food, watching the Abbot's soldiers lying by their evening fires. He knew it would be some while before he could get near enough to Odo and his sister to carry out further orders - but William had made plain what was to be done.

AVIGNON

Now that the party had arrived in Avignon, they no longer felt at risk. For the grey man it did not matter whether he had to carry out his orders in Rome or elsewhere, as long as they were away from William's land or friends - he just had to find the right moment. From now on he would blend fully into the Abbot's closest group until no-one questioned his presence. They all settled, in utmost content, at a large inn.

Avignon intrigued Judith, but she did not dare to venture abroad unless in Odo's company. It was Bertha who was allowed to roam the narrow streets, returning to Judith with tales of the throngs of people, petitioners, envoys, money-changers, notaries, lawyers, officials of the Curia and of other courts, builders and adventurers - together with thieves and money-lenders, prostitutes, astrologers and necromancers. She had a wonderful time, and Judith heard all about it second-hand.

Several days later Judith and her brother dined together, sitting alone after the meal, talking about the future.

'Word is coming through that William has turned to England. He won't have much time for me now. We'll carry on to Rome, as planned, though.'

Judith was thankful that they would again be on the move; the enforced delays had exasperated her. But his next words surprised her,

'Then, after a rest in Rome - and if the news from Normandy seems promising - maybe I'll return home again.'

'You'd risk that?'

'It might be worth my while!'

'Why? What's to gain for you?'

Odo laughed and refilled his goblet.

'More than is immediately obvious, my dear. You see - William can't be in two places at the same time, and he'll be in need of every diplomat he has. A diplomat who is also an Abbot would be even more useful. William is very keen to strengthen his ties with the Church - he has made peace with the Pope, built a monastery at Caen, and has given so much money to strengthen his duchy that he could contemplate a successful foreign invasion. He has also freed himself from dependency upon the King of France.'

Judith smiled blithely at her brother, very fond of him now.

'You've been good to me, dear Odo, and I'm grateful. I'll enjoy meeting your friends in Rome when we arrive. Maybe I'll come back, too, one day, when our father is dead ... if you were safe.'

'Are you sure you would not prefer to remain here? I could send on messengers to Apulia to find your Roger and bring him here to meet you. It would be so much more prudent!'

Judith sighed, 'No, I feel I might be wasting time. I'll journey on with you.'

Avignon was an attractive city, not large, but at an important crossroads. Situated at a point on the east bank of the Rhone River where the narrow valley opens into a broad delta plain, north-west of Nîmes, from Roman times it had been a much fought-over prize. When Judith and her Brother Abbot arrived the city was held by a vassal of the Pope, which was the reason, as a churchman, he could feel completely safe.

CLOSURE

'Before we leave this pleasant place, will you prepare an accredited letter - that certificate she required of us - to go to the Mother Superior, to tell her that I am safe and she can destroy the document she holds for me? We can then send it once we set foot in Rome - and I'll feel free of lies and subterfuges with the convent. Otherwise - something may happen, and I'll be caught up with my nun's habit for life! If we don't do it now it will take me months to persuade you to write it once we're in Rome! *Could you do it now?* I know you'd rather write the letter yourself, as you disapprove of my knowing how to write.'

She looked up at her brother, placing a delicate hand on his arm.

Odo of Grantmesnil was in a mellow mood, rested and bathed, full of good food and excellent wine. He turned to a grey, servant-like figure standing behind him in the shadows near the door and said,

'Send for my Chancellor, Peter. Tell him to come with some fresh parchment, and tell him to bring the writing materials, too.'

The man bowed in silence and left the room.

Some while later Peter bustled in importantly, some parchment under his arm: by this time of the evening he had thought to be free, and was not best pleased to be drawn from his gargantuan meal. The small grey man carried the writing equipment. Finally, when Odo was satisfied, both men stood behind him, near the wall.

The Abbot smiled at his sister in the room full of late sun, and laboriously wrote a long letter, full of gossip, to the Mother Superior of the convent. Peter dozed as he stood, filled with good food. He had stood for many weary hours in the past, waiting for his master to finish his interminable letters, and he allowed his head to fall upon his chest in slumber, as he braced himself against the wall. Only the scratch of Odo's quill could be heard.

Just as he was signing the letter, the small grey man took a few silent paces forward, placed a thin steel knife against Odo's back, rammed it home - and left it there.

The Abbot gasped. A gout of blood spurted out of his open mouth onto the half-signed letter and he slumped forward across the parchment.

Like a wraith, the small grey man dissolved from the room, his footsteps pattering faintly on the stone steps - and vanished.

Peter looked around sleepily when he heard Odo's gasp. He had heard no other sound. Now he could see the Abbot sprawled across the table lying in his own blood. He shrieked.

Judith, white as swan's feathers, clasped a hand to her mouth, soundlessly shaking from head to foot. She had witnessed it all in front of her. Suddenly the tears spilled down her white cheeks.

'Is my brother dead?'

No-one answered her, but she flew to his side, felt for the pulse in his fleshy neck, and knew. No longer would Odo parade and gossip and whisper and amuse: the 'Rolling Abbot' was quite still. The worldly man, who was accustomed to going into church with a hawk on his wrist, equipped with tinkling bells, would ride and hunt no more. Fear, now, would be unknown to him.

In fear and trembling for his own safety, Chancellor Peter bellowed out of the window for the Captain of the Guard; suddenly there was pandemonium in every quarter. Judith continued to sit by Odo until they lifted him up and placed him upon a form of stretcher and took him to a chapel nearby. Priests came and went; servants cleared the gory mess. Bertha was called, and waited, speechless for once, behind Judith's chair. Chancellor Peter, afraid of the finger of guilt being pointed at him, babbled to the soldiers.

Judith put out her shaking hand and took up Odo's letter to the Abbess, part signed, now flooded with blood, which was slowly drying around the half-signed name.

Sweet Jesus - *was the letter legal?* And was she to be free?

Without both their signatures upon the release would the Abbess - *could* the Abbess - destroy the document in her keeping, thereby releasing her from any suspicion of being a professed nun?

Several days later, Judith buried her brother with suitable pomp, solemnised by the Bishop, and attended by the Pope's vassal and all his court and clergy.

The church authorities in the city had been much disquieted; Abbot Odo had been immensely popular, if unfamiliar here - his reputation always travelled ahead of him. The murder of such a man was not to be tolerated. So a hastily assembled enquiry was called, where they established that the thin grey man was the assassin - and a stranger to everyone. No-one could recall who had engaged him, he just always appeared at hand when needed; Odo's party were ashamed that they had been so simply taken in. The Chancellor had been told to stay his hand over Odo's possessions, and lock his room, until the grave matter was resolved.

On further enquiry, in private session with Judith, it then became evident who had ordered his death - but it could not 'be proven without doubt'. A Cardinal, who without delay had been sent from Rome to lead the enquiry, decided that it would be unwise, and impractical, to pursue the matter further; instead, a handsome monument would be commissioned and later added to Odo's grave. The Pope wanted no more trouble with the Duke of Normandy, now good and obedient, who was on the point of conquering Maine and was also making overtures to inherit England.

Judith spent much time with Odo's Chancellor, sorting out his affairs, according to Odo's instructions. Some contracts and ecclesiastical artefacts would have to be returned to his monastery in Normandy, and Peter would take these himself, together with some of the soldiers, who wished to return home.

Other soldiers in Odo's employ voted to journey on with Judith to Rome, whereupon they might join up with mercenary bands, or even accompany her further in her own service. They discussed all practical affairs for several days, until there was no doubt in anyone's mind that full justice was done in every quarter.

Then Judith met the Chancellor privately in her rooms, and showed him Odo's secret document heavy with his personal seals. Under the watchful eyes of the Cardinal the three of them unrolled it, breaking the seals.

It was a Codicil to Odo's Will. He had made Judith his heir.

Peter was clearly shocked by the existence of such a secret document unknown to him, and began to protest about its legality. But the Cardinal ordered Odo's Chancellor to take some servants to Odo's rooms, and return with the sacks of gold. They were also to bring Odo's clothes, his personal plate, and everything else that they could carry. The Cardinal smiled behind his hand: this time he, not Odo, would be carrying gossip from Church to monastery and back again.

Eventually they all returned, overloaded, and deposited it all around Judith as she sat by a large table.

'And the leather bag?' asked Judith, 'Where is that?'

'Which leather bag?' answered Peter. 'I know of none.'

'Fetch it immediately!' said Judith, with a steely look. 'I know all about it and so does the Cardinal. You wouldn't wish to be branded as a thief, would you?'

With a muttered curse the Chancellor did as he was bid, returning with a very heavy leather bag, with monstrously large seals and fastenings, placing it upon the table in front of Judith. The Cardinal and she examined the bag, seeing it addressed to Judith in Odo's hand, and having Odo's thumb-print deeply imbedded in his personal seal.

The Cardinal picked up the Codicil again, calling in Odo's servants as witnesses, and read it out aloud to everyone present. All eyes were upon the unopened bag.

The Codicil disclosed that, as he was unmarried and had no children, Judith was named as his heir. Some of Odo's land reverted to his father, some to the Church. There were various generous bequests to his staff. But all the wealth and possessions he carried upon his person on this journey were to go, 'in brotherly love', to his sister Judith, and 'in concern for her welfare'.

In time, reluctantly, the Cardinal left. Then Judith dismissed Chancellor Peter and all Odo's servants, telling them to go and pray for Odo's soul. Peter sneered, but left.

When everyone was gone, and soldiers were posted outside her door, Judith sat in the solitude of the flower-scented room, filled with evening sunlight. She had never felt so isolated in her life. She genuinely missed her brother. But the question of her own personal freedom was uppermost in her mind, and whether her half-signed document was legal.

At last she reached forward and began to pick at the seal upon the large leather bag, crumbling it away with a small knife and her fingernails. Loosening the tight cords, by and by she managed to open the neck of the bag. Then she lifted up a corner of the base slightly and very cautiously poured out a steady stream of loose gemstones onto the table, like an infinitely precious rainbow, winking and blinking in the last light of day.

Right in their midst was another note from Odo, stating that should she have it in her hand, life must now be over for him: he had bought the gems for his own security when in Rouen, frightened that William might punish or destroy him. But, with this immense wealth, willingly given from the grave, Judith, too, would become secure. Best of all she would, no longer, be dependent upon their father. No-one had known anything about Odo's private fortune, but her. And now she owned it all.

Behaving like a merchant, Judith selected a large pearl and carefully put it into her mouth, tasting it, and was thankful to find it was sweet - so it must have come from Oman: if it had been salty it would have come from the Red Sea and been inferior. Then she dropped it into some wine, and, rather than floating as fakes did, it sank to the bottom of the goblet in a satisfactory way. No doubt about it, it was genuine and immensely valuable. And so was everything else.

It was a freedom of sorts.

ROBERT, DUKE OF APULIA, AND ROGER

Duke William of Normandy had conquered England and, eighteen months after, his fellow Norman, Duke Robert of Apulia, embarked upon the crucial siege of Bari.

The Anglo-Saxon population of England found the new regime under William harsh and vexatious. The crown attached itself to the land like a parasite, sucking up its resources. The almost unlimited power of the post-Conquest king created fear and misgivings even among his Norman vassals, in danger of losing their fiefs by arbitrary distraint.

Nor was the Duke of Apulia, as Robert had now been proclaimed, a man to under-estimate; for twenty years he had fought over all the mountains and valleys of southern Italy and most of Sicily, but there still remained one or two isolated pockets he could not subdue. Very quickly indeed the people of Bari discovered that they had a worthy opponent, who used most unorthodox procedures. This time it was Robert's pride more than his pocket, which was at risk.

Bari was the capital of Byzantine Langobardia and headquarters of the Greek army in Italy. It was by far the largest, richest and best defended city in all the south, the jewel in the crown of the Byzantine holdings: rich people resident there even had lamps made of gold imported from Constantinople.

The leaders of the walled port relied almost entirely upon their cosmopolitan fleet, filled with ships of all categories and sizes; through them they traded, travelled widely, and were known throughout all the other Mediterranean ports.

With their reputation built up over many centuries, linked with their ties in Greece and Byzantium, the people of Bari knew the owners of many other ships, in other ports nearby, who might be relied upon to come to her rescue. The stalwart, cocksure people behind their walls had every reason to be confident that this upstart Norman Duke would be perfunctorily tossed aside by the experienced citizens of this centuries-old city: no more than a handful had heard about England and 'the other Duke.'

Robert immediately created a wave of reverse propaganda, putting it about in the fish markets up and down the coast that he had a deplorable lack of sea-faring knowledge. It was true that he hated the sea, a hatred bred into him by Tancred, but it did not mean he had no ships. He had fought in Sicily, Calabria and Apulia - all around the coast of southern Italy - and now he knew a great deal about warfare by sea. The Bariots, safe in their haven, only judged Robert as a conqueror by land.

Whilst learning the benefits of sea power, Robert had begun to collect ships from the start of his long campaign in Italy: much of his fleet had been used as nothing more than transport vessels to and from Sicily, serviced by Greek crews from Apulia, but all of them had been prepared prior to his proposed siege of Bari and were lying at anchor at Sipontum, northwards, up the Adriatic coast. Robert, always unconventional, thought and planned the siege as a military commander, using his fleet like an army; the Bariots had no conception that he had a small, well-disciplined navy at his disposal.

The moment the brothers had parted, after their meeting with the Pope, they had become closely united. Young Roger had been left in charge of the overall preparation of the siege, and, after some months, had tied up the landward side of the city like a neat parcel, the people of Bari took no heed, simply using their fleet as normal to trade and bring in supplies.

Duke Robert stayed on in Rome, after the long meeting with the

Pope and then the even more extended conferences with counsellors and men of commerce. At the end he rode off to Aversa, to the castle inherited from his brothers, to exchange views on money management with his wife; her brother, the Lombard Prince Gisulf, might be persuaded to become an ally and gain from the siege - if Gisulf lent sufficient wealth beforehand.

Between battles, Sichelgaita had provided Robert with a son, fondly named 'Roger' by Robert; his wife would have preferred a more Lombard name. But the nervous, easily frightened child was soon nicknamed 'Roger Borsa,' because of an unfortunate habit, evolved during his earliest years, of bringing out his purse and counting his coins. That did not please his mother, either. His two unlovely sisters - they each had goitre - taunted him unmercifully, and as the years passed by he became cunning and deceitful, apart and withdrawn. His two enormous parents would tower over him in the most intimidating manner, urging him to succeed ... but he had no aptitude for the abilities they held dear. Sichelgaita became frenzied by disappointment.

Duke Robert had once brought Mark - now universally called 'Bohemund' - to the castle at Aversa, but it was a fatal mistake. The contrast between the boys was too remarkable. Bohemund was the elder, and twice Roger Borsa's size. But he came reluctantly, confused and resentful of his position as a proclaimed bastard - it was hardly of his own doing.

Roger Borsa, although years younger, continually referred to Bohemund's illegitimacy in public, but always out of Duke Robert's hearing. Sichelgaita was apt to encourage this, and slyly taunted him as well. Bohemund, until then having innocence and charm, gradually developed a bitter and twisted side to his character, which was to bode ill in the future.

Although the 'uncanonical' situation had been explained to him at length by his parents in the kindest way, in his unformed mind he felt an injustice too great to bear: there was no denying he was Duke Robert's son. After the years of his father weaving stories to him about his future inheritance at Aversa he found himself overwhelmingly jealous to see his young half-brother in his rightful place, leaving him with no place, nor hope at all.

Dispossessed, hounded by Roger Borsa and scorned by jealous Sichelgaita, Bohemund eventually begged his overtaxed father to allow him to return to Alberada in Calabria. Robert saw that he was simmering with unhappiness, but they were too much alike to communicate with ease, and he let Bohemund go without fully realising the problems; besides, he had overwhelming difficulties of his own. The conquest of Bari occupied all his thoughts.

So Duke Robert and Roger met up, as arranged, in the Hauteville camp, outside Bari's strong city walls. They sat under a eucalyptus tree by the Adriatic Sea, occasionally slapping their strong brown arms as the mosquitoes feasted. Only Jacques and Pierre were permitted to attend them.

The siege of Bari was the most important operation that any Hauteville had been engaged upon in the fifty or more years they had swarmed over the south, and at times like these Robert decided that his and Roger's partnership would have to be amicable if they were to succeed. Dispassionately he saw that they needed each other and, as good Normans, they should forget all past differences and fight shoulder to shoulder - until the next time. In his heart he had every confidence in his younger brother, certain he wouldn't fail him.

Meanwhile, during all his travels and battles, Roger had written regularly to Judith from the moment he had left Normandy, pouring out his heart to her in stumbling sentences, telling her of every adventure, every new sight. The letters had all gone to her in the care of the Count of Evreux, and the Count, with a harsh laugh, destroyed them all - having read them: it gave him comforting proof, however, that Judith's whereabouts were unknown to the Hautevilles as well as himself.

He had known from the beginning that there was a juvenile attachment between the pair, but he had never once mentioned Roger's name. To have done so would have dignified him, given the liaison some significance. By destroying each letter as it arrived he was blotting out any possible substance to the romance. If there was no communication at all, he felt sure that they would get over it in time. Although he never needed to explain his actions to any higher authority, he felt they were justified, especially since Judith's escape.

Six months before, after the conference with the Pope, Robert had agreed that his young brother might send for Judith: his prospects were good enough. He had written, ecstatically, but there had been no reply. He had previously been worried for many months that no replies to any of his letter had reached him, only fragments of news from his mother whilst she lived, but there were many hazards along the route that could account for the lack of them. This invitation to join him in Apulia must surely rate an answer - and yet no news came.

Then, one day, a messenger had arrived from Normandy, bringing news that the lady Judith had long disappeared and her father was in a towering rage ... no one dared mention her name. There was talk that she was dead, had become a nun, was wedded to a Hun, that disease had disfigured her face, that she had lost her mind ... the tales were endless. Roger was bewildered. Preparations for the siege at Bari mercifully exhausted him so the days fled by. Robert made him travel hither and thither, mustering up men, materials, crews. He became gaunt with fatigue and lines deepened about his sensitive mouth. Robert watched him, wordlessly.

Now, at last, the beginning of the siege was truly under way. It was August, the hottest month of the year. No-one deemed it honourable to launch a siege at that moment, when they deserved their annual rest, but 'wasn't that typical of the unscrupulous Duke of Apulia and his brother, Roger?' It looked as though there would be a long, cold winter ahead, and many conventions overturned.

PLANS FOR THE SIEGE

A duplicate of Robert's initial proposals were under lock and key, together with his costs and timing: the original remained with Roger. As he grew older he realised more clearly how the preparations of any battle, the minutiae, were of paramount importance, especially when the stakes were mountainous: gone were the days when he would rush in, heedlessly. Months had gone into the preparations, now he was prepared to share his most secret schemes with Roger, whom he had grown to trust at last. Even so, Robert left nothing to chance.

'This is my secret plan for success. Now, at last, I can share it with you!'

Robert smoothed out a large patch of sand between them as they sat, which had been wetted with sea-water.

'Here is the city, here is the port. See the way it juts out as a narrow promontory northwards into the sea?'

He made another design on the smooth sand.

'Now, look at the plan of the city itself - the great walls here ... and here ... and here.'

He drew with a sharp stick.

'We've dug the ditches all around, we're comfortably out of range from spears and arrows, and we've encircled the city like a neat, tight necklace. Only the harbour is free.'

Roger was all attention. Robert continued, engrossed,

'What they're all relying on is that they can get away to sea at any time. They are also convinced that supplies can come in by sea when they wish. But none of them know we've a fleet of our own, lying in wait. Now, have you those iron chains?'

Roger nodded.

'Each ship has more than enough! One end, in every case, is now firmly attached - the other is loose, but ready!'

'And is each mast of oak, not pine?'

Roger assured him they were.

'And is a coin of lead placed beneath the step of each mast? For I'll take no chances with ill-luck here!'

'I placed each one myself.'

Duke Robert grunted as he swept the sand clear of marks, leaving no tell-tale signs.

'At dawn then, when the sun begins to rise in their lazy eyes!'

They prepared to eat, then slept in their tented camp by the sea. Back to back Jacques and Pierre sat upon the sand in the dark, watching over them, in spite of the multitude of soldiers surrounding them.

The next dawn, just as the heat was beginning to simmer upwards from the stone walls and uneven cobbles, the white sea-haze parting as the sun suddenly thrust itself up over the horizon, a long line of ships in close formation swooped down towards Bari.

Behind the barricades children laughed and shrieked a welcome. Men shouted, too, then taunted the Normans within earshot with the news of approaching friends. The women, ever practical, decided to cook a good midday meal to greet the unexpected friends who appeared to be coming to rescue them. The sun shone in the watchers' eyes as they strained to follow the curious sight of ship after ship apparently edging in closer and closer around the city's port. As the ships closed in, all the citizens cheered their arrival.

Finally one ship nudged the jetty which marked the southern-most part of the harbour. Some sailors leapt out and made the vessel fast to a huge iron bollard, then, faces set, stood on guard like soldiers.

One by one, in formation, boat after boat threw out lengths of rope to their neighbours to the north. As the sailors hauled in the heavy wet ropes the puzzled people of Bari saw that each rope held, at its end, a lengthy iron chain.

The men pulled everything in, ropes and clanking chains, securing them tightly, winding them around the main mast. Then the rowers brought the last vessel right up to the far jetty - and moored fast.

And now, with sinking hearts, the Bariots realised that they were completely encircled by the Norman invaders. Looking back, they were reminded that, by land, they were menaced by all the expert foot soldiers. Now, by sea, there was a chain-linked barrier of ships, crowded by unknown sailors, armed, grim and unsmiling. Not only was there a girdle-like barrier, but also the interlinked ships moored to each other provided a short-cut bridge for the Norman soldiers to cross if they so wished.

Abruptly the shouts and taunts of the Bariots died away and a deep silence followed.

Duke Robert, the Guiscard, head up, and easily seen by all, laughed in their faces, satisfied. Now the siege of Bari had truly begun, and the people there would rue the day that they had defied him.

Then he looked down at his inspiration, the family ring: the lion's paw encircled by chains. He thought about Tancred.

From now on, however, Roger could continue in full command and co-ordinate the wait ahead, he'd earned the position and was fully competent. Within a few days he alone would make a detour to be with Alberada and Mark again, high in the cool mountains. It would be a secret, happy bypass, before facing the intensity of Sichelgaita and more affairs of state. But Alberada would be the first to know! And he'd take her bracelets, or would it be a woven golden belt this time? He couldn't wait to see her face. But he did not know what to do about Bohemund; trouble lay ahead in that direction.

MATTEO OF BARI

No-one at Avignon had heard word of the current problems in south-eastern Italy, at Bari in Apulia, but it was to affect all Normans in time. It affected poor Matteo, sailor of Bari, from the outset.

He was a little man, muscle-bound, the colour of mahogany, with high-polished cheek bones and fierce grey eyes. He leaned against a cart, putting one hot foot slowly onto a spoke of the ragged wheel. He was deathly weary. The horse was dead in the shafts.

Oh - this siege, this cruel siege! In the city lived his old mother, his wife and small sons. Yet here he was, outside the city's walls, not knowing whether they were alive or dead. He could neither go inside, nor get them out.

When the siege of Bari had started he had been away, chasing swordfish - his favourite catch - down into the Bay of Otranto. Never before had he sailed so far from home, his boat cleaving the clear green-blue waters, sometimes accompanied by dolphins and flights of sea-birds. He had followed a school of swordfish, successfully filling his boat - then unloaded at Brindisi, where he sold them at such a profit it made his eyes stand out. They took his octopus, too, and several pails of mussels. That meant he had enough money for the winter months. Thanks be to Saint Nicholas.

With a sense of urgency he had gone on board once more, sailing further south, picking up the school again as he rounded into the bay. A second sale back at Brindisi tempted him into the wine-shops for two nights, the better part of his money tied in a cloth around his waist. Two weeks after his departure, he had headed back up the coast to Bari, slowly and contentedly tacking across the warm and sunny, almost windless sea. But, once close to his home port, men ashore urgently shouted to him the news - 'Bari under siege' - and that he was to land south of the city to save his life.

Shocked and frightened, he left his boat with friends at Mola di Bari and continued on with a local carter who was now in the pay of the Hautevilles. The man carried wood for siege-works - platforms, ladders, firewood and planks for lining the newly-dug ditches around the city. His horses strained so hard to pull the heavy loads, and now this one was dead.

Matteo could hear the inhabitants calling from the city, shouting and whistling. He levered himself from the cart, stumbling along until he could clearly see some of the city dwellers marching up and down the thick outer walls, some with arms cradling gold and silver treasures. Small boys were polishing the shiny metal, angling it towards the sun, trying to blind the invaders. Larger boys were hurling insults at the impressive Hauteville brothers as they stood below at the head of their army, and aiming to hit them with sharp stones.

Robert shouted to them with authority; this type of encounter spurred him to a peak of good humour,

'Thank you, thank you, good citizens! My grateful thanks to you! Look after those treasures well for me - you won't have the pleasure of owning them much longer!'

He and Roger both knew that the siege was to take a long time - maybe several years. Ah - but the spoils at the end! Robert thought of nothing but the gold plate, treasures and prestige:Roger tore his thoughts away from the miserable deaths to come.

Matteo craned his neck to see Robert and Roger ride away from the city walls. His long memory sought, and found, the teasing answer to a sudden flash of recognition,

'That's my colossus on the beach at Santa Margherita - I'm sure of it!'

But he knew he would not eat at Robert's table that day.

Searching, searching, he thought he could just see one of his small sons on the top of the walls.

Weeping, alone, he knelt and prayed.

JUDITH'S NEW COMPANIONS

With advice and help from the Bishop, Judith joined a large party bound for Rome. It was headed by a man named Pantaleone, who was a rich young merchant of Amalfi; he had travelled far and wide. Other small groups of merchants or travellers hastened to join them, so that they set out as an extensive company, which would ensure them from attack. The spy's work was done; William of Normandy had given no orders regarding Judith.

After careful deliberation Judith decided to put away her nun's habit and resume her own garments. Until she arrived in Rome she thought, her many inherited possessions, guarded by her own soldiers, made it unbelievable that she was a poor nun; travelling naturally clothed with such an entourage made her marginally less conspicuous. With Odo dead and buried, and having left behind all areas where her father could harm her, she felt safe at last. Besides - she had not worn modish dress for over three years and longed to look appealing again,

As they bumped along the rutted road Judith thought, ironically, that she was now completely free. Since she had been born she had been escorted everywhere. She used to be escorted, as a child, by a nurse to see her mother - before she died; escorted by her ladies or servants to banquets in the castle; even escorted to the convent, and then taken on to Avignon by her brother: apart from her decision to escape from her father, her life had always been organised by others on her behalf.

Now no-one was taking her anywhere; she was going to Rome by her own choice. She had made enquiries about other groups leaving Avignon for Rome, enquiring about their size and security. She had been to see the leaders of some of them, and then declined to join them, always for some sound, practical reason.

Finally, with the Bishop's help, Pantaleone, the rich young merchant, had been presented to her and she found him sympathetic. Several times they had met, and every time she had felt at ease with him, could talk to him quite freely, that their minds seemed to touch. She was surprised at the extent of his experience. She was also surprised at his friendly approach towards her. Cast spiritually and intellectually adrift, women were confronted with the closed ranks of a masculine society, governed by a thoroughly masculine theology and by a morality made by men for men - but Pantaleone was different.

'My lady,' he said, 'you are far too gentle to travel alone. But with our soldiers joining together we'll all be well-guarded. We've both got a purpose, and, as the Bishop thinks it's fitting, we could be partners in this journey - what do you say? Shall I take care of you and your group and, in return, we can be company for each other when we stop at the end of each day?'

Judith looked dubiously at him standing there, dark-haired and full of carefree laughter. What sort of a man was this, before her? He seemed unique to her. She said,

'What kind of company had you in mind? I'm unused to the company of young men.'

'Well, we'd retain our separate establishments, of course, but perhaps we can sit together sometimes when we eat? Or occasionally mix with some of the more entertaining travellers?'

Judith thought that that was reasonable. Pantaleone happily continued,

'Perhaps you could tell me stories - sing a song - I don't know! I don't even care! I'm sure that just being in your presence would be a delight ...' he looked at her attractive face, innocent of artifice or guile. 'We're both young and we have our lives ahead of us … time enough when we're old to be sombre and careful! I'd enjoy your company on our journey through to Rome - shall we travel together then?'

Judith was aware of a most curious inward sensation. As a motherless child she had always been older than her years, without younger siblings, and had always had to be conscious, under her father's eagle eye, of her social position. She was even too dutiful to take a companion or servant into her confidence; besides, it would be unfair to them, the gulf would have been too wide to bridge. So her inner thoughts were permanently disciplined into silence.

Then, her busy time at the convent had been filled with anxieties, doubts and prayers; and real intimacy with the nuns had never been considered - even Sister Sophia knew little about her. Her journey with her brother, much older and more worldly than her, had proven interesting, but their progress had been fraught with political harassment - finalised with murder.

Now, for the first time, freedom and youth beckoned. And the graceful young man before her seemed to share a congenial background, albeit from another country, with the same conventions and manners. She smiled, then, calm and strangely at ease. He saw the transformation taking place, and said,

'That's better! Your life's ahead - let's enjoy this adventure with light hearts!'

Days went by as they journeyed along, and Judith opened her mind and her eyes at long last and became fascinated by the life all around her. Every third day they needed to stop, to rest the horses and buy fresh provisions: no-one was in any great hurry. Servants set up their tents and appetising smells came wafting into the evening air; cooks from different regions vied with each other, and as they meandered further south, the food seemed flavoured more orientally, strong enough at times to burn the unaccustomed tongue.

In the evenings it was the time for merrymaking, with a variety of people passing to and fro. None of the other parties came from as far afield as Normandy, so the medley of cosmopolitan voices kept Judith alight with interest: mostly they were merchants with their laden animals, and often Judith made impulsive purchases. Bertha pleased herself more than she could ever remember and Judith sometimes found her almost asleep on her horse.

One time they were joined by a colourful troupe of strolling players, who would acrobatically tumble and juggle by their side, prepared to sing their lilting songs and mournful ballads through half the night - if handsomely rewarded. They were on their way to a fair at some cross-route, and they joined the motley throng for safety.

Judith's life became serene. Her wealthy companion had persuaded her that there was no reason to forego the pleasures of life when she had the means. His attention was caught by her group of attendant soldiers, her multitude of servants - especially the cooks - and her large baggage train. He watched how they efficiently set up the spacious tents when they could find no suitable accommodation in the small towns through which they passed, and the way that Judith was pampered by all at hand. And all the time he wondered why she was voyaging alone.

Some of Bertha's time was devoted to attending to Judith's needs, but they were few, and Judith was happy, and let her go about her carefree ways with an indulgent chuckle. With men who attracted her Bertha flirted with abandon. With the most desirable she went further; but she knew her only permanence lay in Judith's service so all amorous adventures were merely transient - and all the more enjoyed.

Many people in the party came from different areas, so Judith began to learn their sparkling languages, and tried to understand their individual patois: Pantaleone helped her greatly. Her cooks experimented, too, creating toothsome dishes for her of some of the local delicacies, plucking oranges or lemons from nearby groves to add zest, or roasting kid with herbs and rosemary in yellow-green olive oil, beneath umbrella pines. Yet when her entertaining companion was with them, her cooks would sometimes present familiar Norman dishes instead, and witness their joint delight and surprise. All types of food now tempted her palate, so the lines of strain on Judith's face disappeared, smiles - even laughter - now came easily to her and she slept soundly each night.

PANTALEONE'S FRIENDSHIP

Much of the journey took them alongside the coastline, which meant there were no hills to climb: it became airless and cloyingly hot.

'You sing like a bird, Judith - thank you for those songs tonight!'

Smiling as she laid aside her flute, Judith sat elegantly on her cushions, under eucalyptus trees, sun-browned, eyes dancing; her cheek glowed with the faint tint of a wild-rose petal and was curved with its curve. Pink and cream, soft as a syllabub, she was utterly at peace. Pantaleone lost his heart to her.

Now that all conventions had been observed, and as day followed day, and they rode together, knee to knee, their conversation had at last, inevitably, become more intimate. In time details about his life came to the fore and others about his parents and their many ramifications of trade in Amalfi and abroad. He was their roving ambassador, successfully probing far and wide: he would soon be setting up another offshoot branch at Constantinople, so the tentacles of their business would curl throughout the Levant.

Through his words Judith learned how he had gained his experience, and she looked at him with wonder. It was the first time she had chanced upon a rich family who had no allegiance to any court, and, realising that there was a prodigious disparity between them, she enquired further.

In the beginning he told her of his initial eagerness to be trained in medicine - he burned to do that: he would have much preferred that way of life to being a merchant. But he was an only son, so his parents impressed upon him that he should continue in his father's footsteps, to search the world for newer luxuries; it was an adventurous and often dangerous life but the family had prospered greatly.

Nevertheless, he told Judith, his parents failed to understand his conflict. They lived such contented lives in such comfortable, yet constricting circumstances, that he felt they could never understand his point of view. His travels had opened up a world to him where poverty and disease predominated - it wrung his heart - but he couldn't convey to them his concern, however hard he tried.

'Of course my affluent life is phenomenal for me, and I appreciate it. But my conscience is ever troubled by what I see and I feel I should - I ought - to work more for the poor and sick. I've discussed it with my parents, but they prefer a dutiful son. Besides - I doubt if my mother has even ventured into the old part of our own city of Amalfi: my father warned her that it would be too dangerous. She doesn't know what the squalid areas are like. She has no notion of terrible diseases - afflictions - real poverty! My father knows more, but he averts his eyes. This I can grasp, but - how the innocent suffer! God help the poor ...'

'Does God help? I've often wondered if He helps people, or treats them all the same, bestowing on them the same opportunities? That way the rich can use their wealth to alleviate the ills of the less fortunate. You could do this couldn't you? With your wealth you have more power than if you were a doctor. Are you not better fitted to be a merchant?'

The conversation turned to ethics and morality. They discussed their opinions in depth and at length, unafraid, now, to put half-thoughts into words. Medicine and healing formed a bond between them.

After several more days Judith recounted the fact that she had run from her father and threats of a loveless marriage, and spent some time in a convent preparing to be a nun. She never mentioned Roger ... just in case.

'I was torn! I wanted to become a nun for the wrong reason ... because it seemed so safe. But then I knew that my destiny wasn't wrapped in that quiet building, but lay far away. Obviously I could have taken the safe way out, but I was driven by a sense of destiny. I suppose, too, that my vocation was simply not strong enough.'

He listened to her gravely as she added,

'I spoke to several of the nuns about their conviction. One said to me, 'You hear it. You know it.' Another said, 'It's not up to yourself, really, it's a force you can't control.' And yet another, 'It might not be your personal choice. It is in the end. But not in the first place.' And a fourth told me, 'I've been thinking about it for some time, I don't think I can escape it now.' Before I left I realised how many of them were torn by doubts - and yet, once they faced them, their lives as nuns were immeasurably enriched for them. But I had insufficient faith to leave my world, and sometimes I feel ashamed.'

She sighed, remembering a world left far behind.

'It's the same for me,' said Pantaleone, 'when I think of studying medicine it's because I'm driven by a strong need to experiment with herbs and drugs, to cure diseases. If my father ever permitted, I could do this within the Church's walls. But I can't become a monk, either, for I quarrel in my heart over some of the Church's doctrines.'

They talked some more about the Church's teachings; mostly they spoke with reverence yet, when they dared, they also spoke confidentially about their doubts. Gradually their lives became enmeshed.

PANTALEONE'S PERIL

Pantaleone said one day,

'As we both feel so deeply, and as we're both so wealthy, let's give money to the poor and sick *before* we die - not wait until afterwards?'

Then Pantaleone told Judith about the chapel cave on Monte Gargano in Apulia, where, with his devout parents, he had been to worship in the past. He painted word pictures for her of the forest-clad wildness, the sea and bright white cliffs and caves, the legend-filled islands. He explained about the descending path cut in the rock, reaching down into the mountainside and leading to the grotto of Saint Michael and all Angels.

'One day,' he said, 'I'll leave money for the Church there to make an entrance to the grotto, like a modest porch. But, before that, I'll send for some bronze doors from Constantinople - or go and fetch them myself - and they'll be mounted at the bottom of those steps, across a little landing. The doors will have pictures engraved on them in silver, showing people from our religious books - our saints, our preachers - and they'll be open to everyone who needs help. I hope they'll last forever!'

Radiantly, in his enthusiasm, he looked at her and rushed on to say,

'Then, as pilgrims pass through my shimmering doors they will be in even greater awe of the wonderful grotto. Perhaps they'll leave a more generous offering in the boxes for the poor?'

'Will I ever see your cave, I wonder?'

'Of course you will, Judith,' he said, 'after you get to Rome. It's only just across the mountains - and then a little further!'

She laughed at his description; her roaming across Europe had already taken her so far. Thoughtfully he continued,

'My doors will also serve to make every one aware that in the Gargano there could be built a centre for the care of poor people's health. The miracle of Saint Michael has brought thousands of people there, by God's design: perhaps, if we could make it a centre for treating diseases, it might become a minor miracle through man's design? Other people, in centuries to come, may be inspired, as I have been, and the lesson passed on.'

Judith was surprised by his serious outpouring.

'Your ideas are very powerful. You've painted a persuasive picture of what one ought to do with one's individual talents. Yet, perhaps I'm more impressed by the fervour in which you say it, tonight you're different, in some way, to the person I first met. You haven't made any light-hearted jokes, have you?'

'Yes, you're very astute, and I beg your pardon - my thoughts have carried me away!'

'Yet ... isn't there something more?'

Pantaleone looked uncomfortable.

'Yes, there is. I have a fever - and my body aches. Tomorrow I'll be well again, more myself and light-hearted!'

But he was not.

Pantaleone was not well again the next day and the party delayed their journey; he remained with his own group, not speaking of what ailed him, and not seeing Judith at all. The day after that it was beyond doubt that he was very ill. He could not leave his bed. One of his servants ventured to ask Judith to pay a visit to their master, and when Judith did so she could see that his eyes had sunk deep into the sockets and had lost their spark.

Judith lost no time to send for her box of herbs and potions. With great care she laid them out and mixed some simple remedies. To begin with, she boiled up willow leaves and roots, to help reduce his fever, and at first he swallowed it, pulling a twisted face; but at least he slept afterwards and took a little nourishment when he awoke.

That evening, when the fever returned, Judith decided to let Pantaleone's blood, for he had suddenly become unconscious. First she tied a bandage around his arm so that the veins of his forearm swelled up. As she was about to cut the exposed vein with a sharp knife she saw that part of his arm was badly swollen and, in the centre, were two small holes. At once she knew - he had been bitten by a snake. But what kind? And when?

There seemed only one remedy - he had to be cupped.

Judith wasted no time. She took her pewter cup and greased the edges all around. Then she dropped burning coals into it until the cup was red hot. Gritting her teeth, she inverted the cup over the snake's bite, which developed suction as the burning material consumed oxygen and the pus was drawn up through the skin's opening. It seemed to afford him a little relief, yet Judith knew that treatment had come too late as the poison was already freely floating in his body. That night she gave him opium, and he slept fitfully. But he had not regained consciousness. Then he began to ramble in his speech, talking in several languages, speaking of strangers.

Judith was filled with horror, certain that the charming man was going to die, she dressed his arm with wine and vinegar; she made a paste from the mould on a loaf of bread and spring water, and bound that on too. She forced him to drink a purge of waybroad and plantain, elder rind and salt, all dissolved in ale. As each remedy was made she prayed to the Apostles and offered up innumerable paternosters in the belief that these would benefit the application of the medicines: when she had plucked the herbs in the convent garden she had made the sign of the cross when each was eased out of the earth by hand - to use a knife would have cancelled their medicinal properties, so she was informed. She could not have done more.

Day after day he rambled, struggling against restraining arms, his curly hair now lank and long. She spoke to other women, but none had her knowledge of medicine: one woman even said accusingly,

'The way you look after him you'd think you'd been trained!'

The illogical terror that the Church might somehow reclaim her showed in her face for a moment, so she shouted back,

'Get away! You're no use to us! God's breath - can't you see he's dying?' She had never shouted at another being before, and was left shaking. And the woman, frightened of infection and scared of death, slunk away - with a sideways look. Finally, one almost unbearably hot day, he lay still all day, his eyes closed and hardly a murmur passed his lips. Once she heard him say,

'Judith ...'

But when she answered he didn't know her and faded away again. At last she called to Bertha.

'I'm going to have to use that special potion that Sister Sophia gave me! Please bring it to me - quickly!'

'But - my lady! That was for you alone ... you know it! You can't give it to a stranger. Think what Sister Sophia would say? Or Reverend Mother?'

Her eyes widened in hysteria and her childlike hands clenched.

'He's no stranger any more, Bertha, we've been like brother and sister all these weeks. Bring it! He needs it now ... I can feel him dying in my arms!'Bertha brought the precious phial, pulling off the bindings around the stopper, gave it - protesting afresh - into Judith's hand. For a moment Judith paused, considering this drastic move: but only for a moment. His head fell back over her arm. She prised open his slack mouth and very carefully and slowly, tipped every drop inside. Once or twice he swallowed involuntarily, then his head rolled back against her shoulder.

'Go, now, and rest. I'll call you if there's a change.'

Nothing happened for a long while. Was all that precious liquid too late? Was it all wasted? Completely limp, he breathed in scarcely-heard shallow sighs. Dusk descended. They were huddled on a sandy beach, at a distance from the others, quite near the sea's edge, longing for cool air. The stars began to come out against the early night sky; the noise of the general caravan died away as everyone settled to sleep. Exhausted, lulled by the rhythm of the waves, Judith fell asleep against a rock, with Pantaleone held in her arms.

Suddenly alert, arms aching, she realised the man she was cradling was weeping. Looking down she saw slow, heavy tears sliding down from under his closed eyelids. She placed her healing hand upon his forehead - it was miraculously cool, the fever had gone. Unknowing if he could hear her or not, she whispered,

'You're safe now. You've been ill a long time ... now it's time to rest. I'll send for some broth.'

She held him close for another moment, then laid his flaccid body down on the warm sand.

His convalescence was going to take some while, testing her newly acquired skills to the utmost - but she believed he was going to live. It seemed that the grotto of Monte San Angelo in the Gargano Mountains would be receiving their bronze doors after all.

But soon a new problem became apparent. She could see, too clearly, how attached he had become to her and the bond that had formed from his dependence. It was eventually to show daily in his eyes, his clutching fingers, as she nursed him.

She had never mentioned Roger; Pantaleone had been told her destination was Rome and the convent - but not the reason why. Now she had to decide her priorities: finding Roger? Or looking after Pantaleone, who clearly loved her?

Dreams of Roger filled her heart, dreams now dimmed by the weary wait. Compassion for Pantaleone she had in abundance, but there was no quickening of her nerves, no fresh tremble in her bones when she met him each day. But he was a wonderful companion and there seemed no end to the variety in their conversation.

So - which man was it to be?

JUDITH AND PANTALEONE

Amalfi, furiously bustling and noisy, rivalled Pisa, Genoa, Venice and Gaeta as a major naval power in trade with the East: it was also a sublimely beautiful city in the late summer sunshine.

Judith sat with her erstwhile patient and his parents on the spacious open roof of their house. It was shaded by reed thatch, decorated with brilliant flowers, pink and orange, which entwined through the supports and thick, meandering trunks of vines. The scent of jasmine was heady, making her feel languorous in the warm air: now and again a tiny white flower would float to the floor after a heavy bee had finished with its nectar.

Pantaleone's mother and she had been tasting from a dish of Persian sweetmeats arranged upon vine-leaves. Her fingers were sticky, so she washed their tips in a bowl of sweet water in which small flowers floated, then took up her decorated parchment fan, attached like a flag to a carved ivory handle, and twirled it idly.

The sound of bells seemed to encircle them as they sat in their inertia upon the rooftop eyrie; church bells pealed, there were bells jingling on harnesses of horses and mules, and there was the single deep bell from the cathedral some way off. Even when the bells were stilled thought Judith, there always seemed to be music in Italy - even when none was to be heard. Pantaleone spoke to her in a thready voice out of the silence.

'Will you walk with me? I especially want to show you something.'

'My son, are you well enough?'

His mother moved up to him, as he lay there so frail and tired, running her hands across his neck and shoulders, smoothing his clothes, patting his cheeks with the tips of her loving fingers.

'Leave it, leave it for a few more days? For my sake? You're my only son - I couldn't bear you to be ill again - you've hardly recovered! Give yourself a little more time, eh?'

He stood and kissed her soft cheek affectionately.

'I'm well enough now, mother. Don't spoil me so.' He smiled into her eyes. 'If I don't strike out now I'll be an invalid all my life in your tender hands! Is that what you want me to be?'

Mischievously, he looked into her devoted face. She couldn't resist him at moments like these.

'Oh – go along with you then!'

Judith rose quietly to stand beside him, ready with a smile to go wherever he meant to take her. His mother looked at them pensively; they looked to her like a promised blend on the horizon.

Her son, with his dark, curly hair, stood tall and willowy, his skin still slightly transparent; dressed in outer clothes which combined greys and creams, with a finely striped under-garment, embroidered with silvery threads, seemed a sympathetic, yet unintentional, tonal match for Judith. She stood beside him in sunny colours, palest fawns with lemon and apricot, a long gold scarf in her hand to match her long, bright sunburnt hair, caught up with a filigree comb. What a splendid pair they made, thought his mother, with a conspiratorial glance at her husband.

Judith was all too aware of the significance of these looks and they troubled her.

She had nursed Pantaleone back to health, such as it was, with deep devotion, eventually aware that it was the first time in her life that she had actually served and tended any one person in need other than herself. Day followed day as she and Bertha offered him tempting and nutritious morsels of food and healing drinks; they had regularly bathed his sweat-soaked body with gentle hands, then massaged sweet perfumed oils into his dry, flaking skin. It had taken a long time before he was well enough to be lifted again onto the shaded cart, padded with down, and to journey on.

Most of the time he lay exhausted and silent, watching the evening fires flicker, the dust motes dance in the last light; listening to the subdued noises of Judith's servants nearby, and the occasional clamour of the gulls.

At night he was often too tired to sleep from the day's jolting, and lay there with his lids half open, looking between his lashes towards Judith's tents. She would sometimes awake early, rise up to see if there was anything he needed and smile tenderly at him, joyful that he was alive.

But she gradually began to feel a deep concern about him, dependent as he was on her every movement. He was still far too fragile to travel alone, even with his attendants. She concluded that she should hand him over to his own family at Amalfi. It meant a radical change of plan; she had really wanted to stop for a length of time in Rome, to make her enquiries about the Hautevilles, especially if anyone knew the whereabouts of Roger. But it now seemed clear to her that she should take her patient to Amalfi first. That meant a long detour southwards. And, who knew? Perhaps she might stay there for a little while?

As they travelled slowly along the coast road he did not speak very much, but smiled - and looked. Judith tried to amuse him when he was mildly fractious. She sang some jaunty songs, accompanying herself with a little pipe in between verses; she told him hilarious folk stories from Normandy, and made up others from her fresh young imagination. She tended him night and day, Bertha taking her turn when she was too tired to go on, tiring him, in his turn, with her endlessly cheerful conversation and mindless burbling: he let it wash over him, grateful for her selfless care.

When he was most ill Judith had taken his hand, warming it with her own, willing life back into him. Loosely held in hers, his hand seemed passive, half-dead. She firmly closed her soft fingers over his long ones, trying to get the blood to reach the tips, massaging each little pad of flesh until a faint flush of colour was seen. It became a habit, every day when they met: his hand lay there, mute, appealing - she picked it up and smiled at him encouragingly.

'Get better! Get better!' Her heart repeated.

He lay back, the tension oozing out of him as he closed his eyes, letting her pick up his hand ... *willing* her to pick it up.

Later, she realised, their actions became reversed. He had begun to take *her* hand instead, turning it over and over in a lack-lustre way, looking at every line or threadlike vein. She had to force herself to stay very still, neither to withdraw nor clutch at his, becoming aware of the increasing intensity which throbbed between them, unspoken, but emanating from him like a driving force. No, she thought, this *must not be allowed to happen...*

She began to take care to nurse him with both hands, so he couldn't imprison one of hers, or to keep a small distance between them in the evenings when she sang or told her beguiling stories. The intentional change was infinitely gradual - the first time she ran towards him with a tiny injured bird in her hands, so he had to hold it ... not her. She moved to another side of his litter, and said she had done so 'to keep out of the sun' or she made him eat his food himself, rather than lazily being fed by her, laughing gently at his efforts, and busied herself with another platter and knife, or with peeling fruit. Little by little she distanced herself; the change was so gradual that it was almost imperceptible. But he knew.

On the rooftop he enticed her disarmingly,

'I want to take you to our famous cathedral, there's something there I want to show you,'

Out in the street they wandered, crowded by servants... it wasn't safe to walk alone in a busy port. They were surrounded by a multitude of races, not only from many nations but dealers and Jews and monks and marketeers - all around the Mediterranean the ports were much alike. Some of their men walked ahead, others to each side. Judith and Pantaleone sauntered together, side by side, not touching, coccooned.

'Our cathedral is very old, over two hundred years! My ancestors helped raise money for it, in return for all the good things they've gained. It's named for our Apostle, Saint Andrew, the brother of Simon Peter. Sadly today he lies in Constantinople, which we believe to be dangerous ... it seems the Muslims are approaching. Then what will happen to our beloved Saint? *How* we long for his body to rest here.'

When they drew close Judith saw the long flight of steps ahead, wide and shallow, but travelling up and up.

Concerned, she enquired,

'Can you manage those steps?'

'Yes, if I take them slowly.'

Pausing now and then, as if to admire the streets below, they climbed the many steps. One last effort and they stood out of the sunshine in the huge porch.

'There!'

He pointed. A shaft from the dying sun danced on to the bronze doors, picking up the silver lines, lighting up the whole area. She stared at them. Huge, partly open, leading into the darkness beyond ... and the flickering candles within.

Each door was astonishing, thick as two interlocked fists, of pure polished bronze. Divided into compartments, with raised and incised decoration, they gleamed with a soft-gold satiny translucence: There was a vast handle and even heavier locks.

'These will last for ever, don't you think? They were brought from Constantinople last year, ships owned by my father and me carried them here ... we feared they would sink in some dreadful storm! It took a great many oxen to pull them finally up the steps - they had to heave away for days.'

He smiled quietly to himself, glancing sideways to see Judith's reaction.

She was astonished. Pure amazement shone in her face, there was nothing contrived in her appreciation.

'Are these the sort of doors you want to give to Monte Sant' Angelo?'

'That's why I brought you here, I wondered if you would remember?'

'Of course I do! I might forget some things - but I wouldn't forget sharing your precious dreams ... how could I?'

She went forward, touched the bronze, cold, in spite of the day's sun, under her exploring fingers.

'Oh yes! These would last for ever!'

'For the glory of God!'

A bell tolled overhead, clear in the late evening air, one deep note.

'And that's an omen. Did you know, here in the south, we believe that a tolling bell symbolises the voice of God, urging you to the gates of paradise?'

She turned and smiled at him, her face illuminated by the final dying light of the sun, setting in the sea. Behind him the horizon swam in a kind of gold-dust haze reflected from the sinking sun. Glinting gold on gold, she shimmered like a firefly.

'Then I suggest you name your future bronze gates for Monte Sant' Angelo 'the Gates of Paradise'.

He looked at her, a last questioning adoration pouring from him.

But he asked her no question in speech.

She stood her ground, still and quiet, and her steady gaze flickered once and then turned back to the bronze doors. At least he had had his chance, and realised he wouldn't win her. Neither spoke. It was enough. Under his breath, resigned, with his heart in his eyes, he murmured,

'Then 'The Gates of Paradise' they will be.'

But he knew the gates of her heart were not to be opened for him. For a long moment they stood, understanding. Then they turned together, slowly walked down the long flight of steps again. It was over: honour had been satisfied. Now she could go on with her search for Roger, lovingly - willingly - released.

And the gates would be ordered, by him in Constantinople, in person.

PREPARATIONS FOR A VISIT: SICHELGAITA

Not too far away from Amalfi, as the crows flew, Duke Robert, elected leader of all the Normans, was reluctantly preparing to receive the Pope's envoy. After having conquered all of southern Italy, and setting up castles and forts in many cities, Robert had finally taken the city of Salerno in southern Italy and made it his capital. This day he and Sichelgaita were deep in preparations for the important visit. He glanced at Sichelgaita, and said fretfully,

'His Holiness' envoy will be entertained right royally with every nuance of protocol. I don't care what you feel - *you will do as I say!'*

'But he's your enemy! He's going to harm you. He'll go back to the Pope and make mischief between you both. I know that.' she shouted.

'What have you got against him? He looks perfectly normal to me! And he is only doing his duty by His Holiness, acting for him, not for himself.'

'You don't know - he has so many political ambitions for himself, so many plans ...'

'How do *you* know?'

Sichelgaita spoke slowly, dreading being hurt by his reaction.

'Once I was approached by him many years ago. He wanted to marry me ...'

Robert shouted with laughter.

'Marry you? *Whatever for?* Oh - for your money! And for breeding. I suppose it's possible! *What a laughable pair you'd have made.'*

It was said with deliberate scorn.

Sichelgaita had recently born him a third daughter. All were curiously sickly, two tiny sons had died - only young Roger Borsa lived to re-count his money: Robert did not care for any of them. He felt savage.

She flinched. Nothing showed on her face, she had trained herself ruthlessly in self-control. She had expected an emotional snub. His continuing relationship with Alberada and Mark - Bohemund - had been reported to her by a well-bribed spy, and it was all like an open sore. She cursed herself for flagellating her own feelings, but couldn't stop. How many more insults would she have to endure? Couldn't he see what she held within her? What else did she have to do to make him have the slightest fondness for her? The honey never worked, so she foolishly used vinegar: she stung back,

'At least I didn't make use of him and then cast him off like a dirty, used glove – like Alberada ...'

He swung at her, hitting her across the face, his heavy silver ring opening her skin.

'You unspeakable bitch! Don't insult her with her name on your lips; you've a tongue like a poisoned dagger.'

She smiled sleepily, her lids drooping. Sometimes aggression had made him interested in her, found him leaping on her for sex in sheer frustration. It wasn't what she wanted, but it was better than indifference. He made no further move towards her. Furious - she spat at him,

'Did you think I don't know everything about you?'

Her nostrils became so white and pinched that her uneven breath whistled through them.

'Well', he said, more slowly, enunciating every syllable, 'let's face it, you're not one of our prettier specimens of womanhood so you've nothing better to do than plot and scheme.'

She became the incarnation of anguish and hate in front of his penetrating eyes, a shell so full of despair and love and pain that her humanity was transcended by it, a body inhabited by a spirit that was cursing God.

'And' he said, remorselessly, 'you try too hard.'

He turned on his heel, cloak swinging wide, and left the room. He had no intention of discussing anything personal with her; it was difficult enough to force her to do as she was bid.

He understood Sichelgaita's reluctance to house and entertain the envoy. His Eminence the Cardinal reminded him of a cool, dry snake, slithering on his belly, head twisting from side to side, missing nothing, ready with his poison. How much better if he was not going to come! Yet, now his arrival was imminent, he had to be treated correctly. To treat him with friendliness would be different - personal - but to treat him with strict protocol would mean Robert could show his enmity, yet remain in the right. Order in both affairs of state and law was everything, you all knew where you were. And stony silence, to Robert, inferred a calculated insult.

Striding through the Great Hall he was aware of the many servants cleaning, sweeping, dragging benches, laying down fresh herbs on the plaited rushes. There was a cacophony of noise which heralded a great social event - and he was better out of it, astride his horse, in the clean air of the mountains: time enough to be the centre of the scene in days to come. He shouted for Jacques to join him, knowing he would ride behind quietly, having over the years absorbed his mood through the pores of his skin.

The misshapen dwarf ran to Sichelgaita, clutching at her skirts with soft, pudgy fingers. He reached up and pulled her girdle.

'Mistress?'

'No, get away now!'

She marched away, leaving the tiny man flopping to the ground: she was still trying unsuccessfully to regain control of herself.

'Make time for me, I've a warning ...'

Sichelgaita strode on. A 'warning' indeed. What sort of ruse was that to attract her attention and be rewarded by a sticky sweetmeat? Indignation clouded the dwarf's face, seen in the uplift of his quivering chin, in his tightly clenched little hands.

She had worked herself to the bone to make the Cardinal's visit a spectacular success. Yet her husband treated her like a hireling, she thought, *damn him to hell!*

Seething, she immediately summoned her two suppliers of luxury foods and spoke to them in a way she fondly hoped they would never forget; then she left the most senior of her ladies in attendance reeling under her displeasure; following that she brought blushes to the cheeks of the deferential Sergeant-at-Arms of the Great Duke who had unfortunately smiled at her - and finally she rent to shreds a costly crescent-shaped fan and smashed the amber handle across her knees. She decided, then, that she felt better.

At last she arrived in her solar, ready to speak to the household Comptroller and oversee the arrangements for the highlights of the Cardinal's coming visit. If Robert wished the event to be regal and outstanding, then of course she would comply. At the same time she would get her own way - somehow! - To protect Robert. It would have to be extremely subtle, which would surely prove dangerous.

The Comptroller bowed as he entered.

'Have we any idea of how many retainers the Cardinal will bring with him?'

'I believe it will be a dozen personal staff, madam, and a squadron of soldiers; probably seventy-five all told.'

'All right, then - we can deal with that number easily. Now, I want to have a check made about the lighting. For this visit I will only have beeswax candles used in all areas occupied by the Cardinal or ourselves.'

'Including the Hall, madam? It will be expensive.'

'Including the Hall.'

The sun was brilliant by day but when darkness fell she wanted to let light fall on every detail in case of trickery: rushes and oil-lamps could fail, beeswax was much more reliable.

'And for the final banquet, do we have sufficient peacocks?'

'We do, my lady, you gave me sufficient notice - and we have some spare.'

'They'll look magnificent when they decorate the high table.'

'Shall we use the singing birds, too?'

'Oh! Yes! I want the table to look like a garden in Byzantium! We'll put the little trees with their silver and gold leaves on either side of the peacocks; be careful to keep all the tail-feathers lying behind them - and then we'll put the mechanical birds beneath the trees, so they will sing on our arrival. Set one of the pages to see they sing again and again during the feast.'

'I will, madam.'

'Although we have no fountains, put the gold and silver fingerbowls between each guest, and float in each of them a flower of some beauty.

'It will be done, madam.'

'And has my gift arrived? I thought I saw strangers in the courtyard.'

'Our messengers from Constantinople came yesterday, bringing it with them! But - oh! Madam! At what cost!'

'Yes, I doubt if I'll ever pay out so much for anything again. Have it brought in.'

The Comptroller helped Sichelgaita unravel a great parcel on the table. The precious object she had ordered, so long awaited, had rocked its way across the seas, suspended in a case of wood and packed all around with shavings and fabrics and dozens of small airy coils of straw like birds' nests. At last it stood amidst the piles of wrapping material and she gasped with delight.

It was perfect! Just as she had ordered.

THE GIFT

It was a huge glass goblet. Glass! That precious material which was so difficult to make and could so easily shatter. Yet in Constantinople they still had the secret which the ancients invented, and this piece had been ordered many years ago. It was majestic; far finer than Sichelgaita had ever seen before.

The goblet stood about ten inches tall, doubly cased. The outer sleeve lay about a knuckle's width outside the inner, miraculously and mysteriously held in place, carved into layers like open flowers, geometrical, yet graduating in size until the smallest lay at the base. The colour was a faint green, as though deep water had been stilled for a moment, then frozen.

To hold it, and to protect if from harm - enriching it immensely as it did - there was a belt of gold firmly clasped around its waist, with four hinged gold bands meeting underneath, attached to a circular gold foot. All the polished, shining gold was finely engraved, then set with gemstones tightly clasped in open gold boxes.

Sichelgaita slowly checked the gems, counting out all twelve on her long practical fingers.

'Sardius, topaz, carbuncle ...' she turned it slowly around. 'Emerald, sapphire, diamond, ligure, agate, amethyst - *what a glorious colour* - beryl, onyx and jasper.'

She breathed a sigh of relief. They were all there; each seemed immense, and correctly placed in order. In between the large gems were smaller pearls in circular settings, which broke up the massy glitter of the precious metal.

She had had it made as a gift for Robert, simply to show her devotion. All the gems mentioned in the old Jewish *Book of Exodus* had been gathered there because they were closely associated with the great virtues - truth, honesty and so on, and made up the exemplar of the perfect man. They were much discussed in general conversation, and everyone knew the attributes of each gemstone.

Pope Gregory the Great had linked the gemstones to the Nine Orders of Angels: sard to the Seraphim, topaz to the Cherubim, jasper to the Thrones, chrysolite to the Dominations, onyx to the Principalities, beryl to the Powers, sapphire to the Virtues, carbuncle to the Archangels, and emerald to the Angels.

To Sichelgaita, Robert equated the diamond, hardest and rarest of all gemstones, bettered by none. Sichelgaita's much-studied lapidary told her,

'It giveth to a man that beareth it strength and virtue, and it keepeth him from grievance, meetings and temptations and from venom. Also it keepeth the bones and the members whole. It doth away any wrath and lechery. It enricheth him that beareth him, enricheth in value and in good. The diamond is most worth to be holden upon for witless men and for defence against enemies. For that beareth it shall the more love God.'

Robert was Sichelgaita's ideal, *the perfect man*, so she had spent much of her personal wealth to have this treasure made. The glass, naturally, would be worthless if attempts were made to melt it down, but the craftsmanship was beyond price. She wondered if Robert would grasp the whole goblet's significance; realise the subtle compliment she was paying him? The last thing she intended to do, now, was to tell him outright.

'Madam - it's so fragile!'

'Yes, that's partly its value. It's like searching the world for one perfect flower, which would die the day it was plucked.'

She looked dreamily to the burnt grass beyond the castle's walls ...

he had never even given her a flower. He had never given her anything at all of his own accord; especially anything of himself.

'Will you give it to my lord Duke on Sunday? It's a feast-day.'

'No, I think it should wait for some more suitable occasion. Probably some time when his Eminence is here.'

The little dwarf pushed open the door a crack, whining,

'Won't you listen to me now?'

She stood between the goblet and the dwarf's gaze, although he was not tall enough to see precisely what had emerged from all those enigmatic wrappings, saying,

'Close that door. Leave that creature outside.'

The Comptroller kicked it shut.

'Now, we'll discuss certain points about the food. Then the entertainment.'

Together they worked on through the day, making decisions, assigning duties, organising every minute detail so that the visit would be flawless.

The dwarf slumped onto the floor outside the solar, grumbling beneath his breath, shrugging his plump shoulders feebly as he sank down. Time to be heard later, perhaps - *but not too late!* And now, he thought petulantly, he could feel a headache coming on...

THE CARDINAL

The day of the Cardinal's visit dawned sullen and hot. Thunder rumbled erratically across the mountains, the air was very still and humid, the leaves hung limply on the trees and no birds sang.

His Eminence's showy entourage spent a very long time arriving, winding its slow, stately way through the countryside, contemptuous, evidently bored by its own progress. Workers on the land stopped as he went by, doffed their simple hats, and bent their modest heads in lowly admiration and fear. They knew exactly who he was, how old he was, how much money he would throw out as largesse from Rome. When he came near, they paused to stare, to pass the back of a hand over a sweaty forehead, or to draw a nose between two fingers. He thrust a hand into the depths of his garments - it emerged with a fat silk purse that sang of gold pieces. He swung the purse gently to and fro by the metal ring that girt its middle, then carelessly flung a few small coins into the dust; it was precious little - but then, precious all the same! They picked it up with simple dignity, after pausing a moment, showing that they only cared for the money, not him. He was not interested in their opinions, stated or otherwise. The procession continued on disdainfully.

To honour protocol Robert rode in state a short way to meet him, then to escort him back to his magnificent castle: this one was in Apulia, where he was Duke. Flags hung absolutely motionless, colourful against the painted wooden poles and grey stone walls. The device on his ring was painted onto shields, azure blue in the background, superimposed with the golden lion's paw encircled by golden chains, and hoisted onto every available space. He was singularly his own man! No-one would be allowed to forget that, in spite of being an ally of the Pope, he was Norman born and bred - and proud.

The broad roads which led to his castle were swept, herbs strewn and mixed with fresh flowers along the Cardinal's way; branches of bay and laurel were there, too, brought down from the mountains. There was no need to look at them, he knew they would be there, they were his due. Heralds stood on the ramparts of the castle in brilliant tabards which duplicated the Hauteville device, beating vast drums. The resonance built up to mingle in syncopation with the rumbling thunder far away. Harmony was manifestly absent in all the strident cacophony, and ostentation was paramount.

As His Eminence rode across the heavily armoured drawbridge a single knife-streak of lightning flashed across the sky, lighting up the dull day with crystal brilliance. An instantaneous crack of thunder followed. The horses started, some leaping sideways, others clattering ahead in mutual fright, some lashing out with their heels. In the general confusion the scarlet-caparisoned Cardinal swayed in his ornate saddle and almost fell. Robert reached out his huge hand, grasped the silk-fringed reins and pushed the skeletal body back firmly into place. He held his own horse steady by the vice-like pressure of his knees - clearly the Cardinal could not ride with any dexterity. Then he removed his helping hand - fastidiously.

His Eminence smiled thinly, relieved, yet hating having to say,

'I thank you, my Lord Duke.'

Robert bowed, coldly, contempt showed briefly on his face for the seeds of deceit and corruption, like light and shadow that he perceived before him. He said nothing, bar the empty phrase,

'May you live forever...'

Inside the castle Sichelgaita stood watching from her solar window, waiting with her dwarf for the procession to arrive. Her braided hair was damp, sweat filmed on her forehead. As she feasted her eyes upon

Robert, she ached with a longing, unassuaged - his indifference being an incurable wound in her heart.

The pudgy little dwarf sidled up to her, pulling a face, making her smile a little. He was older now, the lines prematurely etched in deep furrows across his lowering brow and folded fat cheeks; his hair was thinning, greying, his heart afraid of losing the capacity of being amusing ... even dwarfs had a season. He had a devotion to the gigantic Sichelgaita which he could not justify, only acknowledge with unspoken adoration.

'All right - what is it? What's this warning?'

'Madam, it's difficult to tell you - but I foresee some great calamity!'

Sichelgaita smiled again. Now that the initial preparations were resolved, she allowed time to be diverted.

'Oh yes? What kind of great calamity?'

'The Hauteville family could be brought down - I feel that that would be a calamity! I don't know what's going to happen - but there's an ominous feeling in the air. Can you hear any birds sing? Or the wind? Have you been able to hear anything these past few days, bar thunder? My lord Duke's new dog lies in the corner of the room, whining: I don't like the look in his yellow eyes. The cats have left the kitchens, our pretty caged birds are fluttering about, beating their wings against the bars, trying desperately to get out. No-one knows what will happen, but the atmosphere is laden with fear. All the beasts and birds are frightened - except you, who have been too busy to notice. That's my warning.'

Standing straight, heavy and tall, Sichelgaita had listened intently, then looked about her in thoughtful silence.

She could see, now, his words were true.

But what was to happen? And when? Animals sensed disaster long before humans, she knew that, and the dwarf was sensitive to both and could put this perceptivity into words; the warning must be heeded, the responsibility was now hers - she must tell Robert without delay.

She had her chance when the preening Cardinal had been taken to his rooms to rest. A deep couch awaited him, covered with fine sheets and pillows made of down; nearby were jugs of cool sherbet and dishes of starchy powdered jellies from the East, known as 'abhisa'. If he wished for anything further, he had only to tell his servants, who would call the Hauteville serf who sat outside his door.

Urgently she told Robert everything; he neither laughed not contradicted but listened as carefully, as she had listened to the dwarf. Sichelgaita was reminded yet again that, when faced with danger, Normans banded together and fought to the death side by side. Perhaps, for once, she was being treated like a Norman? She remembered a similar feeling, when fighting beside Robert in Sicily: just once, only the once - a vivid sense of partnership. And from her performance on the battlefield, from that day onwards, she had been known by all military personnel as 'the lady of the golden boots'.

A CONFERENCE

The visit began peacefully enough. The Cardinal spent much time in conference with Robert, dealing with less personal matters first.

They lounged on low seats built up with many cushions, in the Eastern style, and nibbled at salted almonds or crisply fried caterpillars, whilst sipping chilled drinks from tall goblets. At other times there were dishes of raisins from Jerusalem, olives from Palmyra and apples from Syria: Sichelgaita changed the selection each day, and when the apples were placed before them the Cardinal saw that the central one was gilded.

The Cardinal's eyes under the sandy eyebrows travelled round the room. They were dead, expressionless eyes, the whites were grey and his cheeks were like marble. He missed nothing. His mind clicked like an abacus. He was a vulturine, oppressive tyrant and took his time.

The papacy had become increasingly dependent on this alliance with the Hautevilles from which it could not escape, and the Normans on their side had been quick to appreciate the solid advantages they might obtain, be it in Spain or Italy or Sicily, by posing as the champions in a Holy War - as they were now doing in the siege of Bari.

The full implications had also influenced William of Normandy - to the extent that William fought at Hastings under a papal banner, and with consecrated relics hung about his neck. The venture had been made to appear - and in Western Europe was widely regarded as such - as something in the nature of a crusade.

Today, uppermost on the Envoy's agenda was another Holy War - the creeping occupation of the Muslims - the Seljuk Turks - across the former Byzantine province of Asia Minor, now known as Anatolia.

This frightening occupation was first led by the Abbasid Caliph Harun Ar-Rashid, 250 years earlier, but recently the rapid progress of the Muslims was becoming an avalanche of disaster. The Muslims swept aside all minor sects of Christians as they drove effortlessly across the mountains, then efficiently down the plains to the sea coasts. They took slaves, as was the custom, but were generally benign. However, the ruthlessness of their blanket conquest was ominous in the eyes of the Western Church.

The Cardinal confided,

'Up until now the Church had always believed in tolerance and that no violence should be perpetrated upon a man's conscience. But now we are dealing with heretics, and heresy is treason.'

'But,' countered Robert, in wonder at this attitude, 'surely the Church intends no persecution of others?'

'More to the point,' retorted the Cardinal, glad to get off the subject of persecution - of which he was in wholehearted agreement – 'can men of different faiths live together in a single state and society? The Church is increasingly aware that there are three main groups outside Christianity: Jews, heretics and Muslims. I don't believe we want them amongst us is this country. And the Muslim occupation of Anatolia is terrible - I have spoken to His Holiness, urging him to destroy pagan cults and root out unbelievers by confiscating their property and putting them to death.'

Robert's eyes widened.

'Do Muslims kill the Christians in their path?'

'Not as yet, but the threat to some of our precious Christian tombs in Anatolia is obvious.'

Aware that his guest was a fanatic bigot, Robert pressed him further,

'Do the Muslim rulers intend to break them open? Desecrate the bodies? Or merely remove them elsewhere?'

'They assure us they would not.' said the Cardinal reluctantly. 'They say they have no use for them - as yet! But I have grave doubts. These are early days, remember.'

'Does the Church believe their words to be untrue?' asked Robert, wonderingly; any Cardinal might become the next Pope, or direct foreign policies for a weak one in office, and he needed to know the inner thinking of the Church.

'We've no real proof to the contrary, and we know they are still relying on the trade the pilgrims bring - but we believe that they can be powerfully cruel people.'

'But,' said Robert, who had many cultivated and erudite Muslim friends, 'I've always understood that the word of a Muslim, once given, is their bond?'

'Yes. So they say.' said the Cardinal, who had no friends, fidgeting with his rings. 'But the Church is most uneasy all the same.'

Robert changed direction with his questions.

'Which is the most important place of pilgrimage in your estimation?'

'There are many, but the least well-defined is Myra, on the southern coast, where old Saint Nicholas is buried, the former Bishop.'

'The seamen of the coasts hereabouts hold him as their patron saint. Surely, if this business gets out there will be much trouble? Have they anything to concern them, do you think?'

'His Holiness is deeply worried, but that is in confidence, my Lord Duke. If affairs become even more formidable I privately believe that His Holiness might request your help about the matter of Saint Nicholas ... but in what capacity I could not, at present, tell you.'

'Have you ever seen or tasted the liquid in his tomb? Legend had it that it smells of flowers and tastes sweet.'

'I've seen it - there are containers of it in Rome. But I've never smelled it: His Holiness did both some time ago, assuring us it was a miracle. However - the miracle of Saint Nicholas is very far away, and there's nothing we can do about it now.'

The siege of Bari was to be discussed in full, later, and Robert's slow progress minutely investigated. It was being very costly for both sides. Fortunes had changed hands several times. Then, unhappily, the Greek-Bariot leader had managed to escape at dead of night - Hauteville sailors had been given generous draughts of drugged wine and had slept: for a short while the pontoon was briefly safe for the Greeks to step across their slumbering bodies to another ship and eventually to reach Constantinople. Here the Byzantine ruler had agreed to help him organise an expensive relief expedition to save the people of Bari, and their own Greek citizens, and a fleet of fresh ships had sailed to the rescue.

The Normans had word of the approaching fleet, engaging them off the coast of Monopoli, sinking twelve. Whilst they were engaged, another, smaller Byzantine fleet had sailed north and approached Bari, breaking through the collar of boats and bringing with them a new ruler and much-needed supplies. It was as if the past year's siege had been for nothing, and the Normans had been made to look surprisingly foolish and abnormally inefficient.

But Duke Robert, away in his castle, yet all-knowing, gritted his teeth, insisted that Roger should carry on under orders patiently, and refused to give up. He had never been beaten and he wasn't going to allow it now. The provocation festered in Robert's brain.

Bari, he vowed, would be theirs, even if it took a lifetime.

THE DWARF

The little dwarf later came sidling up to the waiting Sichelgaita again. A blown bladder looked grotesque in his hands, with silver bells a-jingling: she thought no sight was more pitiful than an ageing dwarf who no longer found life amusing.

Drooping wearily, he wriggled in discomfort.

'Another word, my lady?'

This time she gave way at once, following the pathetic miniature man into a small room, filled with cold food waiting to be placed upon the tables: there was no-one there, except one servant on watch - who was told to leave.

'My lady, I've just been in His Eminence's room.'

'You stupid oaf!' Sichelgaita raged at him. 'You've no right to use that secret door - what if you'd been caught by one of his men?'

'It was something he muttered under his breath to his priest when he walked into the castle,' the dwarf persisted, 'he hardly saw me underfoot in the crowd. It seems he was displeased by being held in the saddle by my Lord Duke when the lightning flashed on his arrival.'

'But that was days ago! What did he say?'

'I am aware it was days ago,' said the dwarf with dignity, 'but His Eminence is a man of zeal and ambition, and that is a dangerous combination if it's aligned against his Grace.'

'I quite agree, my little manikin - tell me more.'

'He said 'That's the last time he'll patronise me!' So I thought I could learn more if I stayed near him.'

'And did you?'

'I believe so, my lady.'

'Well, come along then, what happened? There'll be a new cloak for you for this - I appreciate loyalty.'

Sichelgaita gave him her full attention, which was rare.

'When I listened by the secret door, His Eminence and his priest were talking about the siege of Bari. At the end I heard him say 'When I make him sign the paper to hand over the control of the siege to me it will be the beginning of the end for him! No-one will respect him any more after they know the Pope has taken away his position. Then he will gradually be forced out of the south.' And there was a smile in his voice, madam, like a contented cat.'

Sichelgaita's mind reeled.

'Did he say why they would force him to relinquish command?'

'It was something to do with money, madam, and over-running his allotment.'

'I see ... thank you, you've done well, you'll get your cloak and it will be trimmed with fur.'

She lowered her hand to stroke his greying hair in comfort, then turned away in great distress.

To hand over his command would be the greatest dishonour to Robert. She knew about the desperate affairs at Bari, but at no time had there been any suggestion that his command was in jeopardy. Well aware that the budget was overrun, she knew that he had poured his own money into the coffers - perhaps he hadn't told His Holiness - out of pride? He was capable of that. Success meant everything to him.

What was at stake was *time*. As usual.

Time for the new policies to take hold. Those new policies, as he had confided in Sichelgaita, included the fact that Roger had been sent to muster a new fleet to lie off the coast, poised to attack a heralded

Byzantine fleet, fresh from Constantinople, which was said to be approaching Bari, ready to rescue the city at last. But that could happen at any time in the near future. What was happening in her own home was happening today, and it was essential to control events before the Cardinal took them into his own steely fingers.

How could she deflect the threat to Robert's career? Give Robert more time? Almost certainly nothing would be done between the Envoy and Robert for a day or two: protocol demanded that there would be a number of great banquets to eat in his honour, as emissary of the Pope, entertainments of various complexities had been laid on, there was also the hunt. Whether His Eminence took part or not was of little consequence, the form had to be observed. It might, in fact, be three days or more before they actually sat down and discussed affairs at Bari in confidence. She would just have to bide her own time, pray for some better news from Roger at Bari. And make contingency plans. In the meanwhile the lowering weather would have to be endured, too.

Three days later there still had been no news from Roger and the weather had not changed. Rumbles of thunder rolled along the hills, up and down the valleys, echoing in the caves and growling like a rabid dog if you laid your ear to the earth. Night and day it continued, sometimes growing closer, sometimes fading almost right away - but then, inexorably, returning. Many people developed headaches, as if the thunder had entered through their ears and was circling inside their bony skulls, unable to find a way out again. When would the storm break?

Sichelgaita had finally - reluctantly - worked out her emergency plans to save Robert. They were not attractive, but they were deadly efficient. As a climax to the festivities she had personally invited His Eminence to a Peacock Banquet to be held on the last night he would stay at the castle, instead of an ordinary farewell meal, and he had happily accepted the invitation. He loved his food. Not many people could afford to breed peacocks, then slaughter them for a guest - even the Pope had not been known to give a banquet such as that. He was conscious of the honour it implied. And she meant him to be.

She had been proud of their collection of peacocks as they had pranced, high stepping, before their castle's gate. She had often thought of their strut and pomp, picturing herself as one, admiring their glitter and the rattle of their spread tails. Now their ugly screeches were silent, and their feathers were ready to decorate their trussed bodies, spiced and cooked to perfection - in death to seem more lovely; blue and lustrous turquoise, shimmering on aromatic foliage.

Robert was surprised by the decision to provide the peacocks for the banquet and wondered at her motives, but left her to make the household decision. During the past few days the Envoy had not once referred to Bari, and this was gradually becoming an insidious, underlying threat. He knew that his campaign was at its lowest ebb, that he had overspent wildly, and that - in most people's estimation - he had no hope of bringing the curiously untidy siege to a victorious end. But only a few knew about Roger's reserve fleet, and he had unbounded confidence that a victorious end was near: as he did not trust the man, under no circumstances whatsoever would he confide in the Envoy and tell him about his plans.

But Robert was primarily a man of action, and the enforced waiting in this sullen weather made him extremely short-tempered and on edge. If only good news would come whilst the Envoy was present!

Why was the atmosphere so heavy? When would the rain come? The thunder rolled on, never stopping; the lightning flashed about the sky indiscriminately, the animals continued to fret and fuss, cowering with wild eyes. Hot dust rose from the burnt ground outside, hovering like a brown mist. There was no drop of moisture as the storm held off.

THE BANQUET

The banquet was due. The castle was elaborately decorated with branches of sweet-smelling leaves between the wall-mounted flags, held together with fine bark; small flowers were mixed with herbs on the floors; all the servants were newly-dressed most richly, and wore blue and gold ribbons tied on their shoulder. A huge lion's paw surrounded by chains was carved above the mantel, and incense, which protocol demanded, hissed upon the logs, expensively scenting the air.

Gradually the Great Hall, swelteringly hot, became filled with all the party, staring agog at the blue-green peacocks in their pride, with their long tail-feathers lying at rest below the miniature gold and silver trees. The guests looked to the roof, to see where the sweet birdsong came from but then found the mechanical birds, too, beneath the valuable trees. Amongst the tankards and cups and colourfully decorated food were sweet walnuts and chestnuts and filberts, truffles and mushrooms and kale. Many of the guests had never before seen such a sight; peacocks for the table were legendary, but events like this were unique.

Great silver-rimmed mazers of fruit - pomegranates, apricots and lemons, lay between the brilliantly-plumed creatures as well, some on different levels of height, with elaborate sweetmeats and shakers of spices set around the pewter platters. Much of their food was adapted from Byzantine recipes, thick and rich, heavily spiced, often sweetened with honey; and those that could afford them wore jewelled knives in their belts for eating, made in the Muslim taste. Some of the drinking horns were of silver, and the rinsing bowls for the fingers and mouths of the chief guests were of turned ivory. At a side-table, where the bulk of the food was waiting, an enormous boar's head took central place, and two gilded swans faced each other from either end above the multi-coloured dishes.

At the high table were three carved chairs, and only three, each with arms; coverings were thrown over them of loose lengths of gold brocade: His Eminence was to be seated in the centre between Robert and Sichelgaita. By now it had been agreed that Robert and the Envoy were to confer the next day about the siege of Bari.

Sichelgaita and Robert awaited His Eminence, who slowly processed with his party into the Hall, taking his time with almost scornful indulgence, his long face like a blanched almond, and his breath puffing sour. Eventually they were all seated and the festivities began.

A bard took up his lute and began to sing about the food as the dishes were handed around,

'First a roasted kid, a yearling,
With its innards firmly strung,
And, upon it, well to season
Tarragon and mint are hung...
Lemons, too, with nadd besprinkled,
Scented well with ambergris.
And, for garnishing the slices,
Shreds of appetising cheese.'

His voice soared into the rafters as his rhythm changed:

'Here capers grace a sauce vermilion,
Whose fragrant odours to the soul are blown ...
Here pungent garlic meets the eager sight
And whets with savour sharp the appetite,
White olives turn to shadowed night the day,
And salted fish in slices rim the tray.'

By now the general conversation had overtaken the singer's voice, and he subsided as they ate their fill. Their choice, as well, came from moussaka and maghmuna and couscous, spiced with wines and wafers, pheasant and guinea-fowl and turtle-doves, pastries and subtleties in the form of fanciful lions and eagles and crowns. An ox was being roasted out in the open for the Envoy's soldiers, and the Hauteville servants and serfs ate almost as well as their masters that day.

Above all, the company were conscious of Robert's dominant presence there, experiencing, for a brief passage of time, the smell of a vein of silver and the taste of a shower of gold.

Sichelgaita was well content with her banquet and display. Normally she would dismiss southern Italian culture and cooking with a sniff, insisting that it was primitive, provincial, uncourtly and ill-bred - of no interest save as objects of ridicule. This time, she felt, they could rival Rome.

She got to her feet, to everyone's astonishment, quelling the singers and entertainers with one look; she appeared like a tower, looming over the snakelike cleric beside her.

The entire Hall simmered into silence. All that could be heard were the mechanical birds and the rolling thunder, which seemed to come nearer and nearer.

Sichelgaita's gown woven through with silver was incandescent in the candlelight, rich jewels set in gold shone in her hair. On both her hands were heavy rings and at her belt hung carved coral ornaments. Her time had come, she calculated, although no-one had expected her to speak. She had to pitch her voice above the thunder rolls.

'Your Eminence! My Lord! Normally this is the time for us to pass the loving cup around the tables. But today I have an especial present to give to my husband, to mark our wedding anniversary ... and we are honoured to share the occasion with His Eminence here. I ordered this gift from Constantinople several years ago, to be made up to my expressed desires and design. It recently arrived - mercifully unharmed! It is, need I say? of inestimable value, but it was made to symbolise the quality of my regard for my husband. Several years have passed since I first ordered it, but my respect remains the same. *Bring in my gift!'*

Her voice shouted the order across the Hall, and as she did so the thunder suddenly ceased outside, cutting off like a knife. For a moment there was total, utter silence.

Robert was shocked. *It was their wedding anniversary?* They had never celebrated it before. Nor had he ever given Sichelgaita a gift, believing that if she had wished for anything - she had sufficient wealth to buy it for herself. What was she up to?

A group of servants had gathered by the big doors. They parted, to allow a stately procession to pass through, headed by the Grand Chamberlain and the Comptroller. All those close to them drew in their breath,

'Ooooohhh ...' was heard on all sides, and 'oooooohh ...' again.

The procession walked in at a stately pace, pride showing in every gesture, every step, every face.

At last the crowd could see that a broad wooden door was borne between the staff, a raised protection all around the edge, and the wood covered by a woven black cloth. The bejewelled goblet from Constantinople was enthroned on top, creating a sensation.

The glass seemed as cold as a piece of carved ice, the encircling gold band and sturdy foot shone and sparkled, the gems gleamed with royal menace - the whole throng gasped at the sight,

'Aaaahhh ...'

Robert got to his feet in astonishment as it was carried slowly nearer, his eyes locked onto the treasure. And he had never even given her a ring. Suddenly he was genuinely aware of the great honour

Sichelgaita was paying him - and of its underlying meaning. His Eminence's eyes glittered with envy and anger, a cruel smile pasted on his thin lips.

A lone drum-beat accompanied the goblet's progress around the Hall and to Robert's place at the High Table; all the company were awe-struck.

This was a brilliant move on Sichelgaita's part, thought the Cardinal. No-one could fault her graceful elegant gesture, yet the orchestration of her moves seemed just too organised to be true, the churchman sensed a contrivance worthy of a great atrocity. A few hours later and Robert would have been publicly humiliated by him, yet here was his wife presenting this incomparable goblet to her husband as if it were a hero's laurel wreath: he had badly misjudged his own timing and swore, expertly, but under his breath.

In the extraordinary atmosphere of stupefying silence Sichelgaita walked forward and took hold of the huge goblet. She slowly turned it around with deliberate intent, so that Robert saw all the twelve gems, and left it with the great diamond facing him. Then she ceremoniously placed it in his waiting hands.

It was filled with wine almost to the brim. He looked into its icy depths, felt the sharp carving of the outer flowers beneath his thumbs and the intellectual pull of the enormous polished gems. It was very heavy.

This was an overwhelming public statement of esteem. He found it vastly, touchingly, revealing - at last. He was devastated by the discovery, and his own reaction to it. He had always, deliberately, denied himself the possibility that Sichelgaita could love him as Alberada did, unselfishly ... afraid that any love that he could offer would be divided and therefore diminished - and both women would be destroyed by the division. He had no concept that love had no extremities.

He gazed at Sichelgaita across the cup, unsmiling. There was a new way of looking in his eyes, a new knowledge dawning. Sichelgaita blushed for the first time in her life, the red blood shot up from the toes and suffused her body quickly to the roots of her heavy hair, leaving yet another fine film of perspiration. She was completely unnerved, totally vulnerable. Her knees trembled and grew weak. She was afraid she might faint.

This time he accurately focused on her, and into her inner depths. Her scarlet face was not contrived, but it was defenceless, brave in its total honesty. Now he truly understood. And there she stood, shaking, wishing that this scene could have been in private. In the concentrated hush of the Hall, where everyone craned their necks to watch, he spoke to her alone,

'Thank you. That's inadequate, but it comes from my heart. Later, I'll say more.'

Sichelgaita swayed, drowning in his gaze.

Robert continued, just as quietly, but heard by all,

'In the meanwhile - let's use this magnificent treasure as our own personal loving cup, shall we?'

Slowly, looking deeper into her eyes, he began to raise it to his mouth, and put his lips to the rim, and drank deeply.

Handing the goblet back to Sichelgaita, he bowed.

With sparkling eyes she, too, drank.

Then, as planned, she resolutely turned towards the third person seated at the High Table; she was manipulating something in her hand - yet held the goblet aloft for all to see.

The avaricious Cardinal was mesmerised by the unimagined beauty of the goblet as she slowly lowered it. He remained silent, staring at it, and licked his lips, his eyes examining every detail and his mind estimating its worth.

Sichelgaita waited until he paused, staring at the great diamond, then caught his eye and held it - mesmerising him, with a question in her eyes: he found he could not turn away from them. *What could be the question she asked of him?*

As they gazed at each other, a tiny phial of poison was released from under her hand into the wine, but he did not see it, nor did anyone else. She had practised her action over and over again.

She knew, too well, that Robert must win his race for Bari before the Cardinal disgraced him - even if she, herself, was eventually condemned to death for the Cardinal's premature and painful end: to preserve her husband's honour she was prepared to make the final sacrifice for him. She spoke out with icy malice and a slight catch of her breath,

'Your Eminence! As our most honoured guest, I offer you this unique loving cup! You will be the only one beside ourselves to drink from it.'

She carefully handed it to the Cardinal, who took it from her with both hands greedily.

But there was something about Sichelgaita, her look, the strange way in which she had turned from him, at such a crucially emotional moment, that Robert sensed was unnatural: an intensity glowed from her rigid body like a lamp. He knew she had no scruples, and swiftly pieced together that by loving him with such abandon she would go to any lengths to help him. But he could countenance no crime against the Church under his own roof. His powerful voice rang out,

'Stay! Wait! Sichelgaita, as the generous donor of this wondrous goblet, *you should have a second draught ...*'

Foiled, knowing herself discovered, she furiously tried to pull the goblet from the Cardinal's hands. But, confused, he would not release it willingly, his mouth open in surprise. For once, she did not know what to do next ... but clearly Robert must be obeyed in front of all.

As they struggled, all of a sudden the goblet slipped between their fumbling, grasping hands. For a moment it rose - airborne - then its mighty weight plunged it to the floor with a shrieking crash, shattering it into a myriad of razor-edged shards. Her face was a ghastly chalk-white.

Robert and Sichelgaita stared at each other, horror-struck, standing like a couple of fighting cocks. The Cardinal subsided onto his chair between them, gibbering and shaking. The wine spread quickly across the floor, staining Sichelgaita's silver shoes.

At that moment, a breaking roll of pure noise, burst into the Hall like a tidal wave.

Before anyone could utter a word there was a furious cracking sound and the ground beneath their feet began to swell and move, like mounting waves. The mighty walls started to crack, dust rose off them in uneven clouds. Beams began to crash from overhead as everyone raced frantically to get out of the building - out into the fresh air,

'An earthquake! Run! Save yourselves!'

Those that could reach the doors ran fast, pulling friends with them, leaping over benches, skidding against others - screaming, panicking in terror. The High Table was near other doors and, as the stone entrance shook and buckled, Robert swiftly grabbed his wife with one great sweep of his arm, and pushed her out into relative safety.

The rooms burned. The ceilings crumbled. Barrels caught fire and their hoops burst. The peacocks flared in mercurial flames and turned to dust.

Outside, parts of the castle walls crashed down, a yawning chasm gashed open across the grounds, obliquely to where Sichelgaita stood - she teetered on the edge, horrified, as several of her servants fell down inside the wide abyss in the earth ... which then closed back, trapping them for eternity; screaming.

Robert had followed her into the night. She turned to him. They looked at one another, faces weirdly lighted by flames, a harrowing uniting.

They walked away, then, and stood in the shelter of a great boulder, older than time. There, slowly, Robert took the shaking Sichelgaita into his strong arms and held her, silently, and did not let her go.

Several hours later they felt safe enough to go inside again. His Eminence had not appeared in the hideous confusion, but they found him, petrified and still in his chair, the gold girdle of the cup in his hands, a beam across his blood-stained throat. He had meant to die with a disdainful smile, a bored twitch of indifferent lips - so he had always fancied. Instead, he had died with his face purple, glazed bloodshot eyes and a protruding tongue: saliva and blood had trickled in a foam onto his richly gilded robes.

Just below him lay the dead dwarf in a fur-lined cloak, a ruby clenched in his useless, elderly fingers.

JUDITH

Judith had been riding for weeks in the cloying heat. Flies nipped her patient horse's flanks, sending it snorting sideways, dancing with kicking steps, as it tried to evade their savage stings; and the sweat ran in rivulets down both horse and rider. Her companions were sadly thin in number now, dangerously so; she had left much of her goods and wealth in safe hands in Rome. Bertha had lost some weight and was often grumbling under her breath. Now and again she dared to reprove Judith, hands on hips, and jolly red face puckered into a very mask of determination.

Having left Pantaleone at Amalfi, Judith had made her way north to Rome and Odo's sister convent, which was awaiting her with open arms. They were astonished to see her dressed as a high-born lady, and not as a nun: explanations followed immediately, in a torrent of laughter and gesticulations.

There she spoke lengthily to the Mother Superior, confessing her sin of taking part in the fraudulent documents prepared at St. Evroul-sur-Ouche to ensure her safety. The Mother Superior in Rome owed no allegiance to the Count of Evreux and, impishly, praised her fellow-Abbess' ingenuity. Judith placed her own document in the Abbess' care, for now she needed it no longer: it was not, however, destroyed. But she kept Odo's certificate in its place of concealment, showing it to no-one.

There, too, to Judith's dismay, she also heard of the Abbess' peaceful death in Normandy, in hushed attendance by all the nuns and congregation of the mother convent. But Judith decided not to mention the most secret document of all, folded amongst the convent's chest of nuns' professions and dowries and land grants and rent books: that would have to wait - it was too complicated to deal with now. Perhaps it need never be mentioned, the Abbess' name never besmirched, to remain an intriguing legacy for the future researchers.

Much of her time together with the Mother Superior was spent in discussing the implications of Odo's murder, and how it would relate to the convent in Rome. Judith offered a princely sum as a goodwill gift, in memory of Odo - which would 'resolve any temporary difficulties for them' until all matters were settled: she was requested to become a patroness in reparation for her sins, and, to both parties' satisfaction, left it there forever.

Then the cheerful Abbess assisted Judith in selling the valuable plate inherited from her brother, together with Odo's clothes and robes and other masculine possessions: the huge price they fetched was very gratifying.

The Abbess was conversant with the Hauteville fortunes and misadventures, and acquainted Judith with Roger's part in the siege of Bari. She divulged, with superabundant details, how Christianity's fate in south-eastern Italy rested on his ultimate success - no-one in Rome could countenance a reversion.

As she now was assured that Roger lived, and breathed, albeit fraught with danger, Judith joyfully made plans to travel on, across the Apennine Mountains. Now that he seemed so close at hand it prompted her to count up the time since their last encounter, to consider how she, herself, had changed through her many experiences - and suddenly she was afraid of her own emotions; doubt, at times, had crept in - especially after she left Amalfi and Pantaleone. Would Roger, she asked herself, have changed as well? What could the future hold? Was she free to make a choice?

Judith's quest for Roger gained in its intensity as she rode through the stifling heat, driving herself, and her companions, beyond reason. Climbing the mountain passes, changing exhausted horses, speaking to the guard of the attendant soldiers was all achieved at a pace the party had not experienced before, and seething resentment could be felt at the haste. The journey developed into a forced discipline, all that was important, she felt, was to pull back the distance between them as fast as possible and see Roger face to face.

Passions she had never known coursed through the marrow of Judith's bones in the unfamiliar surroundings of southern Italy, as day followed day. With no intimate friend to ride by her side she had no other distraction than to think of Roger: she became physically exhausted, her nerves were at screaming pitch, and she sorely missed Pantaleone's companionship and light-hearted conversation. The emotional door at Amalfi remained open.

Finally, once over the mountains, and having travelled across the long, flat and arid plain of Apulia, she arrived at the Hauteville camp outside Bari. She was full of hope, fractious, wildly impatient, and was again bitterly disappointed - neither of the Hauteville brothers were there. She raged, then wept bitterly.

On making enquiries about Roger she learned that 'he had been slightly wounded and was being cared for in another place'. Where this was, no-one would say. She tried bribing people to tell her, but to no avail, it seemed they genuinely could not have known. Blinkered, drowning in thwarted hopelessness, she desperately journeyed back through and over the mountains again, this time determined to find Alberada in her small castle in the mountains of Calabria.

The first news of Alberada's whereabouts had come to her when she was leaving Amalfi; garbled, it was true, but still she felt that of all the family, married or unmarried, perhaps she would be the most trustworthy person to question, and she longed to meet her.

She prayed to God that Roger's wounds had healed. But now she was afraid to consider whether he still wanted her to be with him or not - it had been such a long time since they had last met. She felt no longer a girl. Indeed, not even young, but helpless and bewildered.

As she rode higher and higher through the mountains, she rounded a corner and saw the lake in the valley. It was not until later did she find the castle perched above one end of it. Long and narrow, at one end a bar rose up, a vast ridge of earth and sand. The water was pure and absolutely still, with dense woods on its rocky rising western bank, and pasture sloping more gradually down on the east.

When she first came on this broad water she stopped, enchanted, looking at what would forever be the place where her heart would return. She saw the lake through some trees in a small meadow, and between the smooth grey boles shone the water on which the sunshine lay in flecks and sparkles. Near the shore rafts of dark-green saucers floated, leaves which supported a freight of red and creamy lilies; other flowers, star-shaped ones of mauve, covered the ground beneath the trees and across the water hung a thin pennant of blue smoke from some far-off fisherman's shelter.

She neared the lake, the path had been hewn here and there through rock and splendid pines towered over her, the trunks rough like crocodile-hide, and the outlandish roots gripping for anchorage. Some had fallen during the recent earthquake, and the soil had been heaved and torn in a great area round about; it must have been terrifying for many creatures of earth and air, like the death of a mighty one on whom many simple lives had depended.

Now that she drew closer the woods began to peter out and the rock faces were seen to be clothed with cascades of pink flowers, with dark green fleshy leaves. At the lake's shallow edge it was so clear that she could see the wading birds' feet, and the dark shadows which were fishes, now poised, now darting. She rode cautiously into the water, her horse gratefully stretching down to gulp the cool liquid, so she slid off his back onto a smooth, flat rock. Holding her reins she told her attendants that the day would end here by the lake, and they would rest and eat.

Judith and Bertha wandered on alone for a short while along the banks of the deserted lake, which mirrored the cloudless sky; untrammelled birds soared in the blue gulfs, free as she felt not free, and she longed for life to lift her up, to take her out of the enclosure of her mind.

At last they reached a tiny cove, merely a space between two hedges, recluse and cool, a trickle of water falling with hardly a sound as it steadily passed through a little culvert of stones into the pellucid lake. Flowers grew, lifting waywardly against the blue sky, and ferns, lusty in the damp, fringed the cove's perimeter. The broiling sun had no power here, and a few clumps of starry flowers bloomed in the mossy shadowed bank.

Judith stood looking down into the lake's edge. The slight flow set her image wavering in the crystal water; white stones covered the bottom, gleaming invitingly, and she was overcome by a pagan desire to lie in the cool stillness. It was just after the noon of the day and of the year, it seemed that no-one came down this byway; the cove was as secluded as a room. Quickly she slipped out of her clothes, damp with sweat, and walked into the water with naked feet, shivering slightly, her arms folded about her breast. She stood for a moment, wrapped in her own embrace, her heart beating heavily at her hardihood, thinking of embraces more warm and carnal. Soft, unshelled, she lay down in the water, her unbound hair streaming about her, and let it flow sensuously all over her.

JUDITH AND ALBERADA

Days later, rested and refreshed, Judith and Alberada walked slowly together along the stony ramparts of the castle, warm to the touch, in the cool evening air. Now and then they glanced over the breast-high walls, down the steep and lush mountainside, where trees cast long shadows on the grass and tangled undergrowth. Above them, creeping vines clambered up the trunks of trees, swinging from one tree-top to another, allowing the merest threads of late sunlight to filter through their matted canopy. Against the castle's sturdy walls an exuberant fig had thrust its roots, and the sight of it made Judith yearn, irrationally, for her childhood home - and reminded her, unnecessarily, of Roger again.

The broad track which led to the castle curled and twisted steeply upwards through the trees. In the other direction a smaller pathway led towards a sturdy wooden jetty by the end of the lake. Shaded by elms and poplars, the thickets thereabouts were filled with songs of nightingale, black-cap and oriole. Although it was such an isolated place, Robert protected Alberada well and an invincible bodyguard permanently kept watch.

Every day fresh water was brought to the castle, except when on rare occasions, in the depth of winter, the water froze. Beside the castle's upper walls was a cavernous tank, always full, in case of emergencies: Robert left nothing to chance.

On the ramparts lay several carved dishes made of stone; they were flat and low, the length of a man's sword. They, too, were filled with a hand's depth of water. In the early evening when the slight breeze dipped over the walls and wafted across the dishes it doubly cooled the air. Sometimes Alberada would sit close to one on a cushion, dabbling her hand idly in the water to become cooler. Now and then she would splash some of the tubs filled with greenery and lemon bushes that she had grown to amuse herself, and bees played, darting hide-and-seek in the secret places of the flowers.

During the mellow evening the women watched the last patch of sunshine in the centre of the ramparts where two or three small blue dragonflies, brilliant as jewels, poised and darted above the cool depths of the shallow dishes, sipped on the wing, or made flashing excursions towards the delicate flowers. The last gossiping chirrup of birds was dying away as the sun dropped suddenly out of sight behind the mountain, and the sky, orange-tawny in the sunset, shaded down to a deep pearly-grey. The fragrance of lemon was all around, melding with the musky perfume from the nearby firs, together with the scent of cooking food and charcoal and drifting wood-smoke.

Both women had looked up as a last blush in the heavens floated like a veil rapidly pulled away, then died down almost as fast. A scurry of wind raced through the trees, twitching the ends of the leaves as it hastened elsewhere. Abruptly a thin sickle moon emerged, tremulous, in the night sky, garnished with a faint sprinkling of stars, growing increasingly bright. It was a limitless event put on each evening which Alberada loved, and never failed to admire its variety. She pictured the canopy spanning over Robert, too.

Alberada and Judith conversed for hours together: it was a comfort and delight for them both. Alberada assured her that Roger was not wounded at all, that the rumour had been given out as a diplomatic ploy, and he had really left to seek out Robert for more money: the siege was so extended and the new fleet making its way had been delayed by storms.

Although comforted, Judith was wearily afraid that she would have to travel back again to Bari to find him. But Alberada coaxed her to stay for a while, to rest and become strong after her endless journey from Normandy to the foot of Italy; telling her that Roger had built himself a castle of his own at Mileto nearby. It was more than probable that he would return to Bari via his own home - and he always called upon her when he did.

Judith was hesitant, but gracefully complied. She found Alberada's company enjoyable; besides, it was invaluable to know all the Hauteville news. Yet, now that Roger seemed to be so close, her emotional fatigue became even more serious, to the extent that she almost feared meeting him. She knew this to be senseless, but was at last beyond reason, eaten up by her obsessive search.

Every day Judith went back down the mountainside to her tiny cove, accompanied by Bertha, whilst Alberada saw to her household duties. Sometimes she waded in the water, sometimes she just rested against a tree and daydreamed. Tonight she was restive, unable to remain tranquil, tapping her fingernail unmindfully on the stone. She stared over the wall into the gathering gloom, sensitive to the unknown.

Sudden movement far away in the distance caught her eye. Was that, she wondered, a group of horsemen on the track? She peered down into the twilight, which was growing quickly darker by the minute.

'Alberada! Do you think ...?'

'It's too difficult to see! And the pine-needles muffle the horses' hooves.' By her side, standing tip-toe, Alberada strained to see what was happening. 'You may be right - I think we'll have visitors tonight, but no-one is expected.'

She turned to run lightly down the steps, looking back at Judith, calling out as she went,

'Why not stay here? I'll send your woman to you when we know who it is. I think it must be friends, for no warning has been sounded from the valley.'

Judith paced along the walls increasingly agitated. The slowing horsemen could now be heard, but not seen, because the night fell so fast. There were sounds of bits jingling, of horses snorting, of animals passing through undergrowth - occasionally a muffled shout. When the newcomers arrived they had to pass through the castle gate positioned the other side beneath the tower, unable to be seen from where she stood. She waited with her heart in her mouth as the dusk grew to velvet darkness: she was like a wraith in a ghost world, twitching at her skirt, tapping, tapping.

The young moon now glimmered more brilliantly above the castle: the ground was as lifeless and as light as dark velvet. The trees had lost their shapes and become a rampart of blackness that loomed up in the darkened shield of the sky.

The indecision became unbearable. Suddenly she found she could control herself no longer and she took to her heels and fled. She ran pell mell to her room and bolted her door, retiring to an inner - silent - chamber. She refused to let Bertha come in or answered her calls. Whoever it was who visited she could not confront them - not now, perhaps never! In her passionate distress she could not separate the all-too-precious dream-life that had now intermingled with the real. She lay in her lonely room that shadows from another source were beginning to invade from every corner - just a space filled with shadows: and a horde of invented doubts beleaguered her mind, pinpointing her emotional frailties. She wrestled sleeplessly with her unrealities and to no avail.

The next day, very early, she stood in her secret cove, having left a slumbering Bertha puffing contentedly. In the castle, blurred with exhaustion, she had listened to every baffling sound, been alert to every faint footfall: here, by the familiar lake, she knew she would be alone and in control of her situation - only Bertha was aware of this, her secret place.

As she listened to the rapturous singing of a lark, high amongst the trees, she was conscious that the dew still lay on the leaves, some flowers had petals curled, awakened; the faint daylight was slowly creeping through the leaves and branches, pushing away the grey shadows, and the undergrowth rustled.

Seeking peace, release from the snapping tension which had built up in her for so many weary months, Judith found tranquility in the beauty of nature's scene. Gratefully she sat down on a fallen tree trunk in the dappled light, the long grass wherein flowers grew supporting her simple gown, and she laid her tired golden head against the humid mossy bank and slipped into a deep sleep at last.

JUDITH AND ROGER

Time passed. A bird cooed, the lake water lap-lapped regularly against the stones, the sun rose higher, falling through the leaves, eventually alighting on her sleeping face. Roger had waited patiently all night outside her room, out of sight. He had followed her agitated and trembling run down to her secret cove at dawn, quiet as a shadow, and now watched her in silence.

Hungrily, once she was asleep, he looked at every gentle curve, every nuance of colour, every strand of hair. She seemed much changed: just as beautiful, as lively as his memories, but older, of course, and thinner, too. He watched entranced as she slept, easily as a child. In the pale transparent light, arched eyebrows, curved lips, slender hands loose in her lap, were a remote and fragile elegance. His heart's desire, at last before him, became real. He thoughtfully fingered the cross about his neck, and waited - until she began to stir and he could wait no longer.

She raised her eyes, and saw him standing in front of her as if in a dream - barely recognisable - regarding her wordlessly, but with a smile behind his questioning eyes.

She came unsteadily to him in the early sunlight, her dress rustling with the sound of fallen leaves in the wind.

She stood from him a breath away, and put her slight hands up to his shoulders once again, after so many years - as if to reassure herself that the figure before her was a man and not a ghost. Once again, like a rapier through her tired body, she became aware of how he looked at her; half-smiling and steady, with a remembered gaze which was both a question and an answer. Love, not so young this time but patently enduring, blazed out again like a heath catching fire and was instantly remembered by both.

'It is you!' she said. *'It is you!'*

'Yes, Judith, it is.' He answered, and looked gravely down at her. He saw that her eyes were blinded with wild unshed tears, which she would not allow to fall.

So they beheld each other for a while in silence, until he opened his arms, and she went into them with a sigh.

Hearts pounding together, she spoke, her words muffled in his clothing.

'Didn't you want me? Why did you never send word?'

Roger rested his cheek on the top of her head and gently replied,

'Let me, in turn, ask why you never answered my letters?'

Pushing apart, they stared at each other, round-eyed.

'You wrote to me? Always to Evreux?'

'A thousand letters; but you never responded. I was never told that you might have moved away or become betrothed.'

'I never received any,' murmured Judith, knowingly, 'my father must have destroyed them - it's the sort of thing he would do in his anger.'

'In his anger?'

'I ran away. I ruined his great ambitions. He was bound to be angry.'

Roger pulled her slowly towards him again.

'There's so much we have to talk about - and we can, now we've found each other. In the meanwhile, let me answer your first question! I've always wanted you as my wife, I've always dreamed of you, and I've always remembered everything about you. Now - tell me - do you remember this?'

And, gently, he kissed her.

Her lips parted in pleasure. She remained still, in his encircling arms, and waited.

'And this?'

He kissed her, then, as he had kissed her in the castle's grounds, within the encompassing boughs of the fig tree - deeper and deeper, until they abandoned themselves in a sensuous, voluptuous world of their own.

Later that evening they met again, more formally. This time Judith wore much of her finery from Normandy, her more precious jewels, a silver-encrusted gown and a golden coif. This time she had bathed in warmed scented water in her room, singing softly to herself, had been smoothed in pungent oils by the voluble Bertha, and had shining, rested eyes from a deep and dreamless sleep.

This time there was no confusion, no jangling nerves or tendency to tears as she glided into the Hall. Everything to her was tranquil, glassy, time had slowed down - it was like the moment after one has dived deep down into water and has not begun to rise to the surface. A tiny pulse still jerked erratically at her slender throat, but her hands were folded and still. Roger absorbed it all.

Half way through the evening meal there was sudden tumult. Robert de Hauteville, Duke of Apulia, the most powerful man in southern Italy, strode into the small Hall and pandemonium roared. Young Bohemund streaked across and stood close to his father, his face alight, but then he turned away, tormented by jealousy, remembering Roger Borsa's place in his father's life with resentment. He went out, then, and joined some of Robert's knights in the military quarters.

Alberada's face was radiant as she greeted him, pressed, momentarily against his warm body with desire. In time she would coax Bohemund to re-join them. In this castle, who could doubt it? Robert had come home.

That same evening, as the moonlight waned, the four of them

continued walking up and down the castle's ramparts. Duke Robert and Roger had taken turns in questioning Judith about her journey, about her brother and affairs in Normandy; briefly she answered all that was asked of her, but offered nothing more, believing in her new-found wisdom that some secrets should remain unuttered. In their turn they told her about their lives, especially about the siege of Bari and the lack of funds to bring it to a successful conclusion. It gave Judith the chance to offer a considerable loan, once she realised that Roger would immediately be torn from her again. Laughing – amazed - the brothers accepted her offer with immense gratitude.

Then Roger, for the second time, proposed marriage to Judith with stars in his eyes - the same stars that Fressenda had once seen.

Three days later, Roger and Judith, blazingly happy, were wed at last in the incense-scented chapel of Roger's castle at Mileto. The ceremony was witnessed by the rejoicing households of both castles.

Duke Robert and Alberada quietly watched them, shoulder to shoulder, with leaden hearts, trying to quell the bitter-sweet memories of their own enchanted wedding years before. Their glowering son Bohemund stood, immensely tall, to witness the ceremony under duress, awkward and rebellious. He was long-limbed and lank, all wrist and ankle, with a cormorant throat, and he chose to stand against another wall, away from his parents.

That wedding night was a revelation to the bride.

Bertha's earthy stories had been hair-raising, and she had been half-inclined to believe them. Anticipating this, Roger first made Judith lie beside him, folded in his arms, and go to sleep. She was very frightened - he saw that quite clearly. Her distress had increased throughout the evening. Her miserable self-consciousness resurfaced again, wiped out all desire, if desire she'd ever really known. So he anticipated her needs; gave her tenderness rather than passion, and provided a safe shelter.

His arms were around her, as when he had lifted her into the bed. His body was strong, his shoulders broad and his strength compressed her against him until her trembling ceased. She became lost in her eggshell fortress; all her thoughts and fears and fancies she gave to him in trust as complete as love itself. So he just held her, unmoving, until the warmth of their bodies made her relax and let go into deep and comforting slumber.

When the night was at its darkest he woke her very gently. Then slowly, he began to make love to her.

Together they discovered then the rapture which lies far beyond any false summit of excitement. He guided her through the difficult ascent, waiting for her, gentling her, honouring her with his absolute attention until, when the climax came, in ecstasy their bodies locked. Their individual journeys had ended, and in the last delight they met finally as lovers. They experienced an intensity of peace they had never before known.

Later, during their brief time together, he could remember the most awe-inspiring sense of fulfilment, lying as it were on the summit of their own private mountain. For longer, he could clearly remember waking, in streaming sunlight, with such a sense of his own comfort and peace, such wellbeing and delight in himself, that the fleeting revelation of this being the first time he had ever woken thus was almost impersonal - seemed remote and insignificant; he didn't stop to question it, although he remembered turning to her, finding her smilingly awake, with closed eyes, and knowing it could only have been the same with her. He moved an arm and held her close in their precious private world

INTERVAL FOR ROGER AND JUDITH

So the pitifully few private days and nights became fast in their thoughts, although they discovered that any emotion, if it be sufficiently strong, is elusive, not accurately memorable, and that the memory of it only serves to conceal the core or essence of violently felt experience: it did not matter, the last few days made up for all the months and years they had endured and the loneliness could now be over. They hungered for the years ahead together.

Again and again they both remembered the time of their solemn marriage ceremony, where every word, every pause, took on its own significance. Until Roger had to leave, those words and promises were recalled by them both, which they whispered to each other countless times, and half-murmured into each other's hair or fold of cheek or neck between times of sleep - like an enchanted spell.

There were also memories of their happy wedding banquet, where they all spoke of Normandy and Hauteville and Evreux castles; although nothing was said at the time, no-one believed they would ever see them again. Duke Robert took care not to mention Sichelgaita's treasured cup, but the premature death of the Cardinal was related with relief: the Pope had sent no replacement and the possibility of Duke Robert's removal from command was never mentioned.

ROGER AT BARI

Three days later Roger turned on his horse, waved a last time to Judith, and rode fast towards Bari. His hopes were high.

His devoted but grumbling servant, Pierre, had asked for permission to turn off to visit a shrine in an Apullian *trullo* village that they were passing, and join up with him within a day. Roger knew the area, had visited the shrine himself, and relented - with reluctance. He was aware of Pierre's strong religious convictions, often finding him kneeling overlong in prayer. The man looked troubled as he rode away.

From a bird's eye, the *trullo* village revealed itself like a collection of large beehives, all the houses being a similar size, and circular in shape, built with thick walls and cone-shaped roofs made of limestone slates finely packed together without mortar. Like a honeycomb the houses were all interlocked down the narrow lanes, the community inward-looking and protective of each other. At the sight of a stranger they scuttled down into their round houses like beetles, fastening their narrow doors and, like troglodytes, sometimes clambered down into their own cellars, many of which joined the cellars next door, and pulled down their wooden floors over their heads and fastened them.

The shrine in the *trullo* village had once been pagan but now, turned Christian, it was equally venerated. Pierre had visited it several times, finding some ease for his conscience during the terrible siege of Bari; the carnage, during the past three years, had greatly distressed him. The priest there would hear his confession. Then he would hurry on to join Roger.

At noon Roger ordered his party of men to stop, to rest. Needing solitude he strode to an isolated bamboo plantation, curious with moist aridity. Everywhere the thick-grown ranks of reedy bamboo showed spiky leaves, shivering at intervals, curling down like shade itself. It looked dry, but you could smell the damp. He searched for scorpions. The hot afternoon silence weighed. At this hour no-one was abroad. The bamboo grew just higher than Roger's head, the un-nodding plumes motionless, so that all around he had a hedge of green and cream against the immense azure sky. There was no sound at all, even the insects and mosquitoes were sleepy: once a lizard darted like a living emerald across a sun-baked rock. He sat, ate, considered the siege's future, and planned his campaign in detail.

The heat visibly simmered, transparently radiant. He was bemused by his emotions, mostly rare happiness - which came pushing in, and which he had to be alone to savour to the full. He completed the last detail of his plans in his mind and slept heavily in the noon of the day.

When he finally rose to leave he scared some giant grasshoppers that hung in clusters in the dried bamboo and nearby dead thistles; they started off with the noise of a covey of partridges, and his horse shied and bucked.

Two days later he had arrived at his destination at the Norman camp outside Bari, when the moon was behind the clouds. He came cloaked and hidden. Now was the time to conclude the siege, and Judith's money and promissory notes, strapped to his back, were vital to success; he had much to achieve.

For several days Roger saw the waiting traders and suppliers, paying them their dues, thanking them for their forbearance and making arrangements for the summer campaign he knew would be ahead, this time almost certainly in Sicily. He longed to return to that land, he loved it and felt his destiny might lie there.

Then he spoke to his men, distributing their pay, praising them, prodding the known loafers, enquiring about their families - a joke here, a clap on the back there - until he knew that they were heartened and ready to make one last effort for him. All at once the whole camp began to go about its business with a lighter, quicker step, with purpose in every tread.

A fortnight later, in their turn, the people of Bari, so despondent for years, now changed overnight as well. One night there suddenly appeared to be some celebration taking place in the besieged city - an occurrence which astonished the onlookers: flaming torches were seen on the ramparts, singing was heard from behind the thick walls. Yet, after almost three years of siege there was little for the inhabitants to sing about - what could be happening? Roger sent his spies to report, led by Pierre, but to him the reason seemed quite clear: if the Bariots were celebrating, they were doing so a trifle too early.

He was convinced at once, with his heightened perceptions, that the besieged citizens of Bari must have received word that some attempt at rescue was at hand from the Bariots' Byzantine allies. *He knew it*, there could be no other logical explanation. Ever-impatient, passionately volatile, the Bariots seemed exuberantly relieved and couldn't help showing it in their ingenuous, thoughtless way.

Roger gave orders to treble the watch by the lookouts, whilst his own ships were permanently kept at the ready, just out of sight of the city. Every Norman was on the alert.

That night, alone, he ate fish wrapped in leaves, cooked between hot stones, as he watched across the dark sea. Half in a trance from staring so long at the inky water, he physically sensed an ancestor ghost of a Norse long ship floating by; he even unstirred in his imagination the ghost of a great vanished river up which it had swum with muffled oars several hundred years before.

From days long gone, the words of a heroic saga returned to his mind, an Icelandic song about the history of the world, handed down by bards, which ended with,

'That was the dawn of time, when Ymir lived;

There was no sand nor sea, no salty waves,

No earth beneath nor heaven above,

But an empty nothing, and nowhere grass.'

But as he returned to consciousness the mists rolled back again and only the bright stars shone coldly down onto an empty sea. He remained watching.

'They'll come this way,' he said to Pierre, 'I feel it in my bones; they're near at hand.'

In the depths of the night there was a frantic call from his lookouts that they saw *'The lights of many lanterns, shining like stars at the mast-tops!'*

Instantly Roger sent word to Duke Robert, who was at nearby Trani, to be present at the kill.

Within an hour he took his fresh new fleet to meet the expected rescuers. His sailors were well-armed and rested; more important still were their high hopes, buoyed up by Roger's evident confidence.

Roger directed the naval action himself, brimming with happiness and expectation as his vessels tore across the waves to meet the slack enemy: no-one had expected them to attack at night. But attack they did. They would have attacked at any time. In the molten silver of the sea the final battle was one-sided.

Of the twenty Greek-led Byzantine ships involved, come to rescue the people of Bari for one last glorious time, nine were sunk and not one was able to penetrate Bari's harbour. Roger, on the Hauteville flagship, concentrated his attack on the Greek leader. After a flamboyant battle carried out with storming passion and verve, Roger triumphantly captured his vessel.

This was a victory of enormous importance. The impact, he knew, would crush the rebellious people who were left alive in Bari - and destroy them. In eager anticipation he, and all his ships, sailed back in exultation to the port, his prisoners manacled to the thwarts.

At last the great moment dawned when Roger showed what was left of the Byzantines to the beleaguered citizens of Bari who outlined the walls of the city with fallen hearts, hungry beyond measure and in absolute despair. He displayed the leader of the enemy ostentatiously roped high up against the mast as they sailed to shore, his other ships fanning out behind him from either side in an arc of triumph.

Then, after Duke Robert had given him a hero's welcome, together they paraded the remaining enemies all around outside the city's walls, marching them in chains from one side right around to the other, whilst he and Duke Robert rode alongside, smiling wordlessly, and without weapons.

It was clear to the commanders within the sickened city that there was now no hope - that they had, after all the years of torment, betrayed themselves. In self-disgust and ultimate humiliation they finally sent messengers to the Hautevilles, asking terms. In their hearts they expected no mercy.

At long last, Duke Robert and Roger entered the gates of Bari, triumphant. They could afford to be magnanimous, and they were, in their fashion. Bari now was a western Christian city at last and for good, allied, through them, only to Rome - no longer dominated from Constantinople. Both Pope and Holy Roman Emperor were gratified, but the Hauteville brothers were to receive the glory - and the rich rewards.

Bari's capture, too, signalled Roger's release from dependence on Duke Robert: in the future he could build his own empire, with Judith by his side, and a clutch of well-deserved titles in his hand. His intention was to take - and own - Sicily, especially now that Robert was becoming older.

Expansively his elder brother clapped Roger on the back.

'We've had some fine adventures recently, haven't we? I think that our father would be pleased if we ventured on to visit the grotto chapel of Saint Michael in the near future - don't you? We've never been there, and I'd like to see the place where all this began for our father. I must be getting soft in my middle-age! But - will you come?'

Roger smiled, asking,

'You're not going straight away to Alberada?'

Duke Robert shifted in his saddle, looking uncomfortable.

'No, nor to my lady wife.'

Roger was startled to hear Robert call Sichelgaita by that personal term: it was a new departure and sounded remarkably intimate. Duke Robert continued,

'The eyes of all Europe are on us this time, and many will take a lead from our actions. I'll see Alberada later. I'll send Jacques to her, he can spend some time with Bohemund, to sharpen up some of his skills, now he's grown so tall and strong. In fact,' he said gravely, 'I believe I'll leave Jacques with her and Bohemund from now on, I need someone I can trust to be there always - especially now that I have less and less time, and Mark - Bohemund - is becoming so difficult in my company.'

Robert sighed heavily.

'Sichelgaita expects me, too; she should know about the victory, and I think I should tell her about it in person. But first let's give thanks where it all began, in St Michael's chapel.'

So the diplomat had taken over at last. How strange, thought Roger, Robert's nature has changed: he'll be a great man yet. He could scarcely wait to send for Judith, but it would set the seal to give thanks at Monte Gargano and also in remembrance of their father.

'Yes,' he said warmly, 'let's do just that. We can offer up our gratitude - it's long overdue. But let's travel in a grand manner, and take our time for once?'

Duke Robert concurred,

'We'll give the Pope a chance to read our reports first - that will give us a period to consolidate the restructuring of this benighted city - much reconstruction will be needed after so many years of siege. Then I know His Holiness will arrange to see we're suitably welcomed in the Gargano. We might have to wait a month or so. But I think - on this occasion- it would be better to make it all official, don't you?'

Roger gave a shout of laughter.

'Yes.' he said, 'as Bari's the very last city in southern Italy to be taken by us I think that would be most appropriate!'

They turned to look one last time at defeated Bari as they entered their camp on the outskirts, and they saw the smoke of burning houses, which had first risen skywards in a great upward rush, but now, pallid, pressed down by the evening dew, trailing earthwards in a long, twisted wreath, like a dragon crawling sulkily to his den.

ST. MICHAEL'S GROTTO

Bari, humbled but cleared of the detritus of war, saw the brothers leave the city in easy elegance. Watched by saddened men with deeply lined faces and wistful eyes, their bones showing through their worn clothes, the two brothers and their large party of attendants rode slowly through the city one last time, to leave by the northern gate for their journey to Monte Gargano.

Matteo, now a middle-aged sailor, had slipped back into Bari again when it surrendered - with little hope. After all those weary years he could not bear to watch the victors. His life had turned to ruin - his children had all died of starvation and his wife, maddened, had thrown herself from the ramparts to perish on the rocks beneath. Forced to make a fresh start, he had bargained for another fishing boat and deliberately turned his back on Duke Robert and Roger as they noisily rode north.

Two months had passed, the city's affairs had been handled with due tact and considerable generosity, after the commander of the city had been humiliated in front of all the people and several of his assistants imprisoned, leaving no-one in any doubt who were the conquerors. Food had been brought in, the dead had been decently buried or re-buried, the sick had been succoured, much to their surprise, and the Bariots found the peace terms impressively generous, which shamed them.

The Hautevilles had been fighting for years and years without respite, and both knew that the conquest of Sicily would have to be their next target but, just this once, they would travel amicably together without drawing their swords. The siege of Bari was over, their men were left to see that no revolt would ever be successful there again, and the ghost of Tancred beckoned; Judith had chosen to return to Alberada again, until Roger was free for her to join him.

With a clatter of hooves the two brothers rode nonchalantly across the irregular cobbles, impressively clothed, the sun glinting on the metal parts of their horses' harnesses. The soldiers they were leaving behind shouted a last, loyal salute. They took fifty others with them, all mounted, for all Apulia knew they were travelling fast, but in peace, to the holy grotto; besides, all the land between Bari and the Gargano was now owned by them and nobody would dare to challenge them.

Outside Bari they stopped for a short while at an old Roman fountain in a plantation of young sycamores, drinking deeply of its icy waters, and filling leather containers for the hot journey ahead. Next to it was a grove of orange trees, so they stocked up with their fruit, too: they knew the route before them was very dry.

They travelled for several days along the Adriatic coastline, hoping to catch the sea breezes, eating a filling variety of fresh fish each night in small seaside villages whilst frogs croaked loudly. Now and then they had to turn inland, for the ground was marshy in places, resulting in clouds of mosquitoes 'as big as birds', where people worked the salt-pans. Here the sea seemed idle and lazy, as it slowly ebbed and flowed up the inlets and narrow estuaries; the salt workers worried that the whole area would silt up, calling to the Duke and his companions as they passed not to forget their plight. As they skirted Santa Margherita, Robert remembered Matteo and the meal they had shared, and he recounted it to Roger with amiable indulgence.

In the main they avoided the scorched plain of Apulia, empty, with its burning limestone desert; this time they played up to the *fare figura* - everything for effect - that the ordinary people loved, knowing that everyone liked to be stared at and to stare. Occasionally they took their noontide break beneath the shade of a carob tree, whose thick-clustering leaves yielded a cool shelter; these trees, flourishing in the stoniest of land, were planted with hope where nothing else would grow, and some were very old. Pierre collected their seeds to take to the clergy at Monte Sant' Angelo: he knew they could use them as a unit of weight.

As the brothers travelled, so they reminisced about the many past battles and the possible ones to come, assessing their mistakes and planning the days and weeks ahead. From their horses they could see miles across the flat plains, agreeably surprised to discover how much wheat was sprouting up, and how many fine horses were grazing on their land. Ever mindful of their father's advice, they had seen to the extensive breeding of horses, sometimes mixing them with Arab stock, and now they knew they could reward their soldiers with fresh mounts when they arrived at Sipontum.

Within a week, and trembling with excitement at the honour, the Bishop met them at the sanctuary of S. Maria di Sipontum, to show them the Byzantine statue of the Madonna and Child, and then took them to his modest palace. Small and plump, the cherubic Bishop looked like a grey-haired baby with pink cheeks crazy-paved with smile lines.

The brothers found their quarters comfortable, and were content to lie in soft beds at night and eat food which could just as easily be found on the tables of Venice or Alexandria, spicy and eastern in flavour. A small fountain bubbled in the courtyards, date palms sighed and skittered overhead and the cicadas kept up a piercing thrumming during the evening hours before the velvet night crashed down and nightingales sang and all the while the small wavelets lap-lapped upon the shore.

For three days they remained there, as the Bishop paid court, and they, in turn, patiently attended to the citizen's pleas from the town - their town, and the countryside surrounding them.

Most particularly they dealt with the peasants, clad in shawls, however sweltering, and wearing clouted leggings of ox hide against the scratches from the thorns and cacti bordering their paths. They had scuttled in from the land nearby, clearly frightened by the city dwellers of Sipontum - with their flashes of enthusiasm - that they considered shifty and ungenerous. The peasants seemed to have a sense of contentment in their sheer adversity; their talk and dreams were of things of the soil and they knew nothing save the regular interchange of summer and winter with their unvarying tasks and rewards. Providence prescribed for them a life of endless monotonies; unending toil, exposure to heat, murrains and pestilences. A journey to the city, and a word with the Great Duke, was terrifyingly exciting and never forgotten. The brothers attended to every small triviality with justice and patience and the people returned to their homes in relative gratitude.

Their own soldiers, whilst watching and listening to the Hautevilles, were deeply surprised. The Normans, especially the Hautevilles, were usually in such a hurry, never stopping, leaving the boring business of government to deputies; this time they were showing great indulgence and taking their time. But a new era in Hauteville affairs had begun, and it was being suitably marked - for these were just the people over whom the Hautevilles had cruelly but consistently ridden rough-shod.

The excited little Bishop was to come with them up Monte Gargano to the village of Monte Sant' Angelo, for it was in his diocese: besides, he wanted to tell the great brothers all about the tale which had happened so long ago, as his predecessor, Bishop Laurentius, now St. Laurence, had kept careful records. They, in their turn, were eager enough to hear what the Bishop had to say, and they wanted to hear about the sacred legends of the Archangel Michael; both brothers, as boys, had visited Mont St Michel, off the coast of Normandy and not far from their own home.

Now that their great moment had come they took their pilgrimage most seriously, cleansing themselves the night before they travelled with utmost care, then prostrating themselves in the Bishop's chapel for hours in prayer.

During the coolest part of the day, just before dawn broke, the Bishop led them on foot from Sipontum around the coast to the base of the Gargano range of hills, then pointed upwards.

'Look up there,' he said, 'that's where we're heading, to that village at the top.'

Obediently they stared upwards, the rising sun catching the corners of their eyes. The village seemed very small, insignificant, and not far away: today Monte Gargano was unaffected by the tepid and unwholesome breath of the *scirroco*, and they could clearly see the giant primeval trees in the forests beyond.

Here a man could travel for days and never penetrate the dark forest, *the Foresta Umbra*, nor see another man. Ghostly, filled with secrets, the sun normally shone on the coastline below, yet above the first few hundred feet the mountains were often veiled in this same grey curtain of vapour and soft, echoing calls. Monte Gargano was a place of jolting confusion, where new springs of water suddenly appeared from a rock, where it was only too possible to fall hopelessly into a hole filled with old human bones, where even local countrymen could get lost in a sudden enveloping fog on an otherwise brightly sunny day - and where people seemed to be afraid that they could not truly call their souls their own. Thunder, too, would often rumble around the valleys for days, imprisoned, threatening, struggling to escape.

As they walked, shortening their step out of courtesy to that of the winning little man of the Church, so the Bishop chattered on,

'There was this farmer, my lords, and he used to graze his cattle on these slopes. One day he was up here and the *scirocco* - the sea mist - suddenly came up, in spite of it being a hot day, and after he had woken from his sleep in the afternoon he found he couldn't immediately see his most prized bull. He called to his son, who told him he thought it had wandered further up the mountainside. Stupid boy! He ...'

The bishop paused for breath; he wasn't used to walking uphill quite so quickly, and talking, too. Politely the brothers waited.

'Well, anyway, he told his son to take the rest of their cattle home, down the mountainside, and he would go along and get back the bull – but he couldn't find it! He could hear it alright, stumbling up the mountain, kicking down small pebbles as it went. So he hurried after it, and he was deadly afraid.'

'Afraid,' said Roger, 'why?'

'Well, it wasn't natural! The farmer knew the mountain's reputation ... didn't you know it yourself?'

'No,' said Roger, 'I didn't know it had any fame before Saint Michael's advent.'

'Oh yes, good gracious me yes, it's been famous for thousands of years before Saint Michael came here. There has always been the Oracle's shrine here!'

He paused to gauge the effect of his tale on the brothers. Greeks abounded in the area and Greek legends were as equally well known as Christian ones. The Hautevilles clearly understood the significance underlying his words, he was sure that they were impressed.

'The Oracle's shrine was a very special place where you could go if you had worrying dreams. Each sufferer would go alone, bringing a black ram to the shrine, and he would sacrifice it to the Oracle's shade. Afterwards he would wrap himself in its skin, then lie down near the shrine to sleep. The next morning, if he was fortunate, the Oracle would have cured him of his dreams whilst he slept. People came from all over the land to the shrine, you know.'

He peered anxiously up at the brothers, cricking his neck, eager for them to understand the antiquity of the place.

'It's not much further Sirs,' he encouraged, 'it only takes half a day to walk up to the village.'

They had zigzagged across the steepest part of the slopes nearing the little group of shacks and caves. The paths had improved since Tancred's time.

Nothing was lost to them as they toiled silently upwards: the grace of the gnarled olive trees, the patches of tiny flowers, goats browsing in hollows around rocks, the occasional dark flame-like shapes of cypresses - and the sweeping view behind them, dominated by the delicate opalescent blue of the calm sea. Ahead lay heavy grey shadows, they had left the brilliant sunshine behind, it was as if they were stepping through an invisible shroud.

'What happened to the bull?' asked Duke Robert.

The Bishop stopped, pointing up the mountain.

'When the farmer caught up with the bull it was standing there, simply waiting for him, at the entrance to a grotto - up here - where the shrine used to be. He tried to entice it down the hill, even gave it some of the nuts he had kept for his meal, but the bull wouldn't give way; *he just looked back at the farmer*. Then, at last, the bull turned and walked away right into the mountain!'

'Walked into the mountain? How could he do that?' asked Roger.

'Oh!' said the bishop, 'there was a gap in the rocks which had been overgrown, but the bull had pushed his way through the undergrowth and found the entrance to the old pagan shrine.'

He gave a dramatic shudder, hoping the great men were being suitably gripped by the telling of his tale.

'Anyway, the farmer couldn't really understand what was happening but he followed his bull, finding himself walking down and down into a cave, where the bull had finally stopped; in fact, he couldn't go any further because he was in this large cave and there was no other way out. By this time, of course, the farmer was so full of anger that he took out his little bow and shot an arrow at the bull's hindquarters - just to give it a shock, you know, to get it to move - but when the arrow was halfway across the cave it turned right about and flew back, imbedding itself in the man's thigh! Would you believe it, my lords?'

The Bishop puffed up the last slope and sat down on a flat rock.

'And then?' said Roger, 'what happened then?'

'Well, Sire,' said the Bishop of Sipontum, wheezing a little, flapping his gown to fan some air into his cherry-pink face, 'there was only one thing he could do... the farmer pulled out the arrow, bound up his thigh, for it was really a very nasty flesh-wound, and then he raced downhill to report it all to Laurentius, my predecessor, almost six hundred years ago.'

'How extraordinary,' said Roger, bright-eyed.

'How messy,' said the Duke flatly, 'what did your predecessor do?'

'Well, your Grace, to start with, everyone in the diocese had to fast for three days - that's natural, isn't it? Then Laurentius went up the mountain, with the farmer and several of his own men from the church, to examine the scene for himself. He went right up to the entrance of the grotto, and there he stopped to pray. As he did so, *Saint Michael himself* appeared before him, winged, and dressed in shining armour, with his sword drawn, and wearing a scarlet cloak. It was absolutely astonishing! They were all terrified.'

'I'm not surprised,' said Robert, 'he sounds like a Norman, born and bred.'

The Bishop looked uneasy, his small round eyes rolled nervously in his small round face; he didn't want the famous story to get away from him, so he quickly continued,

'Saint Michael told the assembled crowd that he was taking the old pagan shrine and turning it into a Christian one, and that Bishop Laurentius was to see that the grotto and cave was dedicated to himself and all the angels. Naturally Bishop Laurentius agreed. Then Saint Michael led them all down into the dark cave which suddenly, inexplicably, blazed with light. In a corner the Bishop saw an altar newly consecrated by the Archangel himself and vested in purple in the ancient Roman manner; the walls were hung with purple, too. Then Saint Michael vanished, leaving behind him, as a sign, his great iron spur.'

'Do you have it?' enquired Duke Robert sharply.

'No, your Grace, it was taken to Rome, for the Pope to see.'

'And then?'

'Then the Bishop commanded that a church should also be built on the rock above the entrance to the grotto, high, high above the chapel cave and dedicated to Saint Michael. And he consecrated it on the 29th of September, in the year 493. All of this you're about to see.'

The Duke acknowledged the conclusion of the tale with an imperious gesture of his hand, almost an act of blessing; Roger clasped the little Bishop around the shoulders, bending low to do so, with a smile of thanks.

THE CONCERT

The famous couple and their attendant soldiers were a target for all eyes, villagers and pilgrims alike, when they arrived in the village of Monte Sant' Angelo with their men.

'Pilgrimages are in the blood of the people' said the Bishop, tapping the side of his nose, 'and they're good for us all.'

Duke Robert ordered that the crowded scene should be controlled. All around were travel-stained old women, replacements for witches; dishevelled, wan and dazed-looking girls; boys, too weak to carry a spade at home, colourless and frail, with mouths agape and eyes expressing every grade of uncurbed emotion - from wildest joy to downright idiocy ... clearly they had all come to the mountain for much-needed help. They scuttled to one side as the party approached, frightened, huddling together and hiding their faces.

The ineffectual buildings clustered around the church were mainly rough huts or caves cut into the mountainside, small and crude, with a sack or a branch from a tree pulled across for protection: outside sat time-worn crones, dealing with domestic chores, peering through the teary old eyes of age, physically too tired to show interest. Some roofed hovels stood out in the village, from which peeped innumerable urchins, many with the swollen necks bound for goitre, and mangy dogs; several larger habitations seemed about to collapse in ruins, doomed to kill the fussy chickens pecking around their foundations, as they crumpled into dust.

The durable church, with its Greek facade, was the only building made of stone, and stood on a plateau in the centre. From it snaked away the straggling village, which seemed painfully built upon its own shoulders, with narrow paths cut between the rocks, and endless uneven steps. It was an ugly place.

Then, having eaten and washed, just as their father had done so many years before, Robert, Roger and their men followed the Bishop slowly into the mountain, skidding now and then on the slippery rock floor.

'We'd better have proper steps cut here,' Robert said expansively, 'it will be our gift and may help the old and infirm.'

Roger could hardly believe his ears.

Finally, holding their breath in anticipation, they walked through into the chapel cave. As they were exceedingly tall, they had to bend their heads, for the roof was so low in places that they couldn't stand. It was surprisingly hot down there, damply hot; strong incense almost - but not quite - covered the overpowering smell of years of sweat and dirty feet, foetid and malodorous, which had lain on the floor of the holy cave: for once the rock-floor had been washed, but a miasma remained.

For this auspicious celebration, two ceremonial stools had been put in the place of honour, before the altar, covered with furs. The brothers first knelt beside them in prayer for a long time, then sat to look around themselves in this pilgrimage centre. A group of monks lined the walls of the eerie place, cowled figures not showing a face, just a ghostly multitude of bowed heads and folded hands. Then the bishop said to them quietly,

'The Holy Father wanted you to receive all honours so some singers have been sent from Naples to this place of pilgrimage; they have sung, once before, in Rome. Their voices are pure, but they have no schooling and they are unused to singing in a cave; they're really only humble fishermen and sing at their work. Please forgive their inadequacies.'

The brothers had not expected such an unusual event in this remote pilgrimage spot. They felt deeply honoured: for whatever gross acts that they did on the battlefield, their faith had never wavered.

When the Bishop beckoned, a small band of men from Naples walked single-file into the cave, and stood in the centre of the roughly circular area. Each wore a simple scarlet gown, flaring gently to the ground. They were bare-headed, and wore no cross around their throats, nor any other symbol to show that they were singers for the Church. They were barefoot, old and young alike.

Grey stone lay all around them, the roof sloping unevenly to meet the floor, so that all was enclosed in shades of grey, sometimes dark, where the stains of water ran through, sometimes light, where worshippers had knelt for hours. Out of the corners of their eyes Robert and Roger could see a few old Roman tombs in distant corners, but mainly there was nothing at all in the spacious, irregular cave, save for themselves and their party of men, the Bishop, the monks and the singers. They all stood looking to the altar hewn from rock towards the further side, on which was displayed a small silver statue of Saint Michael fashioned by craftsmen from Constantinople. But, to give greater accent to the size and shape of the cave, just for this occasion, groups of small earthen lamps with lighted wicks had been placed all around the perimeter, marking its irregularity: some were even placed in small puddles of water as they lay.

After a pause, whilst the leader of the fishermen's choir bent his head in homage to the Duke, one of the singers stood forward, beginning a low chant, quickly joined by another man, who went to stand beside him. In moments the second man's voice took up the rhythm, singing another variation. For a while these two singers sang alone, now and then forgetting that they weren't at sea, and allowing their voices to become over-loud, but soon became accustomed to the cave's dimensions and adjusted their voices accordingly.

As they sang, so a second pair turned and moved off to the left a little way, adding their voices to the firsts pair's, skillfully plaiting them in between, harmonising like bees in a tree. Then a third pair moved far over to the right and lifted their voices higher than their fellows', so that they sounded like drops of ice falling into a silver dish. All the while, the central group were humming in accompaniment, and gradually the humming altered to chanting, penetrating into all the hollows of the rocks or hurrying around the flickering wicks. They re-grouped and sang afresh; as each new section was completed, so a singer might re-position himself, either singing alone or with another companion.

A passionate out-pouring of voices flooded across the cave, voice answering voice, cadences falling at the close of a musical movement and voices interweaving between the parts. A singer near the roof would take up a theme, answered by another at a different level across an uneven space, and then others would intervene, parrying and thrusting, until their tapestry of sound led the full choir to a crashing crescendo.

The visual harmony balanced the feast of sound, for as the glorious tones sought out the planes and hollows of the rocky cave, the brothers were transfixed by the slashing lines of scarlet gown across grey stone, or wondered at the sight of a lamp being held up high above the head of some softly singing youngster, the faint light fluttering like a moth upon his dark curling hair and satin skin.

In the manner of some slow-moving pavane each member of the choir was allowed his share of time to sing his part, and then moved to sing another, in another place, with a new companion. Finally they all took up a place behind the altar as a cohesive group, facing Robert and Roger, and sang their last sequence, convoluted and deep, rising several octaves, until, at a sign from their leader, they all ended together on one pure final chord. Mesmerised and bedazzled, no-one stirred as the echoes died, except for Robert, who shifted his silver ring. They both thought of Tancred throughout.

ROBERT'S PLANS

'Sire, the soothsayer is here.'

So spoke the Chamberlain from behind a confidential hand.

'Tell him to come here,' said Robert, fiddling with his enormous seal, 'and move the company out of earshot.'

The Chamberlain bowed, bringing the soothsayer forward and motioning the vassals and knights, servants and serfs to the other end of the magnificent Hall in his castle headquarters at Salerno. Robert caught Roger's sleeve as he moved.

'Stay.'

Roger stood still at once.

A long black figure approached. It had the aspect of an undertaker coming to measure a corpse; the eyes were like black coins and appeared to weep dimly, the dark hair plastered in flattened curls all over the head.

'Your Grace.' His hollow tones were those of a funeral mute.

'Speak up!' barked Robert. The man was silent. Robert glowered at him.

'There's only one question to which I require an answer.'

The man looked at the famous Great Duke aslant in his seat, with short silver hair and beard. Then he looked at his washed-out blue eyes, surrounded by wrinkles, and saw a sense of guilt and spiritual anxiety there. Still the soothsayer waited.

Grudgingly, Robert asked,

'You ought to sense what I want to know. How long have I to live?'

'For some time.'

The man could say that without dragging deep into his intuition, for Robert exuded a powerful strength.

'What will be the manner of my death?'

The man turned away, his eyes searching inwards and he took a deep breath. From a long way away he seemed to dredge up his quiet words',

'You will be surprised by your final passing. And your coming to rest will be turbulent.' Robert grunted,

'That I can well believe.'

'But,' said the soothsayer, as mirror-images of visions rippled across his face, 'let me also tell you this: as far as Ather you shall bring all countries under your sway, but from there you shall depart for Jerusalem, and pay your debt to nature.'

'Our father Tancred reached Jerusalem,' was Robert's aside to Roger, 'it seems I will, too. But I've never planned for the Holy Land - nor have I the time in the foreseeable future.'

The soothsayer spoke no more and, when recompensed, stole away on silent feet: his face blank of expression again.

'Jerusalem!' said Roger. 'How strange that Jerusalem will feature at your death. It's supposed to be a peaceful city.'

'And 'turbulence' is normal in our lives ... '

Robert moved his gold seal from one hand to another, concentrating on the imperial symbol. As he lounged there, Roger was more acutely aware than usual that Robert affected imperial clothes to wear, as well as always fingered the seal. Clearly he was entitled to neither. He had been told that Robert had his clothes copied in Constantinople from the Emperor's own, and they were very fine.

'Come to my private chamber.'

Robert led the way through the throngs of supplicants and

supporters as his Chamberlain went on ahead. The motley crowd fell back and became silent at his approach. Christian and Saracen, Lombard, Greek and Byzantine, there were a multitude of races in apparent harmony for one brief space, in one great palace.

'It's almost unnerving to see all these people being amiable to each other,' said Roger, 'and - really rather dull!'

'It's certainly unique! And you, yourself, should be satisfied, as much of it is your doing. You've done brilliantly in Sicily. It's taken ten years, but you've subdued almost the entire island and, with your able diplomacy, you've even got the Saracens to return and live in harmony with their Christian neighbours. I'm so proud of you!' Such praise and loud enough for all to hear!

As they unhurriedly strolled to Robert's private chamber, Roger glowed with exultation. Rebellion, he thought, was endemic in southern Italy. Robert was never quite secure enough to prevent it altogether, and never so weak that he could not deal with it effectively when it came - generally calling upon Roger for assistance. Although largely independent, he himself, remained Robert's vassal, and had to do as he was bid. It was very often most inconvenient.

Today, to find Robert in expansive and sunny mood was a rare treat. He felt the weight of his brother's hand on his shoulder, being given a friendly shove; there was an underlying insistence in the push, but no naked aggression. Over the years Robert's punishing ways had honed a hardness into the younger man, in place of his soft expectancy; instilled a vengeful determination where no original retaliation had been envisaged - unnatural for his less steely nature, but now set like rock. He had become wary and watchful, and his hopeful looks very quickly had been lost, yielding to a mature - severe - appearance: his handsome face was now covered with a web of deeply-ingrained lines, and he wore an almost perpetual frown.

Fortunately Roger had an inner, gloriously bright sense of fun: it was his saving grace. Robert had no sense of humour, or the ridiculous, and Roger had, on several occasions, openly laughed at his brother. Eventually - just once - he had called him 'pompous' to his face. But not a second time. When at leisure Roger's sense of the ridiculous gave him, and all those about him, hours of joy and occasional hilarity. Often he could rein in his men by laughter, and in his own castles at Mileto and Messina their roars of merriment would frequently echo to the roof. Judith was enchanted with the life.

'You must have been troubled, to have summoned that soothsayer.'

'I am. I wanted to know how much time I had left, now that I'm becoming older.'

'Time? To do what?'

Robert looked about him, as though even the dancing sunlight was there to spy.

'My lands are secure and flourishing in Calabria and Apulia, and I'm at peace with the Pope and the Emperor.'

He spread his hands in front of him, looking at the veins between the knuckles.

'It has taken a lifetime to be able to say that!'

Yes, thought Roger, it had. Between them, they had taken Catanzaro and Taranto, Reggio and Cosenza, over and over again. They had done the same to Otranto and Brindisi, Aversa, Melfi and Salerno - and all the mountains and hamlets, towns and forests in between. Southern Italy and Sicily were all theirs.

'For ten years,' Robert continued, 'you've been Count of Sicily and Calabria, and for even longer I've been the elected leader of the Normans and Duke of Apulia. Popes and Emperors - so many, I can hardly remember them all - have turned to me for help and decisions and, at this moment, all our lands are at peace. It's almost unbelievable.'

'Isn't that enough? What more do you want? You're the richest and most powerful man in Italy, after the Pope.'

Robert lifted his ageing chin, speaking with all the enthusiasm and bravado of old,

'I want to be Emperor in Constantinople!'

ROBERT'S VISION

'My God!' Roger was awe-struck. Robert chuckled at the expression on his brother's face.

'The last Emperor there has been deposed, as you know. And both the German Emperor and His Holiness the Pope are in dire trouble in their own lands. *All three are weak men!* They've left a colossal vacuum - and only I can win the Eastern Empire.'

'Is that how you've seen yourself these last few months? Is that why you wear imperial garments? And hold an imperial seal, even though you never make use of it?'

'It is. I want people to get used to the idea.'

'I had begun to wonder ...' Roger chewed his lip, as Robert leaned forward to speak, his eyes shining,

'I have the power and ability: I've an army of sufficient size to quell the Byzantines, especially now that they're in disarray, and I've also got sufficient ships to transport us there.'

'It's a dangerous sea around the coast to Constantinople. Remember Tancred! He nearly drowned there and was always telling us about the power of the sea.'

'Yes. That's why we'll not travel far by water, but mostly by land, going from island to island - taking them all by surprise! In that way we can subdue all the land, and all the people, between our coast and Constantinople - the battle will be over before we arrive!'

'Robert - Sire - isn't it too great a gamble? In the past, when you left any place you've conquered, you have known that trouble was going to flare up immediately, haven't you? It happens all the time. And you halve your number of troops by leaving behind a garrison large enough to keep order. You'll have no soldiers left by the time you arrive.'

'Of course it's a gamble! I've always taken a gamble - I'm a soldier, not an administrator: I have to concentrate on tactics.'

Roger fingered his goblet, half-listening to the mellow sounds of Palermo in the distance. Distractedly he said,

'As I see it, the very moment I leave Sicily to bring my soldiers to join you, the Emirs will rise up again. And the moment you leave Apulia, the Greeks and Byzantines will undoubtedly make trouble between them. Can you afford to take such risks?'

'I know what I'm doing, I've made contingency plans for every eventuality - and I'll have Sichelgaita by my side.'

Roger's eyebrows shot up.

'At her age?'

'What's age got to do with it? It's her personality that's worth a hundred men - one look from her and she stiffens their resolve.'

'Will you take Bohemund?'

'Yes, I need him, too. And Roger Borsa.'

'My God - but you're asking for trouble with both of them in camp! I can only repeat,' said Roger darkly, 'you're taking a very great risk.'

'No, I'm not!' said Robert abruptly. 'I'm leaving you in overall command!'

Bemused, the younger man tried to take in the extent of the responsibility being heaped upon his shoulders. He could foresee an amazing future for himself. Then he returned to the unfathomable,

'But - let's return to the beginning again: *why* do you want to be Emperor?'

'It's a holy cause to follow, before I die. To redeem my sins.'

'Another Holy War? Like Bari? Do you mean that?'

'If it's necessary. I can see no future for Christianity unless East and West are welded. I've built up a great fear of the forces of Islam for many years now, and the possible invasion of the Seljuk Turks - word has recently reached me that almost all of Anatolia has been taken by them. If someone strong doesn't take command *here* and *now* I'm afraid that Christianity in the East could be wiped out.'

Roger looked at his brother's serious face and could see his gravity, and how the situation was affecting him.

'There has been talk for many years about Christianity being forced out of the East, we all know that. But can't we leave His Holiness to make the first move?'

'He has no army of any size, and he's a poor creature. Not a soldier, not a tactician - merely a puppet for all those powerful Roman families.'

'What about the German Emperor?'

'He's useless! At present he can't control his own vassals - he wouldn't dare to place a foot outside his own homeland.'

It was true. Roger knew it in his heart. The situation in Constantinople could only be resolved by the energy, audacity and political aptitude of a Norman leader such as Duke Robert, with his pride and cruelty and lust for power. There was no doubt about it, the throne of the Eastern Empire would make a fitting end to Robert's career.

'After all.' said Robert smoothly, 'you know I've attempted to influence affairs to our benefit in that area for years and years ...'

Robert changed the subject.

'I've made most of the advance plans already. My forces are marshalled in two places, Brindisi and Otranto. They're ready to sail straight across the Adriatic.'

'And I'm really to remain, in charge of all Hauteville domains?'

'You are.'

'Then I wish you good fortune! God go with you.'

'STAY!'

Robert held down Roger's forearm as he began to lift himself from his seat.

'There's something else.'

Robert went to sit heavily in his majestic chair, which had magnificently carved arms, flung across it was the skin of a leopard brought from Africa in one of his many cargo vessels. Here and there in the airy chamber were other artefacts from that fantastic continent, which seemed especially to suit Robert's personality; a vast ivory carving of a warrior stood on the table, several drums, painted with brilliant colours, were fastened to the walls and a fistful of shining spears clustered upright near the doors. He smiled, almost embarrassed, reaching to fill Roger's goblet again and looking away. Intrigued, Roger leaned forward.

'How strange, you have something even more private to tell me!'

'Mmm ... yes,' said Robert quietly, 'private and possibly radical: I've been considering this for a long time. My aim is to introduce something totally new into our lives: the soothsayer reminded me of my mortality, so I'm going to deal with this before I leave.'

'So you're trying it out on me - now - as an experiment?'

'In a way - after all, we are partners, and I can trust you. I want you to oversee it all when I'm gone.'

'Well ... I'll not speak to anyone about it until you give me leave. What is it?'

Robert leaned back in his chair, turning to look out of the window, his eyes unseeing and his brow furrowed in deep thought.

'I've decided to have a symbol by which everyone will recognise me and mine.'

'But every one knows you already, Robert! And when you become Emperor you can legally use the imperial symbol.'

'At my death - presupposing I became Emperor - the imperial symbol is given to the next Emperor: that may not be one of our family.'

'But you're so well-known ...'

'People may know my face when we meet, but they don't all recognise my goods and chattels when I'm away. And what about when I'm dead and gone? *Will they remember me then?* A thousand years from now? Will they know what I've owned, or built afresh? I've always built to last. Pioneers tend to be forgotten ...'

'Do you want them to remember? You keep harping on about death.'

'Yes – Oh yes! *I never want to be forgotten.* I've been thinking about that man - you know the one, the man Judith travelled with to Amalfi?'

'Pantaleone, the merchant? Who now lives in Constantinople?'

'Yes, that's the one. Did you know he's recently made a magnificent gift of bronze doors to the grotto chapel at Monte Sant' Angelo?'

'No, I didn't know. But what have bronze doors to do with it?'

'The doors are vast, and damascened all over in silver, like a sermon, and they'll last for ever. They're known as 'The Gates of Paradise'. But, most important of all, they've got Pantaleone's name discreetly engraved upon them, and what is supposed to be his portrait. So - you see - even though he's a lesser man, he's done something to ensure his name lasts forever. And,' he paused, saying quietly, 'I never want to be forgotten, either.'

'You're building the cathedral here at Salerno.'

'That is for God. I don't want the Church to think of me as another Drogo. And I've left money to Venosa in reparation.'

'Well, what about copying the design on your seal ring as your symbol? The lion's paw and chains?'

He shot one quick glance down at Robert's strong fingers, at the branched veins that ran into the valleys between the knuckles, the faint reddish-silver hair upon the joints, the engraved bezel of the great silver ring. Robert wore several other rings as well, of gold with big gems, but the silver one never left his hand.

'That's a private family ring, and the Duppa de Uphaughs of Normandy have a very similar design - for them, the chain does not join in an unbroken circle. Now I want something new - fresh - a symbol of our Hauteville dynasty. And shared with no-one else!'

'That sounds very grandiose!' Roger laughed, looking sideways.

'*Not for an Hauteville*. I'm planning for the future, for the whole family, based on what we've built up, and consolidated, here in the south. Besides, don't forget - I'm ageing. Most people think I'm very old, and sometimes I feel it, too. I'm almost sixty-four.'

'Is this symbol to be used by all of us?'

'In varying degrees - yes. By everyone who bears the name of Hauteville.'

Roger sat thoughtfully, then asked,

'What's your inner reason? Just to show ownership?'

'No - the extent of our family power. I look to the future: you and Bohemund are bound to go on to even greater heights.' Roger believed him.

Robert's harsh voice rose to a crescendo. He got to his feet, began to prowl the room as he tried to explaining the living tapestry of daydreams with which he clothed the secret galleries of his mind, galleries into which he withdrew from the world about him: tapestries he wove and coloured by the aid of his vast experience in the south, and amongst a myriad of different people. It was not often that he expressed himself as he was now doing.

'Over the years out here I've learned so much about the uses of power: I learned a lot by myself, and watching others, but the men who taught me most were some of the Popes, teaching me aspects I'd not dreamed of before. You see, with power there are at least two sides to the coin, sometimes more: power has to be seen, to give substance to order; and power has to be feared, which gives a cutting edge to success. In our case I hope they will combine.'

'You mean us to control more through the mind than the sword in future?' Roger enquired with rising interest.

TANCRED'S RING

Tancred paused, and took his time to reply. 'Yes,' he said. 'Something like that. You see, I believe we must now have a symbol by which we're all known, not only here in the south, but right across Europe. I remember when Tancred told me of a meeting with a Persian in Constantinople, many years ago, and this man showed him a seal ring which had belonged to some ancient ruler ... which our father had copied when he arrived back home. But, to make it wholly personal he substituted our own family emblem. I've many times been inspired by one or other aspect of this ring on my hand, and I've learned from it. But this silver ring of mine is private and very, very personal, a gift from father to son, and I want to keep it that way.'

'Will you give that ring to Mark, our young Bohemund? Or to Roger Borsa? Their enmity will burst into flames one day ... which son will get it?'

'That's one of my problems, and always has been, one which I've decided to solve by creating an Hauteville symbol, to cover everyone who bears our name in the future. Sichelgaita understands about dynasties, however bitter she might have been in the past about other things, for she's come from a famous line of people herself. I want the Hauteville symbol to be shown on *everything* I own, from servants' uniforms to carvings over all my castles and forts. My banners will show it, and my jewels - *everything*! She'll love the panoply.'

Robert was lost in his dreams, saying,

'I'll have a jewelled pendant made for her as well, she can wear it when she feels like an Hauteville, and put it aside when she's annoyed with me! Then my own personal ring of state will be made, as a great

Hauteville seal, and no future document of mine - or ours - or our descendants' - will be deemed authentic unless it is so marked.'

Roger was deeply impressed.

'What vision, Robert. You're the first man to think of such an idea. And you show reassuring confidence in our future, for which I thank you. In using these symbols, you realise, you'll create a fashion; everyone'll want to copy you and family symbols will appear like flowers in spring! Ownership banners will appear on all public occasions.'

'I shouldn't think they'd dare to copy my idea. At least, not in my lifetime.'

Inwardly Roger agreed, but encouraged,

'Let them, Robert, *let them* - take is as a huge compliment! Leaving that aside ... have you made up your mind what this symbol is to be?'

'Yes. This is why it's taken so long; I needed just the right one.'

Robert stopped, almost fearful to give it a word, like freeing a lion from its cage.

'Well?'

THE HAUTEVILLE SYMBOL

'It's to be a gryphon.'

'Good God - why that?'

Robert continued to pace heavily across the stone-flagged floor - his hands thrust into his wide leather belt, thumbs hooked over, his head up and triumphant.

'I've thought it out most carefully, and it's been a difficult choice. I *could* have chosen some sign, like a circle or an arrow-head, but that would signify nothing personal. So I've chosen a living creature, a bird, or an animal, call it what you will - because living creatures are understood by all men and are common to all, even though they're unusual ... d'you follow me?' The younger man nodded, and Robert went on,

'You see, a gryphon is a monster of fantasy, a combination of half a lion and half an eagle. I've planned to present it as an uncomfortable challenge, *to make people think*! To start with, it's mythological and curious, well established in the East, but not as well known here - so it'll initially catch the eye because it's new. And remember, human minds have always been preoccupied by monsters, the unreal, haven't they? Monsters plunder your dreams of reason ... so when it's seen here it's bound, as well, to catch the imagination - don't you think?'

Roger laughed.

'We all enjoy our fantasies ... '

'No - you don't understand; I'm trying to *unbalance people* by the enigma! What I'm attempting to explain to you is *the key* to that enigma.'

Robert stopped pacing and turned to face his brother as he lounged in his seat. He spoke slowly,

'All rational people understand that - to be real - even sacred - *is to remain in place*. To break out, to cross boundaries, is to open the world to the threat of chaos, or to commit transgression: it terrifies people. But, isn't that what we, as a family, have done out here? I've gained power because people feel I'm a monster from another land who's created chaos: I've provided hunger, fever and death for so many people in my lifetime. I'm their embodiment of terror.'

'You bring harsh judgment upon yourself, Sire.'

Roger had never known his brother to speak so honestly and openly.

'Well, it's obvious that I've conquered through fear of the unknown in this country. I've violated boundaries, challenged limits, created new possibilities for existence and, to a certain degree, both ensnared some people and achieved freedom for others. That's what I call power, the manipulation of people and events for my own needs.'

Respectfully Roger nodded in agreement. He found it interesting that Robert mentioned nothing about his elder half-brothers who had gone before him, and done the same. But then Robert was initiating something new, and as the initiator, he should bear the first brand, and be seen to wear the first honour.

Robert went on slowly, emphasising each key word with a thump of fist onto hand.

'But the function of a gryphon is also *protective*. Think of the combination of animals in this one design: you have the proud regal lion at the forefront, both a symbol of the Resurrection, and the personification of fortitude. It is melded, combined forever without division, at the rear, with the equally proud and vigilant eagle. Just as important is the fact that they're both Apocalyptic beasts, so I'm weaving through the design the concept of the unseen protection of the

Church, with whom I'm now obviously linked in so many ways - and will be, even more so, if I become Eastern Emperor.'

'Aha! That's clever. But there's the other side of the picture, too; you don't want to over-emphasise the threat of fear, do you? Monsters are taboo subjects, they cross boundaries, they're beings that fall unnaturally between classes ... think of the humble bat, with its fur like a mammal and its wings like a bird; most people make the sign of the cross when they see a bat. Mystery confuses: most people are as direct as children in their demand for the gist of the matter - and they have a need to see clearly.'

'True,' said Robert, with a rueful grin, 'and many of them cross themselves when they hear my name! But you're right, I won't put fear obviously to thc forcfront, I'll just let it lie silently in wait. So, now, do you understand why I've chosen the gryphon? When times are good - the Hautevilles are protecting the people; when they're bad we must use our gryphon as a weapon against them, to play on their superstitious natures and bring them to heel once more. Whatever the situation they'll be left in no doubt that I'm watching them all the time.'

Robert smiled to himself, then continued with his theme, as though thinking it all out anew.

'As well as that, the symbol of the eagle is so easily understood out here, the people's own ancient badge of power and victory, remembered from the standards of the Roman legions. People don't easily forget!'

He seated himself again, then finished.

'And yet, I don't wish to be *too* closely linked with those historic times: I'm a modern man, *a man of today*! And I aim that, when the Hauteville sign has been displayed right across the land, my banners and flags will instantly be recognised. In a word, our Hauteville gryphon will combine a feeling of safety through familiarity with the old yet instill obedience through the fear of the new. There's no question about it being a talking point everywhere, *everyone'll* discuss it and what it stands for - and not only in this country.'

Roger mused,

'Will your son Mark - Bohemund - as a bastard, be permitted to wear the Hauteville gryphon?'

'I've given thought to him, too: I've decided to have a special version created for him, for I'll add some wings to the lion. That's the attribute of Mark, the Evangelist, after whom he was baptised. Perhaps, then, after all this laborious thought, both the women in my life will be content?'

Robert smiled in gentle mockery, then said softly, as if to himself,

'I hope that all of this has bestowed on me the grace to emerge from my researches more sensitive to the living and more tolerant of the imponderable than historical work usually allows for - but that's a very private wish ... I don't want to sound morbid.'

With his head on one side, he looked expectantly at his younger brother, who nodding back, returned his gaze with awe and great affection. He appreciated how the deep shadows of Robert's fancies had taken practical shape and were reality. Robert's progression from 'gang leader' to 'commander of mercenary troops' to 'conqueror' had been impressive. Now, it seemed to him, Robert might add 'philosopher.'

The future for the Hautevilles looked to be very colourful indeed, a great family dynasty arising in Europe, untouched at the outset by royal blood, yet symbolised across the land with unmistakable emblems of power. Roger was glad to be in at the beginning and would, if God gave him the strength and a long life, carry it on to greater heights when Duke Robert eventually died.

Rising to his feet, he strode forward and embraced his brother wordlessly; aware he had been touched by a moment in history.

'Now - let me help you prepare to take the Eastern throne!'

ROBERT AND SICHELGAITA, CEPHALONIA

'Don't leave me ...'

'I'll never leave you - you know that.'

Parched, Robert changed his position slightly and painfully lay upon his back, looking up at the ceiling.

Where was he?

He reached out a claw-like hand, felt it trembling, found it warmly grasped by Sichelgaita's familiar fingers: this time they were soft and gentle - old. No longer plump.

The ceiling was his ancient battle tent; he was sure of that when the mist cleared. A muddy colour, the cool tent had been used for years, presented to him by some friendly Saracens. He must get a new one, he mused. One fringed side was open to the view across the sea. Where was he?

'I can't remember...' he began, thickly, feeling his tongue swollen in his mouth, 'it's stupid, but I can't remember...where's Roger?' She soothed him with her touch.

'Roger's at home, he's taking care of everything. We've had word - and he sent information about Bohemund.'

'Bohemund? My son Bohemund? My Mark?' It came out as a whisper.

'Yes - you remember that he had this fever before you.'

'And he recovered? Didn't he?'

'He did. We sent him back to Bari; he's champing at the bit to return. Our son Roger Borsa's taken charge while we remain here, he's gone on ahead. He knows your plans.'

'Hmmm ...'

The fever rose again, surging like a powerful wave. He was going away, then, fighting it - muttering and mumbling, calling out inconsistently. Sometimes it was,

'Sichelgaita! To me!'

He was the great commander then, and she was on the battlefield with him, a potent weapon in herself. Sometimes it was,

'Oh Alberada - your soft hair ...' and the knife twisted afresh.

But mostly it was in conversational tone, as if they were discussing a battle plan. He would say,

'Sichelgaita - what's your opinion?' She sat on beside him, waiting, silent.

Occasionally she spooned some liquid into his dry mouth, pouring it between cracked lips and sunken gums. Mostly she waited. She knew his strength; she had done all she could to heal him, now the battle had to be won by himself alone.

Ten years back they had had another crisis, and she had taken it in her stride. Now Sichelgaita wondered, as she sat by her husband's bed, whether he could recover again. He had an Empire to win! His sixty-eight years lay lightly on him.

She bathed his head: he jerked it away when he felt the trickle of cool water - he wanted the water in his mouth instead.

'Wife!' His voice was low and weak.

'Yes, my lord Duke?'

'I was dreaming - I think. *Where am I?'*

'You are on the island of Cephalonia.'

'What are we doing here?'

'For the past four years we've fought our way from Bari, heading for Constantinople... and your future Empire.'

'Four years? *Four whole years?'*

There seemed no point in recounting their adventures, their successes and failures; that could wait until he was better.

'Yes, Robert. It's been hard.'

'My throat's so sore and swollen.'

'Open your mouth.'

Sichelgaita poured in more water.

He whispered,

'Sit beside me.'

Tired out, she sat again, to rest. For just a while he seemed to be lucid, but his voice was scarcely a thread, hardly a voice at all.

'Across the sea,' he muttered, 'What's this place I can see across the water? A light is shining there.'

'No - you're mistaken, it's only a ruined town and no-one lives there now. It's deserted. I've already enquired - in case it wasn't safe to bring you here.'

'You're wrong, Sichelgaita. It's full of people. And the light - it's beautiful!'

The light was drawing him irresistibly, dazzling light of a quality he had never seen before. The light was ahead, in the distance, and he was floating among the sun of suns, glinting off numberless prisms.

'Then, what's the name of *this* place?' He said.

He was wandering once more. He was seeing things she could not see: and for him it was sheer beauty. Stilled like a fly in amber, stricken, she touched his cheek and said,

'This place is named 'Jerusalem'.

Robert gazed across the sea with shining eyes, looking at the encompassing light. To him it was glorious. Beckoning, it invited him to come. Swirling colours emerged from it: it was buoyant and magnetic.

Sichelgaita saw the look of wonder and delight suffuse his old face, which changed before her own eyes. He became young again, as she had known him in his prime.

In surprise and delight, he slipped away easily and quickly, and became one with the light.

She held his lifeless hand until it grew cold.

Then removed his silver ring and gave it to Roger Borsa.

THE JOURNEY BACK HOME

Robert's body was embalmed and laid, packed in salt, in a wooden coffin. Because of his often-repeated request, he was to be buried at Venosa, together with his half-brothers. Two sons remained to them, and seven daughters: none were of much interest. Only Bohemund had been significant to Robert.

With numbing ambition, Sichelgaita confronted the issue with the remaining knights and vassals, and forced them to recognise Roger Borsa as leader in Robert's place. Their half-hearted acquiescence matched her own lack-lustre mood. Retreat for them all was the only course. No Eastern Empire beckoned for Roger Borsa ... he was glad to leave for Apulia.

They set sail north-west for home, leaving Cape Ather behind, the most northerly tip of Cephalonia. The people there altered the name of 'Jerusalem' to 'Guiscardo', in Robert's honour, from where it was again altered, years on, to 'Fiscardo'.

Ahead, leading the convoy was Sichelgaita's ship. Robert's coffin was lashed with ropes to the deck. Most of the time she sat beside it, but when she briefly rested, four knights stood at the four corners. She had hung around the ship lavish drapery of an imperial purple colour, tied with gold: even though he was not to be Emperor, he would return to his own land in style.

At first their journey was calm and stately, for it was during the sunny month of July. The Hauteville floating bier imperiously forged ahead, ships packed with weary soldiers clung to her wash.

As they neared Otranto, the sun became obscured and a sudden storm - a tempest - appeared on the horizon. Sichelgaita was worn out, asleep in a hollow under the decking - there was no immediate reason to wake her - and Roger Borsa kept watch over his father.

The storm rapidly grew wild. The waves became gigantic. The ship began tossing like a cork. Suddenly Roger Borsa noticed the ropes around the coffin shifting and slackening, altering position as one end flew loose. He rushed to hold it, shouting to the others to help him - the weight of the coffin was enormous.

But, as they placed restraining hands on the huge box, another mighty wave hit the ship, which forced it to tilt higher and higher at one side. One knight fell backwards into the sea, and was swept away as he gasped for help, weighed down by his armour. Other knights clung to the mast.

Roger Borsa shouted out at the top of his lungs,

'*Mother*!'

As Sichelgaita furiously scrambled up to join them, the sea pitched the ship up again and Robert's wooden coffin escaped its bonds and was swept overboard as though it was feather-light. It shot away on the top of a passing wave and was lost to sight immediately.

Sichelgaita's mouth dropped open in dismay. Roger Borsa looked appalled. The captain struggled to keep the ship into the wind and prevent them all from drowning, and the rigging shrieked. Although midday, it was dark and cold. Sichelgaita was heard to say,

'No! I will not have it!'

Then she shouted with all her might,

'*ROBERT*!'

Her overpowering call was heard by the company on the other ships nearby, in spite of the howling storm. The word echoed and rolled across the towering sea in a mournful keen.

'*ROBERT*!' She yelled again, '*ROBERT*!'

As they clung like limpets to the ship, the waves drew back like a funnel and twisted about. Amongst them a new wave appeared, cleaving through the funnel of turbulent water, and on the crest of it appeared the coffin.

It was rushing in their direction like a shark.

It poised for a moment, cresting and balancing, then hurled itself unerringly back onto the deck, smashing into pieces against the mast.

Sichelgaita threw herself onto Robert's body, and pinned it down. The wood cracked and splintered afresh, and tore apart, as the salt packing went flying into her hair and face. She clung to him, and held his rotting body under her own. She refused to relinquish him until the storm died down.

When it did, gently coaxing, Roger Borsa prised his father's body from her, wrapping Robert like a mummy in the imperial purple fabric, round and around, for the wooden planks of the coffin had slid back into the foaming sea and floated away. Some hours later, the sun came out again and the waves were still. It had been just another Adriatic storm in summer.

Robert was finally entombed in the family vault at Venosa, with Roger Borsa uneasily heading the long procession.

Behind him paced Sichelgaita, alone, very tall and gaunt, attending her husband to the last. She hid behind no veil and leaned on no companion.

And then came Bohemund, in full fighting armour, his sword left at the entrance to the church. With him strode his uncle, Roger de Hauteville, now the elder statesman.

A Mass was said. The burial prayers were spoken. Incense flared, acrid in the nostrils.

Then, at last, the shrouded body of Duke Robert de Hauteville, the Guiscard, was quietly lowered into the family tomb. And placed on top of his brothers.

His epitaph was to ring round the world for centuries:

Here lies the Guiscard, terror of the world.

It became dark in the Abbey Church of the Santissima Trinita during the funeral, in spite of the hundreds of beeswax candles on all sides. Sichelgaita knew that Robert was far away now, in eternity, and part of light itself.

When they had all left, Alberada stepped forward from the shadows, kneeled before his tomb with a candle in her hand, and wept.

PART FOUR

SAINT NICHOLAS

A group of weather-beaten sailors mended their nets by the harbour walls of Bari; Matteo, elderly now, amongst them.

Fifteen years had passed since the siege and he had grown used to his new family. Now and then, agonisingly, he yearned for the former - especially the children who had died. Three years later he had taken another wife, and there had been babies again in the home. It was a solace, but there was still a gap he couldn't fill, night or day. Why he alone had been chosen to live he couldn't fathom, but he felt that the good Saint Nicholas had been watching over him, and only him. What could he do but trust?

Busy hands, occupied with salty ropes, tangled nets and fish hooks were temporarily idle as the men gathered in the shade of a thick wall, and a white gull, insolent in its youthful white feathers, perched nearby upon a mooring rock. The sun, glorious and splendid, which shone all day in the early summer months, poured out over the beautiful and busy scene a flood of light of a quality and brilliance beyond the imagination of northern sailors: but these gnarled little Bariots were used to it, preferring the shade, dripping with sweat. The majesty of the day, still, glorious and slow, was lost on them with its gratuitous grandeur - every matchless day was taken for granted and God's benediction mostly went unnoticed. Yet the weather at sea was much on their minds as they discussed the fate of their patron saint of sailors - Saint Nicholas.

The Saint's history was fragmented, based much on hearsay and local sailors' tales, yet there was an all-embracing belief in his goodness and power: power to heal the sick, power to save sailors, gentle benevolence regarding children.

Matteo had often asked the Saint why he couldn't have spared his children for him, why they had had to die such a terrible death? Yet, on the other side of the coin, he himself had been saved by the speeding swordfish which had drawn him unexpectedly so far south those fateful days, returning to find his native city under siege. It was an enigma whose only solution was that each man could only be responsible for himself, the weak had to go under. Was it also an omen? Did he have some mysterious responsibility towards the Saint?

This day, the sailors were not discussing the actions during his life, but worrying about Saint Nicholas' ancient bones lying in a tomb far, far away across the deep sea, at Myra in southern Turkey. His tomb was one of the most sought-after pilgrimage places.

Uniquely, his bones rested in a double tomb, one built over the top of the other. The reason was a medical curiosity for which there has never been an accounting: from the earliest days the bones of the Saint exuded a crystal-clear fluid called 'manna', which was sweet to the taste and smelled of flowers.

Every sailor from around every craggy coast, every peaceful inlet, from the Mediterranean to the farthest brittle, icy north knew about this miracle. Saint Nicholas, exclusively, still lived - in that he still produced a fresh and beautifully scented sweet liquid, dripping from his age-old bones. Other saints had lived and died and only great reverence could retain their reputation - but Saint Nicholas, daily, over hundreds of years, gave evidence through the manna as witness to his authenticity.

Once the bones started producing this miraculous liquid, seeping soundlessly out of the tomb, the first tomb had to be opened up at floor level, a hole punched through here and there, allowing the liquid to rise easily into a second structure without anyone being able to touch or disturb the good Saint's bones. This outer tomb, too, had a clear opening, but at the top, so that the liquid might be spooned out when required. Liquid gold!

The Greek monks in charge of the small church at Myra allowed pilgrims to visit the tomb, to pray as long as they wished, to smell the liquid and take some home in tiny flasks. Many inexplicable cures had been accredited to swallowing the pure sweetness, and many lives were said to have been saved by the humility of the pilgrimage.

Now the Muslims had rapidly overrun the entire country and the little church was isolated and at grave risk. In the beginning the Muslim rulers had been tolerant of all Christians, allowing them access at all times, quite glad of the revenue - it brought trade. But some uncouth pilgrims had abused the privilege, insulted the new rulers and generally made themselves tiresome and unwelcome. This created an ugly situation and when the same pilgrims returned to their home countries they blackened the Muslims' reputation, for they naturally gave only their own versions of their adventures. Eventually a slow swell of opinion was voiced,

'Let's band together and go out to save our places of pilgrimage in the Levant, they're at risk!'

And, by default and ignorance, they did genuinely become at risk in time, and confusion reigned. The Church fathers were gravely concerned. Neither the Pope nor the contenders to become Holy Roman Emperor were prepared to confront the gathering forces of Islam. Not yet.

Duke Robert had been told, earlier on, about the possible threat of Islam to Christian tombs: it gnawed at his soul, and he would dearly have loved to have seen for himself how many of the stories were true, and whether any pilgrimage places had actually been threatened. But it was not to be. He had been dead two years, and there was now no more reaching out by any Hauteville to grasp the Eastern Empire. Bohemund was prepared to go to the Holy Land, Roger Borsa preferred to stay safely in Apulia and Roger had his hands full with Sicily.

The group of sailors in the shade of the harbour walls of Bari were fluent in their condemnation of the Pope and the Emperors, crossing themselves again and again as they blasphemed, to save their immortal souls: apparently the Holy Father had decided against sending an expedition to save Saint Nicholas, deeming it politically expedient not to interfere. Word had just arrived and the local priests had informed Matteo and the sailors that day. They were exasperated.

'Then we must go ourselves!'

Matteo shocked himself at his outspoken words; he could not believe that he had voiced them.

'So far? We've never travelled that far - we don't know the seas and currents.' said his elderly friend nervously.

'And where do we get the money for ships?' said a very small sailor with a piercing baritone voice - more often raised in song - and a face rutted with lines.

'The Church will allow none. We have none! So we must ask the rich.'

'The monks at Venosa?'

An older man spoke,

'No, they have none to spare; my brother's there - he told me.'

'The Hautevilles?' a voice piped up.

For a moment there was silence,

The siege could not be forgotten, and it's effects. Each man in his turn had something to recall about the Norman family, all-powerful now, vastly rich. Some hated then fiercely, others had little to hate but could not love - the Hautevilles were unpopular, but reasonably fair in their dealings. None knew any member of the family in person, just their reputations, entertaining a private suspicion that the family were now too grand and proud to give charity to poor sailors, whatever their cause - and especially from Bari. Only Matteo had spent a short while with an Hauteville, when he gave Robert his supper on the beach so many years before. But Robert had been dead for two long years.

Matteo led the men in discussion. Even if it was only in theory, they had to estimate how many men would be going, how many vessels they required, how to convey the bones back to Bari - and how much money they would need in total. They spoke without a break for several days, moving from harbour side to tavern, then back again. Many of the townspeople accompanied them, but when one or other spoke up the sailors shouted them down: Saint Nicholas was *their saint - theirs alone!*

Everyone had a great deal to say - and they were all equally determined to say it: first to approve the suggestion, then to tell of their own convoluted knowledge of the Saint and how he had personally helped them, then to condemn the people within the Church and their cheeseparing ways and, finally, to offer their own advice on how to approach the dreaded Hautevilles.

As the expedition was of major importance it was agreed that a scribe - or perhaps two, for safety's sake - would keep an account of everything that occurred, so that their names would go down in posterity as Nicholas' saviors. Everyone would be equal. More equalising than anything was that not one of them had ever made such a long journey before. It imposed enormous problems and questions - even the duration of the journey could not be forecast. Would it take weeks or months? Or longer?

Forty-seven men elected to go to rescue Saint Nicholas. There was a representative from each ship-owning family whose members had survived the siege of Bari. It seemed a fitting way to select them. They, in their turn, were grateful for their lives and their gratitude was focused on Saint Nicholas. In addition, it was an honour - and an honour for their city of Bari, the first brave men to consider a joint foray so far away. If - when! - they succeeded, all the world would look to their city in respect. This they needed, since their humiliating and final defeat at the siege.

They decided they should take three ships - three, for the Trinity, each with large red sails the colour of a napkin stained with wine. Many provisions and barrels of water were needed for the long return journey and, as they would sail in a tight-knit group, should any vessel have difficulties then there would be room on the other two for its crew.

As for the Saint's bones, clearly - as some of the manna must be brought with them, for the bones alone could belong to anyone; a wine barrel was the only suitable container to hold both bones and liquid. The barrel was to be new and large, untainted, with polished wood inside and out to smooth the last path of the sainted relics: after so many hundreds of years they might be extremely fragile, even disintegrate, in a new casing. Who knows about the behaviour of bones so old? The beautiful new barrel was agreed.

Only the matter of money now remained.

MATTEO AND ROGER

Matteo was elected to approach Roger, currently on a visit to Melfi to consult with other Norman leaders. He had too often spoken about his meeting with Duke Robert years ago, so there was no way he could avoid the duty.

So, fearfully he set off for the majestic castle of the Normans at Melfi, in new clothes to which all of the forty-seven men had contributed equally: men of Bari had been republicans at heart since the first sea wave of time. A meeting with Roger was difficult to arrange. On arrival at the castle Matteo asked to see Roger on urgent religious grounds. Although intrigued, Roger told his seneschal to deal with Matteo himself, he was too busy to see him - but the proudly independent representative steadily refused to speak to anyone else bar Roger: as leader of sailors about to rescue a Saint he felt he deserved better. Roger left him kicking his heels for a few days, then relented - his thoughts were with Judith, he could think of nothing else.

Judith had been ill for months and was limp in the heat; Roger was acutely concerned about her - if only he knew what was wrong and if only he had some proper medicine. All three of their children had died at birth, and this, he felt, affected her deeply, although she never spoke of it. It seemed that her mind was suffering as well as her body - but she remained silent and her body drooped.

Matteo stood proudly in front of Roger, wondering how to ask for such a huge sum of money as all the sailors had agreed they needed. Stumbling, he first told of his meeting with Duke Robert years before.

'You entertained my brother to a meal?'

Roger was amused at the thought.

'Yes, my lord, and he enjoyed it.'

'At Santa Margherita?'

'Yes - when I was becalmed and beached there.'

'I believe he told me about it, when we travelled to Monte Sant' Angelo - he remembered it, too! But this is not the substance of your meeting with me today - what is it that you want?'

There was nothing for it.

'Sire, the sailors of Bari wish to sail across the seas and bring back home our patron saint - Saint Nicholas.' Roger's eyes widened. The idea was audacious.

'And?'

'We've estimated what to do and what to take, but we lack the money. That is what we ask of you.'

'Money to rescue the Saint? I can make no decisions until you tell me all about your plans.'

Roger's interest was aroused. He and Robert had spoken about the pilgrimage sites many times. And Matteo did. He made sure that Roger knew every minuscule detail, and he mentioned every one of the departing sailors by name, and often gave their family history, too. He forwent speaking about his own. Half way through their discussion, Roger cordially invited the old sailor to eat his meal with him. Roger was well aware that Matteo's colleagues would be much impressed.

The details that concerned Roger the most were those about the miraculous health cures associated with Saint Nicholas. He must have a cure for Judith. No doctor in South Italy was able to diagnose her complaint.

But Roger was filled with as much personal pride as the Bariots, especially since Duke Robert's failure to reach Constantinople. What was there in this bold undertaking for the Norman cause? It was such a gamble - it would have greatly appealed to Robert. If he gave money for such a religious enterprise there must be something to show for it -

if not for him personally, at least in the Hauteville name. Had the sailors thought that far, he asked of Matteo. No? Their thoughts had progressed only as far as the rescue, not the after-effects.

Roger enquired with patience,

'What will you do with the Saint's bones when you return?'

'I don't know, Sire, we haven't discussed that between us. I suppose we'll have to give them to the Archbishop to place in the Cathedral.'

'No! If I provide the means to bring back the bones we must build a new church for them - the Church of Saint Nicholas! No, no! *The Basilica of Saint Nicholas* - that's better! And it will be Hauteville money which brings them back, then builds the Basilica. Mark my words, you Bariots may be proud, independent men, but so am I! That would be my return. For the glory of our family, especially my brother Duke Robert; for the glory of God, and for the honour of the city of Bari! Do you agree?'

Matteo could do no less. Enough money, and a promise that the bones would be magnificently housed: Bari to benefit in every way. It was just. It was also very generous.

Roger had two last things to say,

'Bring me back some of the manna for my sick wife.'

'Aye, that we will.'

'And tell me what will decorate your sails?'

'We do not decorate our sails, Sire, the rain would wash it off .'

'This time you'll paint a symbol on them with tar!'

'Yes? In what way? What do you mean?'

'On one side of your sails,' said Roger emphatically, 'you'll paint a great Christian cross. And on the other - you'll paint the Hauteville gryphon. Then no marauder will dare attack you, with both a Christian symbol and the Hauteville support emblazoned on your sails. Your three ships will sail on in safety.'

MATTEO: THE VOYAGE OUT

On Matteo's triumphant return to Bari, the sailors heard his impressively successful story, and cheered him to the echo. Plans for their journey were put in hand at once, as agreed. Then they dispersed about the harbour walls to slip into their small sailing vessels, riding at anchor - unfurling their canvas and sallying forth in amicable couples to scour the azure waters. Life, after all, must go on until they left, and they had missed the early tide.

The journey across the Mediterranean to the coastal city of Myra was perilous and long: but they lost no-one, and were frantic with excitement at paying homage at Saint Nicholas' tomb, and then, their simple minds reasoned, of being able to return home in triumph with his bones. They knew the monks at the pilgrimage church would be grateful.

After they had made land at last, and given thanks in Saint Nicholas' own church, a chosen few sought a meeting with the Abbot in all humility. But, disappointingly, he was absent and a monk, his personal priest, was present in his place. It could not be helped.

They all talked for a long while, first with pleasantries, then to the purpose of their visit; fortunately the scribes could translate when necessary. But when he digested their plans the monk was adamant, or deliberately obtuse, and refused their offer of sanctuary for the Saint. Eventually, hours later, Matteo stood glaring at the monk in exasperation, and lost his temper, shouting,

'Don't you understand? We've come to rescue Saint Nicholas' bones from the infidel! Not to take them away from you personally!'

'No, you can't 'rescue them', as you call it - they're ours! And have been so for many years!'

'But we're taking them to safety ... away from the harm which is all around you here!'

'What harm?' said the monk.

'The threatening hordes from Islam ...'

'You mean the Muslims?'

'Yes.'

'Well, we rather like them! There's no danger here, we're all perfectly safe.'

The monk looked complacently at Matteo, his fat hands folded on his bulging stomach. A few of the sailors that had come with Matteo stood silently at the back of the cool room; he had begged them not to interfere whilst he negotiated with the monks. With great restraint they remained silent. Matteo took a steadying breath,

'I don't think you realise how dangerous your position is Father; other places of pilgrimage in this land have been razed to the ground recently, the tombs pillaged and the monks killed. Why do you think the Muslims will leave you in peace here, over others?'

The monk smirked, gesturing as though washing his hands.

'Because this place of pilgrimage makes money for them, that's why! And provides our own income.' Then, patting his stomach, 'besides, Saint Nicholas guards us well.'

'Saint Nicholas would guard you all the better in a Christian land,' pleaded Matteo.

'No. You can't have him, and that's our final answer!' The monk spoke petulantly, but with obvious deliberation.

Unused to arguing with the clergy, Matteo turned away in despair, he could see that the monks were all old, low-bred and avaricious, and he was at a loss to know what to do.

The travellers from Bari had already been awed by a visit to the Saint's tomb, they had paid for small phials of the manna - Matteo bought a large one for Roger - and watched as the monks pocketed their money quite openly. One or two monks were later followed, only to be found sitting at a tavern by the port, drinking deep. Venal creatures! But there were a surprisingly large number of them in the monastery and church, watching the Bariots with growing interest in their turn. No other large party had journeyed so far in the open sea to make a pilgrimage here, and the Hauteville gryphon was a fruitful source of conversation.

The Bariots withdrew from the monks' presence, as quietly as they knew how, but with deep reluctance. They returned to their ships and had a long conference, eventually arriving at a sensible solution - in their own minds.

Some days later Matteo found himself conferring with the same monk, armed with the sailors' solution, empowered to negotiate again. This time he came to the point quickly.

'We wondered whether a financial reward might be acceptable. What would you say to an offer of money for the Saint and his bones, and we will provide the transport free to Bari?'

The monk distended like a bull-frog, grew scarlet in the face and stuttered,

'How dare you! What insult! To buy and sell saints like fish in a market!'

'How much would you want?'

Matteo persevered with studied patience. He and the others had had plenty of experience buying and selling fish - every day of their lives.

'You wouldn't ever have enough, not even if you went back and brought another ship-load!'

Frothy saliva dripped from the old monk's chin as he puffed. He spat on the floor as Matteo exclaimed,

'That's sheer bravado! We can pay! Probably as much as you ask! We could even have room on board for some of you to return home with us if you wished!'

'But most of us are Greek - why would we want to come to your benighted country? No, no, go away! Stop insulting us like this. Saint Nicholas has lain here for centuries; it would be desecration to remove his bones.'

Matteo tried to interrupt, but the monk was having none of it. He gabbled on,

'Can't you understand, for hundreds of years this has been a holy place of pilgrimage, and we've no intention of altering our way of life. We make a good deal of money for the Church, the Muslims are truly our friends and life is very comfortable for us all. Go away - do! You've absolutely no authority to suggest these crazy ideas to us and, besides, you're being too upsetting.'

Matteo again withdrew with his companion. Their approach had been highly unorthodox, but they could think of no other: probably there was right on either side.

Absolutely convinced of the serious threat to the Saint, they knew they couldn't return to Bari empty-handed, and they knew their fate had been sealed when they were given Count Roger's money. They dared not return without the Saint, pride forbade it, and their home city awaited them with high expectations. Last, but not least, they could never replace the money they had already spent.

Next day Matteo called another meeting on one of the vessels. He explained in detail what had happened, and the dead end they were now in. Once everyone was satisfied that they had done all that was possible, moody silence set in.

'There's nothing for it! *We'll just have to take the bones by force!'*

The sailors were horrified. None of them were men of violence, everyone was pious. All they wished was to move the Saint's bones to safety, in honour and prayer. The blind doggedness of the monks had surprised and appalled them; they had expected to have been welcomed with open arms, as saviours. Instead, they had firmly been told to leave.

Now after much soul-searching and vote-taking, their course of action was determined: the Saint's bones would have to be taken - captured - by force if necessary, and rushed back across the seas to Bari. They prayed Roger was right and the Hauteville gryphon would again protect them: some storms at sea would be inevitable.

All day they worked out their plans. Two men were to roll and carry the wine-barrel up to the church during the day, leaving it outside, covered, behind a wall. Others were deployed to stand guard as four men hacked open the tomb. Everyone had to be ready to fight the monks: old and feeble some of them might be, but there were many more monks than sailors, and some were young and muscular.

But who would volunteer to plunge his arms into the inner tomb, fish about in the sweet-smelling liquid to find the bones - and draw them out? Were the bones attached to each other? Would the liquid pour out of the eye-sockets? Should it be necessary to break the bones to withdraw them? Was the liquid slimy? Could any gobs of flesh remain in the bottom, or would any have floated to the top? How could one know, when other miracles had taken place?

Their imagination reeled.

Eventually the men told Matteo that he should do it, as he was their leader. It was an *honour*! He shuddered with black horror. Gagged, was sick - again and again.

MATTEO AND ST. NICHOLAS

Century after century those bones had lain there, undisturbed, oozing the famous liquid day after day, relentlessly. If the Saint had still been a living Bishop, Matteo would have found the greatest difficulty in coming near him, would have nervously stammered too much to speak to him - far less touch the hem of his cloak. Now he had been elected to grope for the saint's bones, at dead of night, after his companions had broken open - desecrated - his holy tomb: it was exactly what they had all hoped to avoid for the Saint.

Yet - what choice did they have? The monks were adamant in their opposition.

That evening the captains slowly steered each vessel, quite openly, out of the harbour and anchored off shore. The sails were trimmed, their gryphons facing onto the harbour; tide times were noted and fresh water was taken on board. All the people ashore had been told they were off the next day, and would be going empty-handed, apart from fresh provisions, which they duly loaded: Hauteville money jingled in new pouches. The local people were used to the continual comings and goings by pilgrims and took little notice.

Matteo's men were rowed ashore in small skiffs and melted into the crowds as night fell, each remembering his rendezvous position. The greatest worry was that the moon was full and the sky was clear.

In silence, just after midnight, the men casually drifted away from the inns and taverns and gathered in a group by the church door. With little difficulty they broke the rusty lock and forced it open. Rushing inside with Matteo, four men with pickaxes began to hack at the outer tomb; whilst two men manhandled the barrel, rolled it crookedly across the stone floor and placed it close by. The rest guarded the main entrance.

The moment the noise of smashing mortar and splintering stone was heard, several of the monks ran out, half asleep, raising the alarm. They had grabbed an extraordinary array of defending implements, lying about them right and left. Outside the church the moon fell brightly on a maelstrom of fighting men; inside the light was very dim.

Matteo held a lantern high above his head whilst his companions feverishly smashed and hacked, until the outer tomb was broken down, and the flower-sweet manna scented the air all about. One man kept muttering.

'Oh God, forgive me! Sweet Jesu, forgive me!' as he worked with desperation.

'Matteo! The pitcher! Fill the barrel!'

Matteo reached out with the pitcher in his reluctant hand, dipped it into the liquid - which almost overpowered him with its scent - and baled out the crystal-clear manna into the barrel. He could distinguish no floating flesh.

'Fill it up! They won't believe they're Saint Nicholas' bones without it!' another shouted.

He baled away as best he could, half-filling the barrel in the dusty crush of heaving men. It was stifling.

'It's open! The tomb's open! Can't you get your hand in?'

Matteo shuddered, replying,

'Yes, but I can't get any bones out! *Think of his head!* His skull - the hole's too small - open it further!'

They strengthened their efforts, levering with agonising slowness.

At last there was nothing left for it any longer. Matteo slid his arm into the stone tomb, reached down, felt something hard - held it - brought out an arm bone with clutching fingers at one end. As he lifted it out of the tomb, the wrist bones gave way and the fingers fell sharply onto his head, scattering onto the floor. He screamed.

'Go on, man, go on!'

Another sailor grasped his shoulder.

'Hurry – I can hear the fighting growing closer!'

Until he died, Matteo never forgot the sensation of lifting out the Saint's bones, terrified he would reach soft, spongy flesh. He never knew if he had taken out all the bones, for the light was so dim, the men were panicking about him, tearing each bone out of his hands as he withdrew it, ramming each into the barrel, filling it with manna.

'I think that's all.'

'That's no good, Matt, feel about the bottom... have one last feel!'

He swept his arm back into the jagged hole of the inner tomb, felt along the bottom, into each corner, finally picking up one last jointed toe. He threw it into the barrel, his clothes were soaking wet and sweet, and he called out.

'Ram home the lid!'

The fighting had grown closer. The monks had broken through the ranks of sailors outside. Men shouted, metal clashed on metal, there was utter confusion in the steamy, moonlit night. Unexpected by the monks, the sailors rolled the barrel out of a side door, guarded by six fresher men, who rumbled it down the hill as fast as they could and onto a small rowing boat, as the others fought each other by the entrance to the church.

At a signal, the battling sailors broke off the fight and followed, some wounded, others holding them up, and stumbled and blundered down the hill to the harbour. Miraculously all were brought aboard the sailing vessels, some badly hurt and losing blood.

Then the saintly barrel was lashed to the mainmast, anchors heaved aboard - and they were off!

They left a group of disconsolate monks panting by the water's edge, shouting irreverent, impotent curses, promising punishment by excommunication whilst Matteo kept being violently sick overboard. He felt his debt to Saint Nicholas had been paid in full. No-one had the slightest doubt that Saint Nicholas would see them safely home.

And, in time, he did.

JUDITH AND ROGER

Whilst the sailors of Bari were fighting for Saint Nicholas' bones, Judith was fighting for her life ... and fast losing her own battle. Her medicine chest had long been exhausted; she was well-known for her skill and generosity in nursing the sick. For her, now, it was just a question of time.

Meanwhile Roger was walking miserably along his castle's walls, head down, deep in turmoil.

The air was quite cool, rain had fallen recently and the sky was still grey. He fingered his small gold cross about his neck absent-mindedly: without doubt, he knew this in twisting anguish, Judith was going to die, and there was absolutely nothing he could do about it. She was his reason for living, he still passionately adored her; the realisation was purgatory.

Day after day Judith had become lighter in his arms. Her body felt like a tiny bundle of spiny feathers, the unlined skin became taut across her lovely face, highlighting her beautiful bones. Every feature of her face still waited, as it were, for the strokes of time's chisel.

Her golden-brown hair alone was unchanged, making a curtain for him to bury his head, to hide her from his despair. Fatigue and anxiety dogged him, sleep denied him, instead he would sit wretchedly on a chair beside her, waiting in his gnawing grief for the next day to dawn - as if it would bring some hope with its arrival. Now he knew with deepening bitterness that probably there would be no more dawns, that there was perhaps only an hour or so left to them; his desolation was unfathomable.

They had never discussed her condition; all they did was look deep into each other's eyes. She spoke little, just followed Roger with her huge eyes as he moved about her rooms. She denied there was much pain, but never laughed, hardly smiled, yet she was always there for him to speak to as a sounding board. For years she had followed him in his campaigns, concerned only for him - no-one else. Several times they were besieged together, in danger of starvation; once they had only one cloak to share through the winter months. She hated warfare, never glorying in it as Sichelgaita did, but she never complained.

The quality of stillness about her, her patient waiting, stirred him most ... her acknowledgement of the fate that awaited her; she had no strength left to fight.

Tangled filaments of energy, drawing in the life-force, had petered out through congestions and blockages. The cancer in her body had spread like wildfire; drugged with opium against the pain, she had lain, almost lifeless, for days. Today she had refused all relief, for she needed to be lucid and able to speak.

Loyal Bertha, now crippled with arthritis, had tearfully told him that the end was near. He could stay away - or be with her until the final breath. Every day he had waited for the manna from Saint Nicholas to cure her, but now it was just too late to be of any use. He braced himself to go to her rooms for a final time, not knowing whether his strength was needed for her or for himself.

He quietly approached from the shady side of their enormous bed. She lay still, in the centre, a delicately embroidered cover across her body, her fragile arms lying by her side. The slight noise he made was enough for her to open her eyes, smile faintly with tranquil lips at him. She gestured him to sit beside her. Instead, he knelt, and put his head near hers.

'I have something to say to you, Roger. Can - can you hear me?'

Her voice was very low, breathless.

'Don't talk now, don't tire yourself.'

'I've no time left. I must say these things.'

She put out a slender hand to him, the skin transparent as a fish, a tiny lavender-coloured thread of blood still just beating beneath.

'You must know that I'm dying?'

He reached forward, touched her brow with his lips.

'Don't. You're breaking my heart. I can't bear it.'

'Nor I. But, during the years ahead, I will watch over you from beyond the grave, until we come together again.'

The effort to speak was almost too much for her and Roger had to bend close to hear. He smoothed her hair from her face, his dark eyes swimming with tears in his strong, sunburnt face.

'But first hear my confession.'

Roger couldn't believe his ears. How could his blameless wife have something to confess? Her lips twitched faintly at his astonishment. She covered his hands with her own, a tiny gesture of comfort.

'When we first promised ourselves to each other I told you about the wise woman, who warned me that my faith would be curiously wrapped up with my love. That I would have either the one, or the other - and I would have to choose. Do you remember that?'

He nodded gravely.

'And then you gave me the gold cross...'

His voice seemed to echo in the silent room.

'But – I never told you my secrets about the convent.'

Slowly, increasingly slowly, fighting for each breath, she recounted the story of the convent, how she had been party to the forging of the document affirming she was a nun - to save herself. Then she told him about Odo's death.

'Fetch – that – cloak – behind you.'

Bertha had put it ready. Roger turned, reached for the travelling cloak, hidden for years.

'Open the hem.'

He did so, breaking the thread with a snap.

'Take out – that document.'

He withdrew the rolled up parchment, opened it out, then saw the half-signature drowned in blood.

'All my life I've never known if I was still in jeopardy. But I swear I never took my vows. Yet, I dared not confess, it was too hazardous - we might have been excommunicated or parted. So no priest has shriven me from blasphemy: I've been so fearful of the fires of hell.' She lifted a hand to her brow, then went on, her whispers slowly fading.

'One day, if you can, go to the convent at St. Evroul-sur-Ouche and ask for my final paper, signed by Mother Superior Montgomery and witnessed by Sister Sophia: that will prove, once and for all, that I never took my vows.'

She closed her eyes, exhausted, remembering those days.

'I've always loved you, but we've had no children that lived: perhaps because I've been afraid. I felt I had to pay, for ... I may have sinned ... the bride of Christ ...'

She looked up at him enquiringly.

'Will ... Christ forgive me?'

There was the faintest flush now upon her ivory cheeks, the eyebrows over her wide eyes were lifted a little in further questions; her lips were parted for speech that did not come.

He, too, had much to say and yet found himself without a word. And so they gazed for a moment in silence, to be remembered for eternity.

She made one final effort.

'There was no choice. I'm so ...'

With an infinitely tiny sigh, her voice stopped.

He looked at her beauty, now set in its marble continuity of perpetual sleep. He took the gold cross from around his neck and placed it in her still hands and closed her tired eyes. His desolation overwhelmed him and, in silent loneliness, his heart broke.

Later, he took a bronze coin, freshly minted, and placed it in her mouth and gently closed it: Charon needed his fee to take Judith's spirit across the river Styx.

BOHEMUND, SICHELGAITA AND ALBERADA IN BARI

A tumultuous, long-awaited welcome greeted Saint Nicholas' bones when they finally arrived at Bari. The Hauteville family had arranged for a fitting ceremony of thanksgiving a few days hence and everyone was invited. Bohemund, now Duke of Taranto, was in charge.

Word had come to Bohemund, leader of the Hauteville forces in Greece, that the bones of Saint Nicholas were to be blessed by the Archbishop of Bari on the 8th of May. Then the basilica would be built around and above them. As Roger and his nephew Roger Borsa were summoned to attend the Pope's consecration at Rome, Bohemund himself was to uphold the Hauteville name. For once he was centrally placed, as he should have been all along. He intended to make the most of it.

Bohemund was as large and tall as his father and uncle before him, with an immense barrel chest. He was as fair as Robert - he kept his thick fair hair close-cropped - but he had his mother's eyes and dark eyelashes: women went mad for him. He was now twenty-seven and still filled with turmoil inside, which he could not resolve or put into words: but it included envy, and hatred, and a thirst for revenge. But he was more in control of himself. His father had once taken him aside and said,

'There are two pieces of advice I can offer you - no more! And if you can remember them you'll be a wise man and successful, too. Firstly: never risk the lives of your men or horses. The second is; never embark on any battle that you aren't certain of winning - run away instead.'

Bohemund was shocked by his words, but he was right! He took no risks. His inner passion, now, was to confront the forces of Islam in the Holy Land - there, he was convinced, lay his future. But today, this glorious sunny day in Bari, was a high point of his life. He aimed to savour it to the full.

Hundreds of people, men, women and children, jostled on the harbour walls at Bari in the brilliant sunshine, or peered down from every available window or roof or rock where they could see the action. They had all dressed in their finest clothes. Some were pilgrims from afar, carrying tall staves, about which were garlanded circles of bread for their journey. Others had placed fir cones from Monte Sant' Angelo right at the tip - a sign of another pilgrimage; yet others carried no stave, but crawled in humility all along their route, licking the ground in front of them, their tongues bleeding.

A small wooden sailing vessel had been constructed, and placed on wheels on the broad quayside. It was a replica of Matteo's fishing boat, named and freshly painted with bright colours, filled with flowers. Flags flew from the mast in red and white, the colours of the proud republican city of Bari, and many of the onlookers, too, wore red and white. A flock of Hauteville gryphons fluttered everywhere.

On each side of the boat waited the forty-seven berry-brown sailors, all dressed in uniform dark blue leggings and jerkin, covered by a scarlet cowl. The city fathers had donated the garments to the sailors when they had returned in triumph with Saint Nicholas' bones in the wine barrel. They had neither wanted, nor received, any other reward ... glory sufficed! Even so, they intended re-telling their stories for years ahead, to anyone who offered a glass of wine; but that was traditional, for anyone who had a tale to tell.

The Archbishop, most carefully and reverently, had examined the contents of the blessed barrel with his fellow churchmen; he had read the scribe's eye-witness accounts of the adventure and he had spoken to all forty-seven sailors individually - and pronounced the bones to be genuine.

Now the smooth-polished barrel was strapped to the mast of the boat on wheels, and two ponderous black oxen with gilded horns, incongruously decorated with garlands of flowers around their necks, were being backed into the shafts. The last part of the Saint's journey was about to take place: one of the scribes who travelled with them to Myra recorded it was the 8th of May 1087.

The procession set off in tumult.

The oxen heaved, yet the boat would not shift: forty-seven men lent a shoulder to its sides and, the hesitation over, it began to grumble along.

Children shrieked, especially all those who could claim a relationship, however distant, to the heroic sailors. Men prayed, some with tears streaming down their cheeks - for what reason they knew not; women sang chants from their own locality, often unintelligible to anyone else, and drums thrummed and banged.

Tension rose higher and higher on that glittering day in May.

At the head of the procession the stately Archbishop led the way with a self-conscious parody of humility, surrounded by a huge body of pious priests, taking a lead from him. A convocation of bishops were there with their clergy, and a congregation of abbots with their sober monks; a lone but impressive representative from His Holiness the Pope fought to take a suitably elevated place, decked out with all the panoply that the Vatican could muster.

It took them all quite thirty minutes to pass along the short route - two hundred metres - from the harbour to the site of the designated basilica, for each person wished to be acknowledged and spaced from the next; the crowds, used to this, obediently obliged with frantic acclamation. The noise was indescribable.

Then came the holy caravel with the attendant sailors, Matteo at their head, tired and triumphant.

Finally came the people of Bari and the pilgrims, who had heard, in some unfathomable way, of the day's celebrations. The pilgrims came from across Italy where the Christian faith was passionate and, indeed, from all across Europe. Mainly they arrived from the coastal towns of Italy and Greece and Illyria - some from other countries - where sailors depended upon their patron Saint.

Finally, the pageant arrived in the huge piazza. Here, in the past weeks, Hauteville men had hurriedly cleared away some broken-down old hovels and fishing lofts and sheds, and had newly laid the area with stone flags. The Hauteville family had donated the site, re-housing some fisherfolk, and providing the money to erect today's colourful decorations and flapping sailcloth awnings. Huge sums of money had been put aside, with enormous publicity, into the care of the Church, for the various stages of the basilica about to be built: half the religious establishments of Europe had heard and were suitably impressed and envious, and longed for as reputable remains to fill their own coffers.

At one end of the echoing piazza was a makeshift altar, a richly gilded table, on loan from the Archbishop, and a simple chair for the Pope's representative, over which was thrown a golden stole. To the north of it was placed a fantastic marble throne for the newly appointed Bishop, created in a vibrant mixture of styles, awaiting a decorative mosaic to be laid around it in the basilica-to-be. There was no other seating.

The Archbishop led the way up to the altar and turned to face the oncoming populace, the churchmen clamorous about him, fussing and pushing, wanting to be noticed.

Soon the black oxen staggered into view, hauling the laden boat as it clattered into the entrance. Its wheels squeaked stridently in the hollow square, screaming as it turned on the stones. Finally it was halted, fifty metres from the clergy, and the restless oxen were fed with some straw to keep them quiet.

From the other side of the piazza another procession began to make its way towards the Archbishop in great solemnity.

Majestic Bohemund led the way, drummers and heralds before him. Handsome and proud, he wore no armour today, but the richest of clothes and jewels, with a swinging fur-lined cloak that his father had left him. His fingers were stiff with rings, chains were strung about his neck, falling to his waist, and his clothes smelled headily of pure gold.

Beside him was elderly Sichelgaita, in equal finery and a waft of perfume, pearls picking out the pattern of her gown, the metallic embroidery winking and blinking in the strong sunlight, and her jewels competing for attention. No-one could see her wispy white hair beneath her jewelled headdress.

Both looked honourable and solemn. Sichelgaita represented Roger Borsa, Apulia's absent Duke; Bohemund continued to resent her presence, but he respected her by now, especially having fought side by side with her on several occasions. In stately fashion they slowly paced forward, hand on hand. They didn't speak.

Members of the Apulian court followed them, so extravagantly dressed and bejewelled that many Bariots could not believe their eyes ... but they were glad that they had paid their city that honour.

Bohemund at last saw the person he searched for amongst the crowds, someone standing alone: behind her stood Jacques, bent, ever alert. Searchingly, Bohemund looked at Sichelgaita, carefully measuring his words as they came to a halt.

'For a moment I must leave you. There is someone I must acknowledge in all honour - but she won't come to me, I must go to her. Can you be forbearing? It's my mother.'

Sichelgaita looked across the piazza, with hooded interest, at a still, small woman who stood to one side of the crowd, dressed soberly in simple, dark clothes. Then she glanced at Bohemund, who had not moved, but waited for her answer. He continued to gaze enquiringly at her and, after a moment, she bent her head, slowly, confidently, in agreement, although the knife turned once more inside her. It was the first time she had ever seen Alberada.

She heard herself say,

'Bring her forward, if she cares to come.'

Bohemund motioned to the courtiers to stay in attendance to Sichelgaita, then walked purposefully across to Alberada in the crowd, who fell back. When they were close he looked, smiling, into her loving face, it had been some while since they had last met. They were very close.

Lifting her hand, he bowed low and kissed it.

'Mother.'

'Mark.'

'Sichelgaita invites you to join her. Will you come?'

Shocked, she whispered urgently,

'Oh no! I couldn't.'

Bohemund said with some intensity,

'She fervently supports Roger Borsa's career, as you know. This is something you can do for mine - will you? All Europe watches. I need the recognition if I'm to prosper.'

He smiled at her the way that Robert did when he was young, with a lifted eyebrow. For a brief moment he was there beside her. Her heart melted. She could refuse him nothing. She bent her head in agreement.

'In that case ...'

The whispering, murmuring crowds parted as he escorted his mother to where Sichelgaita stood, isolated in the centre of the arena. He lifted each woman's old hand in his and held them there.

'Greetings.' said Sichelgaita, quietly. 'Peace. Especially here - today.'

Gracefully Alberada inclined her head.

'Yes.'

She uttered no other words. Just the faintest of smiles set alight her uplifted face.

Bohemund slowly turned, and with Sichelgaita to his right, and Alberada to his left, he paced forward to their designated places in the piazza.

When the Hauteville court had been settled, the Archbishop raised his hand, called Matteo and the sailors to bring forward the barrel from the painted ship. All forty-seven men managed, somehow, to touch the barrel as it was reverently carried to the altar. There was a chorus of sighs as it came to rest in safety at long last.

Then all the crowds of people were permitted to join the celebration, and they swarmed into the piazza until there was no space left at all. They were impossible to control. Eventually they were restrained enough for the Archbishop to make his voice heard.

There, amidst the heady scent of manna and incense mixed, communion was shared between them all in that hot, sunlit situation. Later the great basilica of Saint Nicholas would be built here, magnificently simple, a fitting resting place for Saint Nicholas' unstinting bones.

Alberada gazed across the shifting, kneeling crowds, all penitent heads bent and eyes closed. Forlorn, she longed, achingly, for Robert, more now than ever, the knight who was lover, wise counsellor and paladin.

Sichelgaita, too, was thinking about Robert, recalling the moment that he was freed, his body just a sheath left behind and his spirit soaring like a bird, higher and higher towards the compelling light. She felt forsaken.

Bohemund's eyes wandered to the people of Bari, joyful that the Saint's bones were now secure in a Christian country. Building the basilica would give much needed work to many, and everyone in the city would benefit from their presence in the future - if not for centuries.

The Hautevilles, firmly entrenched in south Italy as a stable dynasty, had their Hauteville gryphons hung everywhere: Robert could never be forgotten.

Bohemund took a deep breath, full of sea air and incense.

Roger and Borsa were to attend the Pope's consecration the very next day in Rome - that would bring complications for them all.

And he, Bohemund, would return to Greece.

After that - further East? The Holy Land? His blood quickened at the thought.

GLOSSARY

Abhisa: also known as **Rahat lokum**, or (today) **Turkish Delight**: a sweet with the consistency of starchy jelly.

Ambergris: wax-like substance from the intestines of sperm whales, used mainly in perfumery.

Betony: a plant (**Stachys Betonica**), credited with medicinal and magical virtues.

Board: slab of timber, later known as a 'table', at this period generally placed upon trestles.

Candles: made from clarified mutton fat. In Autumn, servants or children gathered rushes from the banks of rivers or streams: laid to dry, they then peeled them, cut them into lengths of about a foot, dipped them several times into the hot melted fat from a spit (into an iron grease-pan), then left them to dry. In use, they were held in metal rush-nips. They burned for about an hour. Wealthy households and churches had candles of beeswax.

Carob: (Ceratonia siliqua), tree of the pea family, native to the Eastern Mediterranean region and cultivated elsewhere. It has red flowers followed by flat, leathery pods (3 – 12 inches long) which contain hard brown seeds which were in general use as a unit of weight. Nowadays the word is used in the gemological world and changed to 'carat', 'Karat' or 'K' when indicating purity of gold and other precious metals.

Catapan : Greek/Byzantine ruler.

Clare: spicy and aromatic drink with a base of hot red wine.

Condottieri: mercenaries - professional soldiers for hire.

Couscous: grain dish from the Mahgreb.

Couvre-feu: literally fire-cover, a large brass or copper cover put over the fire at night, then rekindled in the morning with a bellows. From which comes 'curfew'.

Destrier: Frankish war horse.

Ergo: therefore.

Eskalaton: scarlet woven fabric.

Fare figura: loosely translated to 'everything for effect'.

Fief: unit of land parcelled out by a lord, in return for homage and a commitment to a defined amount of military service.

Forestra umbra: literally 'the dark forest'.

Fuller's earth: a white clay, mixed with a strong alkaline solution, made from ash, called lye. This was beaten with battledores into dirty clothes to clean them - when they could not be washed.

Galen: Greek physician (b.129AD, d.c.199 AD) one of the most distinguished physicians of antiquity.

Gambeson: a military tunic of leather or thick cloth, sometimes padded.

Gonfalon: title of the formal head of civic administration, literally meaning 'banner bearer': originally of German origin.

Greek fire: clay pots filled with incendiary liquid, very volatile, catching fire spontaneously when wet, even burning on the sea.

Half-dead disease: illness of the heart and circulation.

Hauberk: mail shirt, sometimes incorrectly referred to as a 'chain-mail' shirt.

Heart worms: death by heart attack or disease.

Herbal: a book about herbs, used for both medicine and food.

Jongleurs: jugglers, singers or entertainers.

Leech book: book of healing.

Legate: the Pope's ecclesiastical deputy.

Maghmuna: see **moussaka**.

Manna: sweet liquid, smelling of flowers, said to drip continually from the bones of S. Nicholas.

Moussaka: (also **maghmuna**): a layered dish of mutton, onions and aubergines.

Mortrew: (because they were made in a mortar). Boiled white meat or fish reduced to a paste, mixed with breadcrumbs, stock and eggs and boiled again until it thickened, then sprinkled with pepper and ginger before serving.

Nadd: a mixture of Persian perfumes.

Oriental: the modern 'Middle East' in the 11th century, anywhere east of Constantinople.

Pale: boundary of land.

Pantler: type of butler.

Pax: peace.

Piano nobile: generally meaning the state or public rooms on the first floor of a house.

Rahat lokum: now known as Turkish delight.

Reeve: a minor official appointed by a landowner to superintend.

Salve: to clear away unwanted food etc after a meal, saving it for re-use in soups etc or for distribution to the poor at the gate.

Seneschal: a senior official in the household of a great noble.

Serf: from the Latin *'servus'*, a slave.

Simony: the practice of buying or selling ecclesiastical preferments.

Sirocco: a sea mist.

Soap: a mixture of sand, sifted ashes and linseed oil. Fine toilet soap was scented with herbs in the kitchen or still-room and kept in wooden bowls.

Strategus: Greek/Byzantine ruler.

Table: a painting or picture, on wood or metal.

Trencher: from the French 'trancher', to cut: thick slices (about 6' x 4') of stale bread which served as an absorbent plate, upon which the food was placed in front of each individual. Further trenchers were always available. After each meal, unused trenchers were given to the poor at the gate.

Trullo: a one-storey, small circular house, with a conical roof, and sometimes with cellars: still to be found in Apulia

AUTHOR'S NOTE

Today you can still see much that has endured of the Normans' story in southern Italy; although Apulia and Calabria are fast being developed, nothing can really change the mountains or coastline, climate or history. The Hautevilles and their adventures in the 11th century are fact, I have merely picked out a few episodes to clothe with words.

Several religious/political events had far-reaching results, such as the Conference at Melfi. The Papal elections were first standardised at that time, partly emasculating the power of the Holy Roman Emperors within the Church; and the consanguinity laws later reached out to influence (among many others) King Henry VIII's divorce from Catherine of Aragon and the setting up of the Church of England.

The 11th century gryphon of Robert de Hauteville is still seen in many places, carved and inlaid, and it is also to be seen as part of the arms of the city of Melfi. Determined to stake his claim, he was one of the first to develop a hereditary symbol as an identification device; from the second quarter of the 12th century in Western Europe heraldic designs were found more generally applied and rapidly gained popularity.

Norman castles and towers do, now, 'litter the countryside,' some later built over, others left as stark silhouettes against the Italian sky. There is a wealth of Romanesque cathedrals, mostly on or near the coast of Apulia and sober tombs of the family, suffused with *gravitas*, lie inland, as recounted, at Venosa and elsewhere.

The translation of the bones of St. Nicholas in 1087 (one of the most popular of saints - also known as Santa Claus – who wears today the colours of the republican city of Bari, red and white) was witnessed and written about by no less than three contemporary observers, among whom was John the Archdeacon.

Peter the Hermit is said to have preached about the First Crusade on that memorable day in the piazza, and the giant Bohemund himself (later Prince of Antioch), with no fewer than five other grandsons and two great-grandsons of old Tancred de Hauteville in his train, led the huge Norman contingent to the Holy Land on that crusade.

Every year, early in May, the citizens of Bari reenact the saga and miracles of St. Nicholas in a brilliant, unforgettable pageant, although it is sadly becoming more sophisticated and catering to the tourist. Even so, an early voyage of exploration in the area, culminating by attendance from the 7th to the 9th of May in Bari, makes a small section of the astonishing history of the Normans come to life.

Pantaleone di Mauro (b.c.1030 - d.c.1071) is the first Italian businessman of the Middle Ages of whom any information survives, known not only for his diplomatic activities (about which I have not written) but also for his philanthropy. He became a bitter enemy of the Normans. He also became the head of the Amalfitan community in Constantinople. In 1209 the bones of St. Andrew were brought to lie in the cathedral of Amalfi.

The bronze doors at Monte San Angelo, damascened with silver, the 'Gates of Paradise', were erected in 1076. They are still there, as you step into the grotto chapel deep within the mountain. An interesting exhortation was added to the base of the doors, from the craftsmen to the priests, asking them 'to see that the doors were cleaned at least once a year so that they might always shine brightly'. They give details of Pantaleone's involvement. I once attended an event here, which involved the famous Padre Pio, just before he died (and was later canonised).

Incidentally, 1087 was the year that William the Conqueror died, on September 9th at Rouen, and it is interesting to consider that, had William been just a few years older, he might never have bothered to conquer England, but might have joined in the conquest of Italy instead.

One of Roger de Hauteville's eventual sons (he married three times) was crowned King Roger II of Sicily. His daughter Constance married the Emperor Henry VI and, in turn, their son became Frederick II, Holy Roman Emperor. So the religious and political circles were completed.